Brothers Black 5
Felix the Watcher

BLUE SAFFIRE

Perceptive Illusions Publishing, Inc.
Bay Shore, New York

Blue Saffire/Perceptive Illusions Publishing, Inc.
23 Chris Matt Ct
Bay Shore, New York 11706
www.BlueSaffire.com

Publisher's Note: This is a work of fiction. Names, characters, places, and incidents are a product of the author's imagination. Locales and public names are sometimes used for atmospheric purposes. Any resemblance to actual people, living or dead, or to businesses, companies, events, institutions, or locales is completely coincidental.

Ordering Information:
Quantity sales. Special discounts are available on quantity purchases by corporations, associations, and others. For details, contact the "Special Sales Department" at the address above.

Brothers Black Book 5: Felix the Watcher / Blue Saffire. – 1st ed.
ISBN 978-1-941924-50-1

I will wait for you. You were made for me so I will wait for you. I will wait for you to remember. I will wait for you to lose your anger. I will wait. I'll be waiting because with you is where I belong.

—Blue Saffire

Next

Carmen

My head is spinning. Nellie and Wyatt definitely had a story worth listening to. I'm in awe of the two. I think it's so sweet how Wyatt handled knowing Nellie was about to lose her mom. Their love is a powerful one. You can see it in the way they look at each other.

I'm literally fanning myself as the two take off to get lost somewhere. I think it's adorable how they can't seem to keep their hands off each other. I hope to find that someday. Someone to love, someone who loves me back with so much devotion.

"A penny for your thoughts."

His warm breath fans the shell of my ear. Sending a chill up my spine. I close my eyes.

I won't dare to think that Ryan is the one who will give me that type of love. I won't be fooled by these love stories. This is my real life. I'm not living in the fairytales come true that Bean, Kamara, and Nellie have shared with me.

I'm not going to fall victim to the lust I feel for this man. Ryan is dangerous. I can feel it with every fiber of my being. It would be easy to fall into the comfort of the trap he's setting for me.

Once I do, I'll be the one nursing a broken heart and hurt feelings. I'm not going to fly too close to this sun. I know for a fact it burns.

"Nellie and Wyatt have a great story," I force out, not wanting to reveal my true thoughts.

"Yeah, it's crazy. I never thought I'd see my brother fall so hard. I mean, there was a time when Wyatt just didn't care." I turn to see him shaking his head with a smile on his full lips. "But it's a good look for him. I've never seen him so happy in my life."

"Your family sticks together. I like that," I muse out loud.

"Yeah, it's the way Mom and Dad raised us."

He shrugs.

I think on his words. My father raised me and my brother to be proud of our family and to be there for each other. However, I've always felt a little like an outsider. My dad may spoil me, but I can't help having the feeling that my brother is in on something special.

It's like Dad and Nelson have a secret society I'm not a part of. If you listen closely enough, you can hear it in the way Dad calls my brother by name. Never Nelson, his American name, but Neruson or Ne my brother's nickname. Dad calls his name with such purpose—like there's meaning behind Ne's name alone.

I guess that's another reason I've been trying to create my own thing with film school. Sometimes, I just want desperately to make my father proud. Maybe then we can have our own thing like him and Ne.

"Where'd you go, gorgeous?"

Ryan's voice pulls me from my thoughts. It's like velvet caressing my skin. I have goosebumps covering my arms.

"I'm here," I say, waving him off.

Ryan twists his lips, giving me a sideways look. I hold my breath, waiting for him to call me on my bullshit. Something else I'm getting used to around here. Skepticism is still written all over his face when he responds to me.

"The party's getting ready to wrap up. A few of us are heading to the pub. If you're not too tired of stories, Felix and his fiancée will go next," he says.

I whip my head in the direction of Felix and the pretty girl I've noticed clinging to his side. The one he kissed earlier at breakfast. I had no idea they were engaged.

How on earth did I miss the rock on her finger?

It's huge, twinkling back at me as her hand rests on Felix's cheek. Felix has a possessive hold on her waist as he looks down at her with a secretive smile on his lips. She says something to him that makes his eyes light up.

My heart races when he places his forehead to hers. It looks like he's trying to breathe her in. They make a gorgeous couple. I tilt my head a bit. It seems like all the Blacks date women of color. At least all of those who I know are dating. I hadn't thought about it until this moment.

Felix's fiancée, I think I heard someone call her Kaye, has a pretty red bone complexion. She's bronzed but her skin has strong hues of red. Her black hair is silky with a wavy curl pattern. It's swept up on top of her head in a bun now, unlike this morning.

If I didn't know better, I would say she's Hispanic or perhaps some type of mid-eastern decent—but I do know better. Kaye looks more like one of my cousins on my mother's side. I'd bet my Prada bag she has some type of Caribbean heritage.

I don't think she's Asian. Possibly she does have some Hispanic background. I might go as far as saying she's Samoan, but I question that just a bit. Again, knowing my family.

Kaye is absolutely a mixed baby like me.

I watch as a cocoa brown colored little boy runs over to Kaye. He squeals something out, but I can't hear it from where I stand. He runs right into Felix's leg, wrapping himself around it.

John appears snatching the boy up in his embrace. The boy throws his head back in laughter. Kaye looks at the child with so much love. As if he were the most precious thing on earth.

It only takes seconds before Felix plucks the little guy from John's arms, placing him on his hip. Felix places his other arm around Kaye, pulling her in closer.

They look like the picture-perfect family. Yet, I don't know any of their relation to the boy. My mind runs wild with the possibilities. I narrow my eyes. I don't believe Felix to be the boy's father. Though, I could be wrong.

I'd say the little fella is about five or six. He's so cute. I noticed him playing with the twins earlier. However, I was too engulfed in Nellie and Wyatt's story to stop and think of who he might belong to.

"I can see the wheels turning." Ryan's words startle me as they get closer to my ear. "You're either wondering what our little family will look like or you're questioning my brother's little unit. You're probably thinking Felix has been hiding a kid like Toby's ass."

I turn to see the mirth in Ryan's eyes. I shake my head at him, trying not to allow my mind to go to what our children would look like. I chide myself for allowing him to plant such a seed. It will never come to that between us. When we return home, I plan to stay as far away from Ryan as I can get.

"I don't think that at all." I address his words about Felix's little family, ignoring his other statement. "Although, I have to say, I'm curious now."

"Oh, trust me, their story isn't one to be missed." I take notice of the twinkle in his eyes.

"So the pub it is," I reply with a shrug.

CHAPTER ONE

Secrets of a P.K.

Kaye

Almost six and a half years ago …

I feel trapped. It's been that way all my life. To the outside world I've always had to look perfect, act perfect, be perfect. On the inside, I'm a mess.

Or at least that's how I feel. I'm afraid of my own shadow. I want to be something that I'm not and I'm in love with someone that's not my someone.

Yup, an entire hot mess.

It's not easy being a P.K.—a Pastor's Kid. My daddy has been a pastor all my life. I've never known anything other than being the Pastor's daughter.

Imagine a six foot four Samoan, raised on the streets of Compton by his foster family. Now that same thugged out

Samoan has turned over a new leaf to be a leader in the community, but you can still see the thug in his eyes if you test him. Yeah, that's my daddy. You'd be a fool to try him.

Raises hand.

My brother tries my father too. We push buttons just to see how far he'll let us go, but we never push too far. Well, I don't. My brother, he's another story.

I just like to drive my daddy a little insane. Heck, I've been dating the same boy since my last year in junior high school because I know it pushes all of his hot buttons. My father can't stand Alberto.

"That boy is reckless, entitled, and arrogant as the day is long. You and your brother need to leave him to his own devices," Daddy normally rants.

Alberto is all those things. That's exactly why I chose him. Well, I have other reasons. I kind of stumbled into my relationship a long time ago—like literally.

It's hard not to feel stifled in my home. Knowing you're rocking the boat just a little can be like a drug. One hit and you just have to see what else you can throw into the pond to see if it ripples back.

Yup, I've tested being a rebel, but I've never gone too far. I want to. I want to have a freeing life like my big brother. A life that brightens the smile on my face with each day.

Danny's smile lights up the world around him. It's because he lives his life and doesn't apologize for it. Someday, I plan to be more like my brother. Outgoing, adventurous, a lover of life and the experience of it.

Which lead me here. In the apartment of the one guy, I've had a crush on all of my life.

Felix Black.

Just saying his name in my head makes my heart flutter. All the Black brothers are drop dead gorgeous. You go from hot to super-hot with the bunch of them.

Although Felix isn't the Black brother that all the girls run after first. He's too quiet and always has a book in his hands. Most of the girls in junior high and high school didn't think they could hold his attention.

There's just something about Felix that lets you know he's out of this world smart. It's not just a look, it's a persona. You know how you have people who pretend to be so smart?

Those people who are always giving wrong information and talking too much. Yet, there's that one quiet person in the room who has a secret smirk because they know that other person is full of shit. Yeah, that secret smirk belongs to Felix.

As I look at him now, I can see why girls were always so apprehensive to try to date him. Felix has a quiet strength about him that's intimidating. Something that's so hot and sexy, but mysteriously silent. Those long lashes—so dark and thick—casting shadows over his cheekbones. His golden eyes are sharp and watchful.

I love moments like this when he has on his glasses. He doesn't wear them often. He started wearing contacts when he went to college.

I'm here in his apartment so much I catch the rare moments when he does wear his frames. Moments when he sits in this apartment for hours reading into my deepest darkest secret. Turning through my pages over and over. Reading my words again and again to help me find what's missing.

Okay, okay, when I say my deepest darkest secrets that may be the writer in me. Then again, my father would be the one to think it's a dark sin best left in the shadow it comes from. Felix has been the one to encourage me otherwise.

I want to be a romance author. Not just any romance. I want to write the good stuff.

I haven't told anyone else. Not even my big brother. Felix is the only one who knows. He has kept my secret for years. Just one more reason to love him.

"This is good. It's really good. You're getting better and better," Felix murmurs as his gorgeous eyes scan over the pages.

"Be honest. I know you read it already, *speed-reader*," I tease because it's the truth.

Felix reads three times as fast as the average person. It's insane. He retains all the information and details, as well as the comprehension of the context. I know he's gotten to the part I'm most nervous about.

He places my writing journal on the coffee table and swings those eyes on me. Taking his glasses off, he studies me. I'm holding my breath. It's the same problem as always.

"It's still missing," he says simply.

I fall back on the couch and groan, throwing an arm over my face. I knew it before he said it. This is driving me insane. I'll never get it right.

"Maybe I should start writing something else. Maybe this is God's way of telling me this is wrong," I whine.

He lifts my arm from my face, looking down at me. I feel my pulse race from the simple touch. My heart is hammering. I try not to look down at his full lips, focusing on his gold orbs instead. I would give all the money in the world to run my fingers through that thick dark hair and push that beanie off his head.

Stop it, Kaye!

Ugh, my thoughts always get so crazy around him. I don't know why. I'm just his best friend's nerdy little sister. Felix has been so sweet to me for years. I've been taking advantage of that fact lately.

He'd probably put me out and get a restraining order if he knew I come here more to feed my crush than to have him read my books. I've gotten into the habit of writing ten thousand words a day just to have something to show up with.

"God is telling you no such thing. You're not giving up. I just told you, you're getting better," he says reassuringly.

"Yeah, but you're not talking about *that* part. You're talking about my world building and character development," I huff.

A grin comes to those gorgeous lips. He's laughing at me. I want to disappear into the couch.

"Kaye, you can't even say it. It's sex. It's not hard to say. You're having trouble writing your sex scenes," he says, mirth dripping from his words.

"You don't have to laugh at me," I murmur through my hurt feelings.

"I'm not laughing at you," he says, letting a chuckle slip. "Okay, okay, maybe just a little. It's just … I don't know. Not the writing, it's the actually sex in the scenes. You sound like you have no idea what you're doing."

"Maybe because I don't," I say, pouting in frustration.

His brows draw in. Those eyes … I've never seen anything like it before. It's like you see the exact moment he locks in on you and starts to read your soul. I turn away to prevent him from seeing yet another of my secrets. The one secret I don't own all to myself. If I did, I'd tell him.

His long fingers go under my chin, turning my face back toward his. I can see all the questions in his eyes. I've opened a can of worms. I know Felix and once he wants to know something he doesn't stop until he gets to the bottom of it.

"Help me understand," he says in that deep voice that does all types of things to my belly. "I want to help you with your writing, but you seem to be stuck here. I don't understand why—"

"It's nothing. I should just write sweet romance and stop trying to go for the shock factor. It's not like my father would ever let me publish it anyway," I reply.

"You're a grown woman now. You can make whatever decision you decide to, Kaye. I know your father has always been strict, but I don't think he would have as big a problem with this as you think," he says gently.

"You can't be serious," I scoff.

"I am. Besides, your books would feel like they're missing something completely if you go the sweet route. You have something here. It's like the buildup and chemistry is there, but when you get to it mechanic—"

His words cutoff and he homes in on my face as several thoughts race across his features. Intrigue, confusion, and shock. I feel like I'm shrinking into myself.

"I should go. Thanks for reading the pages for me. I'm going to go work on it. I'm thinking about submitting this time," I rush to say and move out of his reach to get my journal.

He places a hand on my arm, causing me to turn to look back at him. The hum I feel travel up my limb and through my body is absolutely insane. This … this right here is why my buildups are so amazing. I write them from moments like this. When I'm around Felix and I feel this charge, it's … it's something I can't fully describe and trust me I have tried.

"Wait, are you saying you've never—," he starts to ask.

Thank God for cell phones. Mine rings, saving the day. It was a slip of the tongue that has gotten me here. Now I'm going to have to wiggle my way out of this.

"Hey, Danny," I sing into the cell phone so grateful to my brother.

And then, my world starts to fall apart. Anyone who knows my family knows that my brother and I are super close. I'd do anything for Danny. Anything.

Felix

There is no way Kaye is saying what I think she's saying. At twenty there is no way she's never been kissed or fucked. I mean, come on. Kaye's body has starred in more of my dreams than I care to admit.

Yeah, I know Pastor Porter has been super strict on both Danny and Kaye. Still, I'm having a hard time believing what I think she's hiding. This isn't adding up in my head.

For one, I know her boyfriend has been sexually active. Yeah, not even going to get into that one. Alberto and Danny both confirmed that Kaye and Alberto had broken up during that one time. Danny being Kaye's brother and super close to her, I believed him and went on to mind my own business.

Okay, that's a lie. I went on to plot my chance to finally ask Kaye out. She was away at the church's women's convention. I was going to ask her to a movie when she returned. To this day, I don't know how she and Alberto made up so fast.

Probably for the best. Not only is Kaye my best friend's sister. She's been dating my other best friend off and on since junior high school. I can't blame Alberto.

Just look at her. Kaye is gorgeous. Those dark brown eyes, her clay brown complexion—more reds mixed in with that bronzed brown color. Her black hair can go from looking like thick silk to one big curly mass of wool. Either way, she's always gorgeous—and I've seen it all. I've crushed on her for years.

Most people mistake Kaye and Danny for being Hispanic. They're not. They're a mix of Polynesian, Jamaican, and African American-Creole. Their family gives them a uniqueness of their own. Their home is full of cultures that have colored my life since I first made friends with Danny in kindergarten.

My Irish-Scot ass has had a thing for curry goat, jerk chicken, and roti since I was six—thanks to Grandma Reid, Kaye and Danny's maternal grandmother. Their maternal grandfather is the reason I love gumbo and cherry wine. I can sit with Grandpa Reid for hours and talk cars and computers.

I care for the Porter family as if they were my own. It's the reason I've hidden my feelings for Kaye for years. Even before she started to date Alberto, I kept my feelings a secret because of the family. Honestly, I was crushed when the two started dating.

Which brings me back to my questions. If I go by the way Kaye writes love scenes that would suggest so much that Alberto isn't doing for her. Yeah, I've always said something is odd about their relationship. I also know how bias I am, so I tend to turn a blind eye to anything concerning their relationships.

Stop overthinking, Felix. She's probably saving herself for marriage. Her father is a Pastor, you know.

I know all of this to be true, but I also know Danny threw all of that out of the window. He got his dick wet as soon as he could. I remember all the porn he would sneak over to Alberto's.

Like John, Danny has a singular taste when it comes to his porn. However, unlike with John, I couldn't get into a lot of what Danny liked to watch. Still, I know for a fact he's no virgin.

Honestly, I can justify the lack of sex. Kaye's a girl. Losing her virginity should be special. If she's waiting for marriage, I respect that. It's just … yeah, something isn't adding up.

The wheels turn in my head. Conversations with Alberto, Kaye's writing over the years. Sure, Alberto could be lying on his dick, but with Kaye simple kisses in her writing seem a bit off.

They would have kissed at some point over the years, right?

"Slow down, Danny. Okay, okay. I'm on my way," Kaye's voice pulls me from my musing.

She hangs up the phone and starts to gather her things. Her hands are shaking. I'm instantly on alert.

"Hey, is everything okay?" I ask.

"I … I don't know. I … I have to go," she rushes.

"Oh, okay, sure," I murmur. "You want me to drop you off? I was going to see my mom anyway."

"No, thank you," she says, as she shakes her head.

If I'm not mistaken, I think I see tears gathering.

"Kaye, what's wrong? Do you need me to come with you?"

"No, no," she says quickly, shaking her head. "I'll call you later. Okay?"

"Should I call Danny?" I persist.

"*No,*" she says frantically.

I draw my brows. There isn't much I haven't gone through with these two. When Grandpa Reid had a cancer scare, I was there with them.

When Pastor Porter talked about moving the entire family across country, I was there. I sat writing a petition with Kaye and Danny to get their dad to see why they needed to stay. Granted, Pastor Porter's words to us were, *I'll do what the Lord tells me to do.*

We spent weeks in their treehouse praying the Lord would tell him to stay put. The Lord heard us. Pastor Porter was offered a better opportunity here in California.

Through all of that I was there. I can't imagine why Danny wouldn't want me to be there for him now. I look down at my phone to see if I missed a call.

Nothing.

I shrug it off. Maybe it's a brother, sister thing. My brothers and I can get like that. I'll check in with Danny later.

For now, I let everything go. My questions about Kaye's personal life and whatever could be going on with Danny. After all, there's always tomorrow.

CHAPTER TWO

Devastated

Felix

Six months later ...

I sit up with a head splitting headache. I drank way too much last night. I reach for my head, and it all comes back to me.

The car accident that took the lives of my two best friends, my brothers coming to be there for me, and the tattoos. We all got tattoos last night.

I reach for my ribs and close my eyes. I have my reasons for placing my tat there. My mind shifts from my night with my brothers to Kaye. She wouldn't answer my calls last night.

To tell the truth, I haven't seen Kaye in months. Not since that day she rushed out of my apartment. Things have been weird between me and my friends.

I had planned to go to that party last night to see if I could close the gap that seemed to be forming between me and the guys. Alberto hasn't been around much lately. The one time I did link up with Danny, something was off.

I've known these guys all my life. I can read them just as well as I can read my brothers, my own flesh and blood. Danny was hiding something. He seemed so stressed out and then he asked me for that weird favor.

"Felix, promise me. If anything ever happens to me. You'll be there for Kaye. Watch out for her for me," he said.

"Dude, what the fuck?" I had replied.

He only slammed the shutters down so I couldn't look into his eyes. He sat and waited for me to make the promise and I made it. He would never have to ask me twice for something like that.

Kaye will always be special to me. If I wasn't crazy about her, I'd say she were like a sister to me. I drop my head in my hands. I feel so guilty for having thoughts like that.

Pushing that guilt aside, I reach for my phone to try Kaye again. Again, her phone goes to straight to voicemail. I run a hand through my hair and blow out a breath.

I make a face at my own foulness. I need a shower and to brush my damn teeth. Then, I plan to go pay my respects and see what I can do to help out.

Kaye

My soul aches in ways I could never explain. I've lost not one but two of the most important people in my life. Yet, I can't return home. Six months ago, my brother asked me to do something for him that I still can't believe I said yes to.

In my heart, I wonder if he'd still be here if I'd said no. Daddy always says the women in our family are enablers when it comes to Danny. We help him get away with murder.

A sob tears from my lips. This time he was trying to save a life. I don't know what happened in that car, but I can't help feeling like Danny and Alberto made a trade. I've told two huge lies in my life, and they have both landed me here.

Alone, scared, and without my big brother to make it right.

"What are we supposed to do now?"

The lack of emotion in her voice makes me want to turn and pounce. Some people are so selfish. The precious air she's breathing is a blessing. I would kill for that to be Danny standing there watching me, but it's not.

"We continue with the plan," I reply just so she'll go away.

CHAPTER THREE

Laid to Rest

Felix

A week later ...
I look around for the millionth time. Something is wrong. Kaye should be here.

Never in a million years would I think she would miss her brother's funeral. I can't wrap my head around it.

At first, I thought maybe she was in the restroom or something, trying to pull it together. When we loaded the casket into the back of the hearse and there was still no sign of Kaye, I couldn't focus on anything else. I started to panic and think that something happened to her.

I was only able to relax after overhearing Pastor Porter telling someone that Kaye was devastated and she wouldn't make it in time. Still, something isn't fitting together. You don't grow up in a family's home without learning a whole lot about that family.

There is a quiet anger beneath it all. Pastor Porter is holding so much in, I think he's going to bust soon. Granted, finding out that Alberto's blood alcohol level was enough to keep him from behind the wheel is enough to consume anyone with rage.

However, I see something else. Something beyond what he's dealing with on the surface.

"You all right?" Wyatt asks beside me as others start to leave the grave site. "You want to head out?"

"I'm okay," I murmur. "Can you guys give me a minute? I'll be right there."

"Yeah, you got it, man. Anything you need," Noah replies.

I give my family a weak smile. I'm grateful that they all took the time to be here with me. My mother steps forward and I bend so she can kiss my cheek.

This has been hard for her. Danny has run through our home hundreds of times over the years. He was another one of the kids she took in for her own.

"I love ye," she whispers.

"I love you too, Mom," I reply.

She and my brothers turn to leave. I turn to look at the Porter family. Mrs. Porter and Grandma Reid look wrecked. I think about turning away to let them have this time. I'll catch them at the house.

Just as I go to turn, Pastor Porter turns. He sees me and waves me over. I nod and move to join them around the hole their son has just been lowered into.

"Good to see you, son," Pastor Porter says.

"Tanks, Felix. I know Danny would've wanted you to be one of 'em pallbearers," Grandma Reid says with her thick Jamaican accent.

"Yes, he would have really—"

Mrs. Porter can't finish her words. I feel my own tears stinging the backs of my eyes. I hate seeing her in so much pain. She's been like another mother to me.

"I'm here for anything you all need. Don't hesitate to ask," I say.

"You can go get my granddaughter and bring her back home," Grandpa Reid grumbles.

"Daddy," Mrs. Porter snaps.

Grandpa Reid rolls his eyes and grumbles something under his breath. I don't miss the daggers he shoots in Pastor Porter's direction. Warning bells go off.

"Is everything okay with Kaye?" I ask.

"She's been doing some mission work. She wouldn't have made it back in time for the services," Pastor Porter replies.

"So the good Pastor is a bold face liar now, ay?" Grandma Reid says.

"Mama," Mrs. Porter hisses.

Grandma Reid sucks her teeth long and slow. Her body language tells me a whole lot. Grandpa Reid looks like he's restraining himself. I've never seen this kind of tension between these four.

"Gyal, mi held mi tongue for months. Now, yuh ave one pickney in the ground and the other yuh drove from ar home," Grandma Reid snaps.

"No one drove her from her home. She chose to be fast and where has that gotten her. A dead—"

"Don't you do this here," Mrs. Porter snarls. "Not at my son's grave. You will not do this *here!*"

"We'll see you at the house." Pastor Porter nods at me and turns, ushering a broken Mrs. Porter away.

Her pissed off looking parents follow behind them. Again, all their body language telling a story. I read what I can as I stand watching them walk away. I don't know what's going on, but I know for sure I'm going to find out.

Where the hell are you, Kaye? What's going on?

Kaye

My face is soaked with tears. Today hurts so much. I watch as my family walks away to climb into the waiting limousine. I want to rush over to jump into Felix's arms. One hug from him would make this all just a little more bearable.

I give a weak smile when a memory of my brother and Felix giving me birthday hugs fills my head. I lived for those hugs when I was younger. What I would give for one now.

Instead of rushing out of the shadows, I wait. Felix stands there for about ten minutes more before all his brothers return to surround him. My heart breaks into tiny pieces on top of the already shattered pieces, when they have to support Felix to walk away.

He has always been such a good friend to Danny. Bitter rage builds when I think of my brother's other so-called friend. I don't know if I will ever forgive Alberto for this.

I drag my body over to the open grave of my brother. I drop to my knees beside it, wiping a hand under my nose. I can't stop the tears from falling.

"You didn't think I wouldn't show up, did you?" I give a tearful laugh.

My lips tremble as I stare down at the casket inside the dirt. I can't believe this is where my brother will rest his head forever. This is so unfair and wrong.

"What happened, Danny?" I sob. "Why'd you get in the car with him? You had to know he had been drinking. What were you thinking?"

I punch the tops of my thighs in frustration. This shouldn't be happening. I shouldn't be here saying goodbye to my brother.

I lie on my side and let the tears flow. I wish there were something I could do to change this. I'd give anything to make it right.

"You deserved better than this, Danny. I don't ever want to love someone if this is where it lands me. You deserved so much more than this," I cry out.

CHAPTER FOUR

Overwhelmed

Kaye

Two weeks later ...

I'm so tired. I didn't think it would be like this. It wasn't supposed to be like this. When Danny asked me to do this, he had a plan. It was all supposed to work out differently.

I just don't know what to do now. If I go home, I'll have to explain. Explaining will lead to questions, questions will lead to answers I just can't give. Danny trusted me. I need to do this in his memory.

Besides, things have been said. Words have cut to bleed and left wounds that have not yet healed. As much as I need help, my pride won't allow me to go back with my tail between my legs.

I groan when the doorbell rings, causing all chaos to break loose all over again. I'm going to kill whoever is at that door for stealing my hard-won peace. I drag my tired body up the hallway of the small apartment I now live in.

"Maybe that's that selfish heifer," I mutter.

Though I doubt it. I've never seen someone run so fast—not even a glance back. I huff out a breath to release my frustration. Thinking about the past, no matter how fresh it is, isn't going to help me.

When I open the door, I freeze. I should have known he would find me. I know I look a hot mess, but that's the least of my worries.

Yet, as I stand here staring up into those golden eyes, I'm at a loss. He looks so good. That beanie strategically placed on his head, covering his thick locks.

The front of his hair peeking out in an artful tousle that covers just a bit of his forehead. He has on a black leather jacket on that lean swimmer's body, over a gray t-shirt. A pair of blue jeans clinging to his long legs and black boots on his feet that tell me there's a chance he rode a bike here.

It's not fair that he always looks so good. I mean seriously. He must roll out of bed in the morning singing and dancing like he's the star in a movie.

Yes, *Grease* pops into my tired head. I need sleep. My thoughts are a random mess.

I don't know whether to be relieved or panicked. I settle on being able to take a shower.

"Come in," I whisper when I find my voice.

Felix

I found her. I'm still having trouble with what led me to her. However, the scene before me reveals that my source was way more than accurate. Kaye looks exhausted and the small bundle in her arms won't stop screaming.

I step into the apartment and close the door behind me. I look around the place. It's not the greatest, but it's not horrible.

I'm still trying to wrap my mind around all of this. I feel like I'm in an alternate universe. At any moment someone is going to tell me this is all a joke.

"Why wouldn't you tell me?"

The words are out of my mouth before I can think better of it. Kaye looks too tired to think, least of all have a conversation about anything. She could probably use a good shower too from the looks of the stained up t-shirt she has on.

"It's a long story. Not everything looks as it seems," she says tiredly. "Right now, I need you to hold Dashawn while I take a shower and maybe a brief nap."

With those words, she places the tiny baby in my arms and turns for the back of the apartment. She just had a baby. My best friend's baby. I should feel like a total perv for staring at her sexy brown legs and the swell of her ass beneath her t-shirt.

I should but I don't. I can't take my eyes away. The little dude lets me know he doesn't appreciate it, as he gets louder, demanding my attention.

I tear my eyes from Kaye to look down at the little baby in my arms. He's cute. Of course, he would be with a gorgeous mother like Kaye. He has her nose and lips, with a head full of jet-black hair.

His little face is starting to turn red with his loud cries. I think, trying to remember how mom shut my younger brothers up when they would scream down the house. I actually remember something from dad, not mom.

I move over to the couch and start to shrug out of my leather. Sitting down with the little guy still wailing in my arms, I lay him down on the couch. Moving fast to make quick work of tearing off my t-shirt before he can roll off the cushion or something.

It's warm in here. I unwrap him from the little blanket he's in and get him out of his tiny shirt thing. I fumble with the snaps for a second before pulling it free and getting it off him.

I think I start to sweat from the fear of hurting him while trying to undress him. I'm as gentle as I can be, careful of his head. All while he shouts at me like I'm the world's biggest idiot.

I have no idea how such a tiny human has reduced me to feeling completely incompetent. I decide to leave his little mittens on. I think they have a purpose. Scooping the crying baby back up, I lie him on my chest and lean back on the couch's back rest. He quiets down a little. His cute little face still screwed up. I start to rub his small back to see if that helps.

This is working. You got this, Black.

He gives a little yawn, his lids close and the crying stops. His small back starts to rise and fall with his sleeping breaths. I'm pretty pleased with myself.

Round one, win goes to Felix.

I brush a finger across his little cheek. It's so soft and he's so adorable. My eyes move to his little ear, it's two toned, dark at the top. He's not as dark as Kaye, but not as light as Alberto.

Dashawn.

He smells really good. I touch his tiny covered hand that is resting on my bare chest. It flexes a little within the mitten under my light caress.

I touch a lock of his hair. It's silky to the touch. I can't help scanning his face to find traits of Alberto.

A jealous pang hits me in the chest. I think Kaye and I would make beautiful babies. I close my eyes as that thought floats through my head.

I shouldn't be jealous of a dead friend, but I am. He left a great woman and a beautiful baby boy behind. I think back to the last time I saw Kaye.

She was pregnant then. She had to be. It hurts that she didn't say anything at the time. I can't believe I read into her words so poorly.

It goes to show how off my game I am when she's around. Kaye turns my thoughts into mush. I've been trying to relive that day over and over to see how I got things so wrong.

I wonder if Danny found out about her being pregnant and freaked out. Maybe that was why she didn't want me to come along. That could also be the reason he never answered my calls that day.

I'm still trying to gather the details in my head that will make this all make sense. I wish I could turn back time and be there for her while she went through her pregnancy. The little guy on my chest makes a sighing sound as if he agrees with me.

"Don't worry. Uncle Felix is here for you now. I'll make sure you and your mommy are always safe and okay," I murmur to the sleeping baby.

His body snuggles down into mine, causing my lips to curl into a smile. I can do this. I can help Kaye. I guess now I know why Danny asked me to look after her.

Kaye

I feel human again. I never knew a shower could be such a blessing. I stumble out of my bedroom in shorts and a t-shirt feeling like I can take on the world.

I still could use a nap, but it's been too quiet out there. I need to make sure Dashawn hasn't eaten Felix and teethed on his bones. Oh God, he's going to teethe someday.

I groan internally. I don't know if I'm built for this.

Oh, Sweet Baby Jesus.

I skid to a halt. My heart feels like it might burst from my chest. My panties are definitely useless. I rethink being built for motherhood. My ovaries are pulsing as my eyes soak in the sight before me.

Felix is on my couch shirtless. The baby is out of his onesies covered in only his diaper and one of Felix's palms. They are both fast asleep.

I feel my face melt into a warm smile as I try not to coo out loud. I feel the tears on my cheeks before I can ward them off. I haven't had time to break down since Dashawn was born.

I've wanted to, but I haven't had the luxury. Lifting my t-shirt, I wipe the tears from my face. When I drop my shirt, something catches my attention.

I move closer to get a better look. I lick my lips when those abs and that tight v come into view. Felix has the words Brothers Black tattooed up his right side, running over his ribs.

My fingers itch to touch the ink. I wonder when he got it. The last time we surfed together it wasn't there.

I would know. I've studied that body enough to tell you the number of freckles he has on his back. I look at his muscled arm lying limply beside his body and long to have it wrapped around me.

I could use a hug so badly. I'm just on the verge of falling apart. I probably would have within the next few hours if he hadn't shown up.

I can't help myself. I need human adult contact before I crumble. I climb quietly onto the couch and snuggle into his right side. He stirs a bit but doesn't wake. Placing my head on his shoulder, I close my eyes and silently cry myself to sleep.

CHAPTER FIVE

You Don't Know

Felix

I feel something small resting on my chest and something much larger weighing down my side and shoulder. When I open my eyes, it takes me a moment to remember where I am. My fingers flex protectively against the baby's back.

When I look down, he's chewing on his tiny mitten covered fist while staring up at me. I grin at the little guy. He's awfully quiet but I'm not going to complain. I look to my right to see what the other weight is, only to find Kaye snuggled into my side.

All her hair is brushed back away from her face into a ponytail. Her full lips are parted, a peaceful expression covers her features. She looks so beautiful in her sleep.

Her lips are only inches away, all I have to do is lean in and have a taste. I lightly brush my lips against her forehead instead. When I pull away my eyes drop to her lips again.

I wonder if she's ever felt the charge I feel whenever she's close to me or when I touch her. A tiny whimper breaks me from my thoughts. I look back at Dashawn. His face is tightening up, ready to start wailing.

"Hold on, little guy," I coo at him, rubbing my hand on his back.

I gently pry my body from underneath Kaye's, trying not to wake her. I feel the loss of her warmth immediately. Dashawn starts to whine in my hold, causing me to get up and start away from Kaye. I want her to sleep as long as she likes.

"Hungry, little guy?" I ask the baby.

Looking at the clock, I've been here about three hours. I hadn't fallen asleep for that long. I make my way into the kitchen to learn the lay of the land. I freeze as I see the empty bottles on the counter.

Oh shit, she could be breastfeeding. I'll have to wake her if there's no milk in the refrigerator. I open the door and almost sag in relief to found more bottles with milk. I take one out and look round.

I'll need to heat this in that pot. Cool.

I move over to the pot of water sitting on the stove. I dump it and refill it, not sure why I take the extra step. This little guy is starting to squirm, he'll be screaming soon if I don't hurry up.

I'm running on autopilot as I get the bottle warmed. I don't know where I come up with all this knowledge of caring for babies, but I have the bottle tested for temperature and the little guy sucking the bottle down before I know it.

Don't leave him gassy.

Nodding at my own thoughts, I remove the half-finished bottle and start to pat his little back. Not getting any results, I try a little harder. He lets out a big belch that has me looking down at him in awe. I start to smell something foul.

"Aw, come on. I thought we were becoming friends," I groan.

Sticking a finger in the back of the diaper that's swallowing his little ass, I peek inside pulling a face immediately. This little dude has some real shit with him. I look back at the living room longing for Kaye to get up but knowing I'm not going to wake her.

"Come on," I huff.

I start out of the kitchen to find the bedroom and his diapers. I pass by one room. It's dark with the door half open. I note that it's another bedroom and there's a bed inside. I go to the room with the open door and the lights on.

I look around and the place is a mess. Baby things everywhere. This is so unlike Kaye. She's a neat freak. Her room has always been spotless. Danny used to pay her to clean his room so he wouldn't be placed on punishment.

"Looks like I got here just in time," I murmur to the baby. "Let's clean your stinky little ass and then we'll get to this room."

Kaye

I wake to the aromas of bacon and something sweet. Uncurling from a ball on the couch, I stretch. I freeze the moment I realize Dashawn is not with me.

Panic seizes me. I jump up from the couch to rush toward the kitchen where the smells are coming from. I breathe out a relieved breath when I find Dashawn safe in his bouncer that's sitting in the center of the kitchenette table.

He's fast asleep without a care in the world. Felix has his t-shirt back on, while standing at the stove flipping a piece of what looks like French toast. My stomach growls at the same time Felix turns toward me.

"Hey, sleepyhead," he croons, a hint of a sexy rasp in his voice.

I love it when his voice does that. It happens when you catch him coming out of deep thought. Just a whisper of roughness to his already deep voice. My nipples tighten just from the sound brushing against my ears.

"Hey," I say, dipping my head and placing my arms across my chest.

"He'll be up again soon. We should probably eat fast. I'm on this last bottle, not sure how to make more or if you're pumping or planning to just breastfeed," he says, his eyes dropping to my arms over my breasts.

"How would I do that?" I blurt out.

His brows mirror mine as they draw in. He walks me over to the table as he places a plate down. I inch past him in the small space to sit in the chair he has pulled out. He goes to cut off the burner and fix his own plate, before sitting across from me.

"They didn't give you classes or something? They should have helped you get him to latch or whatever. We can get you one of those pumps. Maybe YouTube or google how they work," he says once seated.

I crease my brows deeper. Tilting my head at him, I then search his face. I snap my head back when understanding hits.

My shoulders sag. He's just like my father. Making assumptions.

"How did you find me?" I ask.

His jaw tightens a bit. He places his fork down, sitting back in his seat to cross his arms over his chest. I know that look. He's pissed.

"The question is ... why the hell did I have to find you? What's going on with you, Kaye? Why would you run off and not tell me what was going on with you?

"Why weren't you there for the funeral? Why is there no name on the birth certificate for his father? I get being mad at Alberto for what he did, but the Perez family should be helping you—"

"Wait, how do you know there isn't a father listed on the birth certificate? Oh, wow! That's how you find me. Shoot." I rub my temple.

"Seriously, that's what you have to say to all of that," he growls.

I lift my hands up to halt his anger. He has this all wrong. Maybe he didn't jump to conclusions like my father.

He assumed based on that document that led him to me. I lick my dry lips and get ready to spill the truth to the only person I think I'll ever be willing to tell. Felix is known for keeping other's secrets.

I've trusted him with my own. Now, I'll trust him with my brother's.

"It's not what it looks like. Dashawn is not my son. Well, I didn't give birth to him. We just made it look that way.

"His mother used my name and information to use my insurance. My dad is pissed at me, but he hasn't cut my employee benefits from the church. Not yet anyway," I explain.

Confusion takes over his face. I chew my lips nervously. If anyone were to find out what we've done, we could be in big trouble. Yet another reason I can't go home and tell the truth. My father would have a coronary.

"*Kaye*," Felix drags out on a groan, rubbing the back of his neck. "What the hell have you gotten yourself into? Hold on … he looks just like you."

"Yeah, he would. He's my brother's son," I reply.

Felix unfolds his arms and drags a hand down his face. I can see the stunned look in his eyes. All of this is nuts.

I'm still trying to wrap my head around it and I'm the one living through it.

"Tell me what the heck I'm missing. You're clearly in over your head. I have a feeling Danny wouldn't want you to be living like this," he says, holding a hand up to gesture at the apartment I now call home.

"I wasn't supposed to be here. After the baby was born, I was supposed to be moving into a nicer place. Danny was going to take care of everything. Alberto was going to cover the bills," I say to my hands in my lap.

"Wait, Alberto knew about this?" Felix asks, clearly in shock.

"Yeah, there's a lot more to the story," I respond. "Alberto and I were never a real couple. I … one summer, you guys were like fifteen. I wanted to be wherever you guys were. I rode to the beach house hoping to find you guys.

"When I got there, I got the surprise of my life. I didn't know what to do or think. I just stood there with my mouth open. I mean—"

I shake my head at the memory. My young innocent mind couldn't put the pieces together back then. I was confused and freaked out.

"When Alberto's eyes lifted to find me, he looked like he would be sick. Danny was the next one to look up. My brother looked like his world was about to crumble. The girl was the last one to notice me. She just giggled, pushed them off and tossed her clothes on." I pause to look up at Felix.

He's watching me intently. No expression on his face to reveal what he's thinking. I bite my lip feeling like I'm about to betray my brother.

"For months, I couldn't get the image out of my head. Danny on top of that girl and Alberto on top of Danny." I shake my head trying to clear the image even now. "Danny sat me down and tried to explain. He told me he wasn't gay, but my father wouldn't understand him being Bi. He and Alberto had been a thing for a while. They found girls who would agree to sleep with both of them.

"Alberto freaked out. He thought I was going to run and tell. He kept saying his dad would kill him. I don't know what made me do it.

"I had just gotten into it with my dad over something really stupid. My idea to get back at him was just as dumb. I knew me dating Alberto would piss Daddy off.

"I told them I'd be quiet about it if Alberto helped me to push my father's buttons. They were all for it. I'd unknowingly offered to be Alberto's beard.

"I found out later that Alberto's father had been getting suspicious. They were already afraid and needed to figure something out. As the years went by, I saw and heard some of the things Alberto's father said and did to him.

"I kept up the ruse as much to make my Daddy angry as I did for Alberto's sake. I noticed his dad was a little easier on him as long as we were *dating*." I make air quotes as I say the last word.

"Yeah, he's an asshole," Felix grumbles.

"You can say that again. We had tried to call it off once. His father berated him in front of a bunch of guests at a dinner party. Danny and I had only been there because Alberto asked us to come.

"I made the mistake of saying we broke up and all hell broke loose. I was in near tears for Alberto by the end of the night. Then there's my father.

"Danny was so scared Daddy would lose it on him. He and Alberto were in a relationship for years. They had a few steady girlfriends from time to time, but they remained a couple or whatever, forever. I say whatever because they swore they weren't boyfriends." I stop to rub my forehead.

"I can't for the life of me tell you what they were thinking. Christa was one of their steady partners. She and her family are members at Daddy's church—"

"Yeah, I know her," he replies. "I've seen her with Danny a time or two."

"She's Dashawn's mother. Those idiots weren't using protection. She got pregnant and started to threaten to expose them both. She knows Alberto's dad is a big-time producer and his mom is an actress. She wanted money for the abortion and to keep quiet."

"She was blackmailing them? Why didn't they come to me?" Felix asks, pain lacing his words.

"Danny wanted to. Alberto didn't want you to know. He gave her the money, but Danny couldn't live with her killing the baby. That's when they dragged me in. Christa said she would be quiet about everything if no one ever found out she had the baby.

"The last time I saw you was when Danny asked me to do this. To pretend to be the baby's mother until he could figure something out. Christa and I would stay out of view while she was pregnant. Danny said he'd take care of everything afterward.

"I know how crazy this all sounds. It was crazy when Danny asked me to do it. At first, I told him no. I'd gone to the house with him so he could come clean with everything. Things just didn't turn out as planned," I scoff.

"What happened?" he coaxes.

"We got to the house, and you know Daddy. He can sniff out when something is wrong. He pounced on me before we could get a word in.

"Called me irresponsible. He knew I'd let that boy get me pregnant one of these days. I've never seen a penis other than that day I walked in on Danny and Alberto.

"How the heck could I be pregnant and irresponsible? I've done everything my father has asked me to do all my life. Even when I try to be bad it falls flat.

"The one thing I love to do, I'm too afraid to do because I know he wouldn't approve and there I sat being berated and thrown under the bus for something I didn't do.

"I snapped. If I was going to be blamed, I might as well protect my brother. I got into it so bad with my father, he threw me out. Told me go stay with my spoiled baby's daddy.

"Alberto wanted Christa as far away from them as he could get her, so we flew here that night. I was so mad. Danny knew I didn't want to go back, that's when he promised me a nicer place once the baby was born," I say, wiping at my tears. "That never happened."

"I walked in on one of their threesomes before. Not like you did. They were both having sex with the girl. I was so pissed.

"I thought Alberto was cheating on you. Danny covered for him …"

His words trail off and he stares into thin air. Knowing Felix, he's thinking of all the ways he could have helped if he'd known. He takes his beanie off to run his hand through his hair then replaces it.

"I—"

My words are cutoff by my nephew's little cries. I go to get up to get his bottle, but Felix places a hand on my arm. That hum seems to be stronger as it zaps up my limb. I lift my eyes to his, but once again he's masking all his emotions.

"Sit and eat. Let's get you guys fed, then we'll figure all this out. I have family here in New York. We'll be calling in a few favors," he says.

"Thank you," I say softly.

He leans in to kiss my forehead.

"Anything for you," he murmurs.

I chide the butterflies in my belly. He means that as a big brother. Nothing more, nothing less.

CHAPTER SIX

Trading Favors

Felix

"Good to see ya," Jamie says, pulling me into a hug.

"Likewise," I reply patting him on the back.

"Logan said yer in need. So the gang is heading in to set ya right. He's on his way, just needed to make a stop. What's up?"

I turn and wave Kaye over. She hesitates for a moment before stepping forward nervously with Dashawn's carrier clutched in her fingers. I give her a reassuring smile. Jamie is my family. I'd only trust Kaye and Dashawn's care to family.

I can't drag her ass back home like I want to. The truth of the matter is what they've done is illegal. She could get into a lot of serious trouble. I need to call Mairettie and get some advice on how to cover her ass on this.

When I know what all we're facing legally, I'll bury this shit so far you'd have to be Houdini to uncover the truth. I need to make sure the birth certificate will stick, and I need to make sure Christa never comes back to cause any problems. She didn't want anything to do with Dashawn, I'm going to make sure it stays that way.

For now, I need Kaye and the baby safe. That apartment in Queens wasn't my idea of safe. One call to my cousin Logan and he had a new place for Kaye within the hour.

I'm sort of grateful Danny made the choice to hide her in New York. I can control things here—even when I'm not here. This is as good as my city as Logan told me over the phone earlier. She'll be more than safe here.

"Kaye this is my cousin, Jamie. Jamie these two are as important to me as Mom, Dad, and my brothers. You get what I mean?"

"Aye, I got ya. This place is as safe as can be. Would put my own sisters here and wouldn't lose sleep. We won't be far away. Anything ya need, ya give us a call." Jamie directs his last words at Kaye.

I crowd her space when his green eyes scan her. I want to make it clear that she's not available. Not that Kaye is mine. I just know the men in my family and Jamie is one to charm the pants off a pretty girl in a heartbeat.

Jamie's eyes twinkle with mirth and his lips kick up into a smile, but he gives me a nod of understanding. That's all I need. I trust him like one of my brothers. We don't get to spend a lot of time together, but we're still close.

"Thank you," Kaye says. "It's nice to meet you."

"Aye, nice to meet ya too, lass," he says, before turning and waving us to follow him. "Let's get the babe inside. Connie is up there getting things ready for ya guys. It's a three-bedroom apartment, but it's a walk up."

"You okay?" I lean into Kaye's ear to ask.

She shivers, turning her head up to look at me. I move closer to share some of my warmth. It's a bit cooler here in Brooklyn. That other apartment will be a distant memory for her now that I'm here. That place was a sweatbox.

"I'm fine." She nods, turning away before I can get a read on her eyes.

I reach for the carrier, taking it from her hands to carry the baby up the stairs for her. We all walk up to the fourth-floor apartment. My eyes are trained on the sway of her ass in her tight blue jeans.

Damn. Does she know how sexy her walk is? I'd bite the shit out of that ass.

I frown at my own thoughts. I'm still sorting through my thoughts and feelings about everything Kaye has told me. The one thing standing out at the forefront is that she was never in a relationship with Alberto.

She's mine to claim.

Guilt settles in as that thought crosses my mind. I never told Danny how I felt about his sister. It doesn't feel right that I never told him.

Just as quickly, my guilt turns to anger. Danny should've told me what was going on. He should've trusted me with the truth. It would have saved us all a lot of pain. Still, I know none of that would've kept the two of them out of that car crash.

"Here we are," Jamie croons. "That's me sister over there munching on the food I bought for ya. Connie, stop stuffing your gub with her food."

"Shut up, Jamie," Connie hisses back. "I'm starving. Cole didn't let me finish me breakfast before he started barking orders. I've been running all day."

"Quit ya belly aching. He sent ya shopping. Yer in heaven and ya know it," Jamie grumbles.

Connie flips Jamie the bird, giving him the evil eye. She wipes her hands off, before rushing over to give me a hug. I return the embrace with one arm, still holding Dashawn inside his carrier.

"Oh, let me see the wee lad," Connie coos when she pulls away.

She bends at the waist to pull the blanket back. Dashawn is wide awake, sucking on his pacifier as he looks back at us. He's an alert baby for his age. His eyes roll over Connie then bounce to me.

"He's adorable. Ya have to come see what I've done with his room," Connie gushes. "Oh fuck, where are me manners? I'm Connie, by the way."

She straightens and pulls Kaye into a hug. I roll my lips trying not to laugh at my cousin. The O'Brien family as a whole is a colorful one. My uncle and cousins give my mother a run for her money. I couldn't tell you who's crazier. Dad's side of the family or Mom's.

I lean in favor of Dad's when Connie steps back from Kaye and looks her over, assessing her from head to toe. A tiny smile kicks up the corner of her mouth. She turns to me with a lifted brow. I groan internally, knowing something crazy is most likely about to come from her lips.

"Aye, I'd be hiding this one for meself if I were ya. What a ride she is," Connie purrs.

Jamie groans. "Ya knickers are safe. She's just being an eejit."

Kaye stands with her brows knit. It dawns on me how heavy Jamie and Connie's accents are. Dylan is the most Americanized of my cousins. He hardly ever slips into the Irish brogue the others do. Dylan sounds like a true New Yorker.

With Jamie, it depends on his mood what you'll get. Cole, or Brooklyn as we all call him, has a heavy New York accent that mixes in with his Irish one. Most times he'll flip back and forth between the two. Although, when back home in Ireland, forget it, all the New Yorker melts away.

Connie, *please*, even I have to listen closely at times. She's the second oldest, after my cousin Logan. They were much older when they arrived here in America. All of my cousins were older and set in their habits when they arrived, except for Dylan. It shows in how each of them have adapted to the States.

"Connie thinks you're pretty and Jamie is reassuring you that you're not going to be mauled by Connie. She's straight. She just likes to tease," I say to Kaye while laughing.

"I'm sorry. I didn't want to be rude," Kaye says as her cheeks heat.

"No, we're being rude. You're family so we didn't think about it," Connie says more clearly. "We'll get you up to speed and then we can bend your ear. Come on. I've gotten the baby's room ready."

"Thanks." Kaye smiles, reaching to take the carrier away. When I don't release the handle right away, she looks up at me. "I think I should change him."

I loosen my hold and allow her to take the carrier from me. Jamie grabs my attention, nodding for me to hang back. My eyes remain on Kaye until she disappears from my sight.

"She hasn't understood a word we said to her, has she," Jamie says humorously.

"Probably not."

"Grand, so we can talk freely. Brooklyn found the lass still here in New York. Big front, slope back, she is. She's burning through her cash like she's Rockefeller. Dylan says she doesn't look good." He fills me in.

"Aye, she just had a baby and she's run off. I bet she looks like shit," I hiss, allowing my own mix of my parents' accents to fall into place. I pause to tamp down my anger. "Ye get the cameras I sent over?"

"Aye, installed and ready to go," he replies with a nod. "Brooklyn gave the order to bring her in at ya word. What do ya want to do?"

"Have Connie and Kate sit with her and make things clear. She can go crawl under a fucking rock for all I care. I just don't want to see her come back out. He's none of her concern anymore and I want it to stay that way. If she breathes a single word about any of this Con and Kat will leave her in tatters on the next visit," I order.

"She fucked with the wrong one," Jamie scoffs. "I'll let Brooklyn know and talk to my sisters."

"Thanks," I reply as the front door opens.

Logan, Brooklyn, and Dylan walk in. If they weren't my own family and I didn't know I could handle myself, I'd probably piss my pants. Not one of them has a smile on their face until they lock eyes with me. Logan gives the big smile, always known for a good laugh and teasing.

"Where's yer lass? Don't have the heart to take the piss out of ya in front of her," Logan teases.

"She's with Con and the babe," Jamie answers.

"Aye, good. C'mere ya rawny fucker," Logan croons.

"Who you calling skinny?" I huff, puffing out my chest.

"Ya," Logan and Brooklyn say in unison.

Brooklyn points at me and laughs. "Ya see this. Kid's got nerve. Comes to our city, asking for favors and then wants to puff out his chest," he jeers.

"Like we won't beat the clothes off of that bird chest and send him back home to Uncle Joe," Logan adds with mirth in his eyes.

We meet in the center of the room and my oldest cousin pulls me into a bear hug, lifting me from my feet to prove a point. I laugh, throwing a punch at his arm when he places me back on my feet.

"Good to see ya," Logan says patting my cheek.

"I'd say the same if ya weren't trying to reddener me," I toss back.

"*Oh*," all four of my cousins bellow out.

"There's it is. That's our little cousin and everyone thinks he's the quiet one. Stop trying to embarrass the lad, Logan," Brooklyn chuckles, pulling me into his embrace.

"Whatever," I grumble good-naturedly.

"Hey," Dylan beams at me as I pull him into a hug.

Dylan is the quiet one. Explosive temper but normally as quiet as I seem. I guess being the youngest of six has a lot to do with it in his case.

"Hey. We have to get in a few rounds before I head out," I say to him causing his smile to grow.

"Sure, sure." He nods.

"When do ya plan to leave?" Logan quizzes.

Kaye

I hold my breath. I've been wanting to know the answer to that question. I appreciate everything that Felix has done for me since showing up. He has no idea how grateful I am.

"I have to leave in a few days. I need to get back to work. I've been handling things remotely, but that's not going to cut it for long," Felix says.

I swear I hear a note of disappointment in his voice. Then again, it could be wishful thinking. I know he's doing all of this as a friend. He'd do anything for Danny, which in proxy includes me.

My heart sinks. I don't know why I thought he would be able to be here longer. I start to feel lonely all over again and he hasn't left yet.

"We have to get ya to the restaurant for a few drinks and a game of Spades," the biggest one in the bunch says.

They're all gorgeous, mostly dark haired versions of the Blacks. The one standing next to the one that just spoke could pass for Wyatt if his hair were a bit lighter. Jamie, the one I met earlier reminds me of a green-eyed version of Braxton, with a dark shoulder length mass of curls. The youngest looking one with the long strawberry blonde hair is the first to notice me.

Dashawn starts to wail drawing everyone else's attention. All eyes turn on me. Connie's heels click against the hardwoods behind me.

"Look at ya all looking like a bunch of bears. Stop scaring the lass with yer loud mouths, ya mingers," Connie sings out.

"Mingers, ya look just like us. So that makes ya ugly too," Jamie snorts.

"Ya wish," Connie snuffs back.

The big one that invited Felix out for drinks twists his lips waving Connie off. He turns for me and moves closer. I have to tip my head back to look up at him, while bouncing my nephew in my arms.

"Hello, Kaye. I'm Logan," he says with a thick accent while pulling a key from the inside of his leather jacket. "This is for ya. Is everything to yer liking? We can get ya anything you need."

"Yes, thank you," I reply, wrapping my fingers around the key to take it. "I think we should be fine."

He's even more handsome up close. His eyes are green like Jamie's, but Logan's eyes tell a darker story. I can tell this isn't a man to be crossed.

"Who do we have here?" Wyatt's look alike says as he comes over to pluck a crying Dashawn from my arms. "Hello there, little fella. Tell yer Uncle Brooklyn what's the matter."

His eyes are a gorgeous green, but again, I note the brooding danger hidden in their depths. Felix comes to my side, allowing me to relax a little. He may be as tall and intimidating as these guys, but I know him. I know he'll never hurt me, or my nephew.

"Cole, what do ya know about babies?" Connie says.

"He's quiet now, ain't he," Brooklyn replies.

My brows knit. He just called himself Brooklyn, but Connie calls him Cole. Felix nudges my side and I turn my face up to him to find his eyes twinkling at me.

"This is Cole, but everyone calls him Brooklyn. Connie just refuses to," Felix chuckles.

"Oh," I reply and nod, licking my dry lips.

"Don't look so scared. We're a big lot, but we're not as terrifying as we look," the blonde steps forward and says.

"Bullshit," Connie coughs behind her hand.

The others try to hide their laughs. Felix places a hand on the small of my back, sending a chill running through me. I try not to let it show, praying they're all too busy laughing to notice.

"This is Dylan. The baby of the bunch," Felix says, pointing to the blonde.

"Ya mean the pretty boy," Jamie teases.

"Go fuck yourself," Dylan grumbles, a small pout on his lips.

The others roar with laughter at his expense. Dylan frowns, his full pink lips twisting and his blue eyes take on a look of annoyance. I notice he's the only one with blue eyes and strawberry blonde hair.

"Boys, boys, lets not teach the babe such foul language," Connie calls out.

All head turn to her, eyes blinking like owls, including Felix. Honestly, Dashawn seems to be mimicking their stare. Connie looks around at them all.

"Aye, yer right. Fuck it," she says with a shrug and everyone starts to laugh again.

I can't help shaking my own head and laughing. Connie is a riot. Once I could understand her, she had me laughing in the baby's room as I changed his diaper.

"Where's Kate?" Logan asks.

"On her way," Connie responds.

Logan nods, then turns to coo at my nephew. I lift a brow. It's kind of sexy to see all of these gorgeous men melt over this tiny baby. I make notes for scenes I want to write whenever I get to pick up a pen again. It's been so long since I've written anything.

It's not easy to write when totally stressed out. I wish I had the time to get lost in my own worlds. As if reading my mind, Logan leans into Jamie's ear then turns to me.

"We have a laptop for ya. Felix says yer a writer," Logan says.

My eyes grow wide as Jamie steps forwards with a brand new Mac still in its box. I look up at Felix and he winks back at me. My heart melts in my chest. I don't know what to say.

"It's loaded with everything you need to write and publish that first book," Felix says. "I told them what to program."

I throw my arms around him and squeeze, burying my face in his chest. Oh God, that may not have been the greatest idea. I inhale. He smells so good. I have to fight not to snuggle into him.

"Hey, don't I get a hug too. I was the one that went to pick it up," Jamie says, causing me to pull away from Felix.

"Don't," Felix says simply, but the command cracks like a whip.

His words run through me. I don't know if he's talking to me or Jamie. I look between the two of them. Jamie has a grin on his lips, but Felix has his eyes narrowed at Jamie.

"Respect ya life, Jamie," Brooklyn says in warning as he laughs.

"It's okay. Ya can thank me later," Jamie winks.

A growl comes from Felix's chest. I take a small step back, shocked by the sound. The room fills with the laughter of everyone else except for Felix.

"This is going to be so much fun," Jamie croons.

"I'd listen to Brooklyn if I were you. You're fucking with your life," Felix warns.

I'm speechless. I don't know how to take the exchange. I know Jamie is teasing Felix, but Felix's reaction seems a bit aggressive for one of a friend. I quickly chide myself for reading too much into things.

Get a grip, Kaye. He is way out of your reach and it could never happen now. He's leaving to go back home and you can't.

Yeah, there is that, isn't there.

CHAPTER SEVEN

Checking In

Felix

A year later ...

I get out to New York to see Kaye as often as I can. It's the reason I made sure Logan found her a three bedroom. I knew I would need a place to stay when I checked in.

The first few months I made the trip monthly. With things picking up at the office, I've had to cut the trips down. I haven't been to New York in about two months.

It's Dashawn's first birthday. I wouldn't miss it for the world. He has gotten so big so fast. Kaye takes such good care of him.

I admire her dedication to doing what her brother asked her to. Kaye is still not ready to face her father. I can't blame her.

I've been to see the Porters and her father acts as if nothing is amiss—at least where Kaye is concerned. He'll talk about Danny and the great son he was, but he won't breathe a word about Kaye. I respect Pastor Porter, but this shit has been pissing me off.

Kaye could use the proper support of her family. Sure, they don't know that the baby isn't hers, but just the fact that it could be should have her father wanting to reconcile with her.

He and Kaye are both so damn stubborn. I don't see either of them breaking down anytime soon. Hell, Kaye has fought me tooth and nail on so much and I'm trying to help her.

For example, I didn't want her to have to worry about things while caring for the baby. She didn't have to work. Brooklyn called me laughing his ass off as he told me Kaye demanded a job.

Kate and Connie were in on it. Offering to babysit so Kaye could get in a few hours a day. When I arrived in New York to put a stop to the nonsense, Kaye gave me that cute stubborn face and I caved.

So stubborn. I see where she gets it from. Grandma Reid asked for me to find her and Pastor Porter shut that conversation down. I wanted to tell her that I found Kaye and the baby.

I also had a few words I wanted to say to Pastor Porter, but I've bitten my tongue because my mother would have my ass for saying what I want to say.

I'll be in my forties and will still fear the wrath of Cassy Black. That woman is not to be tested. However, when it comes to Kaye, I've risked angering my mom.

I'm sure if she knew what I've been up to she'd wring my neck. I frown at my thoughts as I push my key into the lock of the New York apartment Kaye lives in. It always feels like coming home when I come here.

I push the door open and step side. I'm not surprised to find Jamie's ass on the couch or Connie in the kitchen. These two have taken most to Kaye and Dashawn. They want to be here.

What does bring a stunned smile to my face is the sight of Dashawn's chubby little legs holding him up as he moves straight for me. I scoop him up when he reaches me, tickling his tummy and munching on his fat cheeks. He's the cutest kid ever.

"When'd you start walking?" I coo at him.

He giggles and gives me that smile, his tiny teeth and gums flashing at me. He's going to be a handsome young man. Kaye will be beating them off her nephew with a stick.

"He's been walking for about a week now. Or should I say he's been running," Kaye says as she appears.

"Getting ready for the big day, huh," I say to Dashawn.

He makes an excited squeal in reply. I kiss his cheek and place him back down on his feet. I want to see him maneuver around again. I still can't believe he's walking.

I move over to Kaye and wrap an arm around her shoulders, pulling her against my chest. I've missed her. I want nothing more than to dip my head and devour those sexy lips. My mind starts to run off into thoughts of releasing that messy bun while she rides me.

I shut the thoughts down when I start to grow hard. Instead of teaching Kaye all the dirty shit that runs through my head when I think of her, I place a friendly kiss on her forehead. It doesn't help that she looks up at me with that beaming smile.

I look down to see Dashawn hasn't run off, he's holding onto Kaye's leg while peeking up at me. I reach to ruffle his curly black hair. Kaye bends to pick him up and place him on her hip.

"It feels like forever since the last time you were here," she says.

"If he would have waited any longer, I planned to make ya my own," Jamie tosses over his shoulder, not looking away from the TV in front of him.

"Don't start that shit with me," I snap.

"Shit," Dashawn repeats and my eyes budge out of my head.

"Oh fuck, I'm sorry." I look at Kaye and say.

"Fuck," Dashawn mocks.

Kaye rolls her lips to keep from laughing. I can see the laughter in her eyes. I feel like an asshole.

"Relax. He's been doing that for about a month. It's not you. It's Connie's fault," Kaye giggles out.

"Sure, blame me. It couldn't possibly be anyone else's fault," Connie grumbles from the kitchen.

"Con, he's with you all day and the first time he said it was right after you," Kaye laughs.

"Fine," Connie groans. "Still say it was Logan."

"Aye, ya blame Logan for everything. Have since I was in diapers," Jamie taunts.

"Ya may be speaking truth, but no one asked ya," Connie quips.

"What have I done to you, kid?" I say to Dashawn. "I left you with these heathen to corrupt you. Your grandfather would have my as——. Yeah, he'd have my tail."

Kaye giggles, shaking her head at me.

"You've done nothing but help him. I think he's been missing you," she says.

"I've been missing you too," I reply, but I'm looking straight into her eyes.

I watch the pulse in her neck race. I've done my best not to come at Kaye the way I want to. It's getting harder. I think she's become more and more gorgeous each time I've seen her.

I still have some guilt about not telling her brother how I felt when he was alive. I keep trying to convince myself he would be okay with it. I've also been trying to convince myself that Kaye is too sweet and innocence for me to corrupt.

The corruption I want to do to Kaye would definitely have her father looking for me. I want to turn Kaye out in ways that will blow her mind for years, from just one night. I'd give her something to write about.

"Did ya hear me?" Connie calls out, coming into the living room.

"No, sorry," I say.

My eyes are still locked on Kaye's. She looks back at me with a mixed expression. She looks lost, confused, and awed all at the same time.

"I said that the party has moved to the restaurant. The apartment is too small for everyone," Connie repeats.

"Everyone?" I ask with my brows knitted.

"Dae-Dae is quite the popular fella around here," Jamie says.

"Dae-Dae?"

Jamie turns to look at me, a grin on his face. He's being an asshole. He likes to tease me relentlessly when it comes to Kaye. I think everyone expect Kaye has figured out I have a thing for her.

My cousins have homed in on the fact and like to use it to goad me. I try not to fall for it, but Jamie is the best at pushing all the right buttons. I swear, he and Brax really have a talent for it.

"*Da-Shawn*, Dae-Dae," he drags out slowly like I'm the idiot. "Sheesh. Do ya know anything about the kid?"

I give Jamie the finger and turn away from him. Kaye's watching, trying not to laugh. I punch her side and take Dashawn from her arms, moving for my room with my duffle bag on my shoulder.

Kaye

He looks good. I mean, really good. It's been too long since I last set eyes on Felix in person.

Over Skype or Facetime is one thing, but in person. Lord, I need to fan my face. It might just be me, but I think he has bulked up slightly.

He's still lean, but he looks like he has more muscle since the last time I saw him. His ass looks great in his jeans as he walks away from me with Dae-Dae in his arms.

What I would give to see that body in his wet suit.

That body must look amazing moving fluidly on a surfboard, the way I know he does. I miss California. Getting to surf with Felix used to be a highlight of my life.

Since being here in New York, I've taken my nephew to Rockaway Beach a few times. Brooklyn doesn't like me traveling that far alone, so I don't get to go as often as I'd like. Usually, Logan or Connie and Kate will go with me.

Going with Logan is hilarious. He looks so intimidating to everyone else. Meanwhile, he tells jokes that almost make me pee my pants as he holds the straightest face ever.

Being here in New York hasn't been all bad. I've gained a new family. The O'Briens treat me like one of their own. I haven't missed the fact that there's way more to the O'Brien family than meets the eye.

There's always someone here to watch over me and I don't just mean the O'Brien brothers. I've come to know Logan's crew from working in my little office at the warehouse. It took me about a month to notice a few of the guys outside of the apartment building after hours.

While I don't see or hear much at work, my imagination has run wild a few times about the family I've come to call my own. I know they don't play any games when it comes to business, but they're a fun-loving family who loves to laugh together. Much like I've seen in the Black home growing up.

Connie and I have become close. She's like the big sister I've never had. I've called on her plenty of times to help out with Dae-Dae, as she started calling him—when she's not calling him her little husband. I think my nephew has a crush on Connie.

Kate is great as well. She just travels a lot. I haven't spent as much time with her as the others. Jamie's probably the next person I've become closest with.

He may flirt when Felix is around, but Jamie is sweet and protective when Felix isn't here for him to tease. Which leads me to my earlier thoughts. Felix gets so pissed off when Jamie flirts with me.

I know Felix is just as protective as his cousins, but I don't understand why it makes him so angry when Jamie pulls his chain about being attracted to me. If I didn't know better, I would say that Felix's behavior can be a bit possessive. As if I belong to him.

I've tried to tell myself I'm being silly. I've seen some of the model looking girls that Felix pulls. None of them are nerdy and thick like me.

I wouldn't call myself fat, but these hips are not the kind Victoria's Secret offers on their cover. I used to stay fit from swimming and surf, but I'm not going to lie and say I haven't noticed a little more jiggle here and there. Honestly, some days I question whether or not I was the one to have a baby.

Yeah, there's no way Felix would claim me as his. I'm nowhere near the sticks he bar hops with. Not to mention, I've never been to a bar. I'm almost ashamed to admit that.

"Whatcha thinking about?" Jamie whispers in my ear teasingly.

"Nothing," I mumble.

"Sure, nothing my arse," he chuckles. "Ya have a glad eye for Felix."

"A what?" I look up at him in confusion.

Jamie rolls his eyes at me. I'm still learning some of their slang. God help me, I try to keep up when their accents kick in full force. Some days, I'm exhausted from no more than listening.

"Yer sweet on my dear little cousin," Jamie purrs.

"Oh. Wait ... no I'm not," I gasp.

"Aye, ya are," Connie sings from her new spot on the couch.

"No, I'm not." I lower my voice, hoping they take the cue.

"Whatever ya say, lass," Connie giggles.

"He'd turn the world upside down for ya. Ya should take a clue," Jamie says ominously.

"Huh," I say with knit brows.

"Mind ya own business, Jamie," Connie hisses at him.

"What? Come on. They're doing a dance. Don't ya think it's time the music stopped," Jamie huffs at his sister.

"Aye, but I'm not the DJ for this party. Leave it be. The lad's not ready," she replies.

"What the hell is he waiting for?" Jamie mumbles under his breath.

I've caught less than half of what they're saying. Not that I comprehend any of it. I've caught on to how they tend to thicken up their accents when they don't want me to fully understand.

I shrug it off and go to get ready to head out to the restaurant for the party. Jamie was right. Dashawn has a lot of people here who care about him. I'm happy that he has so much love surrounding him.

However, I do feel a pain in my chest as I think of my parents. I picked up the phone to call home several times over the last few weeks. It's been a year since my brother died.

This month hasn't been the easiest for me. I would love to be back home with my family to ease some of the pain from our loss. I wish I could share the life they gained.

Yet, it's that last thought that makes me put down the phone every time. My father is so quick to judge for a man who serves a God of forgiveness. What his congregation sees and thinks has become more important than the things that truly matter.

"You're so worried about being embarrassed. You lost your children and your grandson," I murmur to myself.

I angrily shovel items into Dashawn's diaper bag, swiping at the tears that come unbidden. I promised myself I wouldn't cry today. My nephew's life is something to be happy about. I've learned so much from him in this past year.

I jump when arms wrap around my waist. Only to relax when Felix's cologne engulfs me. I sag into the warmth of his body as he settles his chin on the top of my head.

"How are you holding up?" he says softly.

"I don't know. It hasn't been an easy week," I reply. "It's so insane that she went into labor three days after Danny was buried."

"Yeah, but you have to see the silver lining," he replies.

"Which is? Because I'm having such a hard time finding it," I sob.

He tightens his arms. I feel his lips press against the top of my head. I close my eyes.

I wish he could understand how much his simple touch calms and comforts me. I don't know where I would be without him and the family he has brought into my life.

"Danny was laid to rest in peace. Then three days later his son was born. We can call it a resurrection of Danny. All the best parts of your brother are in his son.

"I mean, he looks so much like him and I swear he does some of the things I remember you brother doing." He gives a soft laugh at the end.

I join with a sad one of my own. "You're right, I guess. He has a lot of Danny mannerisms.

"He sleeps just like him. He gives you that same look, like you're crazy if you say something he doesn't like." I laugh a little more as I think about it.

"He's a great little baby," Felix murmurs.

"Yeah, which is why they shouldn't be missing out on his life. I know we said some harsh things to each other, but they're my parents. He's my dad.

"Either way they know they have a grandson, no matter which one of us he belongs to. It hurts—"

My words cut off when I feel like I can't breathe. This is the part that's been so hard. I've always known my father to be strict and stern, but this has been too much.

He's wrong for this. They both are. My mother should have stepped in or at least reached out to me.

"You and your father are stubborn. Your mother tries to stay out of the line of fire. Not that that's the best way to handle it, but I understand her," he says as if he's inside my thoughts. "He'll come around."

"I've been praying he will. I love your family, but I miss my own," I whisper.

"Yeah, Grandma Reid made me an entire pot of curry goat all for myself. I thought of you while I ate every last drop," he says with humor in his voice.

I turn in his arms and look up at him. He's eyes are dancing with laughter. I pull out of his embrace with a pout on my lips, folding my arms across my chest.

"That's just low," I hiss at him.

"It was *so* good," he purrs and bites that sexy lower lip.

His golden eyes dance with his joy at my expense. Two can play this game. I drop my hip and lift my chin.

"Jamie was telling me about a place in Brooklyn that has great West Indian food. He said he'd take me if Connie babysits for me one night. There's a movie I want to see this week.

"Since you're here, maybe you can watch the baby and Jamie can take me to the movie and the restaurant," I say with a straight face.

All humor drains from his eyes. He moves in to crowd my space, his arms going back around me. My breath is caught in my throat, my heart feels like it's going to pound out of my chest.

"Jamie can watch *my* nephew," he says pointedly. His voice drops and everything he says next sounds so dirty. "I'll take you wherever you need and want to go."

"Oh." Pushes from my lips and I feel like a nitwit the moment the word is out.

Felix's eyes drop to my lips. The air is charged with energy. The same energy I usually only feel when he touches me.

The spark that shoots up my arm, those tingles that spread to my belly—they all seem to have come to life in the room, surrounding us to the point that I can't breathe.

I can't take my eyes off his. When they lift to focus on mine, I feel like their asking a question. For permission?

I want to speak the word, yes, but I don't want to make a fool out of myself. I've been craving Felix for so long, I could be making all of this up in my head. Lord knows, I'm always writing a romance in my mind.

I can romanticize folding socks. However, that doesn't seem to stop my mind from telling my body to react. I lean into Felix like a magnet is pulling on me. I think I'm going crazy because it seems like he's leaning back.

"Hey, ya two coming or not? We need to get to the restaurant. Dashawn's getting fussy," Connie calls breaking into the moment.

I blink several times. Felix seems so far away that I think I indeed imagined it all. He moves to grab the diaper bag but stops.

I look to see what has caught his attention. Following his line of sight, I see my laptop on my nightstand.

Turning his head to me, he narrows his eyes. I know what's coming. I give him a tiny grin.

"You've been writing?" he asks.

I give a nod and shrug, while playing with my fingertips.

"Yeah," I say and bite my lip.

He's face lights up with the biggest smile. I'm always in awe of how happy he gets for me when I'm writing. It warms my entire heart and means so much to me.

"You have that look."

"What's that look?" I ask, as I watch his eyes search my face.

"You're happy. Your muse is back," he replies.

I've had the laptop for almost a year now. I just wasn't in a place where I was ready to write. I felt too broken to create words and stories.

"I didn't know writing would start the healing process," I admit.

His brows draw in, he straightens and moves closer to me. He's watching—always watching. It hasn't been easy to start again. I wonder what he sees.

I've kept my sanity at night while Dashawn passes out in my bed next to me and my fingers fly across the keys. As the words flow, I feel my soul restoring within.

"It's funny. Things my brother would have said to me pop up on the page from the mouths of the characters. It makes me feel like I'm connecting to Danny all over again.

"In those hours nothing else matters. Just me and the words pouring onto the screen." I pause, nibbling my lip.

I'm unsure if I should share the next part. As I look into those golden eyes, I figure what the heck. This is Felix. I've shared so much with him already.

"I'm in love again and it doesn't feel as dirty as it used to. I don't have to worry about looking over my shoulder in fear that my father will find out, like when I was in Junior High—"

"Wait, he found out about your books. When?" Felix asks, concern and intrigue coloring his orbs.

"I never told you about that. It was right before I started to share them with you. It was the real reason you found me crying over my notebooks.

"He found one of the short stories I did. He told me to stop writing them. Then you asked to read one of my notebooks after I told you they were all crap.

"I don't know why I gave you one. But I did and you talked me out of giving up," I say, remembering how nervous I had been when I first gave him that notebook with my stories in it.

"Wow, I didn't know that," he says, brushing my cheek with his fingertips.

"It's different this time. I feel … I feel liberated. I don't think, I just write." I smile up at him.

"You have something for me to read yet?" he asks excitedly.

I drop my head, looking down at my feet. I have something, I'm just not sure I'm ready for him to read it. I know what I'm missing.

It's the same as always. The story and plotline are strong. The chemistry is just missing.

"Ya two are doin' a number on me," Connie says as she appears in the doorway. "Can we please go?"

"Yeah, we're coming," I reply, reaching for my purse.

Felix picks up the diaper bag, placing it on his shoulder. I love that he never cares about carrying Dashawn or his diaper bag around. I turn to leave the room, but he stops me with a hand on my arm.

"I want to read it," he says, the tone of his voice letting me know it's not a request.

"Okay."

CHAPTER EIGHT

Here to Help

Felix

Kaye has gotten better in her writing. I was in near tears on the plane ride back home. She knows how to touch your emotions. Yet, the sex is still so far removed from everything else on the page.

Kaye has it in her to be an amazing author. I want to see her draw that out. She has the talent.

I know the sky is the limit when she just lets go and gives her characters the spark they need. That spark that we have between us. That's what's missing from her pages.

I've been thinking about this a lot. How to get her to pull that fire from within. I want to sit down and talk with her about it on my next visit.

There has to be a way for her to tap into that place that will unlock the words. I would love to see her published and living out her dream. Too distracted with my thoughts of Kaye to get any work done, I open a new browser and start to do a search for writer's help.

I get excited when I start to find organizations for romance authors and critique groups that she can join. Opening a fresh email, I start to copy the links into it to send to Kaye. I don't know if it will address the problem, but at least this will be a step in the right direction for her.

I'm deep into my research for Kaye when I feel someone hovering over me. I turn to find Wyatt over my shoulder, looking at my screen. Give it to my older brother to stick his nose into my business. I minimize the screen and turn to face him fully.

"Romance novels?" He questions. "So you're not building that app any more. It's romance novels now?"

His words are not judging. He's asking for understanding. I love my brothers for that. We may rib each other for everything, but we support each other as well.

"It's not for me. It's for a friend," I reply.

His eyes lock on me and his expression becomes more serious. I groan internally. Something tells me I'm about to get reamed.

"Would this be the same friend who our cousins are looking after?" he says, sitting on the edge of one of my desks.

I have a semicircular set up for all my monitors and gadgets. Most days all my shit keeps my brothers away unless they need something. I wish that were the case today.

"Fuck," I mutter. "How did you find out?"

"Logan and I are the oldest. Don't shit move between the two of us with you little fuckers without us knowing," he replies.

"Yeah, should have figured that. Look this is complicated. I need you to keep this to yourself," I plead.

"I've known since you called in the favor. Logan and his crew aren't the most squeaky-clean bunch. While she couldn't be safer, she's still in the middle of some shit being connected to that side," he warns.

"Yeah, I thought about that. It was my best option at the time," I mumble.

"What's your plan?"

"I don't know. Nothing has changed between her and her parents," I huff. "She's stubborn, they're being stubborn. I don't know what to do, except give them time."

"And the writing thing?" He nods his head in the direction of my computer screen.

"It's her thing. I want to help her out. I think she has what it takes to get her work out there," I say.

"Cool," he replies. He pauses and narrows his eyes at me. "You fucking her?"

I frown at my brother and fall back in my chair. Folding my arms across my chest I stare at him. This would be none of his damn business.

"I'm not trying to be up in your business. I'm only making sure you're thinking straight. Pussy will change how you think," he says.

"Dude, first of all, Kaye isn't pussy. She's a friend and my best friend's little sister. I respect her. Also, Wyatt, no offense but you're not in a relationship to be giving me that kind of advice," I snap.

He tosses his hands up, rocking back against the desk he's propped against. He nods in agreement and tilts his head while his eyes remain on me. I'm fuming but I don't say a word.

"All right, I see your mind is made up here—"

"Made up about what?" I ask defensively.

"It's only a matter of time before you seal that deal. You've had it bad for Kaye for years. You think I don't remember how you used to text her all the time?

"Even though she had a boyfriend and the fact that she was your best friend's sister. Look kid, I'm not here to tell you what to do. I just wish you would have said something to me.

"Not Logan. I'm here to help," he finishes.

"Well, your relationship advice isn't needed. Your track record is shit," I tease to lighten things up, as I try to defuse my own temper.

"Bro, I'm twenty-eight. I haven't seen the pussy worth giving all the rest up for," he tosses back. "But seriously, I'm here if you need me."

"Got it."

Kaye

I've been staring at this email from Felix for almost an hour. It was so sweet of him to do this for me. It also stings a little because he feels I need help.

I'm trying not to overthink that. We all can stand to improve, right? So why am I so afraid to click on these links and find some help.

My phone rings startling me. I look over at it as I sit at the kitchen table. Felix's name flashes on the screen.

I feel the smile that comes over my face. I answer the phone, tucking it between my ear and shoulder. Images of him at work in front of his computers fills my head.

I've been to the Black and Lock office a few times to meet up with Felix. His workspace is like his own little universe in the middle of everyone else.

"Hello," I say into phone as I think of him sitting there clicking through surveillance footage or something.

"Hey, how are you?" he croons back.

"I'm good. Dae-Dae had a tummy ache, so he passed out early tonight," I reply.

"I always look at the clock when you say stuff like that. I forget you're in a different time zone sometimes," he chuckles.

"Yeah, it took some time for me to get used to at first. You sound tired."

"A lot going on around here. Need to get through a few logs before I can head out of here," he replies.

"Then you shouldn't be sneaking in personal calls," I giggle.

"I wanted to check on you. Have you had time to go through that email I sent?"

I chew on the inside of my mouth while staring at the email in question. I want to thank him, but I have questions as well. I click on the first link like it might explode once I do.

"Yeah," I say.

"*Kaye*," he drags out. "I didn't send it to say you're not amazing. I was hoping you could find some support in getting to the finish line. Maybe someone can give you pointers on what's missing."

"We know what's missing," I snort.

"Yeah, well, maybe you can find a critique partner to help with that."

"Not the kind of partner I need," I murmur to myself.

"This is the only option you have," he says with a bit of an edge.

I pull the phone away from my shoulder to look at it. My brows drawn. He must be tired.

"No offense, but I wasn't talking to you when I said that. I also think I could find a date if I wanted," I huff.

There's a pause. His line is completely silent. I look at the phone again to make sure I haven't lost the call.

"Relax. I know you could find a date," he grumbles back. "That's not what I was getting at. I'm here to help, Kaye. I think this could be useful. If nothing else, you'll learn about the business or find a support team that can relate to you."

I stick my tongue out at the phone. He's right and I know it. I'm just being bullheaded about it.

"Yeah," I say reluctantly.

His laugh greets my ear. It's a sexy rumble that has me squeezing my thighs. I miss him. I laughed so much while he was here.

"Let me know how it works out. I should get back to work before I end up spending the night here," he murmurs.

"Thanks, Felix. This was sweet of you. I appreciate it," I suck up my feelings and say. "Goodnight."

"No problem, goodnight."

CHAPTER NINE

Hey Girl!

Kaye

Six months later ...
I joined a few critique groups on a social media site just to feel them out. I happened to click with a couple of authors who stood out. Dean and Lakia always have funny and encouraging posts.

I started to follow them and have read some of their work. Not only are they super cool they both can write their tails off. I wish I had the seasoning their writing displays.

We've become friends over the internet, and they invited me out to a book signing that they both will be making an appearance at. I tried to beg off, but Dean wasn't having it. Not even my one-and-a-half-year-old nephew—or son as they know him—was enough to get me out of this. Lakia has a six-month-old who she'll be bringing along with her so there was no excuse for me.

Not to mention, once Felix found out he got it in his head that this is something I need to do. He has gone as far as offering to fly out with me to Atlanta. He'll be keeping an eye on Dashawn while I get to know the girls.

I'm so nervous. I know I'm going to fan girl. Lakia warned me not to, but I love their work. Dean may not be a huge name yet, but she has the talent.

Lakia, on the other hand, is taking the literary world by storm. I'm so grateful that they have taken to me and my writing. They've given me so much feedback.

Although, honestly, I haven't sent them any pages with my real issues. I'm too nervous. I think after meeting them in person to feel them out, I'll be less reluctant to share.

I'll admit. I'm a bit overwhelmed. I'm glad Felix purchased an event ticket to come along to the signing. There are a few other authors I can't wait to meet, and this crowd is insane.

"You look like me at a tech convention," Felix chuckles beside me.

He looks so handsome with Dae-Dae on his hip. How do you make a light blue denim jacket and matching jeans look like a three-piece suit that's cover worthy? I've noticed the heads turning as we walk around.

"What does that mean?" I beam up at him.

"Your eyes are glowing, and you look like a kid in a candy store," he chuckles. "You're in heaven."

"That bad, huh?" I giggle.

"It's cute. Don't let us slow you down. Have at it," he says, waving at all of the booths.

"Oh, no." I shake my head. "I'll work my way up to all of that."

"Chump," he teases, wrapping an arm around my shoulders.

"Kaye." I hear squealed not too far away.

I turn to see two women in side-by-side booths waving at me. I recognize Lakia from her picture right away. I've never seen a real picture of Dean.

She uses an avatar on social media due to her day job, but I know right away she's the one on the left with the red dreads and the unique freckles—unique to me because I've never seen someone her complexion with such pronounced freckles before.

They're both gorgeous. Lakia is a showstopper with her heart shaped face and oval brown eyes. Her skin is flawless and she's killing that lace front. The only reason I know it's a wig is because the three of us have had lengthy conversations about hair and makeup. Otherwise, I wouldn't know the difference.

It's so out of character for me, but I find myself rushing over into their embrace. I feel like I'm running into the arms of long-lost sisters—we've connected that much over the phone. We're squealing and hugging before I can fully process how I made it across the room so fast.

Felix and Dae-Dae are forgotten until Lakia and Dean look over my shoulders with mischievous looks in their eyes. We've talked about relationships a time or two. When I mentioned that Felix would be tagging along with me, the topic piqued both of their interest.

"Well, hello handsome," Dean purrs.

"Girl, don't start your stuff," Lakia warns with humor in her voice.

"What? I was talking to this little cutie pie." Dean feigns innocence.

"Sure, you were." Lakia chuckles. "Hi, you must be Felix. It's nice to meet you. I'm Lakia," she says, holding out a hand to Felix.

"Nice to meet you," he replies shaking her hand.

"And you must be Dae-Dae." She turns to purr at my nephew.

He nods giving her a shy smile, before tucking his face into Felix's neck. I love it when he tries to act shy. He'll be ripping this place apart in no time.

"Nice to meet you, Felix. I'm Dean," she purrs as her eyes eat him up.

I feel a little tinge of jealousy. Dean is very pretty. She looks like a doll.

She's much taller and leaner than I am, but still on the curvy side. She definitely has me beat in the boob department. I'm a decent B cup. She's rocking at least a powerful D if not DDDs.

"Likewise." Felix nods at her, but his attention turns to Dae-Dae in his arms just as quickly, as he murmurs something to him.

Dean turns to me and widens her eyes pointedly. I've told them that Felix is just a friend. However, because his name has come up so many times over the last six months—and the fact that he offered to come here with me—they've been pushing to know if something more is going on with us.

"We're still going out to eat after this, right? My mom came along this trip to watch Isaac. I'm free to have some adult time with my girls," Lakia says and gives a little shimmy.

"Um, I think so." I turn to look up at Felix.

"We'll be fine. We have a whole night planned," Felix replies with a smile on his face.

"I guess that's a yes," I say excitedly.

"Good, because I'm going to need a drink after this. They already started with the bull. Someone better tell these chicks I'm not for it," Dean grumbles as she rolls her eyes at someone across the room.

"Girl, please. We're not giving any energy to that BS today." Lakia waves off. "People always want it until you give it to them. We about these books. Let that pettiness stew in its own boots."

"Um. You talking all that sh—" Dean looks at Dae-Dae and purses her lips. "You saying that because you're protecting that brand. Which is all good, boo. My name ain't popping like that so somebody can catch these hands all day if needed."

"Why do I bother?" Lakia grumbles shaking her head.

These two have shared with me to be mindful of the back-stabbing and fake smiles in this industry. Lakia has a strict policy. Once they cross her, *they don't exist.* Dean on the other hand has a list of beat downs she wants to hand out.

What I respect about them both, they have told me to watch my back but have never given names. They're leaving it for me to make my own opinions. Never once have they shoved their experiences or feelings on me.

Although, I get the sense that Lakia is the voice of reason in this group. Dean is a couple of fries short from a full happy meal. She's more likely to fly off the handle if pushed.

Trust me, I've heard her go off over the phone once. It wasn't pretty. Dean is actually from New York, but she currently lives in PA. However, that New Yorker came out in full force that day.

"Y'all sure I can let Kaye out with you?" Felix teases.

"I mean, you can come out with us tonight to try us out. If we're good you can let her out with us next time," Dean purrs.

"I think I'm safer with my little guy here," Felix says narrowing his eyes at Dean.

"Oh, Lawrt, please don't have Kaye whip your tail. I like her." Lakia giggles.

"What? She said they're just friends. That means he's fair game. He's fine as hell. You bugging if you think I'm not going to at least shoot my shot," Dean says and shrugs.

My face burns with embarrassment. When I slowly turn to look up at Felix, his eyes are locked on me. He nods his head at his own thoughts before turning to Dean and Lakia.

"I'm going to walk around. You guys enjoy yourselves," he says before turning with Dae-Dae and leaving.

"You know something?" Dean says. "I think you're sleeping on that one."

Lakia fans her face, while watching Felix walk away. She has a huge grin on her face. Again, I feel a bit of jealousy raising.

"Just look at that walk. You know he's packing," she gushes.

"*Girl,* I was thinking the same thing." Dean bursts into laughter.

"Don't y'all have books to be signing?" I mumble.

They both laugh at me, pulling me into another hug before Dean drags me to sit with her behind her table. I watch in awe as my two new friends do their thing. My heart almost exploded out of my chest every time they tell people to be on the lookout for my work.

Real friends.

"We're going to pull that book out of you, baby girl." Dean leans over to whisper in my ear just as I have the thought.

***

"The indie life has been good to me. So has Trad," Lakia says while munching on a basket of fries.

"Indie takes a lot of work, but I feel it's worth it in the end. I've been able to learn a lot. I also think the fanbase is a bit different," Dean adds.

"Mm," Lakia nods, swallowing some of her drink. "Yeah, it can be, but if you come in strong on the indie scene you can make some wave in both ponds."

"I don't know. I was thinking about submitting to a publisher. I mean that seemed like the road to take before I met you guys. Now, I feel like I have more options," I reply.

"Did you get your author page set up? I'm telling you, start building the core base now. Put up some of those amazing snippets you have," Dean coaches.

"Your website, the social media, work on content for your newsletter. Girl, I wish I had gotten to all of that going before things started to pick up," Lakia says.

I jot down notes in my notebook. Again, I'm grateful for their mentorship. I might give this book thing a serious go.

"Thanks, guys." I look up and say with a beaming smile.

"You can thank me by sitting your ass in a chair and finishing that damn book," Dean says with a wink.

"I know, I know," I say and pout.

CHAPTER TEN

Still a Friend?

Kaye

Two months later ...

"I'll see you in a few weeks," Felix says before dipping to kiss my forehead.

"Hey, Felix," Kia and Dean sing in unison from the laptop screen sitting before me.

"Hey, ladies. You whipping my girl into shape?" Felix replies.

"Yup, we got her," Kia answers.

"Good, I gotta go. You ladies be good," he says massaging my shoulder before turning to leave out of the door.

I reach to touch my shoulder that's still tingling. I can still feel his lips on my forehead as well. Those little gestures are starting to drive me insane.

I wish it meant more to him. I'm having a hard time not daydreaming about him when he's around. I purse my lips and blow out a breath.

"You two still in the friend zone?" Dean's voice brings me back to reality.

"Yes," I mutter.

"You still tripping. You know that, right?" she continues. "Did you hear the way he said '*my girl*?'"

"I thought it was just me," Kia squeals. "Phew, yeah. You are missing something there, love. That man wants more than friendship."

"You're both being silly," I huff.

"Okay. We wouldn't be on this computer hashing out these sex scenes if you'd let him put that fire on you," Dean says.

"I know that's right." Kia giggles. "I mean, damn. You don't see the way he looks at you?"

"*Yeeees*, I saw it in Atlanta," Dean says.

"Right, when she called him a friend. He give her that, *I'll fuck the friend right out your mouth,* look." Kia slaps her desk as she laughs.

"Yes, honey. I saw it," Dean chimes in tugging at her t-shirt like she needs to cool off.

"You two have been writing too many of them books. Felix is a childhood friend." I wave them off.

"Pssh," Dean scoffs. "He looks like he's nasty. Like he'll fuck the soul from your body and look you in the eyes the entire time."

"Ow, are you going to put that in a book? That was good," Kia says, picking up her pen.

"It's all yours, boo. Have at it," Dean says. "Back to you. I know we tease you for being a P.K. and for those tired ass sex scenes that my grandmother would toss back at you, but honey. That man be looking at you like a steak dinner. You mark my words he'd put it on you if you stopped calling him a damn friend."

"Why you have to do her like that?" Lakia giggles.

"I hate y'all," I pout.

"She's right, though. We can help all we want but you're not going to get this stuff to where you want until you have some experience, sweetie. And yeah, he would be more than willing to help," Lakia says gently.

I heave a heavy sigh, reaching to rub my forehead. I shove my notebook away to get my frustration out. I don't know why I even bother.

"Okay, okay, I think we've hurt our little sister's feelings. Let's call it a night. I'll send you a link to these vibrators. You should at least explore it yourself if you won't let that fine ass man do it," Dean says while trying not to laugh.

I flip her the bird.

Kia cracks up laughing. "Oh, no. We're corrupting the poor baby. Night, ladies. Love you," Kia says, laughing while she disconnects.

"Night," Dean says while wiping at tears.

I sit staring at my computer screen. I'm not a quitter. I need to figure this out.

It's just sex on paper. Yup, but you have no clue about sex at all. So good luck with that one.

CHAPTER ELEVEN

Facetime

Kaye

Four months later ...

"Miss you, Lix. We go to the park?" Dae-Dae sings to the phone screen.

"I miss you too, buddy. I wish I was there to go to the park with you," Felix replies.

"Come see me and Mama," he says, dipping his face to kiss the screen.

It's so sweet. We talk to Felix every night through Facetime. These two are thick as thieves. Dashawn looks forward to the calls and the visits even more. It's been a few weeks, but I know Felix has been busy with work.

I'm sure he has a social life as well. I try not to take up too much of his time. I appreciate the fact that he always checks in no matter what. He has been on the road and dropped everything to call, if only for a few seconds.

"I'm coming. Promise," he says, his eyes softening.

"How many sleeps?"

Felix chuckles. "One. I'll fly in tonight, and we can go to the park in the morning."

"Felix, no," I protest. "You can't come running whenever he asks."

"You hear something, Dae-Dae?" Felix asks looking around his apartment.

"Felix, he's going to get used to you dropping everything for him. You can't keep spoiling him like this," I fuss.

"Yes, I can. He should get used to it. Do you need anything? I'll probably get in late, but I can make a stop on the way. Everything here is still open," he offers.

"I'm fine. I planned to work on the book tonight."

"Ah, so you need a sexy muse." He winks. "I'm on it."

I throw my head back and laugh. Little does he know he is my muse, whether here or there. He stars in all my books and most of my dreams.

"Whatever, Felix," I giggle.

"What? I'm sexy," he says, feigning hurt.

I bite my lip. I'm not going to embarrass myself with a reply. Reaching to comb a hand through my baby's hair, I lift a brow at Felix. His eyes go to Dashawn, and he sucks that sexy lower lip into his mouth and nods.

"Night, night, Dae-Dae. See you when you wake up," he croons.

"Night, night, Lix. Love you," Dae-Dae replies kissing the screen again.

"I love you too," Felix replies. "See you guys later. I need to square away some things here before I fly out."

"You're so stubborn," I growl.

"Me?" He touches his chest with wide eyes. "Yeah, we'll have this conversation when I get there."

There's a hint of something hidden in his words. I shift on the couch, trying to ignore how his simple words can turn me on. He throws up a salute with his fingers and ends the call.

Dae-Dae turns to look up at me excitedly. His little eyes are glowing. Some days I wonder how in the world his mother was able to walk away from him.

He's my world. I would bend time for him. If I could bring his dad back, so he could have him in his life, I would.

"Go night, night, Mama. Lix coming." He beams.

I kiss his forehead. Secretly thanking Felix for getting Dae-Dae to want to go to bed early. I can get to this book sooner.

"Come on, baby. We'll get you in your PJs and you can go night, night," I reply.

CHAPTER TWELVE

Lesson One

Kaye

Ugh, I'm so frustrated. I've been editing and revising this book for weeks. I finally think I'm ready to jump out the window and submit this one to a few agents and publishers.

Yet, I know what's missing. I've tried repeatedly to rewrite and polish these scenes. Even with help they're missing something. Still each and every time it's the same thing.

I get bored reading my own sex scenes. I'm serious. I've fallen asleep on them several times.

If I don't want to read them, no one else will. Dean wasn't lying about grandmothers throwing this stuff at me. It's all tired and weak.

This is going to drive me insane. I growl and toss the laptop off my legs. Falling back on the bed, I cover my face with my arms.

This is so frustrating.

I hear the door creak open and sigh. I'm training Dae-Dae to sleep in his own bed. I've woken up twice this week to find his foot in my mouth and his head tucked into my stomach.

I still don't know how he opens his bedroom door with those little hands. Brooklyn promised to place one of those safety locks on the front door next time he comes by. I don't want Dae-Dae getting any ideas of leaving the apartment while I'm sleeping.

When I hear my laptop being shifted and the bed dips under the weight of a much bigger person than my nephew, I sit up bolt straight. Those mesmerizing gold eyes are staring back at me.

I instantly relax. I've been so wrapped up in this book, I forgot he said he was coming in tonight. He's a sight for sore eyes. I can use an adult to talk to.

Connie has been busy with her own thing. Logan and Brooklyn have been traveling a lot. I get the impression that Jamie has stepped in to oversee things when his brothers aren't around.

Dylan is so shy. I think I frighten him at times. Besides, he has been getting more and more into his training.

He likes mixed martial arts. I believe he wants to go pro. Without a word, I scoot closer to Felix and place my head on his shoulder.

He puts the laptop in his lap and starts to scroll through. I wince as I see the horrible scene I just wrecked beyond repair.

Felix sighs, causing me to look up at him. His eyes turn to me and they're serious. I bite my lip not wanting to cry.

"I want this so bad. I want to be a writer. I just suck at it," I say with a voice full of emotions.

He places the laptop on the nightstand beside him, before turning back to me. He looks into my eyes for a long moment. I can see him deciding on something and the moment that decision is made.

"You've never felt that spark with anyone? That intense moment that makes butterflies take off in your stomach?" he asks.

I look away from his probing eyes. Hell, yes, I've felt it. I'm feeling it now, with the only person I've ever felt it with.

I'm just not about to tell him that. He lifts my chin with his finger, sending those butterflies into full flight. He leans in until our faces are only a breath apart. If I lick my own lips, I'm guaranteed to lick his as well.

"Tell me you don't feel that?" he breathes against my lips.

"I … I feel it," I whisper.

His thumb caresses the side of my temple down my cheek. He doesn't say a word. He continues the soft caress until his thumb greets the corner of my mouth. He pauses for second, then slowly drags the pad of his finger across my lower lip.

I feel like I might whimper. I feel the pull from the bottom of my belly. His tongue flicks out teasing the path he just trailed with his finger. I gasp in surprise. I lift my shaky hand to wrap his wrist.

He pulls away, caressing my cheek again. I want to follow after him and feel his lips on mine, but I'm too stunned to act.

"That's what's missing, Kaye. That feeling should be in your books," he whispers.

I drop my eyes feeling silly. He's only trying to help me with my writing. I swallow hard, hoping to get my pride out of my throat.

"Oh," I say so softly, I don't think he hears it.

"Tell me one thing," he says huskily. "Is it a religious choice? Are you waiting for marriage?"

I lift my eyes as I blink at him in confusion, not understanding the question. Then I knit my brows deeply. Suddenly, it hits me. I burst into laughter and shake my head at him.

"No. I've just always—" I cutoff, pulling my lip back into my mouth.

I can't say it. I can't tell him that I've always had a crush on him. I've always wished that he would be my first everything.

I know it's a big dream and I need to get real and get over it. I just don't know how. I haven't dated since I've been here in New York, and it's been over two years now.

"I didn't mean for this to happen. I ... I want more. I want to be in a relationship that's passionat—"

The words aren't fully out of my mouth before his hand is locked in the nape of my hair, dragging me to him. I'm straddling his lap in the blink of an eye. Felix captures my lips like a starving man.

It's like an explosion happens in tummy. I feel his kiss in my toes. He's gentle, yet, passionate. He uses his lips to teach mine. The groan that comes from him vibrates throughout my entire body.

I snap out of shock and push my fingers into his hair, tangling them in his silky locks. His tongue flicks against my lips, this time it's like a request for entry. I open to him, allowing him access to me.

I moan as the taste of his tongue against mine strips me of my sanity. I start to grind against his lap. His right hand goes to my backside, grabbing a firm hold to halt me. He doesn't stop the kiss though.

When my hips still, his hand goes to the bare skin of my thigh at the hem of my shirt. I whimper this time, in plea for him to touch me more. I love his kisses, but I need more. I want so much more.

I feel the slickness that starts between my legs. Yet, he continues to keep his hand still. Only flexing his fingers a bit here and there. All while his mouth does the exact opposite. He devours my mouth as if his life depends on it.

He nips my lip with his teeth and tug, pulling a groan from my throat. It stings but feels so good at the same time. I feel the weight of my hair hitting my shoulders and pull away to look at him.

"You're so gorgeous. Tell me now if you want me to stop, baby. Once I start this lesson you can't unlearn what I teach you and you'll never be the same," he says hoarsely.

I cup the sides of his face, pulling his lips to mine. I need his mouth on mine. I mimic the flick of his tongue against my lips.

Felix groans. In the next motion I'm on my back, he's now straddling me. He hovers over me looking down, with so much lust in his face.

My body is humming beneath him. Dipping his head, he kisses my lips quickly but pulls away to look down at me again. He palms one of my breasts over my t-shirt and I nearly lift off the bed.

My nipples are so hard beneath the fabric. I clench my thighs together, squirming beneath him. Felix watches my face as he kneads the mound, teasing the tight bud between his fingers.

"Mama, Mama," I close my eyes as Dae-Dae's voice pierces the air.

I cover my face with my hands and growl in frustration. Not with my nephew but my life. Timing has never been on my side. Felix climbs off me, but when I rise to go tend to Dae-Dae, he leans in to kiss my forehead.

"I got it," he says with a sexy smile.

Felix

I'm grateful for the interruption. I was about to do something stupid. I want more than a quick fuck with Kaye.

What I want we'd need time and patience for. I want her. I want to be the one who gives her that passion she wants to expose.

Now that I know the feeling is definitely mutual I'm not backing down, but I'm going to go about this my way. I care about her. I want more than a quick lesson in lust for her.

I push aside all thoughts of where things were going as I stop outside Dae-Dae's door. Reaching down, I adjust myself. I drop my head back and I blow out a breath.

When I push my way into the room, I find Dashawn sitting up in bed rubbing at his eyes sleepily. When he sees me entering his room his eyes light up. He leaps from the bed headed for me.

"Lix," he squeals.

I find it so cute that the kid's version of my name is Lix. First time he called me that my chest swelled with so much pride and love. Like now.

I scoop him up into my arms and give him a bear hug. His arms go around my neck and he holds on tight.

I've been making it to New York more often. Dashawn asks after me a lot more. I don't like the thought of disappointing him. When he asks, I'm usually on the plane heading this way.

I appreciate everything my cousins are doing so I can make sure this little guy and his aunt are happy. Logan may have told Wyatt, but the rest of my family still doesn't know what I've been up to in the last two years. I prefer it that way for now.

I smile and kiss his cheek. Someday, he won't have to ask for me to come to him. We'll all be in the same place. I'll be patient, but I know it's going to happen. I decided that the moment my lips touched Kaye's.

"Lix, you here. Go to park?" he says excitedly.

"Not now, buddy," I laugh. "It's still nighttime. You should be sleeping."

He makes a sad frown, pulling the perfect pout. He looks just like Danny and Kaye when they were little. I've noted a few times before how he looks nothing like his birth mother.

The Porters have some strong genes. I think of Kaye and wonder what our children will look like. I laugh at my own thoughts.

I can't see me as a father, and I couldn't imagine my brothers as Uncles. Fuck, I hope if I have kids, they're all boys. With our luck, we'll all have a bunch of girls.

"Dae-Dae, let's hope karma doesn't come for me or your uncles back home," I say, sitting on his bed.

"Pop-pop," he says ignoring my words.

"No lollipops tonight. You need to get back in bed and go night-night," I say.

He gives me more of that pout. I swear he's too adorable. If this weren't New York City, I'd get him dressed and take him to the park now. This time of night there's no telling what he might see in the parks around here.

"I'll have to get us a house with a playset," I think aloud.

"Book, Lix. Come sleep with me and read book," he replies, hopping off my lap to get his favorite bedtime story.

I figured I'd be in for the long haul. He's spoiled. Kaye never should have let him sleep in her bed for so long.

Now she's been fighting to get him out of her bed and into his own. When she does get him in here, he usually tries to keep her with him. Honestly, I don't mind.

If I'm in here, I can't be in Kaye's room getting lost in that delicious body of hers. She was on the verge of driving me insane when she was rocking those hips into me. Her lips taste like all that's good in the world.

I mentally shake those thoughts clear as I get comfortable on Dashawn's racecar bed with him. Placing my back to the headboard and bringing my knees up, I pull him into my side to start reading. He's fast asleep before I flip the first page.

Closing the book, I sit to think while combing a hand through his thick curls. This little dude can snore. I crack up to myself as the sound rises.

This could be my life. I could help Kaye raise Dashawn. It's already like we're a little family. There isn't a night that goes by that I don't call to check in and talk to them both.

I know that 'See Lix' means the little guy wants to see me. I know when Kaye gets that look in her eyes she misses me, but she won't ask for me to come to them.

I instinctively know it's when she needs me. Whether just to talk, or to have me around as someone familiar from back home, I watch for it, I know that look of need. I respond every time.

I want to be Kaye's man. I have no questions about that. Dashawn comes with that. So be it, I'm game.

Maybe there's a father in me yet.

Tension

Kaye

"No, Lix. No eat my bacon," Dae-Dae giggles as Felix pretends to eat from Dashawn's plate.

"Then you better eat up so we can go to the park," Felix replies.

I love the smiles on their faces. Dashawn is always so happy to see Felix. That's important to me.

It's one of the reasons I'm sort of happy things ended the way they did last night. I waited for Felix to return. Once my head was clear I wanted to talk to him about what happened.

I care about our friendship and I don't want to ruin it because I'm sex deprived and thirsty. I'm not sure what I was thinking last night. Probably that my first kiss ever was so hot I soaked through my panties.

I was so embarrassed when he left the room, and I found my underwear drenched. I rushed to shave my legs and change my underwear before he returned. I listened for him to come back while I was in the bathroom.

I never heard him. I sat and waited, chewing on the pad of my thumb but he still didn't come back. After a while, I walked down the hallway to see what happened.

I found Felix and Dae-Dae asleep in Dae-Dae's little bed.

My handsome men.

The thought floated through my head bringing with it a dose of reality. I want something that I don't know for sure I can have. Sex is sex.

I mean, Felix did ask if I was waiting for marriage. That can only mean that he's only willing to give me a one night stand. Right?

I went back to my room conflicted and unable to go to sleep. On one hand, I want all that he offered last night, but at what cost? My mind started to circle so many thoughts.

Would this ruin our friendship? Would this live up to all my fantasies? Craziest of all, would I feel like a kept woman once I allowed him to have my body?

I know I don't make nearly enough money to cover the rent here. The money I make barely covers little things for me and an occasional treat for Dae-Dae.

Yet, we want for nothing. Logan and Brooklyn come through here like Santa Clause, dropping off designer clothes and gifts for Dae-Dae. I've never seen my refrigerator empty.

Connie or Jamie always have grocery bags hanging from their hands when they come by. I've never thought twice about it before. I'm so grateful for it.

What if I jeopardize Dae-Dae's security because I'm thinking from my flesh? I would make all the things my father said about me true. Honestly, lately I've been feeling more and more like I need to become more independent.

I've been questioning what I'm doing with my life. Once Dae-Dae is old enough go to daycare I want to know I have more than my little job with the O'Briens. Eventually, my thoughts got so tangled and out of control, I went back to working on my book.

This time I felt like the characters came to life in a new way. I started to see chemistry form between them as images of Felix hovering over me flashed in my head. My fingers flew across the keys as I turned a single kiss into magical words.

For the first time, I had a kiss on the pages worth the read. Then I lost steam. I was almost tempted to watch some porn to see if I could at least fake my way through the rest.

As I typed the words into the search engine, I quickly changed my mind and deleted it. That's not how I want to learn.

"Where are you?" Felix says next to my ear causing me to jump.

I'm so lost in my own head I hadn't noticed him leaning over toward me. I've been avoiding getting too close to him all morning. I can't even bring myself to making eye contact with him.

"Mama go to park?" Dae-Dae saves me from having to answer Felix.

"No, sweetie. I think I need to stay here and get some things done. I'll have lunch waiting for you guys when you get back," I answer.

"Peanut butter jelly," he squeals.

Felix and I laugh at his excitement for a simple sandwich. I had planned on something else, but I can't deny that face. Peanut butter and jelly it will be.

"We're making it easy on you," Felix says.

"Sure, you are. Should I cut your crust off too," I tease to keep things light.

"Nope, I can handle a little crust on my sandwich. I do want milk though. It does the body good," he replies, his words dripping with insinuation.

My eyes drop to my plate. I pick at the pancakes that I can't finish because my stomach is in knots. I don't have a comeback.

"I want swing, Lix," Dae-Dae saves me again.

"We're going to go as soon as you finish your breakfast. Just a little more and we can leave," Felix says.

"Okay," Dae-Dae pouts, but starts to finish his food.

I know he's excited. Normally, this little boy would scruff down his food and ask for seconds. The smile on his face speaks volumes.

"So who's idea was it for you guys to dress alike," I giggle.

"It was a mutual decision. We were on the same page this morning. Great minds think alike." Felix smiles.

"Cute."

"Glad you like it. We aim to please," he purrs.

My eyes flicker to his and I freeze for a second. He has that watchful gaze in place. I'm not ready for my thoughts to be seen.

I'm still too conflicted. I stand to take my plate into the kitchen. I place the plate in the sink and run my hands over my hair. I tug at my messy bun.

I'm startled for the second time when Felix appears placing his and Dae-Dae's plates in the sink. He's standing so close. His cologne engulfs me. I look up at him to find him studying me again.

"You okay?" he asks.

"Yeah, sure," I reply.

He narrows his eyes, causing me to fidget with my tank top. I force a smile and turn to take care of the dishes. He bumps me with his hip.

"I got those," he says.

"Thanks."

"Did you get any writing done since last night?" he asks.

"Yeah, I did. I think I have something good," I reply.

He turns to me with a cracked smile. My chest expands at the sight of it. He has the most gorgeous smile.

Turning the sink off, he turns to me. His eyes drop to my lips. I shift from foot to foot before him.

"So you pulled from our inspiration," he rumbles low.

"I—"

"Lix, I ready," Dae-Dae calls as he barrels into the kitchen.

Felix nods at something in his head but doesn't say a word. I watch as he backs away keeping his eyes on me. Once he reaches Dae-Dae, he gives me one last once over before he turns and leaves.

Once they are out of the door, I groan and slap myself on the forehead a few times. I'm not that girl. I don't think I can just have sex with Felix once and walk away. I need more, but I don't think that's an option.

CHAPTER FOURTEEN

For Keeps

Kaye

I'm still in my feelings when Felix and Dae-Dae return for
lunch. I've turned this over in my head every which way and I
haven't come up with a solution to make it right. I've opened
Pandora's box and now I don't know how to shut it.

"Later, Mama," Dae-Dae squeals grabbing my attention.

I look up from the dishes I'm washing to see him in Dylan's
arms. I knit my brows. They returned from the park with Dylan
along with them.

I thought we were going to hang out around the house and
chill today. It's what we usually do on Saturdays when Felix
comes. We've sort of fallen into the habit.

Now, Dylan and Dae-Dae are bouncing out of the
apartment, my nephew with a big grin on his little face as he

waves. I turn to my side to look up at Felix questioningly. What I find is that heated look from last night.

I hear the front door close, but I'm frozen in place and can't turn to see if they have left out of the door for certain. Felix reaches over me to turn off the faucet. I turn to face him and he places his arms on either side of me to cage me in as he grasps the edges of the sink.

"We're going to have a talk," he says.

"Oh, okay," I reply, looking up at him.

"I could tell this morning at breakfast that you got this all fucked up in your head," he continues.

My feelings are totally crushed. I knew it. I knew it was only a one-night thing. All of that overthinking for nothing.

Reach for the stars and get burned, Kaye.

I place a hand on his chest to push him back. I don't want him to see into my disappointed eyes. I need space. I need a moment to collect myself.

"Kaye," he says my name like a warm caress. On the verge of tears, I look up into those eyes. "What do you think happened last night?"

"I'm sorry. I read too much into it. You were just trying to help me with my books. That's all it was. I understand," I reply.

He ducks his head until we are eye to eye. I can feel his warm breath fanning my lips. I want to breathe him in like I did last night. I feel that pull from deep within all over again.

"Who told you you're reading too much?" He nods his head in my direction with his words.

"I—"

"Nope, baby," he cutoffs me off.

I frown. He doesn't even know what I was going to say. I pout and fold my arms over my chest.

His eyes drop down to the tops of my squished breasts. His tongue peeks out to wet his lips. When his eyes lift back to mine, they're scorching with heat.

"Y … you asked if I was waiting for marriage. I'm not but I don't think I'm ready for a … a one-night stand or anything like that," I says breathlessly.

He makes a disgusted noise in the back of his throat. Next, thing I know his lips are taking mine in a possessive kiss as my feet leave the floor. He moves to the right of the sink to drop me gently onto the countertop.

His strong body settles between my legs. Felix cups the sides of my face as he literally eats it. His tongue, teeth, and lips are all involved in licking, nipping, and sipping from me.

I can only cling to his t-shirt in hopes of not flying away on a cloud of his creation. He kisses his way to my ear. His panting breaths send a shiver through me. His tongue flicks my ear, tightening my nipples against my bra further.

"I asked you that so I'd know if I would be waiting until our wedding night to claim you or if you'd let me turn your ass out now," he hisses into my ear. "You're mine, Kaye. The moment you let me taste your lips, you became mine. I'm a Black, baby. We play for keeps.

"*Lorg a h-uile duine leatha agus cùm i leat leat fhèin.* That's what my father taught us. That's what we live by," he says.

"What does that mean?" I breathe.

He pulls back from my ear and looks into my soul. I feel so much power rolling off of him. Barely restrained power.

"Find her worthy and keep her for your own," he says before leaning in and licking my lips.

I'm not talking about a flick of his tongue. I'm talking a full-on lick of my entire lips. It's nasty, but I like it.

He grins at me when he looks at my stunned face. Reaching down he grabs the ends of his t-shirt and pulls it up over his head. The play and ripple of his muscles is like magic. I've never seen anything so beautiful in my life.

The contrast of his tan skin and the dark hair running down the center of his V is spellbinding. He has definitely chiseled out his body since the last time I saw him shirtless. It looks good on him.

I grin when I see that beanie still in place on his head. It's like his security blanket. I reach out for it, watching to see if he'll allow me to take it off. Felix gets pissy about people messing with his hats.

When my hand comes away with the knitted cap between my fingers, he turns his head and kisses my palm. I feel a tingle run up my arm from the spot his lips touch. Taking the hat, he tosses it with his shirt.

He wraps his long fingers around my wrist, bringing my hands to his stomach. He flattens my palms and eases them up over his abs to his pecs. I follow the path with my gaze.

His skin is on fire beneath my fingertips, it's so smooth to the touch. I bite my lip and smile when his pecs flex beneath my caress. I raise a brow and look up at him through my lashes. He returns the look with a sexy grin.

Nerd my ass.

Felix is as sexy as any of his brothers, if not more so. I never understood why kids at school tried to shame him for being smart. It never lasted long.

If you teased Felix about being a bookworm you usually didn't return to school for a few days, if at all. I love everything about him. I'll take it all just the way it is. Although, I do wish he were wearing his glasses.

I get bold and glide my hand down his side over his tatted ribs. He grasps a hold of my tank top, his eyes on mine as he lifts it slowly. I reluctantly pull my hands from his body to lift my arms over my head.

He doesn't take the shirt off right away though. Instead, he dips his head in and starts to kiss and lick at my stomach. I moan and blush.

I haven't started going to the gym like I planned. I still have tightening to do. Felix doesn't seem to care much. His tongue dips into my belly button, tugging a gasp from my lips.

I feel the bite of his fingers as they drag up my sides. He moves his lips to wrap my nipple over the fabric of my bra. I drop my arms to lock my fingers in his hair, holding him to me.

He groans, drawing the cotton covered peak deeper into his mouth. The sensation hits me right in my core. Like a hot button bypassing all stops, going straight for the win.

I jerk against him, causing him to release my breast to look up at me. He lifts to his full height, completing the task of removing my tank top. It's tossed over his shoulder, forgotten along with his hat and shirt.

I thread my arms around his neck, his lips finding their way to the side of my neck. I wiggle against him, loving the hot feel if his mouth on me and the heat of his body engulfing me.

His hands are at my back releasing my bra. I feel when it's free. My breasts bounce from the fabric, and he slowly peels it away.

Felix gets rid of it too. Then takes a lazy trip from my shoulders down my sides with back of his fingers. My belly tightens. His touch leaves a trail of fire in its wake.

He surveys me closely for my every reaction to him with his eyes. I try to remember to breathe. The anticipation is mounting to a point of cutting off my air.

"Relax," he murmurs. "I'm going to take my time with you."

"Okay." I nod.

He grins.

"Relax, baby," he repeats.

I nod again, leaning in to kiss him. I totally give myself over to the feel of his lips against mine. He deepens the kiss making himself known in a way I will never forget.

Just when I think he can't turn this up any further, he begins to kiss his way down my chin to the base of my throat. He hooks his fingers inside my leggings, peeling them down my hips.

"Lift," he commands.

I raise my butt from the counter enough for him to get the garment down over my backside. I reach to cover my thighs when they're exposed. I just barely had a beach body when I was back home in California. Now, there's more jiggle than I'm comfortable with.

His eyes flicker up to mine and narrow at me, his face twisting. He covers my hands with his, peeling them from my legs. Replacing my hands with his, he runs his palms up to the apex of my thighs.

"I've watched you become a woman. In my eyes, the perfect woman. Every step of the way you've been gorgeous. Every version of you has called to me. I'm going to join every inch of you," he says the last part as his golden orbs go back down to my thighs and he licks his lips.

I place my nervous hands on the countertop, not sure what to do with them now. He steps back and starts on his own pants.

Releasing his belt, then unfastening his jeans to push them down his hips.

He's not wearing underwear.

My mouth falls open when he springs free from his jeans. My brain takes an immediate lunchbreak. There's little to no function left.

I'm sure he's not supposed to be that big. There is just no way that's fitting inside of me. I cover my face with my hands and cross my thighs.

He laughs at me, causing me to peek through my fingers at him. My eyes go back to his huge penis. I shake my head.

Nope, we can't do this. I'm a lot of things, but crazy is not one of them. Like, he doesn't have a starter version?

I need to work my way up to that thing. He moves closer, prying my hands from my face. I look up at him, gnawing my lip. All thoughts of punking out on this have floated out the window.

"Do you trust me?" he asks gently.

"Yes," I answer without thinking.

"Then trust us," he says while scooping me off the counter and drawing my legs around his waist.

My breath whooshes from my lips in surprise. I'm not a light girl. I may not look like it, but I tip the scale at one seventy-five. My grandmother says it's them island gal bones.

It doesn't seem to bother Felix one bit. He carries me to my bedroom as if I'm no bigger than my nephew in his arms. His eyes never leaving mine.

As we make our way up the hallway, I notice music playing for the first time. Ne-Yo's "Good Man," floats out of my bedroom. I suck in a shuddered breath as I absorb it all.

Felix's words in the kitchen, the song, what we're about to do. This is real, not one of my fantasies or my books. I cup the side of his face to make sure he's not going to evaporate into thin air.

He turns his head to suck my thumb into his mouth. My core clenches. The heat from his body and his length pulsing between us doesn't help. It's scorching right through my panties.

The look of pure fire in his eyes only adds to the flames. I swallow hard, feeling like a deer in headlights. I've known Felix to be intense but not like this.

He climbs onto the bed with me still wrapped around him, gently placing my back against the mattress. His lips go to my chin, his tongue coming out to tease my skin. I'm stiff as a board again.

He snakes his tongue down my throat, between my breasts, placing a kiss in the center of them. I realize I'm not breathing when he pauses. I lift my head to look down at him.

He's watching me from beneath his lashes. His eyes command me to relax, causing me to melt into the mattress. As a reward, his lips caress the side of my right breast.

Goosebumps cover my skin. I can't take my eyes off his. It's like he has me in a trance. I watch him watching me as he kisses and licks a path to my nipple.

His hand goes to cup my small mound to give him better access to the peak. When he swirls his tongue around the tight bud and sucks it into his warm wet mouth, my lips fall open and I buck off the bed. His other hand slips beneath me to grab ahold of one of my cheeks.

His long fingers bite into my flesh. My hips start to rock on their own. My peak pops free from his lips.

He shifts to kiss me again, his body lowering to grind into mine over my panties.

It's like he can't get enough of my kisses. I know his are giving me life. I roam his back with my hands, loving the feel of his skin beneath my fingertips.

When he does break the kiss, he does it so quickly. One minute we're locked together. The next he has me flipped onto my belly, pulling my bottom back toward him.

I feel more than see him bite the waistband of my panties to tug them from my waist. I look over my shoulder in time to see him dragging them down my legs with his mouth. He gets them from my ankles and tosses them with his mouth.

Palming both of my cheeks, he gently massages them. Repositioning himself, he dips his head. Licking his way up my thigh to my core.

The moment I feel his heated mouth headed for my petals; I close my eyes. He licks over my folds, before giving them individual attention. The image of him eating a mango pops in my head.

He sucks and nips like he wants the best of the fruit. His groans of enjoyment leave my face burning. His fingers spread me for the invasion of his tongue. His long digits join in and my eyes roll.

"Felix," I say breathlessly.

In my head, this is so much more than I thought would happen. Soon, I'm too lost in my own pleasure to care about much else. I start to grind into his face, and he makes a sound of approval that comes deep from within his chest.

It vibrates through me, causing my toes to curl. My fingers knot in the sheets. My legs start to quiver beneath me.

A silent scream comes from my mouth. My eyes widen and my head falls back.

I promise he just took something vital to my soul, and he hasn't stopped. He keeps going. I'm a shaking dripping mess.

I try to wiggle away and sag into the sheets. He's not having it. Felix bands an arm around my waist and holds me right where he wants me.

I feel my juices gushing down my legs and over his face. Burying my face in the bed, my head thrashing from side to side as an actual scream rips from my throat.

"Fuck, *yes*. That's what I want," he breathes.

I feel him lick from my clit to the crack of my behind before he takes a bite of my right cheek. He doesn't stop there. He drags his tongue up my spine to the nape of my neck. His hands gliding up from my belly to cup my breasts.

Felix nips my ear, breathing heavily against it. Tipping my head back he captures my lips devouring my mouth the way he did my flower. I'm surprise by my taste on his tongue.

It's nothing like I expected. I feel his lips turn up in a smile when I moan and seek to taste more. His rock-hard erection is bumping against my backside.

It's a reminder of the eye full I received in the kitchen. Yet, I'm too jelly to run or stiffen. His kneading hands are only turning me on more and turning my bones to goo.

Reaching for one of my overstuffed pillows, he places it beneath us. Gently, he turns me to lie over it.

My hips are lifted in the air toward him. I get to take him in in all his glory. His tanned skin, that tat on his ribs, the dark trail that leads to more hair surrounding his more than impressive length.

Placing a hand beside my head, he leans into me. His other hand wraps around his base, guiding to my entrance. His eyes are on mine, yet he's not making the next move. I bite my lip, looking down at his girth in his hand.

"Wrap your legs around my waist," he commands leaning into kiss me. "Use them to control me. If it's too much, squeeze to slow me. If you need more, open and pull me in. You're in control."

"Okay," I breathe and nod.

I feel him nudge my folds and close my eyes. He halts his forward motion. I open my eyes again to find him staring intently at me.

"Keep your eyes on me," he says huskily. "We're in this together. Trust us."

I nod and he starts to push in again. He moves his hand from my face to the sensitive button between my legs. I'm so slick it starts to ease his efforts.

He rocks his hips back after a little ways in and I lift my hips for more, not wanting his retreat. He pushes back in, and I question my sanity. I yield to him but not without pain this time.

This time when he moves back out, I don't try to chase him. Instead, I brace myself for his next entry. Felix reaches for my left leg bringing it to his shoulder.

He turns his head slightly, never breaking eye contact. Licking my ankle, before he then sucks the skin into his mouth. Just as I feel his teeth sink into my skin, he pushes all the way into me.

"Felix," I cry out.

He stills his hips, while soothing the bite with his tongue. He releases my leg, wrapping it back around his waist. Leaning his body over mine, he pecks the tip of my nose, then my lips.

His cheeks are red and a vein in his neck has popped. The front of his hair is wet with sweat, sticking to his forehead. He looks so sexy.

It turns me on more. I feel my juices flooding him as I begin to stretch around him. There is a biting pain from him being so far inside me. When I look down, I'm stunned to see he's still not all the way in. I feel him in my back and stomach.

He lifts my face to meet his as he begins to move again. This time when we lock eyes, a soothing emotion comes over me. I feel his care for me, his want for my pleasure above his.

His slow motions speak to all I see within his orbs. I take note that his eyes aren't as gold as usual. They're more black than anything.

I reach to run my hand through his sweat soaked hair. His tongue peeks out to flick my wrist before he kisses it softly. I relax the grip of my thighs, pulling my legs back into me more.

His lips curl as he begins thrusting into me deeper. Pain becomes pleasure and a mass of confusion. I know I need something.

I want more of everything. I just don't know how to ask and for what to ask for. My insides start to pulse around him and I like the feel. I squeeze to make it happen again. It's like a bolt of lightning powers through me.

"Kaye," he groans against my lips.

"Yes," I moan, my nails clawing down his back.

Both of his hands go to the small of my back, pressing me into him as his hips roll into me. I pull my legs back more wrapping them high on his back. My thick thighs cradling him.

When his lips wrap my nipple, I'm done for. My eyes roll back. He picks up the pace and I feel like I'm going to float up out of my own body.

"Oh shit," I scream.

Felix

Her scream is food to my soul. I feel her so close to the edge. I want her orgasm so bad; I can taste it.

I growl around her nipple in my mouth. She's so fucking tight and wet. Her pussy is soaking me with its delicious heat. I want to suck that shit up.

Every. Single. Drop.

I let her peak pop from my mouth. The look on her face is such a turn on. I can't stop myself from working her over. I'm pushing in with ease now.

I watch her with my tongue pressed to my upper lip. She's taking my cock a lot better than either of us thought she would. I'll admit I was a bit concerned for our first time. I knew I'd get in, I just didn't know it would be this fucking perfect.

God made her just for me, I know he did. She fits me as if she were chiseled from my own life force. I lean into her ear nipping it.

"Come for me. Stop trying to hold it. Give in. Give me what's mine," I rasp in her ear.

"Felix, the fuck," she cries out as she convulses beneath me.

I chuckle at her dirty mouth. I like that it's just for me. Although, I've noticed her characters have much fouler mouths than hers.

"You have no idea how long I've wanted you." Floats from my lips.

I slow down, in no rush to finish. I need to savor this. This is the woman I've dreamed about since we were teens. I've wanted her since before I knew I could have her. I've always felt a connection with her.

The same connection that now is off the fucking charts. I've slept with others, but that was before. Before I knew I'd make Kaye mine. Never in my life has sex felt like this.

If I could have one wish, it would be that I could bottle this feeling to have it last forever. I watch her come down off her high, still pushing into her, holding her right on the edge. I don't give her time to touch the ground again.

If I can help it, I'll never let her precious feet touch another surface that hasn't been paved by me. I'm the shield that will keep her safe from the world. Her pleasure is my pleasure.

Feeling my own orgasm riding me too closely, I pull out and kiss my way down her body. I love her breasts. They're not huge, but not tiny. They're enough for my mouth and hands.

I stop to worship them, each in turn. I pay attention to detail. Her left tit is more sensitive than the right. I return to the left one to give it more attention.

Her whimpers and cries guide me through her pleasure like a map. I love having my woman's taste on my tongue. I start to lick my way down to her center, stopping to swirl around her belly button before settling between her legs.

"Felix, don't. I don't think I can take it," she pleads.

I give a dark chuckle. She'll learn to take it and a lot more before I'm done. I haven't even started. I place a kiss to the top of her mound and wink at her.

"Just breathe."

"Felix," she cries out, her hips lifting from the pillow.

I pull her legs around my neck, encouraging her to ride my face. This feast was made for me to enjoy, and I plan to do just that. Kaye never should've let me have a taste.

I'm hooked now.

CHAPTER FIFTEEN

This is Real

Kaye

Sitting on the side of the tub rubbing oil into my skin, I let out a silent squeal. I can't believe what I've been doing all day. I also can't believe how sore and relaxed I feel at the same time.

Today reached well beyond my expectations. I love that he took his time with me. Teaching me along the way. I felt so powerful watching his pleasure as I took control of my own.

Somehow, I know it wouldn't be the same with anyone else. All the feelings I had swirling around in me made every touch worth gold to me.

My face hurts from smiling so hard and my throat is raw from screaming. I caught on after a while that all the screaming turns him on. I'll admit his moans and groans are pretty sexy as well.

"He's eating a burger and fries with Brooklyn, Jamie, and Dylan. No time to talk to Lix. He's with his boys," Felix says as he enters the bathroom chuckling and shaking his head.

He stands over me, cupping the back of my neck to bend and kiss my lips. The kiss is much too quick. After all the sex we've had, my belly and girly parts are still clenching in anticipation. I shouldn't be thinking about him touching me again.

My legs wouldn't even work after we were done. He had to draw my bath and carry me into the bathroom to set me into it. Seriously, I stood and my legs gave out from under me.

"Are we going to go pick him up?" I ask.

"Nope, the little dude is going to have a sleepover with Jamie. He'll bring him back in the morning," he replies.

"He didn't want to talk to me?" I pout.

"He said to tell you not to worry about him. 'See Mama later,' were his words before hanging up."

"I think he's growing up too fast," I mumble.

"Just moving out of the way for brothers and sisters," Felix says with a smile on his lips.

My mouth falls open. I blink at him to see if he's teasing. I'm still not entirely sure that he is.

"You do know that I'm on the pill, right?" I say.

"That's fine for now. Once my family is back home with me, I'll let you know when I think it's time you stop," he says so matter-of-factly.

"When you think?" I lift a brow.

He scoops me off the edge of the tub and starts back into the bedroom. He climbs on the bed, settling me between his legs as he puts his back to the headboard. He kisses the back of my head, while linking our fingers together. He lifts our hands before us, playing with my fingertips.

"You do know this can't go on like this forever?" he murmurs. "I get there are questions that are going to be tough to answer and you have every right to be angry with your parents. Two years is a long time to ignore having a daughter and grandchild.

"But how long do you plan to hide here. Push comes to shove, I'll figure out a way to be here, but our lives are back home. We need to have a plan," he says.

"I don't know. I've been focused on Dae-Dae being safe and happy. I'm still so pissed off at them … my dad. Now, I'm writing again and that will only add fuel to the fire.

"I think I have a chance to do something with my writing. It will be a chance to show my father that God is in everything. To me, it all will be worth it if I make this happen. Raising Dae-Dae right and making a go of publishing.

"I feel like I need to do this before I go back. You know my dad. If I show up with nothing, he'll get on his soapbox and preach about it," I huff.

He's quiet for a moment still playing with my fingers. When he stops, he wraps our locked together limbs around me. He buries his face into my neck and he inhales deeply. I giggle when his tosses his legs over mine caging me in.

"I think I did this all wrong. I know you better than to cage you in. I've been taking care of everything and never thought about how it would look if you went back home to your family with no career or anything." Hhe pauses and huffs before he continues.

"Fuck, you gave up everything for Danny and Dashawn. You never finished your last year in college. Shit, baby," he groans.

"Actually, I did finish. I just never made a big deal about it, and I've been saving to pay off my balance to get the degree I finished," I say quietly and shrug my shoulders.

"You were so excited to walk for graduation. Danny was so happy for you." His voice is laced with pain.

"Things change. The one person who would have meant the most to have there wouldn't have been anyway."

"You and your mom were so close," he replies.

"Yeah, but you weren't there that night. She sat there and listened to him hurl all those hurtful words at me. You know she was the one to take me to get on the pill," I scoff.

"Not because I was sexually active, but because I used to be in such pain during that time of the month. I mean, sure, the pill isn't one hundred percent or anything. But she knew and she never stopped Daddy to question me or what happened."

"Your dad is a hard man to rein in. I'm sure she wanted to. Maybe if she had time to. You guys took off—"

I shake my head cutting his words off. I've thought all of this over so many times. I've played that day over and over.

"My dad may seem like he runs things, but mom is no wall flower. I've seen her step up for Danny over the years without hesitation. Sometimes, I wonder if she knew I was taking the bullet for Danny." I clamp my mouth shut.

After the day we had, this is the last thing I want to talk about. I snuggle back against his chest, taking comfort in his embrace. His silence tells me two things. He's thinking of a way to make this all right again and as always he knows me well enough to know I need a change in topic.

"You're not going to let me do this for you, are you?" he grumbles.

"No," I reply.

"One phone call and I can get your book in the right hands. It would be nothing," he breathes into my neck.

"And nothing is what I would feel like. I wouldn't have done it on my own. I want to know I did this. Think about it, Felix. You just said it yourself.

"I gave up everything. I've been doing for everyone else. I want to do this for me.

"I need to know I did this. Something to call all mine," I say pleadingly.

"I totally understand. It's been a long time coming. I know you'll do it."

"Thank you."

"Kaye?"

"Yeah."

"The goal is to be together. To get you back home. You're amazing.

"Write the book and shut shit down like I know you can. Show your dad what we know," he replies kissing my neck. "I'll be waiting."

My stomach flips. I suddenly feel like I have so much on the line, but I'm hungry for it. I have a reward awaiting me at the finish line.

"I need you to know one more thing," he says next to my ear, sending warmth and tingles shooting through my body. "You can call me all yours."

CHAPTER SIXTEEN

Ready or Not

Felix

I know I'm not right. I just couldn't help myself. I have to fly out tonight and there's no telling when I'll get to see Kaye again.

So yeah. I woke her up screaming and coming all over my face. Just so I could put her back to sleep all over again. It's the way it should be every morning. Snatch a soul, save a life.

With a woman like Kaye to call my own, I'll be more relaxed throughout my workday. Absolutely less likely to kick someone's ass at work. Sometimes those bounties can push you to the edge.

Then there are the other special assignments that make me question the sanity of my family and our government. They know what they send us to do and don't bat a single lash about it. Knowing I have Kaye in my life as mine has already started to make me think more cautiously about everything.

I have an assignment I need to get back to. I'm thinking of approaching things differently. Less risk, less fall-out, that's the goal for this one.

"What's on ya mind?" Brooklyn asks from his seat on the couch.

"Work stuff," I reply.

"Aye, heard yer getting into some muddy waters. Tread lightly. I will not hesitate to go to war if backlash results from this one," he warns.

"Dad already informed me of the thin lines here. I'll get what I need without tipping the scales," I respond.

"My grandfather is a right bastard. Ya just keep an eye out for trouble."

"I will. I'm thinking I may be able to do this one from the comfort of my own home if I play this right," I think aloud.

"Good. Yer the best. Wish ya were working for me," he says.

"Maybe someday. I still owe you guys a favor," I acknowledge.

"No favor owed. Kaye be family just as well as ya. Dae-Dae will always have a set of uncles in New York."

"Thanks."

"Uncle Cole, fix please," Dae-Dae interrupts holding up the remote to the Xbox. The batteries must have died again.

Brooklyn gets up to change them out for him. Meanwhile, Dae-Dae comes to sit on my lap and wait. I've noticed him clinging to me a bit this visit.

I brush his hair back off his forehead and kiss it. He looks up at me with a beaming smile. I love this kid. My heart aches that I'm leaving again.

"I'll bring you a new game next time," I promise.

"Racecars?" he asks with that infectious smile.

"Racecars it is," I say and give him a sage nod.

"*Yes*," he cheers.

Turning in my lap he wraps his arms around my neck for a tight hug. I hug him back absorbing all the good he shares. It's impossible to be angry around this kid.

"Here ya go," Brooklyn says as he returns with the controller ready for Dae-Dae.

"Thank you," he sings and rushes back over to his spot in front of the TV.

I watch him with a smile on my face. Kaye is going to get me for letting him play for so long. Although, I don't think we'll be seeing her for quite a while.

That thought brings a larger smile to my face. She made this sexy purring noise this morning that had me ready to explode. I can't wait until the next time I can make that happen.

"I do want to ask you a favor," Brooklyn says, breaking into my musing.

He has my attention right away, as I notice that he pushes aside his Irish accent. His eyes have a seriousness in them I'm used to seeing for business only. I know what's said next is important to him.

"It has to do with the old bastard. There was a family back home. Two brothers, both married American women. African American women. They each had daughters. I need to find those girls, but my grandfather can't get wind of it," Brooklyn says.

"Do you have names?"

"Deja Walsh and Ciara Walsh. Use the surname Murphy as well. It was their father's maternal grandmother's name," he replies. "I believe it's the name that kept them alive."

"Anything else you have for me to go on?"

"I believe Deja is still in Ireland. Ciara may be somewhere here in the States. Her father was a boxer.

"What you need to know most importantly is not a hair should be harmed on either of their heads. I want to keep it that way. If that bastard finds out I'm asking after them he'll try to make it otherwise.

"I don't need another reason to want to kill my own flesh and blood. He's already collecting a debt he can't handle." His last words come out in a hiss.

"Bro, consider them found."

"Aye, I know."

Kaye

I wake with a smile on my face as I stretch my sore and satiated body. A gasp flies from my lips when I get a peek at the clock on the nightstand. It's darn near three in the afternoon.

I can hear rumbling voices and Dae-Dae's high-pitched giggles coming from the front of the apartment. I can't believe Felix allowed me to sleep in this late. I can't believe I actually slept in.

I'm normally the first one to get up so I can make breakfast and sometimes, have a minute to myself to write. Breakfast and lunch have both past and I'm still here in bed. My mind goes to the wakeup call from this morning.

I thought I was dreaming at first. Felix's fingers were biting into my thighs, while his face was buried between my legs. I remember coming so hard, I thought my chest would explode.

Crap!

Then he put it on me until I passed out. Oh my God. I've been asleep since.

I scramble from the bed. My legs are shaky, but I can stand and make it to the bathroom on my own two feet. I take a quick shower and freshen up before throwing on leggings and a t-shirt.

When I make it into the living room, my apartment seems so tiny. It's full of O'Briens. All the brothers and their two sisters are here. It's like they're having a party and I'm the last guest to arrive.

Drinks are in hand, Connie is passing plates around. Dae-Dae looks like he's on cloud nine as he sits between Felix and Dylan. The three of them are transfixed by a Manga film on the TV. *Bleach,* if I'm not mistaken.

Felix and Dae-Dae have watched a few of the movies before. I think it's a bit beyond his age, but Dae-Dae seems to love watching it with Felix. Kate and Brooklyn are chatting with Logan, while Jamie remains on his cell phone.

Looking around it dawns on me that I've had a family right here in New York. I was kind of homesick after my talk with Felix. I toyed with the idea of calling my mother, but the old familiar hurt rose, and I thought better of it.

I have people who care right here in New York. Sure, I would love to be closer to Felix on a regular basis, but for now, I have things I need to do for me. I need to make something happen for me.

"There she is," Connie sings.

I watch Felix turn his head in my direction. He doesn't hesitate to get up and make his way to me. He puts his arms around my waist and dips his head to place a quick kiss on my lips.

"How are you feeling?" He leans into my ear to ask.

I feel my face burn as I think about what he's truly asking. I look up into his eyes. They're twinkling with mischief and mirth.

"I'm great," I reply with what I hope is a seductive smile.

His lips are at my ear again. He nips it, then licks it soothingly. I coil my fingers in his shirt.

"You're lucky I need to get back. I can still taste you on my tongue," he whispers.

He has a sexy grin on his lips when he pulls away from my ear. I can see he enjoys stunning me with his words. I'm feeling bold so I offer my own dose of shock.

"Maybe next time I can find out what you taste like," I whisper back, looking up at him through my lashes.

I see the instant fire that enters his eyes. He licks his lips moving in closer. Just when he goes to say something else, Dae-Dae runs over to wrap himself around Felix's leg.

We're pulled back into the room and the reality of our guests who are watching us with amused looks on their faces. I groan internally. Felix gets to go back to Cali.

I'll be here for all the teasing and questions. I can see it in Connie's eyes, I'm in for it. Maybe I should leave with Felix.

"Mama, tell Lix stay," Dae-Dae says as he holds onto Felix.

I know how the little guys feels. I'm getting sad too. I know he has to head out soon. I'm a little annoyed with myself for sleeping so long.

"He can't, baby. He'll be back," I reply.

Dae-Dae gives the biggest pout. Felix bends to pick him up, kissing his cheek. From the look on Felix's face this isn't easy for him either.

"I'll come back as soon as I can. I promise," he says to Dae-Dae.

"Come with you?" he replies hopefully.

"I wish," Felix answers, burying his face in Dae-Dae's curls, looking over his head into my eyes. "I'm giving your mama time to do her thing, but when the time is right, ready or not, I'm coming to get you both."

My mouth pops open. I hear the promise in his words and I sure as heck see it in his eyes. Felix has a clock in his head and it's ticking. I'd sure like to know when it's set for.

CHAPTER SEVENTEEN

Who's Ye Fool?

Felix

I smile down at my phone. Kaye just sent me pictures of her and Dashawn. They're making duck faces in one. Dae-Dae is showing off his muscles in another.

I miss the fuck out of them both. Kaye is glowing. She looks so happy. According to her, she's writing up a storm. However, she won't send me any of her new work.

My phone vibrates again. It's a picture of just Kaye blowing me a kiss. I bite my lip and grin like a fool.

"I always find it funny that ye fuckers believe ye can hide things from me. Who's ye fool, Felix? It sure as fuck ain't me." My mother says across the kitchen island, drawing my attention from my phone.

I focus on her face and see her hazel eyes locked in on me. She looks pissed. I groan internally. I don't know how much she knows, but I'm positive my mother is onto me.

"What—"

She lifts the wooden spoon in her hand and slashes it through the air to silence me. I whip my head back, but I shut the fuck up. I know that look too well.

"Don't ye play dumb with me. At first, I thought ye were working and tending to business. Then I started noticing a pattern. Who do ye think audits the books each year? I've seen the flights and the locations. You keep taking ye ass to New York.

"At first, I figured ye were going to hang with Jamie and Dylan. Which is fine. I wish youse boys lived closer to each other. But when I talked to ye aunt, she kept mentioning Dashawn this and Dashawn that. How the wee one loves ye so.

"I kept me mouth shut and just listened. Come to find out there's a girl in New York that ye have the O'Briens looking after. A girl named Kaye. The same Kaye that's been missing with her mother crying on me shoulder for her.

"Aye, I ought cobbler ye, Felix. I have a mind to put my foot clear up yer arse. I would too if ye weren't the child ye are. I trust ye. So I'll allow ye this pass. Now explain to me what me in-laws know that I don't," she demands.

I rub my forehead in frustration, as the wheels turn in my head. I had no idea Mrs. Porter has been coming to see mom.

Hope blooms in my chest. If I can fix this one thing for Kaye, I know it will ease her burdens a little more. I know how much she misses her family. Knowing her mother isn't as closed off about the subject gives me a few ideas.

"Start talking ye rawny wee shit, before I batter ye hoop," Mom growls.

I try not to laugh, she means every word. She'll kick my ass if I don't start talking, so talk. I tell my mother everything as she feeds me brownies and milk like I'm still eight. She takes a seat and listens just like she used to do back then.

"Yer still sweet on that lass," my mother says when I'm done.

I know it's not a question, she's stating a fact. It's the one thing I didn't tell her. I never said a word about how I feel about Kaye, not once. As I look into my mother's knowing eyes, I know I never had to. I get my watchfulness from her.

"I care about her. I want to do whatever I can to make sure she and the baby are taken care of," I reply.

"Again, lad of mine. Who's ye foul?"

I blow out a heavy breath. I might as well be straight. My mother knows me better than anyone.

"Not you. Yes, I'm in love with her," I say.

"Ye have been for years. She's a pretty little one. Her father … now that's going to be ye challenge. He loves you like a son, but he is one stubborn as fuck man. He believes he means well and in principle, he does. It just doesn't always translate that way," she says.

"I want to bring her home. It's been long enough," I mumble.

"Some things we shouldn't stick our noses too far into. Ye bring her home, ye may be bringing her too close to a fire that will run her away for good. Trust me. Her father hasn't finished roaring yet and her coming home will cause her to have to face that noise." She pauses, reaching for my hand.

"She misses her family. They have a grandson they should get to know."

"She also allowed someone to use her name and health insurance. Health insurance her father's ministry paid for. She's listed as the mother of that babe on his birth certificate.

"Coming home means choosing to expose a string of lies and choosing who to protect. Herself or her beloved brother," mom replies.

"She gets hurt either way," I huff.

"Aye. It's a noble thing she's done for Danny, but there has been a web weaved. Yer pressing up against someone's beliefs here. The backlash will have a ripple, it will. Be careful of the stones ye throw at this one," she cautions me.

"What should I do?" I ask feeling lost.

"Watch it all closely. I have a feeling it will work itself out somehow. Ye just don't be the one to force it. She's in good hands. That, I'm glad of," she says, smiling up at me. Patting my hand, she stands from the seat she took when I started to tell her the story. "Ye have done good."

"Can I ask you something?"

"Of course," she says softly.

"I never told Danny how I felt about Kaye. Do you think it's wrong that we're ... "

"That yer shagging his sister now?" she laughs. Patting my cheek, she shakes her head. "If ye only want to have a fuck and test the waters then, no. I don't think it's something ye should do. But if ye love her, like I know ye do. He would be happy that his best friend is the one to take care of his little sister in every way she needs."

"You're sure?"

"Did I raise ye to be a fierce man in everything ye do? Yer like ye father in a lot of ways. Kaye is a lucky one to have ye," she replies.

CHAPTER EIGHTEEN

Missing You

Felix

It's been a rough day. It seems like every time I finished one task something else comes up. Toby has had a lot of shit going on with him, so dad forced him to take some time off.

We've been covering for him since. I thought I'd get to go back to New York sooner, but with the extra load, I just haven't been able to make it happen. I'm frustrated and tired.

It's only been three weeks, but it feels like it's been so much longer. Our calls at night aren't enough. Yet, I know I'm going to keep my word and give Kaye what she needs.

She needs time to at least see if she can build her own thing. For now, I've been doing my best to work through all of it. It's killing me, but I'm dealing.

I give a tired smile to the one thing I've had to distract me. I have good and bad news for Brooklyn. I'm not done. I'll get him everything he's looking for, but it may be harder than I initially thought. Even for me.

"Hello," Cole's voice comes through the phone line after a few rings.

"Hey, you have a minute? I found Deja," I say.

"Where is she?" he asks before I can fully get my words out.

"Scotland," I reply.

"Fuck. Is she okay?"

"Yeah, well, she has been. The grandmother you told me about. That's who she's been with. The grandmother is on her deathbed. Doesn't look like she has much longer. Small village, word is spreading," I inform him.

"Fuck me. Son of a bitch. Fuck," he growls. "What about Ciara?"

"No luck there. It's not looking good. I found an obit for Donald and Iesha Walsh. Two children are mentioned. A baby boy and little girl. The trail goes cold after that. I'm still working," I reply.

"Damn it," he huffs.

"You want the location for Deja?"

"Have I killed a man?"

"I used the secure box. It will disappear in one hour."

"Thank ya, Felix."

"No thanks needed. Let me know if you need anything else," I say and hang up.

I sit staring at my screen as if Ciara will appear. I know the answer is there. I just need to keep digging. I'll turn over the right stone eventually.

I called in favors with my mother's side of the family to verify the information I found on Deja. I know I can trust them. I put that fact in the message I send to Brooklyn in case he needs to reach out.

The McGowans treat the O'Briens just like flesh and blood. Brooklyn knows he can trust them. I've wondered a few times who the Walsh cousins are to Brooklyn.

During my digging I learned that while Angus Walsh raised Deja, she's his adopted daughter. Deja was born in Ireland to a recently widowed military wife. Helen Walsh never returned to the States. Angus fell hard and fast for Helen and they married. Angus was the only father Deja has ever known.

His brother Donald Walsh was a hot cruiserweight boxer. He met his wife on a winning streak. He won a fight in the US and met her in a club his team chose to celebrate in. Ciara was born in Ireland a few years later.

I pull off my glasses and rub my burning eyes. I've been in front of these monitors way too long. I'm not going to pluck the answers out in this state. I need to walk away for a bit.

Leaning back in my chair, I close my eyes. I blow out a breath and push my fingers into my hair. My phone rings, causing me to twist my lips. I just need a few moments of silence, including from my own head.

Without looking, I reach for the phone bringing it to my ear. Anyone calling this phone is meant to have the number, so I'm not worried about dodging anyone. A smile comes to my lips when I hear Dae-Dae singing in the background before I can answer.

"Hey, baby," I rumble into the phone.

"You sound so tired," Kaye replies. "We'll call you tomorrow."

"Hang up and I'll spank your ass next time I see you," I croon into the phone.

I'm greeted with silence from her lips. I know she's still there. Dashawn is still in the background singing. I can make out his words as they're on repeat.

"Mama, Dae-Dae, Lix," he continues to repeat.

"I miss you guys too," I say to her silence.

"He's been driving me crazy for hours," she groans. "I thought hearing your voice would get him to stop."

I laugh. She sounds about ready to pull her hair out. He's only getting louder by the minute.

"And yes, we both miss you. You should get some sleep," she says softly.

"I'm leaving now," I reply as I force myself out of my chair.

I start to shut down, snatching my keys from my desk. I wasn't going to get anything else done tonight. My head is starting to pound from trying to think too hard.

I need to head out for a bounty in the morning. It's way past time to call it a night. I drag my tired body to the elevator.

"Dae-Dae, please," she huffs away from the phone.

"Isn't it past his bedtime?" I chuckle.

"Yes, Jamie came over and got him all hyped up. I'm going to kill him," Kaye grumbles.

"What did he want?" I frown as I ask the question.

"Calm down, killer," she giggles. "Connie asked him to bring over some stuff for Dae-Dae. Those two started horsing around and Dae-Dae has been bouncing off the walls since."

"He'll wear himself out soon," I reply, as I jog down the stairs.

As tired as I am, I should've taken the elevator, but I'm just too tired to wait for it. Besides, I've been sitting at my desk all day since after my morning workout. I can use the stretch.

"Put him—"

My words cutoff as I feel my hackles go up. Something is off. I start to pat at my pockets as if I'm searching for something. Meanwhile, I start to scan the lot.

"Damn, babe. I think I forgot something in the office. I'll call you back," I say into the phone.

"Okay," she replies sounding disappointed.

I have to push that aside for now. I keep my attention on my surrounds as I cut the call and pretend to still be searching my person. I feel the moment someone starts to close in on me.

I keep my head down until the very last second. When they step in to grab me, I throw an elbow back, yielding me a satisfying crunch. Ducking down, I spin around until their back is to my front and I have the dude in a headlock.

"What do you want?" I hiss.

He refuses to respond, his nostrils flaring. I apply more pressure to his neck, cutting off his air. He struggles clawing at my arm. A sound to my left catches my attention.

I knock out the guy in my arms with a solid punch, dropping him to the ground just as another guy swings at me. I duck back out of the way seconds before his punch connects. Deflecting his arm with my left, I shove my right into his face so hard I see his cheek cave under the pressure.

A loud bellow comes from the asshole, but he's not down for the count. He comes charging at me. I lead him in grabbing his shoulders and bringing my knee into his midsection. I bring my elbow down into his back, dropping him to his knees.

Snatching a hand full of his hair, I tug his head back. "Who the fuck sent you?" I hiss in his face.

"Fuck you," he says awkwardly.

A broken jaw and cheek will do that. I grab his face with my free hand and apply pressure. His scream fills the parking lot.

"Start talking before I rip your fucking face off," I snarl.

"H ... his information is ... it's in my phone," he relents. "Last call—"

He doesn't get to finish his words before I slam my fist into his face again. This time knocking him out. I search him for his phone.

My jaw works as I look down at the number in the phone. I tuck the phone away to do some digging once I get this mess cleaned up. Pulling my phone out, I make a call.

"I have a package in the lot at the office," I say simply and hang up.

Locking the place down from my phone, I start back upstairs. This will all be taken care of. I need to know if this number belongs to any of my top list of suspects. I've been making a few enemies lately with some of the favors I've done.

Kaye

I can't sleep. Something was off about Felix's voice when we spoke earlier. He hasn't called me back yet. I'm worried.

I flip in the bed, reaching for my phone to look at the screen for the hundredth time. As if I just happened to miss a call while sitting right here.

Nothing.

I chew on the inside of my mouth. Maybe he just fell asleep. I don't want to wake him if that's the case. He did sound tired.

I know I'm exhausted despite not being able to pass out. I roll my lips and turn them to the side. I'm never going to get any sleep if I can't settle my mind. I know in my heart something is off.

"Fuck it," I huff and dial his number.

I roll my eyes at the voice in my head telling me that Felix and the O'Briens are rubbing off on me. I don't curse nearly as much as they do—thanks to grandma and her bar of soap. I smile at the fond thought of my grandmother.

The smile is followed by a sharp pain in my chest. Felix told me my grandparents returned to Jamaica not too long after Dae-Dae's first birthday. I've thought a time or two about going to stay with them.

"Hello," Felix's tight voice interrupts my thoughts.

I hesitate, feeling foolish for calling. My mouth flaps a few times. I think to hang up. Tomorrow when I talk to him, I'll tell him I rolled onto it in my sleep.

"Kaye, are you all right?" he asks, his voice going from frustrated to frantic.

"I'm fine," I answer quickly. "I … you never called back I was worried. I'm sorry to wake you."

"You didn't wake me. I haven't gone to sleep. I'm sorry. "I needed to take care of something in the office. I'm just walking into my place," he says.

"Is everything okay?"

I sit up in the bed not liking the aggravation I hear as he speaks. It takes a lot for Felix to show he's irritated. Something is definitely up.

"It will be," he gives the ambiguous reply.

"Felix, you're worrying me."

I hear the sigh that he releases. I frown ready to hang up and go to sleep. I know he's okay. I'm not going to be the annoying girlfriend who needs to know his every move.

"I don't want you to worry. If you were here, you'd see I'm fine," he replies before I can exit the call.

"But I'm not there."

"Yeah, don't I know it. I miss you. I could really stand to see your face right now," he rumbles.

"I could come to you," I blurt out.

"You don't know how much I would love that, but now is not a good time," he says, again, aggravation showing.

"Oh, okay," I murmur.

"Don't do that," he groans. "As soon as things settle here and I plug up some shit, I'm on my way to you. And if you want to come here, I'll make that happen too."

"Okay, let me know if there's anything I can do for you. I'll let you get some rest," I reply.

"Actually, there is something you can do for me. As tired as I am, hearing your voice has me hard as a rock. You want to help me with that?"

My breath hitches. I have to squeeze my thighs together. I'm assaulted by images of our time together.

"How can I help you?"

The sound of my own voice surprises me. It's thick and husky with lust. Forget sex addiction. I'm a Felix addict.

I start to bite the pad of my thumb when he doesn't answer right away. I can almost hear him thinking. I fidget my toes together as the anticipation builds.

"Don't freak out when I tell you this. I only use them to make sure everything is okay there," he says.

"What?" I ask in confusion.

"There are cameras in the apartment in all of the rooms. It's the same system I put in all of my family's homes," he replies.

I drop the phone from my ear. I whip my head from side to side, I looking around the room as if I can see the cameras. Tugging my t-shirt over my knees, I curl into a ball like I can hide or something.

"You're joking right?" I say, putting the phone back to my ear.

"No."

"Have you been watching me?"

"No."

"*Felix*," I say in warning.

"I said, no," he repeats. "I can start if you like. Actually, I want to watch you now. Will you do that for me?"

"Do what?" I frown at the phone.

He chuckles. "Never mind."

"No, what do you mean?"

"Will you play with your pussy for me? I want to watch you come," he purrs back at me.

"Seriously?"

"When it comes to that pussy, I never play. I could use the release. It will help me relax. The cams are on my secure network. No one else monitors them," he says.

I sit silently thinking on this. He has cameras in my bedroom. I know what he does for a living. Should it really shock or bother me that he has cameras set up in my home?

I know he takes my safety very seriously. If he has the same system in his family's houses, I should feel like family too. Right?

Although, let's face it. He's not asking any of his brothers to masturbate on cam for him. Is it sick that I'm a little turned on by the request?

"Come on, Kaye. You know you want to. I know you're already wet. Do this for daddy," he says silkily.

I pull the phone from my ear and lift a brow. "*Daddy*," I mouth at the phone. I think we've both just lost our minds. I swear the way he says it has my girly bits pulsing. I'm totally wet for him.

Felix

I can hear the gears turning in her head through the phone line. She's curious and turned on. I move to my desk in my home office and sit.

Logging into my computer, I pull up the cameras in the New York apartment. I hold my finger over the mouse as I hover over the camera that will open up my view to her room. I wait for her to say the words. It's her choice, always her choice.

"Okay," she whispers.

My lips curl into a smile as I click the cam. Kaye comes into view sitting on her bed. She's curled up with her knees in her chest and her t-shirt pulled down over her legs.

My smile grows when I see it's one of my t-shirts. I know it is from the Mobb Deep logo. I was looking for that one.

"You look sexy as fuck in my shirt," I say lazily.

I'm tired, but I need this. Not only do I miss her. Hearing her voice has all my blood flowing in one direction.

I hear her gasp, her head whipping back and forth. I chuckle as I watch her trying to figure out where the cam is. I have a head on view of her bed.

"You can really see me?" she asks, allowing her legs to slide from beneath the fabric of the shirt.

I lick my lips. Those thighs are going to be the death of me. I want to get lost in them for days. I bring up the memory of having them wrapped around me. I can almost feel their weight pressed against me.

"Look straight ahead," I reply.

She straightens her head and stares straight ahead. She knits her brows. She won't see the cam. I use the best. It blends in perfectly.

"Like this?" she asks.

"Yes, take your hair down. I like tugging it while I'm inside of you."

I expect my words to shock her, but I'm just as pleased by the response I get. Releasing her hair to fall to her shoulders, she dips her head and runs her hand through the front. When she lifts her head slightly, she's looking up through her lashes in the direction of the cam.

I zoom in just a bit. She's so fucking gorgeous. The small sassy smile on her lips reveals the real Kaye.

The one I've had the pleasure to unlock. The camera is so sharp it reveals her brown skin and those brown eyes to me as if I were staring at them in the flesh. Unzipping my pants, I wrap my hand around my cock.

I don't stroke, I allow the weight to rest in my palm for now. Kaye parts her legs in front of her slowly, setting my hand in motion. Before I can tell her to, she places the phone on speaker sitting it on the bed.

Then, she lifts the t-shirt up over her head. Those perky tits jiggle as she tosses the shirt aside. I would love to wrap my lips around those chocolate tipped nipples. I watch them tighten more as if I'm there to breathe against them, just before taking one into my mouth.

"You're so beautiful," I breathe. "Slowly, run your hand down your stomach into your panties. Don't take them off yet."

She follows the command perfectly. I lean back in my chair. Spitting in my palm, I then go back to stroking slowly.

I can hear the harshness of my own breathing as I watch her throw her head back and rock against her fingers. The white of her panties is the perfect contrast. Almost as sexy as the sight of my skin against hers.

"Put your fingers in your mouth," I hiss.

She pulls her hand from playing with that pretty pussy and pops her fingers into that sexy as fuck mouth. I think of my cock between those lips. Cursing myself for not having the real thing when I could've.

The ways she's sucking the juices from her fingers, I can't wait to be what she can't get enough of. Sliding in and out of that wet, warm mouth. I start to stroke harder thinking about it.

"That's my baby. Just like that," I groan. "Take your panties off now."

A grin turns up her lips as she reaches to wiggle out of her panties. I growl when the sight of her bald pussy is revealed on cam. She had a bit of a patch when I was last down there.

"Spread your legs wider for me. I want to see you play with it," I say.

She scoots back against the headboard to prop herself up. Her legs spread wide for me. I can see that pretty flower just ready and waiting for me.

She parts the lips with her fingers and starts to play with her clit just the way I made her watch me do. She looks like she knows her body as well as I do. Yet, I know, no one knows that body as well as me.

"Pinch your left nipple, baby," I order.

She reaches for her nipple, pinching it between her fingertips. My eyes are trained on her as her back bows and her hips rock. I can just feel her slick heat sliding up and down on me. Her tits in my face as she rides me. I stroke a bit harder, getting closer.

"Put two fingers in."

Her moan fills the air, echoing in my office. I release my own groan. My eyes focus on the pumping of her hand. I can see her juices dripping. It's so fucking hot.

"Felix," she cries out.

"I'm right with you, baby. Does it feel as good as when I'm inside you?"

She moves her hand from her breast to cling to the top of the headboard. She uses it for leverage as her feet dig into the mattress and she rides her own hand as if it were me. The look on her face is so hot.

She's biting her lip. Her nostrils are flaring lightly. Her lids are fluttering as her eyes roll back.

"No, it's not you," she breathes, before sucking her lip back into her mouth.

"Good answer," I pant at her. "Come with me, Kaye. Come just like you would all over my hard cock when I'm deep inside you. Imagine me inside you and come."

She starts to thrash her head against the headboard. I can see it. She's right there. I wish I were there to catch every drop with my mouth.

"Fuck," I hiss as my own orgasm rushes from my balls.

"Yes, yes, yes," she calls out.

Damn. Only with Kaye. I love this girl.

Kaye

His hissed word is my final trigger. I'm so turned on from knowing he's watching me. I never thought I'd be bold enough to do something like this. Yet, here I sit coming so hard, my legs are shaking.

"God, yes," I cry out.

I slump against the headboard, too spent to move. That was so dirty and sexy. His voice filling the room with his commands.

The knowledge of his eyes on me while I pleasure myself. Hearing his heavy breathing and the sound of him stroking himself were just what I needed.

He's turning me out and I like it. I didn't think I could love Felix anymore then I already did, but I was so wrong. I only want Felix.

"Sleep tight, baby. I'm coming to see you as soon as I can. Promise," he says.

I hadn't realized my lids were closing. I slide onto my side and finally pass out. Thoughts of what just happened bringing a sleepy smile to my face.

CHAPTER NINETEEN

Felix

"So the phone was registered to him?" Brax asks from the conference table.

"Yup," I reply tightly.

"Found two grand cash on those assholes," Ryan says.

I grunt my response. Still too pissed off to speak. From the cams on the building, those two had been coming to the office late nights to watch me. Keeping enough of a distance not to be noticed, they waited until last night to make a move.

I have answers and I don't like them. Those two assholes were sent by an entitled asshole I closed a case on not too long ago. He'd been laundering money from his father-in-law's business for years.

His wife was actually the one who found the first thread that lead to unraveling the trail of over twenty million dollars over the last five years. The husband got greedy and sloppy. It didn't take me long to uncover the accounts and the dummy companies he was filtering the money out to.

The wife begged the father not to send him to jail. I thought it was a dumb ass decision, but Mr. Vector agreed to keep things in house as long as Martin, the husband, returned the money he still had in the offshore accounts.

Of course, Martin agreed—long enough to pack a bag and take off. He left his wife behind and took off with the money. Uncle Rob offered for us to track Martin down. Vector paid us and said he was washing his hands of it.

I called bullshit then and I'm calling it again now. I think Vector planned to hunt Martin's ass down himself. Although, my question has become—why the fuck am I being targeted in the middle of their family bullshit?

On one hand, I'm glad it's none of the other things I have my hands in coming back to bite me. Still, this is the last case I expected to blowback. I don't like it, not one bit.

"You do know when I find his ass, I'm going to fuck him up," Noah grumbles, his arms folded across his chest.

"Exactly," Wyatt adds.

"That's why we're going to keep this one as quiet as we can. Someone is going to come up missing," my father hisses.

"I don't think Martin is the only foul party in this equation. Where is the wife?" Uncle Rob muses.

"Gone," I grind out.

"She was the one to blow the whistle in the first place, wasn't she?" Rob turns to me with a perplexed look on his face.

"Yeah, she was," I reply tightly.

"When you closed the case out was there anything that stood out as a red flag?" my dad asks.

I fall back in my chair. My mind takes me back to that day. It's like the entire scene is playing before me. I rebuild it in my brain to see it just as I did that day.

"Yeah, something did stick out. I just got sidetracked," I murmur more to myself.

I got a hit on one of my top priority cases. Needing to get a handle on that top-secret situation, I put the Vector case aside for a few hours. When I went back later, it was like the path I had been tracing disappeared. It was a small detail, so I let it go.

"There was one account, one of the earlier ones, it had a third designated signer. All the others were just opened by Martin and his sidekick," I say as the memory surfaces. "I remember seeing it, but when I went back to it, I couldn't find it. I shrugged it off since we were off the case."

"This smell like shit. I'll get to the bottom of it," Wyatt grumbles.

"I want to know where Vector's daughter is," my dad demands.

"You and I both," I mutter.

"See what you can find. We'll hit the street," Noah says, standing from his seat.

CHAPTER TWENTY

So Proud of You

Kaye

Six months later ...

My hands are trembling. I've kept this to myself for months. One click of a button and my life could change forever.

I shake my hands out in front of me. I feel like I may vomit all over my laptop. This is insane. I need to just do it. Like ripping off a band-aid.

"Just do it, Kaye," I grumble to myself. "Stop being a chicken. Besides, this will get you one step closer to being with your boyfriend."

Press that damn button!

My inner voice is screaming at me. I don't know which part of me misses Felix more. The part of me that loves to sit and talk to him for hours or the parts of me that love his mouth talking to them for hours.

With Felix so busy with work he hasn't been here as much as either of us would like. We need more time together. This long-distance thing isn't flying it for me.

Yet, I know I'm not running back to Cali without something of my own to show. Hence, the reason I haven't shared with anyone what I'm doing. I'm keeping it close to the heart until I have it figured out and manifested in the flesh.

"It's now or never, Kaye. Just do the darn thing," I huff.

I reach for the mouse and click publish. I feel butterflies take off in my stomach and my head becomes a little light. This is such a rush. I've just published my first book.

I sit staring at the screen biting at the pad of my thumb. This is so surreal. I've wanted to do this since I was a young girl.

Tears start to flow. I wipe at them quickly when I hear Dae-Dae's voice outside the front door. I turn to look at the clock.

I can't believe I've been sitting here this long. I close my laptop and smooth my hands over it. It's one of the best gifts I've ever received.

I've spent countless hours watching YouTube videos on how to make covers. I purchased a program to format my book. Then there are the hours I spent writing the book itself. I could never thank Felix enough for this single gift. It just keeps on giving.

I've taken my dream in my own hands. I want to squeal and do a dance, but Dae-Dae and Connie push into the apartment. I smile at Dae-Dae's excited voice. Then my smile splits my face when I see the reason for Dae-Dae's excitement.

This day just keeps getting better. I run across the room and jump into Felix's arms before he can fully get into the door. He drops his bag before I reach him, wrapping his arms around me and lifting me onto his waist.

I miss him so much I could cry. I cling to him as if he's going to float out the door again if I don't hold on. His embrace is just as tight. He holds me to him, burying his face in my neck.

"Mama," Dae-Dae giggles. "You're too big for Lix to carry."

Felix laughs into my neck. I roll my eyes. That's what I tell him when he whines for me to pick him up. This little boy is growing to be too much. I can't deal with him. He's two and a half going on thirty.

"Come on, ya," Connie says with laughter in her voice. "Let's get ya a snack."

"I don't want a snack. I want to play with Lix," Dae-Dae whine.

I'm still holding onto Felix. I can feel his smiling lips against my skin. Just when I get ready to climb down off him, he tightens his arms and sucks my flesh into his mouth.

"Let's go wee lad. We don't want to be seeing this," Connie replies.

"I've missed you like crazy," Felix groans into my neck. "You smell so good."

"I thought you had an away assignment," I say as he starts for my room with me still in his arms.

"I finished earlier than planned and took off the moment I knew they didn't need me back home," he replies.

"I wish I knew you were coming."

"You aren't happy to see me?"

He steps into my room, booting the door closed. With me still in his arms, he climbs on the bed hovering over me. As soon as I look into those gold eyes nothing else in the world matters.

"I'm very happy to see you," I purr back at him.

"How happy?" he asks, moving to shove his hand into my shorts.

A wolfish grin spreads across his face when he finds me wet and ready for him. It only takes the sight of him and I'm ready. I'd be ashamed if I didn't know what's coming.

Sike, that's a lie. I'm not ashamed at all and don't know how to be when it comes to sex and Felix. I've put on a show for him through the cam more times than I can keep track of. It's become our thing when he has the opportunity and privacy for it.

"Very, very happy, I see," he answers his own question with a deep rich purr that strokes every part of me.

"Felix," I pant. "Connie and Dae-Dae are right in the kitchen."

He reaches for a pillow and hands it to me. A sly grin on his lips. He goes to peel my shorts down my legs.

"Then, you better use that pillow to keep quiet. I need to taste you and that can't wait another second," he croons.

"But—"

I don't get the words out. I have to cover my face with the pillow to muffle my cries. I don't know why I bother. I should know better by now.

Felix

She's just as beautiful in her sleep as she is when she's awake. I love that she sleeps with her mouth slightly parted every time I've watched her. It's so cute.

I've missed Kaye like crazy. Between work and everything that's been going on with Nellie's ex, I haven't had the time to be here like I would like. Everything is changing back home and it's making me want to be here with Kaye more and more.

Or should I say, it's making me want her back home. I question keeping her here. Things have changed. Having Kaye here in New York may be placing a strain on my family.

Logan went missing for two months before we found out he had been arrested and thrown in an Irish prison. The charges are bullshit and I know exactly who set him up. I didn't think that old bastard could stoop so low.

Brooklyn has a hell of a lot on his plate as he steps in for Logan. Things are changing for the O'Brien family as a whole. It's only a matter of time before the Alliance is a real thing. Logan's disappearance is the only thing stopping it.

The backlash from its completion will only set things in motion that I don't want my woman in the middle of. My cousins are dead center in the middle of some things that put me a little on edge when it comes to having Kaye around them.

It was one thing when Logan promised to keep her in the office, but out of family business. He also placed men on the building to watch over her. Brooklyn won't say it, but I think he can better use the resources now. Besides, Kaye doesn't need to be affiliated with the O'Brien name for a while.

I need to talk to her about quitting her job and it might be time for her to come home. It's one of the reasons I made this trip. This is a conversation we need to have in person.

Brushing a lock of hair from her face, my eyes follow the path of my finger from her temple down her cheek. Her skin is so soft. My gaze shifts to her shoulder, the passion mark I left there drawing my attention.

I hadn't intended on marking her. I got caught up in the moment. It's been too long since I've had my hands on her.

It's only been six months, but I know I'm in love with Kaye—I always have been. That love has only gone to another level. It's a deeper level.

She stirs in her sleep, her eyes opening slowly to land on mine. Her lips turn into a smile and she reaches her arms over her head to stretch. My eyes fall to her naked body.

My cock twitches, ready to get lost inside of her all over again. We never made it up for air to go back out to join Dae-Dae and Connie. Connie sent me a text hours ago, informing me she was going to take the little guy home with her for a sleepover.

"Hey," Kaye breathes.

"Hey."

Her eyes start to search mine and her smile falters a little. Lifting a hand to my face, she cups my jaw. I turn my head to kiss her palm, nipping her thumb in the process.

"Don't try to distract me. What's the matter?" she says softly.

"We need to talk."

She purses her lips, reaching for the sheet to cover herself. The action pisses me off. I've waited this long to see that perfect body in the flesh. I only want to see it covered when necessary.

I reach to tug the sheet from her grasp, wrapping an arm around her waist to tug her closer to my body. I can see from the look on her face, her thoughts have gone to the worst possible place. It tears at my heart that she still doubts herself when it comes to me.

"Kaye?" I say when I place my forehead to hers.

"Yes."

"Why do you still doubt the way I feel about you?"

She shifts a little, fidgeting in my hold. Her little tongue darts out to wet her lips, skimming mine in the same gesture. I have to bite my own to keep from getting sidetracked and devouring her whole.

"I … I don't know," she breathes.

I close my eyes feeling like a fool. She may have just answered my question, but her answer reveals so much more. She wouldn't know.

I've never told her how I feel. I've wanted to, but on the phone has never seemed like the right time and when I'm here I've made the poor assumption that she knows from the way I can't keep my hands off her.

Time to set that shit straight.

I open my eyes and pull away enough for us to look at each other. I can see the questions in her pretty brown orbs. I vow instantly that she'll never go another day questioning how I feel.

"I've been in love with you for longer than I can remember. No, that's a lie. I do remember. It was Danny's thirteenth birthday party. You came down the stairs in that pink dress, with this smile on your face.

"I can't explain it. For the first time, I saw you as more than a little sister. I couldn't take my eyes off you. It was the only secret I ever kept from Danny," I chuckle.

Reaching to brush her soft cheek, I then peck her lips.

"Now you're mine. I adore you and everything about you. That simple puppy love has grown into the love of a man who can't breathe without his woman. I love you, Kaye.

"I said we need to talk, but I'm not about to break up with you. I've waited all my life to have you. I'm not letting you go," I say.

Kaye

I'm not sure if I should burst into tears or jump up and shout. He loves me. If only he knew how much his words have just spoken to my soul.

There have been times when my mind has tried to tell me that he's more invested in the sex than in the relationship. I've questioned if he has someone else in Cali or if he only says he's too busy to come see me. I know it's all silly, but sometimes … it happens.

"I remember that day," I choke out. I can't help releasing a small laugh. "I picked that dress just for you. I had a crush on you for way longer than that. I love you too."

He takes my lips in a possessive kiss, holding my body tightly to his. I feel like he's trying to consume me, but I'm all for it. I melt into him and his demanding kiss.

"Say it again," he says against my lips.

"I love you," I whisper.

"Fuck, we need to focus," he groans, dragging me into his lap as he sits up. "What I have to say is important. I'll make love to you after."

I giggle because I swear, he's talking to himself more than me. His penis is trapped between my hip and his stomach, pulsing in need. I want to reach for it, but I know he wants to get out whatever is on his mind.

"What's up?" I ask, pecking his lips.

"Things have changed. New York isn't the ideal place for you at the moment—"

"You mean safe?" I ask knitting my brows.

"Yeah, you can say that," he says, lips pinching as his jaw works.

"I figured that. Logan hasn't been around, and I've noticed a change. My hours were cut, but I'm getting the same pay and Jamie has been around a lot more," I speak my observations aloud for the first time.

Felix narrows his eyes on me. I shrug. He's not the only one who watches everything around him. I'm still in awe of the fact that Danny was ever able to keep secrets from him. I guess when you know someone so well you figure out how to dodge their vigilance.

"I need you to stop working there completely," he says, still watching me.

I bite the inside of my cheek. I had already planned to. According to Dean and Kia, if I want to be serious about writing full-time I need to produce. I need my time to write and get the next book ready. Content is king in the literary world.

When I don't reply he continues. "I've set up an account for you and Dae-Dae. You'll have plenty of spending money. If you need anything more, just ask," he says.

"Felix—"

"Don't. This is not up for discussion. You and Dashawn will never want for anything, ever. I'm not trying to take your independence. I'm making you comfortable while you find it. I'm not going to argue with you about this like last time," he says sternly.

I narrow my eyes at him, but he returns the look with one of his own. His look says he's not above putting me over his knee. I squirm in his lap, wanting to continue being defiant to see if he'll follow through.

"Fine," I finally answer.

Felix cups my face, placing a kiss on my lips. Whatever irritation I feel about his highhandedness floats out the window.

I entangle my fingers in his hair, while he twitches against my thigh. I go to reach for him, but he catches my hand just before I wrap it around him.

"There's something else," he says on a sigh.

"What?" I grumble.

"I want to you to move back home," he says.

"I'm not ready," I reply, shaking my head and moving to get out of his lap.

He wraps his arms around me to keep me in place. I want to relish in his heat, but I'm not falling for it. This is not okay. I'm not going back to California until I can prove to my father that I did something with my life.

"Cali is huge, you don't have to run into your family. We can get you a place in Vegas, Reno, wherever, but I'm not leaving you on a coast away from me with ..." His words break off and his jaw works. "You can't stay here."

I look down into my lap, absorbing his words. He's not saying I have to go home. I just can't stay here.

My mind shifts to earlier today. I don't even know if my book has gone live. I've been locked in here with him since he arrived.

I hold up a finger, signaling for him to wait. Curiosity fills his eyes, but he allows me to get up off his lap and climb from the bed. I pad out to the kitchen naked. Grabbing my laptop and my phone, I then take them back to the room with me.

"I'm all for a sex tape, but it's going on one of my secure devices," he teases.

"Oh, shut up." I laugh, shaking my head at him.

I climb on the bed and open the laptop. When I pull up the dashboard to my KDP account, I gasp and feel my eyes light up. It's live, my book is live.

"You're shitting me. Is that what I think it is?" Felix asks grabbing the laptop.

"Yes," I squeal, leaning into his shoulder to look at the screen.

He clicks to open my actual sales page for my book. I can't explain the feeling I have. My book is published, sitting right before my eyes.

"Babe, you hired an editor? Who did the cover? This shit looks fucking awesome," he says excitedly.

"I hired someone Kia recommended to edit, with some money I saved up. I did the cover," I whisper the last part pursing my lips nervously.

"You did? This looks great. Holy shit. I can't believe you did it." He pauses, a huge smile coming over his face. He turns to me, and I see the sparkle in his eyes. "Your penname is Kaye Blaze?"

"Yeah," I grin.

"I love you so much," he says, cupping the back of my neck to kiss me.

"I love you too," I say when he breaks the kiss to run his nose over mine.

"I can't believe you used my gamer name for your penname," he says, his voice filled with emotion.

Felix has been Black Blaze since we were teenagers, when it comes to playing video games. Danny was Renegade Son. They would play for hours, and I would sit there, cheer them on and secretly crush on Felix.

"It popped in my head, so I went with it," I reply.

He turns to grab his phone from the nightstand. I knit my brows as I watch him. He has the biggest smile on his face. He turns the screen for me to see when he's done.

"You bought it," I gasp.

"Of course. I will always support my baby," he croons.

He turns the phone back to look at it. I grab the laptop to marvel at my book on screen. I can't believe I did it. My phone lights up, pulling my attention.

When I see a bunch of texts and missed calls on the screen, I snatch it up. My heart is pounding as my thoughts go to the worst. I knit my brows when I see it's Kia and Dean.

You on some bullshit!

Is the first thing I read. I whip My head back and I open it to see what the hell is going on. My hands tremble as I read through the texts.

"There's no way," I breathe out.

"What?" Felix asks beside me.

I turn back to the screen and scroll down. I scream. I mean, literally scream my head off.

"What? What?" Felix asks. I point at the screen with a shaky finger. He leans in to read it close. "*Holy fucking shit.*"

He moves the laptop and pulls me into his embrace. I start to cry, I can't believe it. I'm stunned.

"Oh my God! Oh my God!" I sob.

"I'm so fucking proud of you," he says into my neck.

"I'm a bestseller," I sob-laugh.

"Yeah, you are. You're a published author with a bestseller. Just like I always knew you would be."

I wipe at my face, trying to see through my tears. Felix has the biggest smile ever on his face as he looks back at me. I'm so happy he's here for this moment.

"Kia and Dean were calling and texting me to curse me out for not telling them I published. Then they started calling and texting to tell me that I hit the charts," I gush.

"This is insane. How did this happen? I mean, it's not number one—"

"Cut that shit out. First, you've worked hard and wanted this all your life. Second, you wanted God to say that you could do this. I'd say he's answering your prayers. Third, you will be number one. I know it, but don't downplay this victory," he says fiercely.

I cup his face and kiss him. I'm on such a high, I don't want to come down. I'm not where I want to be yet, but he's right, this is a win.

"Can we make love now?" I ask against his lips.

"All night," he purrs.

CHAPTER TWENTY-ONE

You Nasty

Kaye

"Girl, you wrote the hell out of that book. I'm so proud of my little church mouse," Dean sings through the computer screen.

"I can't tell you how many times you had me breathless and in my emotions. Wow, Kaye, just wow. It was amazing," Kia adds.

"Thank you," I say, feeling my cheeks warm. "Coming from you guys that means so much."

"Please, I need to ask you where you came up with some of that stuff. Kaye, you nasty," Dean chimes, fanning her face.

"*Yes*," Kia squeals. "Nasty isn't the word. Hold up. I have a question. Did you finally get the D?"

My face is on fire, I roll my lips and stay silent. I never shared with my friends that Felix and I have started dating. It's been my little secret.

"Ow, I knew it. I knew," Dean says. "You don't go from that bullshit you were writing to straight fire without getting dicked down something serious. Lord, child, when you had him toss her up against that wall—"

"*Yes,*" Kia exclaims. "That was so hot. And his dirty talk was off the damn chain."

"Baby, I'm going to get Dae-Dae," Felix calls as he enters the living room where I've been talking to the girls.

Before I can stop him, he leans over the couch and plants a toe-curling kiss on my lips. I don't so much as bother not moaning into his mouth. When he pulls away, he has his lip sucked into his mouth and the look he gives me has my nipples rock hard.

"Ow, you so wrong. I knew it," Dean shouts.

Felix turns to the screen. "Hey, ladies. Sorry about that."

"You don't have to apologize to me. That shit was hot. Woo," Dean replies, battering her lashes. "Didn't you say something about brothers?"

"Have six of them," Felix chuckles.

"*Damn,*" Kia and Dean say in unison.

"Do they all have eyes like you?" Dean asks.

"Yup, and two have red hair." Felix winks.

"I know where I plan to be for Christmas," Dean sings.

"Girl, you're a mess," Kia laughs.

"Like you weren't thinking the same thing," Dean huffs.

"Not gonna lie. If they'll provide the type of muse Kaye has," Lakia giggles.

"Man, *Felix*," Dean drags out. "I just want your brothers to teach me some moves. Hopefully it runs in the family."

"You guys are making assumptions," I murmur.

Felix makes that disgusted noise in the back of his throat. I'm used to hearing that sound when he doesn't like something he hears. I look up at him and his eyes are locked on me.

He leans into my ear. "Tell them that bullshit if you want. I've read your book, baby. That shit is all me."

He licks his lips at me, then kisses my forehead. Only Felix can chastise and make your panties disintegrate at the same time. I almost forget my thoughts and my friends right along with them.

"Maybe we should go," Kia giggles.

"No, you ladies get back to your conversation. I'm going to go get our little guy," Felix says.

I swoon. Big time, absolutely swoon. I've never corrected Dae-Dae from calling me his mama. For all intents and purposes, I am. However, hearing Felix claim us both is so sexy, I'm rendered speechless.

"Yeah, I told you that one wasn't playing with you." Dean's voice pulls my attention from watching Felix walk out.

"You guys are so cute together," Kia says.

"I don't know what you're talking about," I say, feigning innocence.

"You still going to play this game?" Dean scoffs. "Um."

"So how long do you guys think I should wait before I release the next book?" I reply.

"Heifer," Dean mumbles.

"If she wants to keep her dirty little secret, we'll let her," Kia laughs.

"Thank you," I say, giving a sage nod.

"As long as you keep writing that fire, I'm so good with him putting it down on the low," Kia teases.

Dean falls over laughing. I growl at them both, tempted to end the call. I don't, only because these two have become like sisters and I love them.

CHAPTER TWENTY-TWO

In Depth Lesson

Felix

Two months later ...

Too much shit is going on for me to make Kaye's move happen the way I want to. I've had to keep my focus on a few high-profile cases, as well as the plans for the mission coming up with Briggs.

Once again, my trips to New York have been few and far too short. Many times, when I do make the trip I have to focus on work the entire time. I don't always feel so bad about that.

Kaye has been focused on her next book. The first one has had a great response and with good reason. She did amazing. I've read it twice. While I know our sex favors her scenes, she has made them so much more intense on paper.

I love that faraway look she gets on her face when a story is speaking to her. Like now, she's sitting on the floor with her legs crossed and that look in her eyes. Dae-Dae is with Connie for the weekend, giving Kaye and I time together.

I've been going through files for work and working on some coding for the office system. Having Nellie around has taken some of the load off. She's been going back and forth with me for a few hours to help me get this done faster.

We're just about to wrap up, but I've been distracted the last few minutes as I observe Kaye. Her nose is wrinkled and her lips are twisted. I smile. Something isn't working out the way she would like in that head of hers. I know that look.

I turn back to my screen and finish up. Usually, if I let Kaye talk out the problem aloud, she can move forward. I love watching her mind work.

Felix: *Thanks, Nel. I think we have this locked up for now.*

I type into the private messenger on our closed work system.

Nellie: *Cool. Glad I could help. Let me know if you need anything else.*

Felix: *Don't worry about it. My brother sends me one more text about taking up all your time, I'm going to have to kick his ass.*

Nellie: *Goodnight, Felix.*

Felix: *Night, Nel.*

I close the laptop and place it aside. Moving closer to Kaye, I kiss the side of her neck. She smells edible. She lifts her hand to cup the side of my face.

"What's wrong?" I murmur against her skin.

"I feel like I'm writing the same sex scene over and over. It shouldn't be that way. I want the scenes to be fresh with each book. This is frustrating. I mean there are only so many ways to do it, right?" she says, sounding more like she's musing to herself.

I nip her neck. "Oh, baby. That's a lie. I think I've been a very, very bad boyfriend," I purr. "Where are they? What are they doing?

"In his apartment, watching a movie," she replies.

"Perfect. Class is in session," I whisper in her ear.

Kaye

My skin is tingling from his breath fanning against it. I feel my nipples tighten. I need to be finishing this scene but I'm not going to get anything done with him this close.

I don't have to worry about that as he takes my laptop from my lap. I don't know how long I've been sitting here zoned out like this. I've been playing the scene in my head trying to get it to play right.

"I'm going to need you to come out of your head for this one," he says in that sexy silky tone I love.

He brushes his lips against my temple. I turn to him right as he goes to pull his glasses from his face. I reach for his hand to stop him, shaking my head.

"Leave them. They're sexy. My hero wears glasses," I say with a smile.

He lifts a brow but gives me a broad smile. He gets to his feet, pulling me to mine as well. I stand before him, looking up into his eyes expectantly.

He crowds my space, allowing his body heat to engulf me. I love the warmth that's always rolling off him. It makes me want to curl under him to absorb it.

He brings his hand up to brush my cheek. My lids flutter. I feel like he's touching me for the first time again as the anticipation builds within. He presses his thumb into my lower lip as he tips my head back farther.

"Breathe, Kaye," he murmurs as he bends his head to start a warm trail of kisses down my neck.

When he gets to the spot between my neck and shoulder, he starts to suck the skin into his wet mouth. Lifting my heels from the floor, I'm on my toes trying to get as close to him as I can. Both of his hands go to my backside.

He kneads it before squeezing and lifting me off my feet. I wrap my legs around his waist, placing my arms going around his neck. He captures my lips, using his mouth to massage mine.

I open to him, welcoming the invasion of his tongue into my mouth. He doesn't hesitate to take the invitation. I can feel his all-consuming kiss all over.

He begins to move us, not breaking the kiss. I feel him lowering to the floor, sitting with me in his lap. He starts to lift my dress up to my waist, snaking his hands beneath it.

I go to unwrap my legs to stand, but I hear the tearing sound as he yanks my panties from my body. I gasp, breaking the kiss to look at him with wide eyes. The heat and desire I'm met with caves my belly.

If his eyes could burst into flames, I'm sure this would be the moment when they would do just that. I feel like they've set me ablaze. He watches me with that heated look as I reach down to peel my dress over my head.

His eyes take a slow trip down to my bare breasts. It's like a caress of his hands when in fact he's not touching me. When his heavy hand does land on my hip, I feel the heat scorch right through my skin. I feel his touch in my bones.

I start to rock my hips against him. I'm becoming impatient to have him inside me. He, on the other hand, seems content on dragging this out.

He moves his other hand to my hair. It's out in its natural wild coils. Felix grabs a handful, tugging my head back until I arch into him, my breasts in his face. Tilting his own head, he takes my left breast into his mouth.

The way his hot mouth plays with my peak is enough to shatter me into pieces. He's toying with me in the best way. I haven't stopped grinding against him, trying my best to get some relief.

He claws his hand on my waist around to my butt. The sensation shoots straight to my core. I begin to drip down my thigh.

"Felix," I gasp out and whimper when he slaps my ass twice.

Palming the stinging cheek, he massages it. Never once does he stop the torture on my breast. I coil my fingers in his hair as I stare up at the ceiling. My eyes flutter closed.

He is releases me from his mouth, allowing his tongue to start a trip across my skin. He licks a path to my other breast. I bite my lip and moan when he flicks his tongue rapidly over the nipple.

"Ah," I cry out when he bites down on it.

I begin to quake in his hold. His warm breath bathes my skin as he blows on it to soothe his bite. I'm still shaking against him when he releases my hair from his tight grasp.

Lowering my head, I watch him go to lift his shirt over his head. I slip my hands free from his hair, going to his chest. So warm, always so warm. It's like a blanket you can't live without.

His lips are back on mine, tasting, nipping, driving me crazy. I need him, I need more. I have this sensation like I'm hanging on the edge, waiting for him to pull me up.

I break the kiss, bringing my lips to his ear. "I need you," I whisper.

Felix

Her words are like fuel to my flame. I'm already burning from the inside out to have her. It has taking all my restraint not to take her.

My plan was to take this slowly. Show her how the build can be just as hot as the act, but she's just derailed that plan with three simple words from those sweet lips.

I roll my hips up to show her what's waiting for her. The look that comes over her face is so hot; I would've come from it alone when I was a teenager.

"Up," I command.

She stands before me. I hook her leg over my shoulder. My face is in between her legs before she can say another word. I fumble with pushing my sweats down my legs with one hand, while holding her upright with the other.

"Yes," she cries as she rides my tongue.

She's so wet already. I love that she's dripping all over my face. My own Kaye facial. She can pamper me in that shit any day.

With my pants taken care of, I grasp her ass with both hands and guide her hips. I want her to come one more time for this. I assault her hot zone as soon as I feel her right where I need her.

"Fuck," she screams as her leg give from beneath her.

I chuckle, catching her falling body. I turn her guiding her back to my front. Now she's ready for her next lesson for her book.

Her ass plants snuggly against my pulsing need. Stretching my legs out before me, I nip her neck and wrap my arms around her. Kissing my way to her ear, I take a slow lick of the shell.

"I need you to do something for me. Stay relaxed, but fold your legs cross-legged," I say into her ear.

"Indian style?" she asks with confusion in her voice.

"Yeah." I chuckle at her confusion.

She follows the instructions. Folding her legs beneath her as she sits on top of me. I bite her lobe. Lifting her by the waist with one arm, guiding my cock with my free hand, I bring her down onto me.

Her head falls back. I release her lobe to kiss her cheek. The purr that comes from her lips is my sweet reward.

"Give me your hands."

She reaches for my hands, allowing me to lace my fingers through hers. I can already feel her dripping down my balls. She squeezes against me as I twitch inside her. I know we both need more.

"Stay upright. I've got you," I say before lying back.

Before I can start to move either of us, she starts to circle her hips. I groan and start to thrust up into her. I tighten my hold on her hands to keep her steady.

When she looks over her shoulder with her mouth gaped open, I know she loves it. I swirl and roll my hips, pulling a sex face from her features. I ground my heels to really dig in.

"Oh, *shit.*"

"You like that, baby," I pant.

"Yes, fuck yes," she hollers.

I keep thrusting, wringing her pleasure from her. When I feel her legs start to wiggle on top of me to get free, I know it's too much. I slow down allowing her to unfold them.

"Sit forward. Plant your hands wherever you like," I tell her, reaching to fold her legs back at my sides. "It's yours. Take it."

She does just that. I watch her ass as she starts to wind her hips and ride me. She plants her hands between my legs as she takes just what she wants.

"Fucking amazing," I murmur to my view of her ass bouncing on my cock.

I sit up on one elbow to get a better view. I move my other hand to massages her back, encouraging her to get more into it. The way she starts to move her body as if dancing to her own beat is mesmerizing.

Kaye

He does feel amazing. I feel him in my spine like this. It's a mix of pleasure and pain that's making me question my sanity on so many levels. I don't want it to stop.

I rock my hips up and down on him, making circles between bounces. It feels so amazing I throw my entire body into it. I sit up to cup my own breast, pinching my nipples.

I feel Felix at my back. His warm chest sending his heat through me. He bands his strong arms around me, guiding me to a pace he starts to set from beneath me, taking over. His knees come up as he plants his feet to thrust harder, faster.

"Yes, yes, yes," I chant.

He licks from beneath my shoulder blade up to my shoulder. Planting a kiss at his final destination, he then nuzzles into my skin. He slides his hand between my legs to cup my sex and play with my magic button. My orgasm rushes my body like a runaway train.

"Felix."

My gasp echoes to my own ears as it fills the room. He groans into my skin spilling his hot seed. I spiral into a round of multiples as I feel him empty—so hot.

My heart is pounding like it wants to come out of my chest. I close my eyes as I try to breathe. We always have amazing sex, but that was … yeah. I'm a writer and don't have words for that one.

"Do you think you have enough for your scene now?" He chuckles against my skin.

"I don't pay you enough," I tease.

His reply is a hand covering my sex as he starts to finger my clit.

"I can't, not again," I whimper.

"I'm collecting my tip. You can handle it. Promise."

For the next two hours, he continues to provide plenty of ammo for my scene and then some. I stop complaining. It's a win-win for me. I actually could take way more than I thought.

CHAPTER TWENTY-THREE

Celebration

Felix

Four Months later ...

There are no words for how proud of Kaye I am. Her second and third books have been published and shot right up the charts. I've wanted to do something special for her.

I know how hard it was for her to leave New York. I was finally able to move her and Dae-Dae into their new place. I moved her to San Diego to give her a good distance between her place and where her parents live.

It's a long drive, but I make it anytime I can. I know she's lonely sometimes and she doesn't have as much help as she did in New York. I was able to get Dashawn into a daycare that he loves. It at least gives her the time she needs to write during the day.

When my mom found out Kaye was back on the West Coast, she had a million questions. The moment I told her about the books she was all over helping me throw something together for Kaye. I think she needs to keep busy. It's been hard on mom, not being able to help Nellie snap out of her depression. It's been hard on all of us.

I'm grateful to my mom. I don't think I could have done this without her. Well, I wouldn't have pulled it off the same.

"She's here," I breathe, as I hear Kaye's Benz pull into the driveway.

Man, the fight we got into when I gave her that car. She's my girl, it was her birthday, and she needed a car. I wasn't hearing shit she had to say. It's her car, in her name. That's it.

"Aye, yer in love. Listen to ye," my mother teases.

"Ya haven't seen nothing, Aunt Cass," Connie chortles.

"I'd just like to say now, this family was blessed with some beautiful genes," Dean says dreamily, as she looks at Dylan. "Phew, you're lucky I don't rob cradles."

"Lass, yer going to slip in that drool," my mother teases.

"I just love you," Kia giggles.

"I've taken a liking to ye and yer wee un," my mother replies.

"Would you all shh," I hiss.

Low laughter surrounds me as everyone tries to hide it behind their hands. I roll my eyes. My heart starts to pound when I hear Kaye's keys in the front door.

The only thing that could make this better would be having my brothers here. I get Wyatt needs to be there for Nellie. Toby has some shit going on with him.

Now that I think about it. So does John lately. He was gone before I could make the offer for him to join us.

Noah, Ry, and Brax all had work, which I can't blame them for. They have been helping pick up the slack in the office. Still, it would have been nice to have them in on this.

Honestly, I haven't had time to tell my brothers about my relationship with Kaye. There always seems to be something going on these days.

"Mama, why is it dark in here? You left the lights on," Dashawn says as they walk in.

Fuck.

This kid doesn't miss a thing. I swear, he needs to come work at Black and Lock. I give the signal before Kaye can panic.

Kaye

"Surprise."

I nearly jump all the way out of my body. I was already on edge the moment Dae-Dae pointed out that the lights were off. I turned them on this afternoon when we left, knowing it would most likely be dark when we returned. I hate stumbling around in the dark.

I look around at all the smiling faces. My brain is still trying to catch up. The big congratulations sign helps the pieces to click into place.

"Aunt Connie," Dae-Dae squeals.

"Really, kid? That's all you see," Dylan grumbles.

"Hi, Uncle Dylan," he giggles.

"Oh my God, what are all of you doing here? I mean, I'm happy to see you, but how, why?" I ramble.

"Your man wanted to celebrate his best-selling girlfriend," Dean chimes.

"Aye, he's very proud of ye, lass," Cassidy Black says with a beaming smile.

I rush over to wrap my arms around her. She still smells the same. It feels like it's been decades since I've been in one of her embraces. She hugs me just as tightly as I hug her.

"I'm proud of ye too. You've done well," she whispers in my ear.

"Thank you." I sniffle.

"Look at you," Lakia says when I step back, wiping at my eyes.

"Really?" I huff and laugh. "I just talked to you two this morning."

"And your boo had us on the plane not too long after. I wanted to spill so bad," Dean laughs.

Lakia and Dean wrap me up in a group hug. We hug for a long time. When this last book went to number one, we all sat on the phone crying together. I couldn't ask for better friends.

"I'm so freaking proud of you," Kia says. "You're doing the damn thing and not a word has been weak. That book was straight fire, no chaser. Phew."

"You heard," Dean chimes in. "I've read it three times already. I wish I could pay you for each. Lord knows I should be writing my own books, but it keeps sucking me in."

I laugh, wiping more tears.

"I've been doing my best," I say tearfully.

"You're doing more than your best. I don't think you know how good your work is," Dean says in the most serious tone I've ever heard her use.

"You had me in tears. I was so inspired," Kia says.

"Thank you, guys."

"Ladies, I want to give Kaye her surprise," Felix interrupts.

"Oops, sorry," Dean giggles.

Felix pulls me into his arms. I feel like I'm drowning in his eyes. He doesn't know that just him being there when I published the last book and when I found out it went to number one was the best thing in the world.

"There are so many things I could have gotten you. I thought about it long and hard, but there was something I thought you needed," he says, bending to kiss my lips.

He turns me toward the back of the house. I have the biggest smile on my face. My smile wobbles and tears rush down my cheek. My knees nearly buckle as I watch my grandparents walk out of one of the back rooms.

I rush forward into their open arms. It's like being a little girl all over again. I didn't know how much I needed this until their arms are around me.

I'm crying so hard, I start to rock and moan. I have no words for how I feel in this moment. It has hurt so much that I haven't been able to share my success with my family.

"It's all right, gal. We're 'ere now," my grandmother coos.

"Lix, why is Mama crying?" Dae-Dae asks behind us.

"She's happy, big guy," Felix replies.

"Oh, okay, happy tears," Dae-Dae says as if he has gained a world of understanding. "Who's that?"

"It's your great-grandma and great-grandpa," Felix tells him. "Come on, let's go say hi."

"Look at the pickney," my grandmother says. "'Em a big boy."

I laugh, running my hand under my nose. Dashawn has gotten so big. He looks more and more like his father every day. Danny would be so proud. Dae-Dae is so smart and funny. Just like his dad.

"Em looks so much like, Danny," my grandmother says with a shaky voice.

"Who's Danny?" Dae-Dae looks up at Felix to ask.

"Your uncle," a voice booms behind me, startling me.

I turn to see my father almost glaring at me. My mother rushes forward, pulling me into her arms. She sobs as she rocks me in her arms before I get a chance to register what's unfolding before me.

My eyes haven't left my father's. All I've done. All I've accomplished and he manages to squash it in one look. I close my eyes and turn away.

I've done nothing wrong.

I chant the words to myself. Yeah, I allowed Christa to use my insurance, but I haven't done any of the things my father's accusing looks suggest. I won't be made the villain. Not again.

"Mama, who's that?" Dae-Dae asks.

I open my eyes to look at the little boy who has become my son. He is pointing to my father. I follow his little finger to see several emotions cross my father's face. It happens so fast I can't peg them all.

The one emotion I do recognize is disappointment. It cuts me to my core. I feel Felix place his hand on the small of my back. It should comfort me, but it only raises my anger.

He should have talked to me first. He should have allowed me to prepare myself for this. Honestly, he should have just left this alone.

"I'm your grandfather," my father says as he moves closer. "You can call me Papa."

"Hi, Papa, it's nice to meet you," Dae-Dae says with a huge grin on his face.

My father reaches to run a hand over his hair and cups his face. I can't see my father's full face to see his reaction to his first interaction with his grandson. Still, the ridged stance that he's in speaks volumes.

"Give him a chance, Kaye," my mother whispers in my ear.

I swallow my hurt feelings and nod. Brushing a hand over my hair, my mother kisses my cheek, before she nuzzles it. It's a soothing balm I didn't think she still had the power to offer.

"God is going to bless you for the amazing woman you are," she whispers.

"He already has," I say bitterly.

"Oh, no, my child. You haven't seen anything yet. Eyes have not seen, ears have not heard. Even the stubborn will fall to the truth. You be patient, Kaye."

Dae-Dae's giggle pulls my attention. My father has him in his arms, tickling his stomach. When I hear my father's chuckle, I feel a sting in my heart.

Patience. It's been three years. It doesn't get any more patient than that.

Felix

"Hey," Dylan says as he comes over to the corner, I've placed myself in.

Kaye is pissed. I can feel it rolling off her. If I couldn't feel and see it, I would know from the way she's been avoiding me all night.

"Hey, you heading out?"

"Yeah, Connie wanted to hit a bar or something. I'm going to go with her," he says, shrugging his shoulders.

"Okay, man. Be safe. Thanks for coming."

"I wanted to say something to you," he says, looking down at his feet. "You were looking for Ciara. Brooklyn told me. I just wanted to say thanks. I know you didn't find her, but thanks."

"I haven't found her, yet. I'm not giving up," I reply. "And you don't need to thank me."

"She's the reason I fight," he says with a small smile. Then his brows knit in sadness. "Knowing her dad is gone. It all seems silly now."

"How so?"

"I made her a promise—"

"Hey, are ya coming with me or not. Time is ticking away, and I want to have a wee bit of fun before we have to go back. Brooklyn is like a fly up my arse, never lets me live my life," Connie says and pouts.

She winces, then looks over her shoulder. "Oh, sorry, Pastor," she says. She then turns back to whisper. "Get me out of here."

Dylan and I laugh. Connie has been slipping up all night in front of the Pastor. Mom let a few curses fly as well, but as long as Pastor Porter has known my mom he hasn't flinched.

"I'll tell you about it another time," Dylan says. "Thanks again."

I pull Dylan in for a hug. I wish I had better news to give him about his friend. Brooklyn told me not too long ago why he had me look for Deja and Ciara. I've doubled my efforts since.

Thinking of them turns my attention back to Kaye. She should look happier. This was supposed to be a great surprise.

I fucked up.

Whenever I get close, she finds a reason to move to the other side of the room. She hasn't let me touch her and her responses to anything I say have been short and clipped.

In my defense, I'd only meant to reunite her with her grandparents and her mother. Pastor Porter blindsided me when he arrived with them. He's another one who has been giving me the evil eye all night.

This has not turned out the way I thought it would. The one good thing about the night is Dae-Dae's interest in his family and theirs in him. It's funny but he has been clinging to his grandfather's side, hanging on every word he says.

"Ye did the right thing," my mother says, pulling my attention to my side. "Ye couldn't have known he would come, but it was time. It will work out."

"How can you be so sure?"

"I'm no spring chicken. Aye, I maybe clean on, but I've been around a block or two. I've seen enough to know a few things. He wouldn't have come if he didn't want to see her," she replies.

I grin at my mother. Clean on she is, she's good looking for her age. She has kept her youthful looks, despite me and my hard-headed brothers.

"He hasn't said a word to her," I huff.

"Pride is a powerful thing. It can make ye or it can break ye. It sure as fuck can turn ye around a few times before ye head in the right direction."

I heave out a breath. Taking my cap off, I run a hand through my hair, before returning it to my head. My jaw works as I think of how this night was supposed to go.

"So yer not going to propose tonight, are ye?" Mom whispers.

"Nope."

"Aye, my smart boy. Always give a lass time to calm down. Maybe it's for the best," she chuckles.

"Yeah, Dad would probably be pissed too."

"Aye, he is. He's on a plane heading home." Mom laughs harder. "I told ye this wasn't going to fly. Ye were in a rush."

I groan, wrapping an arm around her shoulders and tugging her into me. She did warn me and now look. It's all falling apart. I bend down to kiss the top of my mother's head.

"One of these days, I'll listen to you," I murmur.

"Aye, ye will."

CHAPTER TWENTY-FOUR

You're a Liar

Kaye

I peek over at Felix and his mom. I wish I had that kind of relationship with my parents. I've always admired all the love and laughter in the Black home.

Cass may run a tight ship, but you never have to question her love for her boys. I know Danny felt that love. He talked about her like a second mom. When I think about it, I can say she made me feel the same way growing up.

Even from this distance, I can see the affection in their relationship as he holds her small frame in a hug. I try not to tear up. I'm just a little overwhelmed.

Here I sit right next to my parents and my father hasn't uttered a single word to me. It's as if I'm not here. I'm glad he has accepted Dae-Dae, but I feel like nothing sitting here. Like I'm invisible.

I wish I could have left with my friends. Kia and Dean left for their hotel. Connie and Dylan just took off to get into some trouble. I'd like to be anywhere but here.

"He's sleeping," my mother murmurs. "I'll take him back to his room. It's been so long since I've placed a little one to sleep."

"It's the last one on the right," I reply.

"I know. It's where we were waiting," she says with a smile.

I take a shuddered breath. It's like the temperature drops in the room as she walks away. I want to follow after her and help. As a matter of fact, that's a great idea. I get up to do just that.

"Don't move, gal," my grandmother says.

I flop back into my seat. I look at my grandparents and they're both glaring at my dad who is glaring at me. I drop my eyes to my lap.

"T'ree years, ay. T'ree years and yuh still cyan chat 'pon the gyal wit' some sense," my grandmother hisses.

"I, for one, can't sit here and watch this," my grandfather speaks up. "Your daughter tells you she's with child and you throw her out. You lose your only son, and you still don't make it right."

My grandmother kisses her teeth and folds her arms over her chest. I know she has more she wants to say. Both of my grandparents look like they're boiling.

"Maybe it's me. I'm from South. We don't do our children like this," my grandfather says.

"Cyan say we gwan like dis in Jamaica," my grandmother scoffs.

"She is my daughter. I'll handle this as I see fit. I don't think this is the time or the place," my father snaps.

"You won't even look at the child," my grandfather presses.

"You left your child to grieve alone. Don't you chastise me," my father bellows and he stand to his feet.

"Because every time my wife and I asked you where the hell my granddaughter ran off to you couldn't give us an answer. You told us to stop asking. *This is my home, if you don't like it, you can leave.'*

"Those were your words. I'm no one's child. You talk to me like one, it's time for me to go," my grandfather says, lifting to his full height and puffing out his chest.

"Daddy, please," my mother pleads as she rushes out to jump in the middle of my father and grandfather.

"No child, I don't like how you've handled this." My grandfather shakes his head. "It's not right."

"What's not right is this girl thinking she's grown and can do things on her own. What's not right is that she didn't come home when her brother passed away—"

"I did come home." I stand and shout. "I was there for my brother like I've always been. I would never let him be buried without me."

"You're a liar," my father turns and barks at me.

Everyone is standing now. The atmosphere is thick with emotions. My lips tremble as I nod my head. I swipe at my tears, but I straighten my back. I'm stronger than this.

"Yeah, I am. Now get out of my house," I say firmly.

My father's eyes look over my shoulder and narrow. I don't have to turn to know who he's glaring at. I can feel Felix at my back.

"You, young man. I've treated you like a son. We'll talk about this," my father grinds out.

"Sir, I respect you like a father, but tonight, I'm going to ask you to respect my home. I think you need to leave like Kaye asked. I'll come to see you so we can talk man to man," Felix replies.

"Living in sin every chance you get," my father snorts.

"Don't you dare," I snap. "Don't you dare. You don't know me, and you don't know what you're talking about."

"I don't recall you and my daughter being married before she returned to my home knocked up," my grandfather deadpans.

"Danesha, let's go," my father snaps at my mother.

"I'll be spending time here with my daughter and grandson. You can go home," my mother says, folding her arms over her chest.

"Bout time," my grandmother sucks her teeth.

My father turns almost purple. He storms out without another word. I stand, staring at my mother in awe.

"Sometimes we have to allow the bull to storm the shop for him to learn his lesson. You and I have some catching up to do," my mother says.

"Aye, ye do. The truth will set ye free, lass. It's time to be free," Cass says, walking over to kiss my cheek, before she turns and leaves.

"Gwan, gyal, we waiting," my grandmother says, reclaiming her seat.

I take my seat and stare at my fidgeting hands. Saying a prayer first for my brother to forgive me, I begin to tell the truth. The whole truth.

CHAPTER TWENTY-FIVE

Good Man

Kaye

It has been a long day. I haven't spoken to Felix in two weeks. You'd think that would stop the man from coming to my home. Nope, I think he has been here more now that we aren't speaking than before.

Well, he did tell my father that this was his home. Yup, I didn't miss that. Just one more thing to piss me off. Now on top of all the other crap my father thinks I've done, he thinks I've been living with a man as well.

Yes, Felix spends the night here when he can. Yes, he sleeps in my bed with me. Yes, I know I've been sleeping with Felix, but it's the principle of it all. If I'm going to be accused of something, let it be the things I've done. That's all I'm saying.

Most of all, I'm still fuming over being blindsided and then made to feel like crap. None of that would have happened if Felix hadn't gone behind my back and forced me to face my father. I've been so mad I won't let Felix explain what the hell he was thinking.

I've let him dictate to me for long enough. And no, I'm not doing this because I can afford to take care of myself now. Although, it's nice to know that I can if I need to. Again, it's the principle.

I love Felix, but he can't just do what he wants all the time. He thinks he's doing what I need, but how can he know that when I don't even know what I need anymore.

Honestly, I'm just hurt and in my feelings. My father called me a liar. I think it hurt more because I am. I've been lying for over three years. I'm tired and it's weighing on my soul.

So much so that I should be writing this book, but I can't think or focus for the life of me. Every time I start to type my mind wanders to Felix or my dad. That night was horrible.

The front door opens, and my frustration rises. Felix walks in with a Cold Stone's bag in his hand. He walks over, placing it beside me.

"I just filled your car with gas. I'm taking the light and gas bills with me. I'll put out the trash after I kiss Dae-Dae goodnight." He pauses with a sigh, leaning over to kiss my forehead. "I'll come to cut the grass this weekend."

All things I didn't ask him to do. He has been steadily chipping away at my armor just like this. If I weren't so hurt by what happened I would have given in already. I miss him, but I don't want a relationship like my mother and father's.

Daddy runs all over my mother when he wants. Sure, she has fought many battles and won. However, lately, all I can think of are the ones she rolled over on. I guess that's because the last time I needed her most she didn't take a stand.

I feel like I'm seeing that version of my mother in my own relationship. Until I sort my feelings out, I'm going to stick to my guns on this. He was wrong and I'm not in a forgiving mood just yet.

He releases another sigh. Then turns for Dae-Dae's room for their nightly routine. The one thing I refuse to do is get in the way of their bond. I know how much Felix means to Dae-Dae and how much Dae-Dae means to him.

When he's out of sight I peek into the bag. A little smile comes to my lips. It's my favorite, Oreo Overload. He even added the caramel sauce on top.

"How long are you going to stay mad at that boy?" My mother's voice pulls my attention.

I turn to see her coming in from the backyard. She must have been in the guesthouse with my grandparents. When I tell you Felix found me a house with more than enough space, I have *more* than enough space.

My shoulders sag a little more. At times he does get it all the way right. I pout as I think of how hard I'm being on him and then I hear my father's voice calling me a liar all over again and I get over it.

"I don't know, but I'm not ready to forgive him yet," I mumble.

"You know he had no idea your father was coming," my mother says as she sits at the table.

I knit my brows as I search her eyes.

"What?"

"Your father overheard me talking to Cassie. She arranged things with me and your grandparents for Felix. I was so excited that I hadn't heard him come into the house.

"You know your father. Once he heard the conversation, he wouldn't let up until I told him what was going on. He's lit up at the mention of you. I thought things would work out differently." She bows her head. "You're both so stubborn."

"I'm not going to let him make me a villain for something I didn't do," I huff.

"I knew that girl was trifling when I first saw her hanging around your brother," my mother says with a frown.

"You know who she is?" I gasp.

This was the one detail I didn't reveal. I told my mother everything except who Dae-Dae's mother is. I sit in shock as she lifts her head and looks me in the eyes.

"I'm a mother. I knew about Danny too. He was so in love with Alberto. He hid it well, but there were moments that he'd slip up and let it show in his eyes. A mother sees things others don't.

"Just like I knew you were in love with Felix all of these years. I had a feeling something was off that night. When you two came to your father. I also had a feeling Danny was tied up in it somehow.

"I've known your father for a long time. God saved him from some terrible things, so he is set in his beliefs the way they've been taught to him.

"I ... I thought I had time to smooth things over. Time to prime your father before sitting him down and easing him into your brother's lifestyle choices. I thought you would cool off and come home—"

"But why didn't you reach out when I didn't? When Danny died and you couldn't … why'd you leave me alone?" I ask sadly.

"I regret it every day. I was so distraught. Losing your brother was like living a nightmare. Then, I … I just. I wanted to. How do I make your father understand this now.

"His only son is gone and to return our daughter is to take his son away again. I feel like I've failed you both—"

"Mommy," I protest. "I understand."

I lift from my seat and wrap my mother in my arms. I know exactly how she feels. It's the reason I didn't want to return. I planned to take Danny's secret to the grave.

If it weren't for Cassie's words, I would've. But I needed to be set free. I've felt trapped for so long. Well before my brother asked me to cover his secret for him. My father held the reins so tightly, I've felt imprisoned to his beliefs since I was a little girl.

"You know we are all always right and wrong," she says through her tears.

"It's all in the eyes you're seeing life through. What's right to one isn't the truth to another. Our greatest challenge in life is having the courage to be wrong and the wisdom to learn when we aren't right.

"Just because it's our truth doesn't make it *the* truth. It only makes it the truth we're willing to accept. That boy has come here every single day for the last two weeks. He talks to you even though you won't answer him.

"He takes out the trash, plays with the baby, don't think I haven't seen him going through the mail for the bills. He does all of that while looking like he might pass out from exhaustion. Then, tells you he loves you right before walking out that door, every time.

"Not once has he forgotten to declare his love. Trust me, I know because I've listened. I've prayed for him to make it home safely every night. Tired and stressed out over his woman not talking to him.

"Baby, you've rubbed enough salt in that wound. He doesn't deserve it. He was trying to do something nice for you and it went wrong, but it's not his fault." She looks into my eyes through her tears. "You hear what I'm telling you?"

"Yes, Mommy. I hear you," I murmur.

"Now, your father. We're going to let his old butt remain salty for a while." She gives a small laugh.

"You get no arguments from me there."

"Go fix things with your man, Kaye. A good wife never brings unrest to her husband's head. Soothe him while showing him the way as gently as you can. Save the silent treatment for the big stuff," she says, standing to her feet and kissing my cheek.

With a grin on my lips, I grab my ice cream and make my way to get my man. I miss him.

However, when I get to Dae-Dae's room, I don't find Felix. Dae-Dae is fast asleep in his bed. His little snores filling the quiet room.

"Did he sneak by us?" I mutter to myself.

I move down the hallway to my room. When I push the cracked door open, I find Felix sitting on the bed, twisting the titanium ring on his pointer finger. It's the ring I gave him when he graduated high school.

We'd gone surfing one time and he wanted to walk through the shops after. He saw the ring but forgot he didn't have his wallet on him. I went back the next day and bought it for him.

"You still have that ring?"

Felix

Her voice pulls me out of my thoughts. I was thinking about when she gave me this ring. I should've seen it then. I'll be honest. I did, but I told myself I was projecting.

Kaye has always been mine. We've danced around this for so long, but in all honesty, we were meant to be together. It's the reason I can't let this go on any longer.

"You gave it to me. Why wouldn't I?" I respond to her question.

"It just seems like so long ago," she replies coming to stand in front of me.

My hands instantly go to her waist. I bury my face in her belly, needing to anchor myself to her. I'm exhausted and I miss the fuck out of her.

"You're talking to me," I muse aloud.

It's a statement, more than a question. Hearing her voice directed at me is like water to an open flame. I've been thirsty for her words, her attention.

"My mom told me that you didn't know my father was coming," she replies.

"I tried to tell you that, but you wouldn't listen."

"Yeah, I know. Some people are just so stubborn," she says with a smile in her voice.

I growl and nip her stomach. Her responding giggle is like music to my ears. Two weeks without that sound has been killing me.

"I'm sorry things tanked the way they did. That was not the night I had planned at all," I groan, lifting my face to look at her.

"I was more angry that you didn't give me the chance to prepare to see my dad or the chance to make the choice," she says with sadness in her eyes.

"When have I ever taken your choice away?"

"Really?" she asks giving me a pointed look.

"Kaye, the few times I've demanded you do something has always been for your good. What you don't understand is … ultimately, it's always your choice. I'll always do what's best to keep you safe and happy, but I won't force you to do anything that makes you unhappy.

"Come on, think about it. Haven't I always been willing to bend when you need it? That's me respecting your choices," I say, trying to show her my point.

"Yes, you're right," she says softly.

"I need you to judge me for the man I am, not the man who raised you."

She whips her head back as if I've slapped her. It's the truth. She's placing me in her father's shoes.

She just stares at me. I hold my ground. I've said what I meant. Everything I've done for Kaye, I've done so she can be happy. I never want to take that from her.

"You're right," she whispers. "I'm sorry."

"I'm sorry too. I should have asked him to leave before you arrived."

Kaye snorts and laughs.

"Pastor Porter would have broken his foot off in your ass," she says through her laughter as she throws her head back.

It's a beautiful sight. I wish I could wake to that every morning. I squeeze her waist, drawing her closer.

"Whatever," I chuckle.

"You know I'm right. I'm surprised he didn't try to shoot you a fade for throwing him out," she giggles.

"Shoot me a fade? Listen to you. Your father doesn't want it with me," I tease, running my hands up her back.

I begin to massage my way back down. She moans as her eyes fill with lust. I suck my bottom lip into my mouth. Tired or not, I want her.

"My ice cream is melting," she holds up the bag. "I should hurry up and eat it."

I lift a brow when she drops to her knees before me. She places the bag on the floor, reaching for my belt. My cock goes crazy inside my pants.

I spring free as soon as she gets the zipper down. She hooks her hands into the waist of my jeans pulling them down my hips. I lift to help her, kicking my sneakers from my feet.

Kaye tosses my jeans over her shoulder when she gets them off. I lean back on my elbows against the mattress. Pushing my shirt up she kisses my stomach, starting a trail down to my waiting length.

My lips are parted in anticipation. I know what Kaye is capable of with that mouth. It's more incredible than all the dreams and fantasies I've had about it.

Her eyes lift to mine, that plump lower lip going into her mouth. I watch as she reaches for the bag, pulling the ice cream out. I can see through the lid it has started to melt. When she opens the top, it spills right over my saluting rod.

Kaye wastes no time diving in to lick the sugary taste off me. I pulse against her tongue, my head falling back as I groan. She licks me from root to tip then back again.

"*Fuck,*" I hiss the word out.

My nostrils flare when I feel her slide her mouth down on me. She swirls her tongue on the way back up. I've taught her well. She knows just how I like it.

"Kaye," I groan, "Damn, baby."

She answers with her own hum. I push my right hand into her hair, clutching her ponytail. I use it to guide her, slowing her down. I'm in no rush to come. I've needed to feel her mouth on my body for weeks.

She digs her small hand into my thighs. I feel her nails drag upward, raising goosebumps. I groan and my head rolls. I start to lift my hips meeting her efforts.

"Oh, yeah," I pant. "Just like that."

After a few strokes things get awkward as we both move, the challenge being her squatting and the height of me on the bed. I tug to pull her from sucking. She looks up at me like I've just committed a crime.

I start to back up on the bed. She catches on, grabbing the ice cream as she follows, climbing up the bed after me. Settling between my legs, she pours the rest of the ice cream down on me.

This time she lets it empty all over my cock and up my stomach. I mentally make a note that I'll be picking up a new bedspread. She's going to be pissed at us both when the moment fades.

"Ah," I rasp. "Yes."

Kaye goes back to work, this time licking and sucking at my balls. I spread my legs wider, bending them at the knee as I watch her get into pleasing me. Bypassing where I long to have her most, she licks my stomach clean.

"Fuck, yeah."

I'm damn near drooling from watching the way she does it. It's not just the feel of her silky tongue on me. It's the sexy, determined look on her face, as she watches me through her lashes that's turning me on.

"Oh, *fuck*," I call out a little louder than I mean to.

When she sucks the ice cream off the tip of my shit, without placing her mouth on it, I lose it. It's the sound of her slurping the ice cream in that's just icing on the cake. I bite my lip and my brows knit in the center of my forehead.

When she dives in and sucks me clean in one pass, I almost propose on the spot. I didn't teach her this shit. My girl has been in that nasty head of hers again.

I love when she has new things she wants to try on me to see if they will work in her books. I would pay to have a front row seat to what really goes on in that brain. She rolls her neck and starts to work me with her hands.

A grin comes to my lips. I guess this is a front row seat, but I'm not about to be out done. I lift to reach for the hem of her shirt, pulling it off. She releases me from her mouth long enough to get the top off.

I hear her shoes hit the floor. Next, Kaye works to wiggle out of her panties and the skirt around her waist. I tug my shirt off the rest of the way.

"Come here," I command.

Reaching an arm around her waist, I draw her lower body toward me. Leaning back, I guide her pussy over my face. I can already smell the lavender oil she rubs into her skin every morning and night.

Bringing her mound down to my mouth, I kiss her fat pussy before opening her folds and having my own feast. The room fills with the sounds of sucking and slurping. Kaye continues to give as good as she's getting as she moans around me.

I start to rock my legs back and forth. I'm getting close. I palm her ass in both hands and really dive in to get her there at the same time. When I feel my own release rushing forward, I suck her clit into my mouth and push my thumb into her ass. She squirts all over my face.

I'm shocked at first. It's the first time it's happened. If I didn't already come down the back of her throat that would have ended me right there.

"Come here," I say, helping to shift her body so we are face to face.

Cupping her face, I lick her lips, tasting the flavor of cookies and cream on her face from the ice cream. I let my tongue linger around her mouth, cleaning up the sticky remains of the melted treat. Kaye snuggles into me, getting comfortable.

I run my fingers up and down her back. I'm not settling in. I'm just giving her time to recover.

"I love you," she whispers.

"I've missed hearing that," I admit.

"I know. I promise to talk to you from now on. Sometimes I'm so busy trying not to be like my father, I end up being just like him. Thanks for not giving up on me," she replies.

"I'm here Kaye. *Lorg a h-uile duine leatha agus cùm i leat leat fhèin,*" I repeat the words I told her, what now seems like so long ago.

"Find her worthy and keep her for your own," she says with a smile in her voice. "I think I'm going to use that in my book."

"Have at it. I just want my royalty. I'll take ten percent, thank you," I tease.

"Bullshit," she giggles.

"Oh my, Kaye. What would the Pastor think of that mouth?"

"Well, since I'm already a heathen in his eyes, fuck it," she says.

I burst into laughter, kissing the top of her head.

"I like my sweet, mouthed Kaye better. The smooth to my rough. The verdict is still out on your heathenism," I chuckle.

"Still not giving you no royalties," she whispers.

"Whatever, I'm already all of your heroes so I'll let it pass this time," I taunt.

Kaye sits up to looks down at me. Laughter in her eyes, she looks at me pointedly. I lean up and take her mouth in a deep kiss.

"Tell me when I'm lying, baby."

"I don't know what you're talking about." She rolls her eyes.

"Fine, let me remind you," I growl, pouncing on her.

I give her one for the books while cleaning us both off in the shower. We made it through our first big fight. Thank, God it's over and I have my baby back. I think we can make it through anything.

CHAPTER TWENTY-SIX

Loyal Reader

Kaye

Five months later ...

This book has been pouring from my soul. I needed to get some of my frustration out. I still haven't spoken to my dad and my mother is still staying with me.

I don't mind having her here. Dae-Dae loves her and spends as much time as he can with her and my grandparents. He loves to listen to my grandmother talk.

I think it's more the musical melody of her voice than the actual accent. It was that way for me as a child. I loved when she would read me stories.

I know I've been enjoying the food, while having my family here. Between my grandparents and my mother throwing down,

I've been in heaven. Felix says he's been needing to put in an extra workout each day as well. I call hogwash. I still count an eight pack.

What's infuriating is that my dad hasn't made things right. Forget about me. He should be making things right with my mom.

I've gained a new respect for my mother. She shows up to church to support my dad every Sunday. To the world the first lady is in place, and everything is in order.

However, as soon as the last hand has been shaken and the church is locked up, she jumps in her car and heads right back to my place. During the week, she's been handling the accounting and payroll right from the office in my house. I think she's taking her own stubbornness to the next level.

I now see I get it from both of my parents. I never had a chance.

"You're not typing," Nellie says beside me.

I point at the sight before us. Who can blame me for losing focus? You'd have to be blind not to stare.

"Can you blame me?" I say, nearly drooling.

"Not. At. All," she drags out.

I've been distracted with watching Felix surf for about a half hour now. We came to the beach, so I'd have a change of scenery, but I'm not sure if this was such a good idea.

I mean, come on. This is not fair. At this very moment, Wyatt and Felix are running out of the water with their boards tucked under their arms.

Neither is wearing their wet suit pulled up, revealing their tanned skin and sick abs. Felix's wet suit is riding so low, I lick my lips as if I can taste his skin. I would love to spend the rest of the day chasing those salty droplets of water all over his body.

I keep waiting for someone to scream cut. They both look like they've stepped out of a movie. When Felix lifts his hand to push his wet hair out of his face, I tip over and lean into Nellie.

I think it's the sexiest thing I've ever seen, until Felix's golden eyes lock on me and a seductive smile pulls at his mouth and his tongue comes out to lick his lips.

"Yup, not going to blame you one bit," Nellie giggles. "I think I see why your books are so hot."

"Insane," I breathe as I watch Felix turn to Wyatt and start to horse around.

"I'm glad we did this. It's nice to get out and breathe," Nellie says, taking in a deep breath of fresh air.

"I'm glad you guys could come. It's good getting to know you," I reply.

"Yeah, I think we had a few classes together in high school, but I was sort of shy," she says.

"You, please, if it weren't for my brother and Felix, I probably never would have talked to anyone." I laugh. "I was just fine with a book in my hands."

"I know, right?" Nellie giggles.

We both sit lost in thought for a bit. I think of how much I missed out on in high school pretending to be someone I wasn't. When I did make friends, it was because I was Alberto's girlfriend. Other than that, I don't think people would have talked to me.

"Does the pain ever stop?" Nellie whispers a little while later, turning to look me in the eyes. "You lost your brother, right? Has it stopped hurting so much yet?"

"Surprisingly, it stings less when I see Dae-Dae do something my brother would do. Most days, life has me too busy trying to breathe to linger on the hurt. We were so close. I would love to share my books and success with him.

"It hurts to know that's something I'll never get to do," I murmur.

"Yeah, I know what you mean. Like, she'll never be there to see her first grandchild. I'll never get to plan a birthday party for my children with her. There are so many things I can't share with her and no matter how my family has grown, no one can replace that," she sniffles.

"It's still fresh for you. Take it a day at a time. No one can tell you how long to grieve, but you don't want to forget to live. You know? Danny would want the best for me."

"Yeah, I'm trying. I'm a lot better now. Wyatt has been so patient. I love him for that," she says, turning to smile at him. "At least she got to see me get married. That will always mean the world to me."

Suddenly, my heart feels heavy. Since I was a little girl, I wanted my father to walk me down the aisle. Maybe even perform the ceremony. Now that we barely speak, I don't think that's an option.

I look down at my laptop to see I have an email. Needing to distract myself from all things somber, I open the email. I smile when I see it's one of my readers. I swear, they always come right when I need them.

It's a really sweet email, thanking me for writing such real books. I'm humbled and reply back right away. I'm grateful for the smile that has returned to my face.

I go to close my laptop to enjoy some sun and continue the vigilant focus I have on my man. However, it pings with a Facebook message. I click over to my author page and see I have a message in the inbox. Already feeling warm from that email, I open it.

Hey Kaye Blaze,

I'm such a big fan. I think I can say I'm one of your loyal readers. I've read your first three books and you are just getting better. I have a traveling book club and we are set to take a bus trip next fall.

You will have a chance to meet readers, sign and sell books, and get to know fellow authors. We have a few other awesome authors joining us. My partner and I were wondering if you'd like to join the line up? You can contact me at the number below.

Hope to speak to you soon.

A fan

I chew on my lip. I would love to meet readers in person and do this. I'm just not sure. I haven't done anything like this before.

Dean is actually talking me into considering a signing she'll be doing. Scratching my head while I reread the message, I ponder it. It wouldn't hurt just to get the details, right? I shrug my shoulders and decide what the heck.

I shoot off a quick message to let her know I will call her tomorrow before shutting my laptop down. I look at Nellie and the smile on her face. I think she's going to be just fine.

The hurt never goes away, but there's comfort in knowing you have an angel up there helping you along the way.

Thanks, Danny.

A Fan

"Yes," I cheer at the computer screen. We needed someone like Kaye. Her books are amazing. She's been building a great fanbase.

I scroll through her pictures on her social media. She just added some of a little boy and a gorgeous guy. I wonder who they are.

I pick up the phone to call Lisa, my business partner. I told her I could get Kaye. This is going to be so big. I can feel it.

"Hello," Lisa answers the phone.

"We got Kaye Blaze," I squeal into the phone.

"Really? She paid the twenty-five-dollar registration fee?"

"She said she'll give it to me tomorrow when we talk. She is so nice, girl. I think we're going to be good friends," I reply.

"Oh, okay. Well, make sure to have her sign off with the deposit," she says hesitantly.

This bitch is always doubting me. I've pulled in the authors we have. She's only brought one person to the damn table. Ugh, I can't believe I have to put up with this.

I suck it up. Once things take off, I'm going to do my own thing. With Kaye signing on to do this event that will happen sooner than later.

"No problem. She would have done it today, but she had to take care of her little boy. Did you see the pictures of him? He is so cute. She said he's a handful, but he's just adorable.

"Oh, I did see her post some new pics. That little boy is hers?"

"Yes, we got to talking in messenger so long, I felt bad for taking up her time. She said he was there asking her a million questions," I reply, nodding my head like she can see me.

"He is cute," Lisa agrees. "Hey, have you started working on the flyers and things? We need to get our numbers up for the readers. I don't think ten readers will be much of a draw to the authors. We need to promote and get more interest."

"Don't worry about it, girl. I got this. I'll have it all taken care of. I told you that's my thing. I'll get it all done," I reply.

"Okay, great. Well, I have to go. I'll call you later."

"Sure, I have a few books I need to ARC. I fell behind talking to Kaye for so long," I giggle.

"Oh, let me know how you like that new Davina Kelly book. I won't ruin it for you, but the ending. It's something else," she says.

"I'll let you know. Okay, let me go before my man gets in. You know how he gets," I say.

"Later."

I hang up and grin looking around my one bedroom. I smooth my hands across the table in front of me. My smile falls.

Getting up I get a can of tuna from the cabinet. I might as well start to prepare dinner. Once I mix the tuna with the elbow noodles I boiled earlier, I get out a dish to place it on.

I take my plate to the table and sit down to eat. Dragging my kindle closer to me, I pull up my man. He's my latest books boo and he has been demanding all my attention. They get like that.

My grin comes back. I'm going to talk to Kaye Blaze tomorrow. We're sure to have so much in common. Her heroes just speak to me.

I bet they're all jealous now.

CHAPTER TWENTY-SEVEN

Recovery

Wyatt

I stare at my wife while she sits on the couch. She's not one hundred percent herself, but she's way better than she was. It's been a big change since we finally talked that night.

I haven't had to hide out to tug one out. Nellie has been more than willing to fuck since our little playtime. A smile comes to my lips. If only she knew how easy I went on her.

My phone chimes, pulling my attention from Nellie. I take a look at the screen to see a text from John. I knit my brows.

This is the third time this month he has texted to say he's out of town for a few days. I know it's not work related. I looked at the schedule about an hour ago.

I noticed he wrapped up his workload and had a few days open. I shoot him back a text to let him know I got his text. After, I sit trying to remember when John started acting odd.

All my brothers have one thing or another going on with them. My head has been spinning with their moods swings and strange behaviors. John is the type to hold things in until he explodes. I know something has already been going on with him for a while, but the trips started—

"*Fuck*," I groan out loud.

"What? What happened? Are you okay?" Nellie asks sitting up to turn and look at me standing in the kitchen.

"Yeah, fine. Just thinking of something," I say, scratching my head.

I don't know how I missed this. He's been different since not too long after that mission with Briggs. Yeah, some shit was going on with him and Missy before that, but the trips and his brooding demeanor started after that mission.

"Hey, what's going on?" Nellie asks as she enters the kitchen where I'm standing.

"It's John. Something is up with him," I grumble.

"You think it has something to do with the girl on the motorcycle?" Nellie asks looking up at me.

"Girl on the motorcycle?" I repeat, knitting my brows farther.

"Yeah, at our wedding. I went inside to go to the bathroom. She pulled up on the motorcycle in front of the house. He seemed like he was waiting for her. They had a heated discussion and then she took off. She was really pretty," she informs me, smiling at the end.

"I'm going to need his ass to start talking. What the hell is going on with him?"

"He's a grown man, Wy," she says.

"So, he's my baby brother and always will be. They all are. I'll be in their shit until I can't wipe my own ass or remember who they are anymore," I reply.

She giggles, lifting on her toes to wrap her arms around my neck. Pecking my lips, she looks up at me with that loving smile. Some days I still can't believe this is my wife.

"I like Kaye for Felix," she says, distracting my thoughts.

"Yeah, he's happy," I reply, thinking about my brother and Kaye.

I can see how much Felix cares about her. He'll probably be the next one walking down the aisle. I saw in his eyes how much she means to him.

I worry about Felix though. Kaye has a lot going on with Dashawn. I never pried, hoping Felix would tell me everything himself. He finally did today as we sat out on the water. I'm still working through it all in my head.

"Now you're worrying about Felix." Nellie's voice pulls my attention. It's a statement not a question.

"I just want them to be as happy as I am," I reply.

"Do you know how much I love you?" she purrs.

"Can't be nearly as much as I love you?"

"Are you sure about that, Mr. Black?"

"Positive, Mrs. Black."

She beams at the mention of her new last name. I love that smile. I feel like I was wasting my entire life away until the day that smile turned up at me in the airport.

"Weren't you talking about some more practice making our own babies on the way home," she coos.

I know she's trying to distract me from worrying about my brothers, but I let her. Talk of our own children and the act of making them possess my brain on mention. I can't wait to see her swollen with one of my kids.

I can deal with my crazy ass brothers later. If John's problem is a girl, I can live with that. I never liked Missy anyway.

My brothers will survive one more day of my not getting in their asses about something. No one's bleeding and they're not in any danger. I'm going to pounce on my wife while she's smiling and talking happily about her future.

Nellie

I've been watching Wyatt all night as he strolls around the house shirtless in his low hanging jeans. I've wanted to get my hands on him and thank him for a wonderful day. I've just been waiting for the right moment.

I think this is the perfect moment to seize. I've totally distracted him. I knew the mention of babies and sex would get his attention. Wyatt can worry about his brothers too much sometimes.

It's something I've learned as we've been married. He tries to act like it isn't a big deal to him when they're off kilter, but it is. I know he just wants to make sure they're all okay. I love him for it.

I wish I had siblings to share all I'm going through with. Maybe it would make things easier. I know having my in-laws has played a big part in my recovery.

But I don't want to think about any of that tonight. Our trip to the beach was just what I needed. Watching Wyatt surf with Felix, getting to know Kaye better, those were all things that made today a good one.

"I sure did have ideas of how we could spend the night," Wyatt replies, dipping to pick me up and throw me over his shoulder.

I yelp and giggle as I bounce against his body. He takes us to the bedroom and drops me on the bed. I land with a bounce. Before I know it, he pounces on top of me, trapping me beneath his big body.

Hooking my thighs over his arms, he wraps my legs around his waist, planting his palms beneath me. I giggle when his stubble tickles my skin. He didn't shave this morning and has more growth than usual.

"You smell like the ocean and fruit," he murmurs against my collarbone.

"We can do this in the shower," I purr.

"Tempting, but I haven't made you filthy enough for a shower," he croons.

"What are you waiting for?"

He growls, taking my lips with his. The kiss is one for the books. My toes curl, I claw my finger at his bare back.

"I need to take my piercings out," he huffs, as if it's an afterthought.

"Leave them," I whisper.

"You sure?"

"Yeah, I want to feel them while I ride you," I reply seductively.

"You're killing me tonight," he hisses.

"We don't want that, do we?" I grin.

"Oh, there is going to be a murder. The vic' is just going to be your pussy," he says, licking his lips.

He starts to move down my body slowly. I can't help but hold my breath. We can do this a million times and I'm always in awe and anticipation of him.

Peeling my sweats from my legs, he follows them down my hips and legs with soft kisses. Moving between my legs, he eases them over his shoulders. I'm squeezing my thighs closed not even seconds later, when he begins his worship of my flower.

He wraps his arms around my thighs to palm them, prying them apart. I rock my hips to the rhythm of his tongue. That tongue ring drives me nuts.

I grip the top of his hair, bowing off the bed, my head sinks into the mattress beneath me. My bare toes curl in the air. I'm convinced my husband was a sorcerer at some point in his life. He is a straight magician when between my legs.

"Wy," I whimper. "Please."

He ignores my pleading, taking and giving at the same time. My pleasure for his own, because a man doesn't eat pussy like this without enjoying the task on a soul deep level. He is eating me like it's a rite of passage.

"Yes," I cry out.

His groans and growls of enjoyment only spur me on more. I ride his face harder, tightening my legs around his head. He allows me to trap him there this time, working his head between my thighs.

Suddenly, my lower body rises up off the bed and I'm resting on my shoulder blades as he holds my lower half in the air. I grab the sheets at my sides, holding on for dear life. My screams turn into open-mouthed silent ones. He moves one hand to my back, massaging and supporting. The other one goes to my belly, splaying against it.

"Fuck, Wyatt, yes," I cry out when I find my voice.

I start to thrash my head from side to side. My orgasm blossoms from the pit of my stomach, seemingly spreading into all my nerves and rocking my bones.

When he finishes lapping me clean, he lowers my body back to the bed. Wyatt stands from the bed, removing his jeans in almost slow motion. I watch him lazily from the bed, with a smile on my face.

Those gold eyes stare at me with so much promise. I suck my lip into my mouth when he stands to his full height, fully nude. He strokes himself upward and those piercings come into view.

I eyeball him, lifting to my elbows. Wyatt will forever be a gorgeous man. Just watching him has my blood rushing through my veins. I wish I could capture the image before me to hold for eternity.

I reach out for him, causing him to move slowly toward the bed. When he climbs back on, he moves over me. Cupping the back of my neck he offers up the flavor of my own juices on his lips.

I take my fill, sipping from him as he devours me. He sticks his tongue out and I suck on it. I pout when he pulls away.

"Turn around, you're going to have to earn that ride tonight," he croons at me.

I waste no time getting on my hands and knees. I have no problem earning my pleasure. I know he's going to do the same without question.

"Mmm," I moan when he grasps my waist and sinks into me.

He always feels so good stretching me. I arch my back, falling in line with his smooth strokes. At least, they start smooth. Soon enough I'm bouncing back onto him and he's thrusting deeper, harder with each pass.

Feeling the tingling sensation of him in my belly, I think of what it will be like to actually get pregnant. As if reading my mind, Wyatt cups my chin and tips my head back. His eyes connect with mine.

"I can't wait to fill your belly with my seed. I know you're going to give me the most amazing and beautiful babies, just like you," he says with so much intensity.

I don't get to reply. He captures my lip between his teeth, tugging and swallowing my cries as they float from my mouth. He rolls his tongue ring over my lip as he soothes it.

Trying not to fall into all that is this man is pointless. I'm putty beneath him. He swivels and thrusts his hips, stirring more than just my sex.

He has mastered my body in so many ways. Always knowing just what I need and when. I claw at the sheets trying to hold up under his assault.

It's useless. I begin to quake and melt into the sheets. When he releases my face, I bury it into the sheets, screaming into them. He slaps my ass, and my orgasm feels like it ripples through me on repeat.

I've never experienced anything like it. I swear my womb feels like it contracts, ready and waiting for his gift. I guess we're getting in some good practice.

I slip from my knees, flat onto my stomach, but Wyatt's not done. He chases my pussy down, still thrusting and searching for his own release. I know the moment he lets lose.

He roars into the room and his hot seed thunders into my body. I shake beneath him coming again.

"Wow," I say after a few moments.

"Yeah, that was … yeah. We're not done though," he breathes in my ear.

I close my eyes and laugh, my shoulders shaking. I can already feel him getting hard again as if we both didn't just come explosively. When I feel his lips on my neck, my nipples bead against the sheets.

"Practice makes perfect," I purr.

"Damn right it does," he replies, lifting up to flip me onto my back.

It's going to be a long night.

CHAPTER TWENTY-EIGHT

Rambler

Kaye

I walk out of Dae-Dae's room with an empty laundry basket. I let my lips flap as I blow out a breath. It's been a morning full of chores. Yesterday's relaxation is long forgotten.

My mother had to head to the church for a women's group meeting. The annual family retreat is coming up this weekend. The women have something special planned as always.

There will be a big service on Sunday. My mother has asked me to join her, but I'm not sure that's something I'm ready for. I told her I would think about it.

My grandparents took off to do their own thing. Granddaddy most likely taking my grandmother out to spoil her. They are such a cute couple. I can only hope to have that at that age.

I think of Felix and smile. I don't think I'll see him today. He mentioned having some work he needed to focus on. He slept over last night but had to leave out early this morning.

I look up at the clock in the living room. I have a little bit of time before I have to pick Dashawn up. He has a playdate after school, so I'll only be dropping him off over his friend's house.

"Oh shoot," flies from my lips.

I totally forgot I was supposed to be calling that reader about her book club thingy. I put the basket in the laundry room and pull my phone out. Sitting at my computer, I find the number from the message.

I dial and start to scroll through my account to catch up on a little social media. A smile stretches my lips when I see a pic of Kia and her little boy, Isaac. He's adorable.

"Hello, hello," the voice on the other end of the phone rushes.

"Hello, this is Kaye Blaze. I'm looking for Bonnie," I reply.

"Oh my God. Hey, Kaye. It's so nice to talk to you. How are you?"

"I'm great. Thank you for reaching out. Can you tell me more about this event and what's expected of me?"

"Sure. We are a traveling book club. We have about one hundred members, we get about fifty percent of that to sign up for the bus trips," she explains.

I look up when the door opens. Felix strolls in with a smile on his face. My face splits into a matching expression. I didn't expect to see him at all today.

I take in his workbag that holds his laptop and I understand that he came to work from my place. He moves over to me with that sexy saunter. Capturing my lips with the dip of his head, he then gives me the best hello ever. I try my best not to moan.

He places his forehead to mine, biting his lip as he stares into my eyes. I flick my tongue out to tastes his lips, causing him to nip my bottom one. I cover the phone and move it away to giggle.

Bonnie is just rambling about other authors who have joined the tour or are considering. She's been dropping names and going on and on. I'm half listening as Felix pulls up a chair beside me and starts to unpack his bag.

Once he is set up, he places a hand on my thigh and focuses on his computer screen. His face is so intense. I love watching him work.

He completely zones out. He teases me about how I get when I'm writing, but he is the same way with his work.

"The readers will be so excited to have you in the lineup. Girl, you did the damn thing in book three. I was all in my feelings." I tune back in to hear her say.

"Oh, I'm not sure if I can do it yet. How much is the fee?" I ask.

Dean and Kia told me there is always an author fee. Some are way more than others. I've been making good money, but I'm not about to do anything that's going to break the bank.

"Oh, author registration is one-fifty," she says.

"That's not so bad." I think aloud.

The event Dean has me thinking about will be three hundred. Granted, that one has a lot more readers attending. One hundred and fifty dollars is doable. The wheels turn in my head. I'm new to all of this.

Maybe I should ask Dean about this one.

I shrug off the thought. Dean has been busy lately. She's getting the rights back to a few of her books and rebranding them. She has a whole lot on her plate. I'm a big girl. I can handle this.

"We want to be reasonable for the authors. You have so much you need to bring and take care of as it is," she says.

"I'll think about it. I have to see what I can do about my son and look into a few other things," I reply.

"What's up?" Felix squeezes my thigh for my attention.

"It's a traveling book club. They've invited me to join them on a bus trip and to sign books and stuff," I reply.

"Is Dean or Kaye going?" he asks.

"I don't know if they've been invited. It sounds fun," I say and shrug my shoulders.

"Don't worry about Dae-Dae. If you want to go, go," he says.

I suck my top lip into my mouth. I'm still not sure. I'm not the most outgoing person. This would totally be something Danny would do.

Do it.

I chant the words to myself. It's for the fans. My readers have been so good to me. I'm humbled to even be given the offer in the first place.

"Okay, I'll do it," I say into the phone.

"*Yay.* I'll send you the form to fill out. My partner will run your card, so you'll just place the information on the form and we'll get you all set," she says excitedly.

I frown. I would much rather just send the money through PayPal. It would be easier and more secure.

I go to say so, but my attention is broken when Felix stands to pull his shirt over his head. My computer pings next, drawing my attention. Kia is messaging me, freaking out about her plot twist. I look at the time on the computer and I need to get going to pick up Dae-Dae and take him to his playdate.

"Listen, I have to go. Can you email me that information and I'll get it back to you as soon as I can?" I rush into the phone.

"Okay, thank you again. I'm so excited about this," she gushes.

"Yes, me too. Thank you. Talk soon," I say and hang up.

A Fan

"Yes." I pump my fist.

She likes me.

I think that went great. I think I named all the right authors to seal the deal. Once I share with some of the others that I have a rising star like Kaye I know they will sign.

I call Lisa and wait for her to pick up. I look at my nails. I can get them done when Kaye sends the money. I already paid the rent with the money from the other three authors I've signed to the event.

"Bitch," I hiss at the phone when Lisa doesn't pick up.

She's lucky I need her for this business stuff. That's okay. I've got this. I send her a text instead.

Me: *Just locked down Kaye Blaze. We had a long talk again. She's everything and more. I think we're becoming great friends. Call me.*

I grin while hitting send. Placing my phone on the table in front of me, I stare at it and wait for her to reply. I start to get pissed off when her reply doesn't come in after two minutes.

"Bitch," I hiss again.

I grab my laptop and log in to my Bonnie account. Technically, I'm not catfishing. I mean, I'm not trying to date anybody or anything like that. So I'm not catfishing, right?

Oh, who cares. The rent is paid and once I book one more author this week, I'll get something more than tuna fish and beans for dinner.

I click on Kaye Blaze's profile and scroll through. She hasn't posted much today. Oh, I know. I'll message her to get her to share the event. That will get me more authors. Yes, nails, food, and maybe a movie this week.

My phone finally buzzes beside me.

Lisa: *Wonderful. Will call you later. Dealing with my son's homework.*

I wave her off and go back to surfing through some of the online book clubs. I narrow my eyes when I see that Kaye Blaze replied to a reader in one of the groups. Their exchange is a bit long. That was five minutes ago.

I thought she was in a rush.

I click on the reader's profile to see where she's from and if Kaye knows her personally. I don't find any connection, but I request the woman anyway. It's best to look connected on social media.

Julie Cummings. She's nothing special.

I inbox her a message anyway.

Bonnie: *Hey, girl. I love your haircut. I saw you and thought to myself, I have to be friends with her. My daughter has been wanting to cut hers like that.*

I get up to warm my beans. I wonder what book I'll get lost in today. Maybe a re-read of one of Kaye's. Her men are so hot. Ross is my favorite.

Yes, Ross it is.

My computer chimes, breaking into my thoughts. I rush to the computer. It could be one of the authors I've been waiting on.

Julie: *Thanks. My sister does my hair. Your daughter should totally go for it. Love that book by Shyann, by the way.*

I grin. I signed Shyann last week. I've been doing some online promoting for her since. My profile pic is of her books.

Yes, I know people, bitch.

Bonnie: *Yes!! That book was fire. I told her it was going to be a hit. I'm on her BETA team. She struggled with the ending, but I was there for her. We were able to hash it out. It was amazing, wasn't it?*

Julie: *Yes! That ending was fantastic. You're going to make me go re-read that one. It's been a while. I thought she didn't use BETAs. I wanted to read for her.*

Shit!

Shyann is one of the author's that doesn't use Betas. I forgot about that. I don't know why not.

We're willing to give our time. Some of the books I've read weren't worth the money they want me to spend. I only read them because I get them for free.

Bonnie: *Between you and me. She has a secret team. It's not a lot of us.*

Julie: *Oh, okay. Well, you are among the lucky. Nice talking. I need to get back to work. These people are driving me crazy.*

Bonnie: *Yes, I need to help the kids with their homework. Talk to you later.*

A notification pops up to inform me that Julie has accepted my request. This is good. I can see more of her account now to see how she knows Kaye.

CHAPTER TWENTY-NINE

Amen

Kaye

I still don't know how my mother talked me into this. Here I sit in the front row like no time has passed and nothing has changed. A smile painted on my face when I'm so far from smiling on the inside.

Praise and worship is the only thing that's helped me not to reveal how I'm feeling. I was able to get lost in God's presence. It's a presence I know.

I've known it all my life. It hasn't left me just because I haven't been within these walls. In all honesty, I feel God whenever I write, when I pray with Dae-Dae, when I sit in the sand at the beach and watch the waves.

God is always there. Only difference today is the fellowship that's devoted to Him that heightens all of our awareness. I've been contemplative of this fact during the morning announcements.

For all the sins my father would say I've committed, I can't say that God has forsaken me once. If anything, God has comforted me and pushed me forward in my darkest hours. The weeks before Felix found me, times when I didn't want to bother Felix, but I was lonely and scared.

God was there for me through all of that. I look down into my lap. I've sold thousands of books, touched the lives of so many. Does that make me so different from the man who stands in that pulpit?

God says he'll meet us where we're at. If we are bound here, how can we be out there to meet God's people on their terms, in the places that make them comfortable? I can't say that I've always been most comfortable in this church, and I grew up in the house of the Lord.

Even today, I have on a YSL black suit and red bottoms, dressed to the nines. My hair is straightened into a slack wrap and my nails are done to perfection. I'm the Pastor's daughter and I look the role, but this isn't me. Not really.

"We're here to celebrate our fifteenth family retreat. Family day has always been a special day here." My father's voice fills the church strong and steady, pushing into my thoughts.

"I asked the Lord what I would speak on for this occasion and he started to talk to my spirit about foundation. Not just foundation, but strength. Strength that comes from wisdom. Strength that comes from love.

"I said to the Lord. Yes, yes, that's good. I can go there and … But the Lord cut me off. He said, Wayne, I need you to look at your foundation.

"I need you to go back. Remember the days before the man you've become. So I sat in silence.

"I sat in silence because I realized that I was ready to get ahead of God and what he was trying to show me. And that's when he began to reveal that I can get ahead of myself often. I've stood here many a times and told you all about my years on the streets.

"How I was placed in a foster home and I had to steal, lie, and do things I won't mention here. I was a young man doing the only thing I knew to survive those streets. It was eat or be eaten.

"I'm not proud of that. Compton almost claimed my life more than a few times. I started to pray to the Lord. I promised him that if he saved my life and got me off those streets I'd dedicate my life to him." He pauses to take a drink.

"Come on now, Pastor. Take your time," one of the church mothers calls.

"All right now, preach," someone in the back says.

"Somehow, I survived and landed in a university with a scholarship. That was the beginning of my foundation. I used all my strength to get there.

"I met the woman of my dreams in freshman orientation. Danesha was a fine young girl then just like she's a fine woman now. I knew God made her just for me," he says to the laughter of the congregation.

"We dated through college, and I married her as soon as I set a foundation for my family. It took strength to get through those first few years. We were young and had big dreams.

"But you see, as God showed me where I've been, it began to reveal something to me. Danesha and I had to learn. We had to go through. We weren't born with that strength or the wisdom that trails cultivated us through.

"Come on, y'all. Ask your Pastor where he's going?" he prompts.

"Where you going, Pastor?" everyone says in unison.

I turn to the deep voice to my left. Felix turns to me with an encouraging smile. I return it weakly before looking back down into my lap.

"Jesus didn't go fishing for nobody. Scripture says Jesus told them to go cast a hook and take up the first fish that cometh. He didn't go catch that fish for them.

"The miracle was in their participation to get that piece of money. Throughout the bible we see example after example of individuals who were participants in their own miracles.

"Yet, I as a father, as a foundation setter, held onto my children too tightly. Instead of telling them to go borrow pots and not a few, so they could pour the oil until there were no more pots to fill, I tried to fill the pots for them. I didn't allow them to stand before the king to make a request on their people's behalf. I spoke for them.

"I didn't tell them to go get the fish and pull the gold from his mouth. I went fishing and I retrieved the gold and took care of their needs for them. I wanted to do it all for them.

"But that took away one intricate part of their experience in the Lord. You see, they had no test to be a testimony. I held on so tight that I hindered their opportunities to stumble.

"And when they started to tug at that tight leash I strapped to them, it snapped back in my face," he says.

I wanted to get up and leave. I knew he would do this. This was why I didn't want to come. I knew he would make a sermon out of me.

Felix places a comforting hand over mine and I lace my fingers with his. He is my rock. My anchor in this moment when I want to shrink into myself.

"I didn't demonstrate strength, nor wisdom at the time. Instead, I became angry. Once again, I got ahead of myself. I lost my son and my daughter in what seemed like one fell swoop.

"Friends and family, something happens when you let anger be your guide. You lose sight of the truth that stands before you. You stop paying attention.

"But the Lord walked me through my past to have me focus on my present and my future and I started to see some things clearly. Say what did you see, Pastor?" he coaxes.

"What did you see, Pastor?" everyone replies.

"That this revelation of strength and wisdom was not my own. This story belongs to my seed. My daughter is a woman with a heart as pure as gold. She is a woman who knows great sacrifice." I snap my head up as his last words reach me.

He's looking down at me and our eyes meet. He nods his head at me and gives a smile. He continues his sermon, but his eyes remain on me.

"I'm getting old, and I'm set in my ways, but I'm still a man of discernment and my own wisdom. I also know when to say I'm wrong. Family, my daughter took a burden upon herself and rose from the ashes of it all like a true woman of God.

"She's a bestselling author—"

"All right now," several people say as applauds erupt, causing him to pause.

"She's a bestselling author. An astonishing author. Now, I'm not talking reading for the faint of heart. Your Pastor did not suggest you purchase," he chuckles.

"You all buy her books with caution. She made her daddy blush to his toes. That young man sitting next to her is going to have to put a ring on it sooner rather than later, if he's behind any of the inspiration," my father jokes.

I burst into laughter as tears roll down my cheeks. Felix squeezes my hand, leaning to kiss the top of my head. Everyone else laughs, murmuring around us.

"My point is, while reading her work, I saw my beginning. I saw the lessons I learned to get up here to take on the young knock heads that need to turn their lives around. I saw the birth of my ministry as I set my eyes upon the birth of Kaye's.

"I saw strength and wisdom. I'm a proud father to say that I'm watching her set her foundation. Baby girl, I may not know it all and I may not know the why, but I know what you did.

"We don't have to stumble through this life the same, but it's important that we stumble. You, young lady stumbled into greatness. If I removed all the passionate moments from your works you would still have a touch that changes lives through words.

"That, my child, is God."

"Amen." Voices lift and hands clap.

I sob so hard snot threatens to bubble out of my nose. I turn my face into Felix's shoulder, and he rocks me from side to side. I feel like the weight of the world is lifted from my shoulders.

I sob my way through the closing of his sermon. I didn't see that coming. I thought he was going to use his words to embarrass and chastise me.

His words mean more to me than he will ever know.

CHAPTER THIRTY

Bestseller

Kaye

Two months later …

This is my first conference as a published author. I'm excited and nervous all at the same time. I'm taking comfort in the fact that Dean is also signing at this one.

Having someone I know in attendance will help me to come out of my shell. I'm naturally a shy person until I get to know you. Then I can open up and be me. This is totally outside of my comfort zone.

I feel like my life has been a whirlwind in the last year or so. So many things have changed, I've learned so much. I'm happy.

I'm also grateful to have my parents back in my life. My mother has come on this trip with me. She agreed to come along to watch Dae-Dae. I didn't want to leave him behind.

My grandparents offered to keep him at my place, but Dashawn is full of way too much energy. He would have worn them out. Besides, my mother has taken such an interest in what I'm doing.

She's been a great help with arranging my finances. Felix has been busy with work again. He was barely able to see us off.

I know that was much to his frustration. I hope we can find more time to spend with each other when I get back.

I've been getting more and more offers to do events on and offline. I want to say yes to everything, but I need to find time to write, and I have Dae-Dae to worry about. Anyone who says having a writing career isn't real work is crazy.

I'm exhausted just thinking about what we have to look forward to this weekend. I hope I can handle the pressure of coming out of my shell to talk to new people.

"Earth to Kaye," Dean says, bursting into my thoughts.

"Sorry," I mutter.

"Relax honey." She reaches for my hand. "This will be painless. I promise."

"If you say so."

She rolls her eyes, waving me off. We are walking to the opening meet and greet for the weekend events. My stomach is in all types of knots.

What if I say something stupid? What if no one knows who I am? What if someone tells me my books suck?

I have all types of thoughts running through my head. I try to tell myself to breathe, I'll make it through this. Still, every step feels like I have on steel shoes.

"Your mom is so sweet. She didn't have to treat me to breakfast," Dean says.

I love her for changing the subject and trying to pull me out of my own head. I don't think I would've or could've done this without her. I latch onto the lifeline she's throwing me wholeheartedly.

"That's my mom. You might as well put your wallet away for the rest of the trip. Besides, I think she's trying to send my father a message with the bill," I reply.

"Are things still tense with him?"

"Tense? You would have to interact with someone to have tension. Things with my father weren't tense, they were a hot mess," I laugh.

I can laugh about it now. A few months ago, I probably would have burst into tears. I think of his sermon and almost do anyway.

"Things are better. A lot better."

"That's good. I'm sure having his grandson around has changed the sound of his tune," she says.

"You might be right there."

My shoulders sag a little. I hate lying to my friends. I've told the truth to so many already. I just haven't told Lakia and Dean.

I go to launch into the story, but I feel Dean's entire demeanor change. The air seems to shift, and I catch the sound of the low hiss that comes out of her mouth. I turn to Dean to see her face is twisting in dark anger.

"Ain't this some bullshit? I told these heifers I wasn't doing this event if she's here. How you going to put me in a room with someone you know I have beef with?

"I wasn't joking when I said that ho better not ever show her face around me again," Dean says through tightly clenched teeth.

I grab her arm just as she looks like she's going to cross the room and act a fool. I have a tight hold on her, but she's trying to get free. I lean into her ear and whisper to her.

"You're here for business. My daddy always says you don't argue with a fool. No one can tell the difference between the two from a distance. Calm down. You don't ever let someone take you out of pocket when it comes to taking care of your pockets. Breathe," I say low enough for only her to hear.

When I look in Dean's face, she looks like she's on the verge of tears. I know that feeling. When you're so angry you want to react and holding back is almost painful.

"You don't know what she's done," Dean chokes out.

"Neither do these readers. You'll look like a crazy woman beating someone's ass for no damn reason. It's not worth it, boo. Today, we go high," I murmur.

Dean nods her head, looking away from me to gather herself. She clenches her fists open and shut as she reins it in. She is visibly still shaking with rage.

I reach for her hand and squeeze it. When she looks back at me, I see the gratitude in her eyes. Dean has a hot temper. I've seen and heard it in action before.

"I don't give a damn about none of this. I'm doing this for you," she says. "But I love you for thinking of my career and looking out for me."

I pull her into a hug. She places her arms around me and squeezes tight. We've grown so close from such a long distance. I love and respect this woman.

"I love you, girl. The best is yet to come for you. Don't lose focus for no one," I say.

She nods her head, pulling away to wipe her face with the back of her hand. She inhales a deep breath, smoothing a hand down her dress. She gives me that sassy smile.

"Let's go stunt on these bitches. After all, my book did just chart with the big dogs." Dean winks.

I grin. We squealed like crazy this morning. She ranked higher than she's ever ranked on the charts. I'm so proud of her.

"Love your crazy ass," I giggle.

Felix

I'm missing Kaye like crazy. I hope she had a great turnout for her signing today. She's been having fun while away with her mom and Dean.

I, on the other hand, have unfinished business on my hands. Not to mention this case I've been working that's getting on my nerves. My instincts are telling me to be patient, I'll get what I need soon enough.

I feel like I've been telling myself that a lot lately, in most areas of my life. Things have been going great between me and Kaye. Yet, I haven't felt like the time has been right when it comes to proposing. I can't explain it.

Have you ever had the feeling like things can blow up in your face at any moment, or like you're one day away from things in your life shifting in a way that will change everything? That's the feeling I've had lately. My gut has never stirred me wrong, it's a gift and a curse.

Pursing my lips at my computer screen, I place my hands behind my head. Blowing out a breath, I feel like I'm watching paint dry. It's like this guy knows we're on to him.

"Come on, you little bastard," I mutter to myself.

"Not the sort of greeting I was expecting," I hear a voice boom.

I look up to see Pastor Porter standing in front of my desk. I look around the office. Noah has raised his head from the papers in front of him. Toby is lost in his phone. Ryan has a grin on his face as he sits back in his chair and folds his arms over his chest.

Little fucker.

He would be amused by Pastor Porter looking like he has come to kick my ass. I stand, holding my hand out for his. We shake and I nod for the conference rooms.

"You want to have a seat and talk?" I ask.

"Don't you think it's about time?" he asks, lifting a brow.

I shrug. "I've been trying to get in to see you. Our schedules have been conflicting," I reply.

He frowns and shakes his head. "Yes, I know. That church doesn't run the same without my wife there. My assistant never brought your calls to my attention. I would have cleared some time for you," he says.

"It's all good. I need to take a break."

I round my desk and start for conference room B. Pastor Porter falls in at my side. I open the door and let him walk in before me.

"Can I get you something to drink?" I offer.

"No, I'm fine. I had a late lunch with my in-laws. You know that curry will rock you to sleep," he chuckles.

"Yeah, Grandma Reid has my pants needing to be let out," I reply.

"I know that's right. I lost weight while they were in Jamaica."

"Have a seat." I hold my hand out, gesturing for the seats at the conference table.

"Thank you. You know I've always liked you, Felix. You never came into my home with disrespect. I think that's what hurts the most," he says, unbuttoning his suit jacket and taking a seat. "You're like a son to me."

"Why didn't you come to me and tell me what was really going on with Kaye? You knew where she was and said nothing."

"With all due respect, sir. Kaye never changed her number. She still hasn't changed her cell number. What was stopping you from calling your daughter and finding out what was going on with your grandson?" I reply.

He sits back in his chair, his jaw working under the skin. I can feel my own temper flare. I've had opinions about this for a long time.

"Listen, you're the father of the woman I love. I don't want to be at odds with you. You and Kaye, both thought you were doing the right thing—"

"It was you." He cuts me off. "You were the one sending me the emails and pictures of her and Dashawn. Letting me know they were okay."

"Yeah." I nod tightly. "She'll kill me if she finds out."

"I'm sure. I wanted to thank you. You will never know the comfort those pictures and emails brought to me.

"At twenty-one Kaye was a grown woman. She made a choice. I let her live her life. Had I known what I realize now, I would have intervened, but I think things worked out just as they should have," he says.

I shrug.

"There were times she would have rather had her mother and father," I mumble.

"When Dashawn is older and you and Kaye have more of your own, you will understand," he says.

I stare at him. He lifts a brow at me and cracks a smile for the first time. He starts to laugh.

"Boy, you think I don't know you are head over heels for my daughter. You have been since you were teenagers," he laughs. "I always thought she was going to come home and say you were her boyfriend. I was blindsided with the Alberto thing. He was such a reckless young man."

"He had a good heart. His home life just sucked," I defend.

"Again, when you have children you will understand the facts, but you will always want what's best for your children. My son would be here to raise his own son if not for Alberto's reckless behavior," he replies.

I draw a hand down my face. While he may be right, Alberto was my friend. Honestly, he is absolutely right, but still.

"Felix, I didn't come here to rehash the past. I came to talk about the future. I knew from the moment I saw Dashawn he belonged to Danny.

"Kaye shouldn't be burdened with her brother's son. My wife and I—"

"Hold on a minute." I raise from my seat. "That's her son! She has raised him from the moment he was born. His mother didn't give a shit and walked, leaving Kaye on her own. She has loved and taken care of Dae-Dae all on her own.

"You're not about to take his mama from him. She's all he knows, and she loves him like her own. Never once did she say she wanted to give him up. I'm not letting this shit go down like this," I bark.

He lifts to his feet, glaring at me.

"Boy, you better remember who you're talking to. Sit your ass down before I whip it and call your mama and daddy to come and whip it again. I'm not trying to take that baby from that girl," he snaps back at me.

I tear my hat off my head and flop back in my seat. The door to the office opens and my dad walks in. He has a grin playing on his lips as he closes the door behind him.

"Told you." My father chuckles, holding his hand out to Pastor Porter.

"Didn't let me get my words out," Pastor Porter mutters.

"What were you getting at?" I huff.

"Ye best be fixing ye tone," my father throws my way.

I shift in my sit. I've pissed my father off. His accent is slipping through. He's not having it when it comes to disrespecting his friend. These two have been buddies for years. They go to basketball games together when they can.

"Cass told Danesha you were going to propose. We know you plan to marry Kaye. We were thinking we could take Dashawn off your hands from time to time," he explains.

I side glance him. He and my father both take a seat. I feel like I'm being ambushed.

"You and I both know that girl is stubborn. Look at where my wife and grandson are now. She won't be able to drag him around like this forever. Her career is just taking off.

"Your parents and my wife and I want to be a support system. We thought she would take it better coming from you. As I said this is not her burden. I don't want her to pass up on any chances and opportunities in her writing career because she thinks she's alone," he says pointedly.

I nod. He is right. Kaye will make every sacrifice she can to take care of Dae-Dae. This has been a concern of mine as well.

"All he is asking is for you to come to us, your family, before you both burn out. We're watching it happen," my father says. "If your mother threatens me one more time over this, I'm going to clobber you myself."

I grin. If Mom is after dad about this, I'm in for it. They're right though. I've been spreading myself thin.

"I'll talk to Kaye," I reply.

"Good. Now, when's the wedding?" Pastor Porter asks.

"Soon, I hope." I smile, rubbing the back of my neck.

"She deserves the best," he says.

"All I've ever known to give her."

CHAPTER THIRTY-ONE

Score to Settle

Felix

Noah and I sit in the darkened living room. Wyatt took surveillance on this one. I've been waiting a long time for this. I wanted to be hands on.

I've always been the quiet one until you fuck with me. Martin Davis and his wife Hallie Vector-Davis picked the wrong one to fuck with. Sending those guys after me was the dumbest thing the two of them ever did.

The light goes on in the foyer, but Noah and I don't move. We wait in the silence of the living room. Voices carry our way as the owners of the home argue.

"I don't know why you always get so mad. He was just complimenting my hair," the woman whines.

I never did like the sound of Hallie's voice. I don't know why I didn't see it before. It's all so clear to me now. Every time I think back on my interactions with Vector's only daughter, I can see the jumpiness, the lack of eye contact, and the pitchiness of her voice.

At first, I passed her voice off as annoying. Now, I can hear past that initial annoying ass voice to what was really going on back then. Hallie was playing everyone. Snitching on her husband was a part of some dumb ass plan.

If I weren't spreading myself so thin, I would have seen it sooner. A mistake I've only made once and will never make again. I'm no one's fool and I don't like the fact that these two tried to make me one.

"He wouldn't have said shit to you if you weren't staring in his fucking face. I swear, I don't know why I brought you with me. I should have left your spoiled, slutty ass right with your father," Martin barks at her.

"Slut, who are you calling a slut?" she hisses at him.

"Trouble in paradise? Awful lot of trouble to go through to end up broke on an island bickering," I speak up, as they cross the threshold into the room.

Martin flips the light switch. Both of their faces drain of blood. It's priceless. A look I'll remember for years to come.

"Listen, this was all her idea. I had nothing to do with it," Martin says, holding up his hands as if he can ward this off.

"Bitch," Noah snorts.

"I'd shut up if I were you," I grit out.

"How did you get in here?" Hallie asks shakily.

I tilt my head at her. My lip curls back. There are a few things I'd like to say to her, but my mother raised me better.

"Who helps their husband rob their father blind only to lose it all? You know you can never go back, don't you?" I say to her.

"Did he se ... send you?" she stammers.

"No one sent me anywhere. I'm not a pet," I reply.

"I want to get the fuck out of here. I have better things to do," Noah grumbles.

"Patience. First, I have a question," I say to Noah before turning back to the dumb ass couple in front of me. "Why call attention to the missing money if you were in on it?"

"Oh, I can answer this one," Martin snorts in disgust. "It's because she's a stupid jealous cunt. She thought I was cheating. To get back at me she took her name off everything and ratted me out."

"I'm jealous? You fucking prick. You just choked a guy at a restaurant. You weren't calling me a stupid cunt then, were you?" She hollers at him.

I roll my eyes at them. I feel like I'm watching a bad movie. They're both idiots. Blowing through five million when you know you can't get your hands on the rest of the money you stashed.

Oh, yeah. When you send guys for me, I'm going to fuck your shit up. The only reason I didn't get to that last five million was because they'd just withdrawn it seconds before I ruined their lives.

"You are stupid. You left your name on one of the accounts. I had to try to clean that shit up. I don't know why I give a fuck. I should have let the old man find out the truth. No, I'm always thinking with my dick. Now look at this shit," Martin barks.

"I told you to send them with guns. You said they didn't need them for the nerd," Hallie huffs.

Noah bursts into laughter. These two are pretty sad. I agree with his earlier statement. It's time to go.

"Wait, wait," Noah says through his laughter. "You sent those guys after my brother to cover your tracks because you didn't remove your name from all of the accounts. So you two could have gotten away if you didn't come for the one person who might or might not have outed you, but without doubt has the power to end you."

"We can work something out," Martin tries to talk his way out of this.

"Yeah, fuck that, you sent goons for my life," I say between my teeth. "At best, I'm going to watch you bleed out."

"Wh … what," Hallie breathes.

I give a laugh. "Nah, I'm joking, dude. Come on, I have something for you," I say, waving them to follow me.

I don't look behind me to see if they are following. I walk out the back sliding doors whistling. It feels good to be on this side. Watching from my mentors can get boring at times.

I hear Noah growl behind me, the shuffling of feet following. I grin. I'm sure the look my brother just gave them killed any thought of running or putting up a fight.

I stop beside the infinity pool. Their flashiness appalls me, but I'm applauding it tonight as it works in my favor. Their neighbors are over a mile away. The sound of the ocean and the distance will be enough to muffle their screams.

I squat next to the pool running the tip of the muzzle of my gun across the surface. We cut the lights out here. The gorgeous lighting that showcases the pool is no longer shining. Looking up, I smile with all my teeth showing.

"Strip," I bark the command.

Hallie takes a step back bumping into Noah's chest. She nearly jumps out of her skin, whirling in a circle before turning back to me with wide eyes. She looks at Martin pleadingly.

"I don't like repeating myself. Do it now or you'll be doing it with holes in your knees," I hiss.

They both spring into action, stripping out of their clothes. Hallie does so while trembling. Martin curses the entire time under his breath. I stand, crossing my arms over my chest.

Placing the gun in my waistband, I pull my knife. Some might think this is cold. Me, not so much. Those guys were not there to play with me. They were there to take my life.

I hold the handle of the knife out to Hallie. She looks at it, then back at me. I see her mind working. She quickly makes up her mind that trying anything stupid with me is useless.

She wraps a shaky hand around the knife. Her eyes look at me with a mix of pleading and confusion. I take a step back.

"Cut him and I'll think about letting you go," I say.

Her mouth falls open. She looks at Martin, contemplation clear in her eyes. She turns to him with her brows drawn.

"You'd really do it, you stupid bitch," Martin snarls before lunging at Hallie and the knife.

I watch in amazement as she stumbles back. Martin manages to get the knife from her, slicing her hand in the process. I can't describe the feeling of anticipation that fills me when he pushes her into the water.

Wait for it.

I don't miss a beat as I halt a charging Martin, placing him in a headlock and retrieving my blade. He struggles against my hold just as Hallie's high-pitched screams fill the air. On cue, the lights come up.

"Thanks, Bro," I say into my earpiece to a listening Wyatt on the other end.

"No problem," he says back.

"What the fuck?" Martins gasps as he looks at the pool before us.

Hallie tries to swim to the edge as she continues to scream. She can give it up. She's not making it out of that pool. Edging closer with Martin in my hold, I slash across the front of his chest.

Releasing him, I quickly slash the back of his knees before taking a step back. Planting my foot in his back, I send him over into the pool. His screams begin to fill the night air.

Piranhas. Nasty little fuckers, but they'll get the job done. Maybe this is why my brothers make me stay behind the computer screens.

"You know your mind is twisted," Noah says as he steps up beside me, speaking to my own thoughts.

"Takes one, to know one," I say with a shrug.

"Truth," Noah chuckles. "I'm going to see what's in the fridge. The cleaners are on the way."

I nod, my eyes remaining on the pool before me. The screams are dying down. When I hear the sound of movement to my right, I cut the audio between myself and my brothers.

I turn to see Norman Vector staring into the pool. He's wearing a look of pure disgust. He was the one to tip me off to where his daughter had been hiding. He didn't want to send his man for this.

"She wasn't my child," he says tightly. "My stepdaughter didn't know any other father but me from the time she was a baby. Yet, she still betrayed me in the end. This doesn't get back to my wife."

"You're not even here," I reply.

He doesn't reply. He returns to the shadows I mapped out for him to follow. This part is between us. Never know when I'll need to call in a favor.

CHAPTER THIRTY-TWO

Conflicted

Felix

One month later …

I walk into the house to find Kaye sitting on the couch with the most perplexed look I've ever seen on her face. She has a book in her lap, with her brows knitted tightly.

I don't think she's noticed me coming in at all. When I note her open laptop and a bottle of wine, I smile. She's researching for a book. I'd bet on it.

When I get closer to her, I see the title of the book. I cock my head to the side and knit my own brows. This was not the type of research I thought I'd find her doing.

I pluck the book from her grasp, drawing a gasp from her lips. She nearly jumps out of her skin. I burst into laughter.

The look on her face is priceless. She looks both shocked and horrified. She tries to reach for the book, but I lift it up out of her reach while reading the page she was turned to.

"Felix, give me that," she huffs trying to jump for it.

I laugh, holding it higher as I squint at the pages. She gives up, placing her hands on her hips, scowling at me. She's so cute. Out of breath and pissed off.

"Why are you reading this shit?" I close the book and toss it on the coffee table.

"You just lost my page," she gasps in horror.

"So what. I can guarantee you that was some bullshit. It doesn't work like that," I reply.

"How the heck would you know?" she grumbles, going to reach for the book.

I place my hands on her thick hips, tugging her to me. My hands glide back to cup her full curves. I've been thinking of getting my hands on all this all day.

When Dashawn asked to go see his grandparents and stay the night, I offered to take him. Kaye looked like she could use a break. I know I've been feining for some alone time with her.

"Have I not taught you everything you know?" I ask with a teasing grin and a squeeze of her ass. "If you want to know about BDSM you come to me. I'll teach you all you want to know."

She gives me a disbelieving look. She has no idea who she's dealing with. I search her face to see if she's truly ready for this.

"How ... why ... you don't know," she stammers as she narrows her gaze.

"I'll let you in on a little Black brothers secret," I say, winking down at her.

"What?"

"John has a thing for the life. When he becomes fascinated with something we all have to hear about it. We've all learned more than we should or need to know about the BDSM lifestyle, thanks to John," I reveal.

"Seriously?"

"Yeah," I say and shrug.

"How … what did you learn?"

"I've been to a dungeon or two. I've topped—"

I cut off when her eyes light up. I can see the curiosity as it blossoms. I take my girl in for what feels like the first time. I'm seeing her through new eyes.

"You want to dominate?" I ask as my own curiosity is piqued.

"Well … my character does," she says, biting her lip.

My brows shoot into my hairline. My cock stirs to life. Kaye's ass in latex or leather, I'm all for it. If this is what she wants, I'll happily give it to her.

"I'm warning you. I'm into that shit. We go there, I'm going there," I say.

Her mouth falls open. I see the second of hesitation in her eyes before she shuts it down. She lifts her chin looking me in the eyes and says the words that take us to the world of no return.

"Teach me."

Kaye

They tell you be careful what you ask for. I should have heeded the warning. I didn't think two simple words would land me in a sex club.

Felix is serious when it comes to his lessons. He explained that most of what I was reading came from novices. If I wanted to learn the truth, I needed to experience it.

But this …

I don't think I'm ready for this. It's a sex club. I look around nervously, chiding myself for my stupid curiosity.

I thought I'd spice my next book up a bit. In my head, my female lead has been flirting with the idea of the lifestyle. Okay, okay, I had questions too. I just didn't think any of that would lead here.

"Mistress, this was sent for you," someone says, making me jump out of my skin.

I turn to find the beautiful woman that greeted us when we arrived.

"Welcome to Club Desire," she had said in a smoky voice.

She looks to be a little older than me. She's very pretty. I'd say she's Middle Eastern. Her dark hair and eyes add something mysterious to her looks.

Hadiyah.

That's the name Felix called her by. I believe Hadiyah has a story. There's a secret smile in her eyes that's so revealing. It's a dark smile that doesn't touch her lips, but a smile nonetheless.

That's when she looks up. I noticed she wouldn't make eye contact with Felix. After he leaned to whisper something in her ear, she stopped peeking up at me.

"Oh, thank you," I say taking the gift box from her hands.

"I'll help you get ready, Mistress. The one is waiting," she replies.

My brows knit. I don't know what to say. Felix led me to this room and told me to wait here. I haven't seen him since.

Hadiyah waves me over toward the vanity. I turn to see the bench seat placed before the mirrored table. I take a deep breath to calm my nerves. I know Felix would never let things go too far.

Hadiyah's movements pull my attention back to her. She has untied her red silk robe and let it fall to the floor. My mouth pops open. She's in a red and black corset and red heels.

I quickly look away. My cheeks heat. I'm so confused about what to do next.

"You can look if you like, Mistress," she says.

"Um, I should get ready," I say, rushing over to the vanity.

I place the gift box down and open it. My eyes nearly pop out of my head when I see the outfit inside. A black corset sits on top. Red heels are resting in the top corners. When I lift the corset, I find black latex pants beneath it.

"This is not fitting over my ass," I mutter under my breath.

Hadiyah giggles taking the corset from my hands.

"The one said you would say that. You have a beautiful body, Mistress. My master would love a scene with you," she says lightly.

I turn wide eyes on her. I'm not letting any man, but Felix put his hands on me. Maybe this wasn't such a good idea.

"Do not worry. You are here to learn. I can see you two have trust. That is very important, Mistress," she says.

My shoulders sag in relief. I chew on my lip, staring into the box. This might not be so bad. Right?

"Okay," I say aloud, more so to encourage myself.

"Can I help you to undress, Mistress?" she asks.

"I ... um," I stammer.

"I am here to do as you wish, Mistress."

"I may need help with the corset," I admit.

"No problem, Mistress."

I fidget with the hem of my shirt before I tug it up over my head. I look at my smaller breasts in the mirror, before peeking at Hadiyah's breasts spilling forward with a little more flesh than I possess.

"Mistress, not to speak out of turn, but I was instructed to help you where fit. I was not always a slave. This is why my help was asked for," she says pointedly.

I turn to look at her. This time she lifts her head and looks at me. There is a different type of confidence I see in this moment. That secret smile is revealed in its fullness. As if she's always smiling secretly because she knows the true power she possesses.

"You were a dominatrix?"

"I still am. When I choose. It's called being a switch. I can top or bottom. I've found a relationship where I choose to bottom.

"This lifestyle is about choices. The right partner will always respect your right to choose. You have been given the choice to be a dominatrix.

"There is power in this decision. It will unlock your confidence. Turn, look in the mirror. What do you see?" She instructs.

I turn to look at myself as I stand there in my bra and jeans. I never did find time to get to the gym. My stomach is a lot pudgier than it was when I was in high school and college. Although, my lower half is much wider and curvier than my top. Last time I got on the scale it read two twenty-five. At five-five I'm packing all of this in a pretty small package.

"I'll tell you what I see," she says when I don't answer.

She caresses my side with the backs of her fingers. It's a light touch, but it still feels a bit intimate to me. I feel like I'm being seduced into her web. The difference in her demeanor has my head spinning.

"You're a very attractive, very beautiful woman. Your curves are gorgeous. Your breasts are perfect for your body. They leave an appreciation for the entire package.

"You have the hips of a life giver. A man could get lost in the feel of them wrapped around his waist and a woman could take pleasure in feasting on all that lush beauty.

"You did not see the heads you turned when you arrived. We noticed." She winks into the mirror at me. "Own your beauty. Do not compare yourself to anyone else. You are who the creator made you to be.

"Make your servants see you and only you. When you enter a room command everyone's attention with that confidence. You learn to dominate like this, you will take life by storm in every area."

I nod my head. Hadiyah moves behind me to unfasten my bra. She helps me with the corset, returning to the meek servant from earlier. I have so many questions.

"I will answer all of your questions later. We will be friends, Mistress. I can see this," she says softly.

I fall silent as she helps me to get ready. When I'm dressed and Hadiyah has finished my makeup and hair, I can't believe the woman that's staring back at me.

I would never have thought I could look so sexy in something like this. My coke bottle figure dares anyone to look away. My ruby red lips call for attention, bringing a smile to my face.

"There she is," Hadiyah purrs at my side.

However, when I turn my eyes to her, she's not looking at me. Her head is bent and she's waiting for me. I stand from the bench seat I've been sitting on while she did my makeup.

"I'm ready," I say.

"Yes, Mistress."

She nods, turning to lead the way. We don't go through the door we entered through. She walks to a door on the other side of the room. When she opens it, she moves out of the way for me to step through.

When I enter my breath is taken away. Felix is sitting in one of two throne chairs. His head bent over his phone as his hair falls into his forehead, he's shirtless.

My eyes lower to his legs, one stretched out the other bent at the knee, completely relaxed without a care in the world. He's not wearing the blue jeans he entered this place in. His long legs are now clad in black leather pants, but his feet are bare.

I raise my eyes back up just as he lifts his head. He has on his glasses. Why the hell is that so damn sexy to me?

His eyes shift from mine to something behind me. I turn in time to see Hadiyah rush forward. I almost forgot about her. I didn't know she would be in here with us.

My eyes follow her as she drops to her knees and bows her head before the two thrones. My gaze instantly moves to Felix. I'm not too sure about having a half-naked woman who looks like her kneeling in front of my man.

However, when my eyes find Felix, he's not looking at her. His heated gaze is on me. He reaches his hand out, beckoning me across the room.

My feet are moving before I can tell them to. Felix's eyes go from heated to hungry as he takes in my outfit from head to toe. I feel confidence flow through me just from taking in his gaze.

I never knew a single look could make you feel so sexy. I think I put just a little more sway in my hips because I'm starting to feel myself. Felix darts his tongue out as a grin hits the corner of his mouth.

He raises from his seat, wearing his own confidence. He saunters toward me sexily, as he meets me halfway. When I stop in front of him, he places a hand on my hip and draws me closer still.

He leans in, inhaling my neck before nuzzling it. I feel his tongue peek out to tease my skin.

"I'll be getting you more latex and corsets," he whispers.

I lift a brow at him when he pulls away to smile down at me. Taking my hand, he leads me over to the throne chairs. He guides me to sit in one, while he retakes the seat he was in.

He reaches to run a finger down the center of my breasts, keeping his gaze on me. I feel my skin pebble under his touch as my breathing shifts. I gaze out of the corner of my eyes to see if Hayidah is looking.

Her head is still bent as she remains perfectly still. I turn my eyes back to Felix. He's watching me closely, the way he always does.

"Let's start with the basics for tonight's lesson," he says. "Hayidah's master offered her to us for tonight. She will be your pet, but she will also help to train you for your desire to be a dominatrix. You will see what I mean by that.

"The first thing to understand is that this is for everyone's pleasure. I never enter play or leave play without satisfaction being the goal and end result for all involved," he says.

My brows knit as I process his words. I don't see how that could be possible. Some of the things I've seen and read. I shudder just thinking of them.

"From some of the things I've read I can't see how that can always be true," I reply.

"Can this shit get sick and twisted? Yes, if you're entering with someone who's fucked up in the head, or doesn't understand the roles and rules of the life. Or if a partner is naïve and doesn't know or watch for limits.

"Miseducation gives the life a bad rep. The best Doms always take care of their pets, slaves—whatever you are more comfortable with."

"Can I call her by her name?" I ask as I frown.

"You can ask her what she prefers. Titles can be gifts. Terms of endearment become rewards. It's an honor to be called Pet, Angel, little dove. Just as stripping her of a title and just addressing her as "her" or "him" can be used to put her in her place—beneath you. Remember, your goal is to please her as much as she pleases you," he explains.

My head reels. I don't think I want to strip of her humanity with the use of a simple pronoun. I remember reading that somewhere. It rubbed me wrong then.

I ignore the part about her pleasing me. I don't want to think about how Felix plans for this to go. I'm holding onto my confidence at the moment.

Thinking of him wanting to sleep with Hayidah will put an end to all of that. The fact that his focus has been only on me is serving to soothe my ego. The sensation of his finger that's still tracing all over my skin is doing a great job of distracting me as well.

I turn to her still in the same position before us. I square my shoulders as I get ready to address her. I pull on confidence I didn't know I had.

"I will call you doll," I say. "Does that please you, Doll?"

"Yes, mistress," she replies.

Felix leans in to kiss my temple. I turn to look at him and see the pleased look on his face. He places his hand under my chin to lift my face, planting a kiss on my lips.

"Very good. You were made for this," he croons against my lips. He pulls away, curiosity glowing in his orbs. "Why doll?"

I look at Hayidah, my eyes dance over her pretty face. It was the first thing I thought when I looked at her. The long lashes, the dark eyes and hair. Yup, she looks just like a doll.

"She reminds me of one," I reply with a shrug.

Felix glances at her and laughs. Turning back to me, he places another kiss on my lips. He deepens the kiss as if she's not in the room with us. I peek out the corners of my eyes and see her head has not lifted.

When he breaks the kiss, red lipstick covers his lips. I reach to wipe it off with my thumb. He sucks my finger in his mouth, causing my girly bits to pulse.

"I don't know if you've noticed, she has called you mistress. That's an honor. She belongs to someone.

"That's one of their rules. She can play when he allows, but he is her only master. No one else gets that right to be called that from her lips.

"Tonight, you will be her mistress. If I allow, she can call me *the one*," he says.

"Why, *the one?*"

He gives me a panty-melting stare. I nearly squirm in my seat, but I restrain myself. A dominatrix would have control over herself, I chide in my head.

"I want everyone in this room to remember, I'm *the one. The one* who *you* love, *the one* who brings *you* ultimate pleasure, *the one* who *you* belong to and *the one* who belongs to *you*. I am *the one*," he says.

His words are like dragging silk against my skin. They are smooth, just the right amount of soft, but they soothe. My heart thunders as I try to mask my reaction on the outside.

His eyes bounce over my face as he caresses my cheek. His thumb takes a slow drag across my lips. I can see him thinking.

"Tell me why your character is considering the life. I want to understand what she needs. What you're trying to learn for her. Then we can play," he says thoughtfully.

I draw my brow in and I look down as I sort through my thoughts. If I continue to stare into his eyes, I'll never find my words. I've been mapping out this book for a while.

"It's deeper than some sexual need. Her husband of nine years has just left her for someone else. She spent years helping him build his company and then, one day, poof. He snatches the rug out from under her.

"At first, she wants to do this to have control over wealthy men, but after a few encounters something changes. I'm working that part out. I think I need to understand more to figure out why everything shifts," I muse aloud.

"Good," he says almost to himself. "I know exactly where to take you."

He turns my face to look at Doll kneeling on the floor. Her chest is heaving silently. A clear sign of anticipation. I'd be lying if I said I'm not intrigued by this.

Again, I wonder what Felix has planned. I'm not in any way about to let her touch him or him touch her. I don't want to learn this stuff that bad. She has been nice, but I can totally see myself having a Dean moment. I'll snap if she puts her hands on my man.

"She's not for me." Felix leans into my ear to whisper, as if reading my thoughts. "Being the bottom is not easy for me. It's not as natural for me as topping. I didn't want to teach you wrong. Your little Doll will help us both."

I whip my head in his direction. My mouth opening. He has a wicked light in his eyes. I search his face to make sure I'm catching his meaning.

No, I misunderstood. No way is he saying what I think. I lose that idea and shake the hot images it brings off.

He winks at me.

"Come, let me show you how this can be fun for everyone," he says, standing and holding his hand out.

Felix

I love that stunned look on her face. This is going to be amazing. Kaye looks stunning. Her hair is slicked back away from her face in a low bun. I have a full view of all her gorgeous features.

The corset and latex pants put her coke bottle figure on display in a way that has me questioning if I can really do this. I want her now and I want her my way.

I have to remind myself that this is what she wants. To learn and understand BDSM, being a dominatrix in particular. I will always give my baby what she wants.

I knew coming here to Club Desire would allow me to do that. I just happened to luck out when I made the call. I had no idea Hayidah would be in LA. She is usually in New York with her master.

Her help is a friendly gift for a few favors I've done back in New York. It's the perfect gift because Hayidah is an excellent sub and I've seen her top in a scene before. She's powerful.

I want Kaye to learn that type of confidence and control. I know she already has it in her. Hayidah is the right person to help me bring it out.

Standing behind Kaye, I stop her in front of Hayidah. Although I want to touch Kaye and command our Doll to watch, I don't. This is Kaye's time, she's in control.

"Tell us what would please you," I whisper in Kaye's ear.

I feel her shiver as my voice washes over her. She collects herself quickly. I watch her as she takes in the playroom fully for the first time.

I know this is the first time she's taken in her surroundings because she was drawn to me the moment she walked in the room. I felt it as she entered. That's the kind of power I want her to leave this place confident in.

I watch her double take toward the knife display before cringing. While our Doll has few hard limits, I'm not interested in knife play. I had a feeling Kaye wouldn't be either.

Kaye moves over to the displays. I follow after her. Giving her room to explore.

My eyes drop to all that ass in those pants. I'm ready to bust through my own. The sway of her hips coupled with the knowledge I have of the weight of those thighs around me almost make me lose focus.

She looks over her shoulder, catching me with my eyes glued to her ass. Kaye smiles and I return it with a half grin. She giggles to herself, turning back for the displays.

"I thought the toys would draw your attention," I say from behind her when she stops. "Why the whips?"

"I want to understand how they bring both parties pleasure," she says.

I reach out and take one of the metal floggers in my hand. Kaye turns her head up to look at me. How can wanting to learn be so sexy? Her inquisitiveness turns me on to no end.

"This may seem like a physical thing. But it's more mental than anything. I can speak from the Dom perspective. For a Sub to give me that kind of trust is empowering and thrilling.

"I get to push her to her limits. Watching her get there is part of the experience for me. Seeing that moment when the mind breaks free. When pain becomes pleasure and everything else fades into background noise.

"It's kind of a false sense of control. You are the one wielding the whip, but your sub is the one with all of the power," I explain.

"So they are gaining pleasure from relinquishing control?"

"I guess you can say that. I've never been whipped, but from observing and being the one with the whip in hand, I would say so," I reply. "Come."

I inhale deeply as we walk back to her Doll. She is still sitting in place obediently. I've observed her remain in that position for hours without flinching, but she won't have to remain that way this evening.

When we reach Doll, Kaye stops before her, lifting Doll's head. I tilt my head as I watch the gesture. She's more natural at this than she knows. The intimacy she's building is key.

"I'd like to understand what a Sub gets from being whipped. If this isn't for you, I understand," Kaye says.

Here goes nothing.

I drop to my knees beside Doll, holding the flogger out to Kaye. I keep my eyes on the floor as hard as it is for me to. I want to see her reaction. I want that look of pleasure I imagine playing on her lips when she realizes I've intended to be her slave all along.

"Please accept my gift, Mistress," I say as Kaye's hand wrap around the handle.

I hear the gasp that leaves her lips. I feel more than see Doll stand. Or should I now say Mistress Doll. I'm already feeling out of my comfort zone, but this is Kaye. If she wants this. I'm here so she can have it.

Kaye

My mouth is still hanging open when Doll moves to my side. I'm confused and turned on at the same time. Felix kneeing before me shirtless in those leather pants that hug his thighs, has zapped my brain cells.

"I'm still your servant. You control the room," Doll says at my side. "Tell me, do you still want to learn to use the whip, Mistress?"

"Yes," I nod jerkily.

"Impact play can go from sensual to extremely erotic. Spanking, whipping, flogging, caning, they all offer different levels of gratification. The key is communication. Both verbal and non," she explains. "Ask him for his safe word. This is new for both of you, it's best to have one."

I grin before addressing him. I move closer, wanting to see his face when he talks to me. I lift his head with the tip of the flogger's handle.

"Tell me your safe word, Angel," I purr.

His eyes blaze back at me, his nostrils flare. All clear signs that he's turned on as much as I am. I know Felix, I know that vein that has popped in his neck. This is taking all his restraint.

In his head, he has probably stripped and fucked me by now—guest or no guest. His right eye twitches, pulling a smile to my lips. I know I'm right.

The fact that I've just stripped his power with a single term of endearment sends blood rushing through my veins. Yes, he is the one, but in the moment, he has offered himself up as my servant and I like it.

"Blaze," he says with a secret smirk playing on his lips.

I squat before him. His eyes drop to my breast, then between my legs before he remembers himself. I note the pained look that crosses his face. It's so damn hot that he's doing this for me. While wearing his glasses, nonetheless.

I want to kiss him all over his face and tell him how much I love him, but I don't want to break character. I tap the flogger beneath his chin, tilting my head to the side as I look at him. His eyes remain on the floor this time.

"Look at me, Angel," I command. He snaps his eyes up from the floor. "Are you mocking me?"

He can't help himself. He licks his lips, while giving me a look that tells me I'm going to get it later. I'm loving this.

"No, Mistress," he replies.

"Your safe word has me thinking that's a lie," I purr.

"I would never lie to you, Mistress."

"Is that right?" I ask tilting my head to the other side.

"Yes, Mistress."

"Do you find Doll attractive?" I ask.

"Yes, Mistress, but you are the most beautiful woman in the world to me. Attractive is beneath alluring, bewitching, tantalizing, or captivating. You are all of those things and more to me, Mistress," he replies.

"While your words are beautiful, you talk too much," Doll says behind me. "If you want to give more than the answer your mistress asks you for, you should ask for permission."

A dark look comes over his face, but he doesn't reply. Wanting to see how far I can push him, I lift up, turning to take a light seat on his shoulder. Again, using the tip of the flogger handle, I turn his face to me.

"Tell Doll you understand," I say firmly.

"I understand, Doll," he replies.

Leaning in, I peck his lips. I can feel that he wants to deepen it, but he holds back. I cup his face and lick the seam of his lips, coaxing him to open for me. I take over the kiss, moaning into his mouth.

I can feel Doll's eyes on us. My mind goes to when I used to get myself off for Felix through the surveillance cams. I break the kiss before I get lost in it.

I stand turning to face Felix again. His eyes are locked on mine. I tsk at him and he lowers his head with a grin.

"We will start lightly, Mistress," Doll says. "You want to hit where fat or muscle protects the body. A little flick of the wrist will do more than you think."

I look from the flogger in my hand to Felix. I don't think I can do this. I don't think I would've done this if it weren't him. I was hoping Doll would just offer the information I want to know once I told her what I planned.

"There are other ways to unlock pleasure," she says when I hesitate. "I can tell you the things you want to know. We can use this time to explore other things if you like, Mistress."

I turn to look at her and freeze. There is a suggestive measure to her tone that I pick up on. Yet, I don't think her interest is in Felix.

Felix

I can sense it when it happens. When the room shifts and the tides change. I look up to make sure Kaye is okay. She is staring at Hayidah with a confused look on her face.

"What do you mean?" Kaye says.

"You like to be watched. There is power in commanding the attention of a viewer. I don't think impact play is for you yet. But making him please you in front of me. That, Mistress, would make you very happy," Hayidah explains. "Am I right, Mistress?"

"Yes." Kaye nods.

I tilt my head. I take in all the things I know Hayidah has noted. How she came to this conclusion. It's all there.

I fight the smile that threatens to take over my face. This has taken an interesting turn. I don't move waiting for Kaye to make a decision on what she wants.

"It is your scene, Mistress. Tell us what you want," Hayidah says.

Kaye lifts her head and pushes her shoulders back. I can see the wheels turning in her head. The flogger drops from her fingertips.

She reaches for Hayidah's hand leading her to the thrones. Kaye takes a seat, tugging her doll into her lap. They make a beautiful sight. Kaye whispers something in Hayidah's ear that brings a smile to her face.

She turns and places a kiss on Kaye's lips. My mouth drops open. When they break the kiss, they both turn to me with sly smiles on their faces.

"Stand up, Angel," Kaye purrs.

I lift to my feet. Hayidah raises a brow at me, reminding me of my roll. I lower my head and come out of the stance that definitely reads of my propensity to be the dominant one in the room.

"Take your pants off," Kaye commands next.

I'm smiling to myself as I start to unfasten my pants. I'm glad to be free of the constraints that have been tripping my erection. Pushing the pants down my thighs, I step out of them.

"Eyes up," Kaye barks.

I look up through my lashes to see Hayidah kneading Kaye's breast. Kaye's eyes are on me. Her expression a mask of control. My cock twitches at the sight before me. Hayidah whispers something to Kaye, causing her to nod.

"Stroke yourself, Angel, but you're not to come no matter what," she orders.

"Yes, Mistress," I reply reaching to wrap my hand around my shaft.

I start with slow strokes as I watch another woman begin to kiss on my woman's neck, while fondling her breasts. Kaye keeps her eyes on me the entire time. Only the rise and fall of her chest gives her away. She's turned on as much as I am.

I lick my lips and my mouth falls open. Kaye taps Hayidah's leg for her to rise. I watch as they both stand. Kaye turns to Hayidah.

"Undress me, take your time. Give him a show," she purrs.

"Yes, Mistress," Hayidah says.

Hayidah goes to stand behind Kaye, her hands gliding from behind Kaye, slaying her stomach. They then make the slow trip up to cup her breasts. My jaw flexes, my eyes squint behind my glasses.

This wasn't what I planned for tonight, but I can't say that it's not hot as fuck. Both of them are gorgeous women. Each beautiful in their own right. Together they are stunning—brown on brown.

I know that look on Hayidah's face. She's more than attracted to Kaye. I understand. It's hard to look away from Kaye. Especially when the shyness fades away, revealing the real Kaye.

I start to stroke harder, faster, when Kaye's tits bounce free from the corset, as Hayidah releases and removes it. Kaye's nipples are tight, pointing right at me. I want to suck one into my mouth.

I feel myself go to move forward to do just that but remember myself at the last second. Kaye's eyes blaze at me in warning. The look is so sexy, I have to slow down my strokes. The base of my spine tingles.

"Don't come," she warns.

Meanwhile, Hayidah has her hands all over Kaye's curves as she peels the latex pants from Kaye's legs. Those thick brown thighs come into view, calling me to be between them. I know one thing for sure, when I get my hands on Kaye, she's going to wish she didn't tease me like this.

I'm going to enjoy every single moment. When I finally get to make her come, I'm not going to stop. That is *if* I let her come.

I love that Kaye steps back into those spiked heels once her pants are out of the way. They have her calves looking amazing, making her legs look longer.

With a wicked grin on her lips, Kaye turns her back to me. She beckons Hayidah to her with the crook of her finger. Again, she says something only the two of them can hear.

I watch as Kaye bends at the waist. Hayidah drops to her knees behind Kaye and I nearly lose it. Hayidah pries Kaye open and starts to feast on that pussy I know so well.

My tongue darts out of my own mouth as if I can taste it for myself. The sweet taste is one I've come to love waking to. The hum that comes from Hayidah's throat is both understandable and envied.

Kaye looks over her shoulder to watch me as I watch them. The sexy look on her face threatens to push me too far. Hayidah begins to knead Kaye's cheeks, while working her head, causing Kaye to suck her lip into her mouth.

"Ah," Kaye purrs.

"Fuck," I groan, not caring that I'm supposed to be the silent one.

I'm not sure how much more of this I can take. I'm ready to call all of this to an end to claim my woman, but the look of satisfaction on her face gives me pause. It's not the satisfaction from the pleasure. It's the look of satisfaction because she's the one in control.

All at once it's like I step out of my body to watch this from above the room. I see everything before me differently. I see Kaye differently.

All her life she's done what's been asked of her. Publishing her books has been the first time she's chosen something for herself. The first time she's had control.

Until now.

This is so much more than something sexual. Just as it should be. This experience has turned into what Kaye needs, not what her character in her book needs.

I have to bite down hard because the gratification of knowing she has this threatens all the restraint I've had up until this point. As if sensing my need for her, she straightens. Kaye strokes Hayidah's hair, leaning down to whisper something in her ear.

Hayidah gets to her feet and heads to the displays, but Kaye and I are focused on each other. She moves to where I'm standing in the room. That confidence and control rolling off her.

Seeing this, I vow to give her this whenever I have the opportunity to. I want to see this self-assurance on her more often. The way it's oozing from her makes me proud she's mine.

Kaye cups my face, staring up into my eyes. I want to lean in and capture her lips. I'd love to smear more of that lipstick all over her face.

"Stop," she commands, halting my stroking motion.

Kaye gestures with her eyes for me to lower before her. I do as she asks. She then tosses her leg over my shoulder. I give her a wolfish grin. It's time I remind her that no one can make her come like I can.

Tilting her hips forward, I start to devour her core. She starts to roll her hips into my face, working in circles. She's offering me her pussy the way I like it. I tighten my grasp as I feel her peaking. Then dive in farther, closing the deal.

"Oh. My. God," she whimpers.

I pull back looking her in the eyes as I lick my face clean. I go to go back for seconds, but she shakes her head. Placing her fingers under my chin, she guides me to stand.

Towering over her, I stand as her waiting sentinel. Kaye runs her hands up my stomach over my chest. Her eyes telling all the things her lips are holding in.

She lifts to her toes, wrapping a hand around the back of my neck to pull me down to meet her lips. My knees feel weak from the moment our lips lock. This woman has all the power in the world when it comes to me.

I'd cutoff my own arm to keep her happy and safe. I mean that shit too. If Kaye hollers, I'm the one who'll come running ready to destroy the world to get to her.

"Show us why you're *the one*, Angel," she whispers against my lips.

She doesn't have to tell me a second time. My hands are on her ass, lifting her onto my waist before she can finish her command. I take her lips deepening the kiss.

Fuck a bed. I want Kaye to remember that I love all her curves. I handle them without question whenever I get my hands on them. Her questioning if I find Hayidah attractive stung. I didn't bring her here to doubt herself or how I feel about her.

The one time she tried to hide her body from me, I thought I made it clear that she's perfection personified to me. I wouldn't change a thing about Kaye. She was made just for me.

I meant what I said. Hayidah is beautiful, but when standing next to Kaye she might as well not be in the room. I prove that as I drive into Kaye, my eyes locked on hers. I can hear the buzzing of the toy Hayidah is across the room using, but I don't turn to see what she's doing.

Instead, I bounce Kaye on my cock, wringing her pleasure from her sexy body with each stroke. I bring her down on me repeatedly. The way her eyes roll into the back of her head tugs at something animalistic inside of me. I growl and bounce her harder.

"Yes, fuck yes," she cries out as she drips down my shaft.

I love it when she loses herself to our lovemaking. I grow harder inside her as her unfiltered words explode from her lips. She so wet. The way her insides are rippling around me, I know she's going to come soon.

"Shit, I feel it, come," I bark out.

"I'll come when I want to," she purrs back.

I chuckle darkly tilting her body back and dipping in for her left nipple. She's coming now. She wanted to see why I'm *the one*. I'm going to show her.

"Felix," she screams breathlessly.

I smile around her peak as she gushes around me. With her body still tilted back, I move to the table on the left side of the room. Placing her back gently on the surface, I let my hands roam her smooth skin.

Kaye smiles up at me, then takes a peek in Hayidah's direction. Her cheeks start to glow as if she's just registering the fact that she's allowing someone else to watch us. It's too late now. We're about to put on a real show.

Lifting both her legs to my right shoulder, I start to rock into her again. I have her full attention now. I work her pussy like the cameras are rolling and we need a money shot.

"Felix, shit, Felix," she begins to scream.

Good thing all of the club's rooms are soundproof. I don't let up, not even when I hear Hayidah start to cry out from pleasuring herself. I ride right through Kaye's next orgasm and the next and the next.

"Felix, I can't," Kaye sobs.

"You told me not to come, Mistress," I taunt.

"Oh, fuck, please come," she groans.

I chuckle, pulling out to shift her to her weakened legs. She wobbles on her heels. I hold her steady as I bend her over the table. Grabbing a handful of her bun, I bow her back, returning into her heat and chasing down my release.

"You want me to come," I hiss in her ear.

"Yes, please," she cries.

"You know what to do. Take it," I rumble in her ear.

Kaye starts to throw her ass back at me as she tightens her walls around me. I lick the side of her face, reaching to play with her clit as I pound deep into her.

We both come, filling the room with the sound of our climax. I roar so hard; my chest vibrates against her back. Kaye squirts all over me. Wrapping my arms around her quaking body, I hold her to me.

"So, what else do you need to know for your books?" I murmur.

Kaye giggles. I nuzzle her neck and inhale her skin. I love this girl so much.

"Actually, I want to learn to shoot," she replies a few moments later.

"Consider it done," I murmur.

CHAPTER THIRTY-THREE

My Rib

Kaye

Two months later ...

My man never disappoints. Felix wanted to teach me to shoot himself, but his workload wouldn't give him the time he felt I needed. He asked his older brother, Noah to help me.

I've always been sort of shy around Noah. He's huge and can be intimidating in size alone. Although, in the last few months I've learned that he's just a big old teddy bear.

He is so gentle and thorough in his teaching. I feel so much more confident than when we first started. I was scared to touch a gun before.

Now, I'm standing here, aiming at the target with nothing but determination and focus. I inhale and pull the trigger. With each shot I tear right through the target like Noah instructed me.

When the clip is empty, I nearly burst with excitement. I made all the kill shots just as he asked me to. I think I'm addicted to this.

I put the gun on safety and place it down. Removing my headgear, I do a little shimmy. Not only do I know how I'm going to write this into my book, I can actually shoot a gun.

"That was awesome, Kaye," Noah croons, holding up a hand for me to give him five.

"Thanks," I squeal, throwing my arms around his waist instead. "You've been so amazing. I had only planned to learn the mechanics. This was so much more than I could have hoped for."

"You're welcome. You're my brother's girl. We'll always be there to protect you, but when we can't be there, it's my job to make sure you ladies can handle yourselves," he replies.

"Yeah, I'm still debating on the self-defensive lessons. You still scare me a little," I admit with a giggle.

"If you can learn to take me, you can take anyone. Nellie and Bean have learned how to take a guy my size down without batting a lash. You're in good hands. I'll go easy," he chuckles.

"Still thinking," I chime.

"Okay," he says with a twinkle in his eyes. "I have something for you though."

I watch him as he walks over to one of the closets at the back of the range in the basement of the firm. The door to the range is slightly opened. Now that I'm not shooting, I can hear the sound of someone in the gym a few doors down where the boxing ring is.

"What's this?" I ask when he hands me a gift-wrapped box.

"Something you've earned," he says.

I move back to my station to place the box down and open it. Inside is a silver case. When I open the case, I find a gun nestled within.

"Don't worry. It's registered to you. Felix already set up a lockbox in the house," Noah says from behind me.

"It's gorgeous," I say as I run my hand over the top of the cold metal. "Thank you."

"No problem," he replies. "Felix texted for you to meet him in the gym when you're done. My girl is on her way down, I'm about to head out for a date. You need anything else before I'm gone?"

"No, I think I'm good. Thanks again, Noah. You've given me so much to use for my book. I appreciate everything you've done," I say, wrapping my arms around him again.

A throat clears, pulling both of our attention. I turn to see Bean standing in the doorway. I remember her from school. Like Nellie, I never had much interaction with her.

The way she's looking at me now, I don't think that's about to change. I go to step away from Noah, but he wraps an arm around my shoulder, tugging me into his side. Bean's eyes narrow on his limb embracing me.

"Rebecca, you know Kaye, don't you? You guys were in the same grade, right?"

Bean's eyes bounce over my face. Recognition doesn't register right away. I tell myself not to fidget. I'd probably be pissed if I walked in on Felix hugging someone else, I don't know or remember.

"Danny's sister," Noah continues trying to jog her memory. "She used to be with Felix a lot."

Her face lights up this time seemingly connecting the dots. My shoulders relax in relief. Noah is very handsome, but I have the Black brother that I've wanted all my life. Bean doesn't have to worry about me.

"Hey," she says, with a small wave.

"Hey." I wave back.

Noah releases me to walk over to Bean. He wraps an arm around her waist, drawing her into him. He leans into her ear to whisper something to her.

They are a beautiful couple. I watch Bean's lashes lower and her cheeks start to glow. When her eyes turn to Noah, I can see so much want in her gaze.

My brain starts to work, my hands itch to get to my laptop. Noah and Bean have just become my muse. I start to plot and plan their story.

"Kaye. Kaye?" Noah's voice pulls me back to the present.

My eyes come into focus. I see Noah and Bean looking at me expectantly. I start to fidget with the hem of my shirt. I have no idea what was said to me. This happens all the time.

"I'm sorry. What did you say?"

Noah chuckles. "Did we just become a book?"

I blush harder. I'm going to get Felix. He must have told Noah about me zoning out when I'm writing a book in my head.

"Um, I—"

"Really? Nellie mentioned you write novels," Bean says.

"Wait, I thought you didn't know who she was," Noah says, his brows drawing.

"I never said that," Bean says shrugging her shoulders.

Noah gives a hearty laugh, wrapping both arms around her shoulders and pulling her into his embrace. He looks at me over

Bean's head with mirth in his eyes. Yeah, we both know this is all totally going in a book.

"I was asking if you think you and Felix want to join us," Noah says.

"Oh, I don't think I can. I have to pick up Dashawn soon," I reply looking down at my watch.

"It would be cool to meet the little guy. Felix says he's quite popular and has a great social life," Noah teases.

"He does. Better than mine. He gets invited everywhere," I say and roll my eyes.

"Well, when he can fit some time into his busy little schedule, we'd all like to get to know him. I can see how much the two of you mean to Felix," Noah replies.

"If you know how much she means to me, why are you holding her up? You told me you guys were done fifteen minutes ago," a shirtless, sweat drenched Felix says from the doorway.

"Dude, aren't you supposed to be sparring?" Noah chuckles.

"I couldn't focus," Felix grumbles, training his eyes on me as he moves across the room.

"I bet," Noah laughs.

Felix flips him off, stopping in front of me. He places his forehead to mine. His wet, sweaty hair sticking to my face now.

"Hey," he breathes.

"Hi," I whisper back.

He takes my lips as soon as the word is out of my mouth. I cling to his wet skin, not caring that he's dripping all over me. We've both been super busy. I miss him.

"Yeah, that's love. He's all gross," Bean giggles.

"Like you haven't climbed all over my sweaty ass a time or two," Noah tosses back.

I laugh into Felix's mouth. He pulls away, rolling his eyes at the other two in the room. I lift on my toes to peck his lips once more.

"You guys should come over this weekend," Noah offers.

"Can't. I got saddled with surveillance this weekend," Felix huffs.

"A new schedule is up?"

"Yeah, Heather plugged in some new shit an hour ago."

"All right, the door is open. I'm heading out," Noah replies, slapping Bean's ass. "Let's go, sexy. I think you need to have a seat for a few hours as a reminder ..."

He leaves the end of his sentence open, but I get the feeling Bean finishes it in her head from the look on her face. I make more mental notes for my book. I'm lost in my head again when Felix's words pull my attention.

"Come get a tat with me," he says.

I turn to him with my brows knit. He can't be serious. I'm scared of a simple needle.

"I think you were hit upside the head."

"Maybe," he says and shrugs. He pulls me into his embrace. "Besides, I said come with me. Not get one."

"Oh, okay. That's different. I have to go pick up Dae-Dae," I reply.

"Your parents can watch him," he murmurs.

"They had him last weekend. I don't want to keep bothering them," I reply.

"They're his grandparents. Let them spend time with him. You need a break," he says.

I narrow my eyes at him. He's not fooling me. He has been talking me into taking Dae-Dae to my parents more often. He cuts my words off before I can point it out.

"You've been going nonstop. You have the new book in the works. That reader from the book tour calls all the time with updates and whatever—"

"Oh my God. You noticed that too," I groan. "Half the time I don't know what she's rambling about. How many times do I have to say I don't know these people or I just don't care? How do you know everyone's business? Like seriously."

Felix laughs. "Yeah, something is off about that. Are you sure you still want to do that event?"

"I don't know," I pout.

"Are Dean and Kia doing it?"

"No," I huff. "Neither of them have heard of her before either. Dean knows a lot of readers and authors.

"This one seemed so nice at first. I let her read a couple of chapters for this book to give a little feedback and it's gone downhill from there."

Felix's brows knit. I can see the wheels turning and his hackles going up. This man doesn't play with my safety.

"What did you say her name is again?"

"Bonnie something. I have to look in my inbox," I answer.

"Where does she live?"

"Georgia, no, wait, Florida or something. I can't remember," I say, trying to think. "I promise you. I honestly don't listen to her."

"Yeah, I know that. I can see when your ass zones out on her." He shakes his head at me.

"I can't help it. Books are always talking. People who know me well, know to just let me be by now."

"Very true. So, about this tat," he says, running his nose against my temple.

"What are you getting?"

"It's a surprise."

"Fine."

"Awesome, I already had your mom pick up Dae-Dae," he says and takes off running.

"I'm going to hurt you," I call after him.

I turn to clean up my space. After putting things away, I lift my gift from Noah. The weight of the box reminding me of what's inside.

Felix is lucky I don't pop him in his butt.

I giggle to myself and start after him. Target practice will be the only time I ever use this thing. I couldn't hurt a fly. Just think, I totally failed at flogging someone.

Felix

I'm nervous for Kaye to see the tat I have planned. When I got my Brothers Black tat on the side of my ribs, Kaye was the reason I placed it there. At the time, it was a subconscious thought.

"Felix, is that—" Kaye gasps when the artist pulls the stencil away.

"Yeah," I say, watching her face for her reaction.

Her eyes fill with tears. She reaches shaky fingers out but pulls them back before they touch my skin. Those full lips tremble and I just want to kiss her.

"I can't let you do that," she whispers.

"You're not letting me," I say with a shrug.

"Felix, it's so sweet but you can't," she retorts.

"Baby, I'm not asking you."

"Why would you want a picture of us drawn on your body?" she chokes out.

"Because you and Dashawn are everything to me," I answer truthfully. "Besides, in a way, you're already on my body."

"Huh," she knits her brows.

I point to my already tatted side. Her brows draw with more confusion. I wave her over to follow me as I hop on the table.

"I got shitfaced the night I found out about your brother's car accident. I was supposed to be with them that night. I had so much guilt and shit going on in my head.

"My brothers were there to get me through it. I know I wouldn't have made it without them. We decided to get the tats, so we'd be able to find each other in any life. This world or the after, something like that.

"I was so drunk, I'm surprised I remember that part. I do remember picking my side. All my drunken mind could think about was Danny asking me to look after you.

"I knew then, like I know now, I would always protect you. He never had to ask me. Almost four years ago, drunk out of my fucking mind, I still knew you were my other half.

"A part of me, just like my brothers. If anything ever happened to me, my brothers would be the ones to step in and make sure you're always okay. They would have your back like they have mine," I explain.

"But I still don't get it," she says softly.

"It may read Brothers Black, but it's placed where God created you from for me. If there is no me, my brothers will cover you. They will always cover you," I reply.

"Wow," she whispers. "Just wow."

CHAPTER THIRTY-FOUR

In My Head

Kaye

"Yes, yes, yes, yes," I sing to myself as I type way.

I'm so lost in this book. The characters are coming to life in front of me. Tweet's, "I Was Created for This," is playing in the background. My foot is tapping as I sway in my seat. I'm writing a powerful scene between my new favorite couple.

Tears are spilling over as I feel the emotions of my hero and heroine. The words are pouring out. I can see it all happening in my head. My scalp feels like it's tingling, and goosebumps cover my skin. Writing is such a high for me. The music is only enhancing the euphoria pumping though my veins.

I type in the finishing touches to close the scene and my mind starts to work on where I want to go from here. Picking up my notes I look through my timeline from the previous book. Chewing on the pad of my thumb, my thoughts start to come together.

Seeing just where I need to go. All the dots start to connect. I'm totally in the zone. I'm vaguely aware of the fact that at some point, I'll have to get up to use the bathroom and to eat.

The phone rings in the middle of me grasping a string of thoughts. Trying to follow the path through without losing it, I pick up the phone—not bothering to check for who's calling. I need to keep this book going if I want to finish on time.

"Hello," I say into the line jotting down a few things I want to hold onto.

"Hey, Kaye," Bonnie's voice greets my ears.

I scrunch my face and poke out my lip. I should have looked at the caller ID. I could've let this call go. I want to get this done.

"Hey, what's up? I'm in the middle of a scene. Do you need something?" I ask absentmindedly.

"Oh, I just wanted to check in and see if you've been sharing the event," she replies.

"Oh, I've mentioned it. I'll have to post or something later," I murmur.

"Oh, okay. Thank you for posting. I want to get the word out there. This is going to be so great," she gushes.

"Yeah, I'm sure it is. I'm excited about it. Listen, I'm working on this book. I'll talk to you later," I say as I read over the last thing I wrote.

"I can't wait for the next book. Your books give me life. I'm still fanning myself over Tristan," she says. "I can't wait until you get to his best friend."

"Yeah, I'm looking forward to writing that one," I say as my mind tries to shift to Lexington's book.

I have to stop that train wreck from happening. I need to stay focused on these characters. If I start thinking about others, I'll get totally derailed and will have to start notes or pages on that story just to move forward in this one.

Not happening today. Nope.

"I'm sure it's going to be hot," Bonnie coos.

"Yeah, we'll see. Well, I'm going to get back to this one though," I say by way of ending this call.

"Girl, I don't know how you do it. You create magic every time. I just love how their stories come together. Not a lot of authors can do what you do," she replies, not catching a hint.

"To each its own," I mumble.

"I was reading Vanity's latest book. It's not as good as the *Clever Love Series*. It just didn't flow. I think it's because she's going through some things in her personal life. Between her health and her husband that has to be a lot," she continues.

"No disrespect, but that's not feeding me or my son. So it's none of my business. I'm about these books that put food on my table. If it's not making me money, I don't have time for it," I say in frustration.

I'm so serious. I'm trying to focus. I don't even know the author she's talking about. Sure, I've seen her books and I think I read one or two of hers in the past, but I don't know her personally.

Even if I did, none of this is my problem or business. My mind is still stringing my book together. I start to filter out the noise that is Bonnie.

"I hear you. I do. It's just some authors could be ..."

I've tuned her out. This has become a pattern with her. I say I have to go, and she starts a new topic. Total pet peeve of mine.

Goodbye does not mean continue. I zone in on my book before me.

Oh yes, want to get that in there. Maybe, I should move this scene down a bit. I feel like I haven't established the connection enough yet. If I add a scene in here …

"I'm telling you. She has no idea what she's doing. Her husband is a good friend of mine. We're working on a few things together. That's how I know her. She used to write so much better, the mess she's been putting out lately though," Bonnie rambles into the phone.

I'm not listening to a word she's saying. This book is talking so loud. I need to get this stuff down. I scribble a few more notes before I put my pen down and start typing again.

"Mmm, oh, okay," I say into the phone.

I think I'm answering in all the right places. She keeps going so I must be. At this point, I truly don't care. She's changed the subject to something else. Some PA or something, but I'm still focused on my task at hand.

I'm lost in the words before me. This book is coming to life. I need to get as much done as I can before Dae-Dae gets home and needs my full attention. I don't know how much time goes by before I tune back in.

"I don't know what book they were reading. I loved *Paradise Is,*" Bonnie says pulling at the edge of my attention.

It's the title of my last book. I wasn't listening to what she was saying before now. I've been adding in words to the conversation here and there trying not to be rude.

I'm on complete autopilot. With a three-year-old and a busy career you learn to half listen and interact. I'll most likely be able to play back this conversation hours from now if I care to, but I'm totally not invested at the moment.

Well, until the mention of my book.

"I'm sorry what was that?" I say, shifting my focus back to the call.

"I was reading the reviews of *Paradise Is.* Those one and two star reviews are a mess," she replies.

I frown at the phone. The last thing I want to talk about while creating is reviews I avoid in the first place. I know I should end this and hang up, but curiosity always kills the cat. Like a fool, I take the bait.

"I don't read the reviews. My friends read them for me and tell me anything that's constructive," I say chewing on my lip.

Felix, Dean, and Kia read reviews for me. I value all their opinions. I know they'd be honest with me. They used to tell me all the time when something was missing. They tell me when a review has a good point about something we all may not have thought about.

I understand not every book is perfect to everyone. There will always be something someone wants more or less of. It's about my craft and what I thought was needed in the end. However, there's always a time or two when the light bulb goes off on a skill I can tweak.

"Oh, I get that. That makes sense because those reviews are a lot of BS. You're an amazing storyteller. I think you captured the heroine perfectly. There was nothing whiny about her at all.

"I mean, I didn't like Amina from Brave Hearts, but Charlese was everything," she sings into the line.

"What was wrong with Amina?" I ask, making more faces.

"*Well,*" she draws out. "She wasn't my favorite. I still liked the book, but she got on my nerves."

I know I shouldn't, but I take my butt right to my reviews. Felix and the girls would kill me if they knew. This is a rabbit hole we all agreed I wouldn't go down.

My shoulders sag as I start to read the reviews. Some of them are so harsh. Not harsh and constructive, but harsh and cruel. I shove my fingers into my hair and place my elbow on the desk before me. I knit my brows as my eyes scan the page.

My blackness is actually being questioned. Wow, I've never *not* identified myself as a black woman. My dad will tell you in a heartbeat that he's a black man, Samoan or not. I've always believed my characters to portray the women I grow up around—Black women.

"This is so wrong. Like, what the hell?" I whisper. "This has nothing to do with the book."

I blink back a few tears while reading one review in particular. It's an extremely cruel one because it's filled with lies and things that never happened or have any existence in my book. Why tell someone to not read my work just because you didn't have a taste for it.

Especially when it's clear they didn't read the book. If they did, it's clear it was without comprehension.

Wow.

"Dude, the fuck?" I hear growled over my shoulder.

I jump, turning my head up to see Felix looking down at me with concern. He cups my face, wiping my tears with his thumbs. Reaching for my computer he closes the browser.

"I have to go," I call into the phone still resting on the desk.

Felix cuts the call, tugging me from my seat. He pulls me into his arms, engulfing me in his presence. I can feel him pouring love into me. I need it so much more than he knows.

Those were some of the most hateful words I've ever read about my books.

"You can't be reading that shit. I thought we talked about this. Dean and Kia told you not to get caught up in that crap," Felix says into my hair.

His words soften as he chides me. I know finding me in tears wasn't something he expected to walk in on. It dawns on me that I'd been on the phone for way longer than I thought—hours.

The madness has to stop. I don't even know what the hell she was talking about half the time. Ugh!

A Fan

I glare at the phone. Her boyfriend just interrupted our moment. I felt like Kaye was about to open up to me.

I could hear it in her voice. We were on the verge of a connection. She never stays on the phone long when he's around.

It's like he forces her off the phone or something. I bet he's abusive. He sounds so controlling.

I dial Lisa. I still have time before I need to call one of my other author friends. She works during the day. I'll catch up with her tonight. Vanity is a mess, she needs me.

"Hello," Lisa answers the line.

"Hey, girl," I chirp into the line.

"Hey, how are you?"

"I'm good. I was having a great conversation with Kaye until her boyfriend came home. I'm concerned about her. I think he may be abusive," I reply.

"What? Are you serious?"

"Yeah, I've heard them argue before. Just now, he came in the house cursing at her and she rushed off the phone. It was so bad," I tell her.

"That's so messed up. She seems like such a sweet girl. She doesn't mention her personal life that much, so I don't know anything about him really. I hope she takes care of herself," Lisa says in concern.

"Yeah, I hope so. I'll check in on her tomorrow. You know, to make sure she's okay. I don't want to cause any problems calling back today."

"Yeah, I don't think you should," Lisa replies.

"It's so sad. She's so talented and writes about love. You would think she would want better."

"You never know people's story. Listen, I have to get back to my kid's homework. I'll call you back later," Lisa says.

"Oh, did you get my email. I want to go over the list of authors I booked," I say.

"I got it. We can go over it later."

"Okay, we need to stay on top of things," I say.

"Yeah, about that. I need to get back to the vendors tomorrow. Something went wrong with the check you sent over and the contract," Lisa says.

"Oh, I'll look into that. You work on the kid's homework. We can talk later, girl," I say quickly. "I have that stuff right in front of me. You don't have to worry about it."

"Oh, all right," Lisa replies, as one of her kids calls for her in the background.

"Later," I sing and hang up.

Maybe I should get lost in a book for a few hours. Yes, that's what I'll do.

CHAPTER THIRTY-FIVE

Just The Guys

Felix

"Hey, Uncle Ryan," Dae-Dae sings looking up at my brother.

"What's up?" Ry replies.

"So I was thinking. Mama says I can only ride my bike when someone is here to watch me," Dae-Dae says, turning it on thick with those big brown eyes.

"Say no more," Ryan laughs.

"This should be fun," Braxton snorts getting ready to follow.

We all know Ryan took the longest to learn how to ride his bike. I think he crashed all our bikes at least once. I still say it's because of his big ass head.

"Don't teach him to lead with his head," John teases.

"I was just thinking the same thing," I burst into laughter.

"Fuck you," Ry hisses.

"Kid, he'll have you in the shrubs," Noah teases. "Let me show you how it's done."

"*Yes*," Dae-Dae cheers, jumping up and down.

"I think he wanted to ask you anyway," I laugh.

Noah grins, shrugging his big shoulders.

I've been watching Dashawn follow Noah with his eyes since my brothers arrived. I think the kid is both fascinated and scared of the big giant. He has been getting up the nerve to talk to him all day.

It makes me think of how long it's been since he's been around my cousins. I make a mental note to have him around the guys more. They've taken to him like I knew they would. It's hard not to fall for the kid.

"Look at you, playing the family man," Wyatt teases.

"Yeah, I guess I am," I say, flipping the burgers on the grill in front of me.

Kaye is out taking some time for herself. I invited my brothers over to the house to hang out with me and Dae-Dae. After all, they've been asking after him.

"He's a cute kid," John adds.

"He's amazing."

"So what's the plan?" Wyatt asks.

"I want to propose. I was going to, but shit happened," I say.

"Okay, well, what about now?"

"Everyone doesn't have to get married just because you are," John mutters.

"In what language did I say they did?" Wyatt tosses back.

"Whatever," John replies.

"You want to tell me what's going on with you?" Wyatt narrows his eyes at him.

"Nope," John responds.

"How's Roni?" Wyatt asks, his golden eyes homing in on John.

John whips his head in Wyatt's direction. They stare each other down for a few beats before John curses under his breath. He runs a hand over the front of his hair.

"You can ask her yourself," John mumbles.

"What does that mean?" Wyatt grunts.

"She'll be here later. You can ask her yourself."

"Why is she in LA?" Wyatt and I say in unison.

"Wait, you know about her?" Wyatt turns to me and asks.

"Duh," I deadpan. "I've been working with Briggs and some of the trainees."

"She's not one of his trainees," John grates out.

"No, because she's yours. What the fuck have you been up to?" I narrow my eyes at John as I speak the words.

"Wait … hold on. So you're not fucking her?" Wyatt asks in confusion.

"No, she's a friend," John grits out.

"I'm totally lost," Wyatt huffs, placing his hands on his hips.

"Don't bust your brain. New York and the compound have been a hard sell. She doesn't trust easily. This … what's going on works. I'm not talking about it," John says in frustration.

"How'd you get this shit by me?" Wyatt pushes.

"Don't. Just leave it for now," John says, releasing a heavy sigh.

"I think I'm going to propose soon." I change the subject as I see both of my brothers getting annoyed.

"Just tell me the time and place and I'm there," John says.

"Yeah, you know I'm always here for you," Wyatt says pointedly, as he stares at John.

"Never a question," John replies to the words meant for him.

"Daddy," Dae-Dae squeals as he runs over to me.

I snap my head in his direction. He stops in his track as if catching his own words too late. He looks down at the ground in front of him with a long face.

I put down the spatula and go to lift him in my arms. Kissing his cheek, I put my forehead to his. It may have been a slip, but I felt it in my heart.

"Yes, son," I whisper to him.

He looks at me, his eyes lighting up. His little arms go around my neck, squeezing the breath out of me. I hold him back just as tightly.

"I love you, Lix," he says.

"Yeah, I'll be getting on that," I say to my brothers as they watch us.

"Sounds about right," John says.

CHAPTER THIRTY-SIX

Life Changing

Kaye

One month later ...

I think I'm going to be sick. I might faint. I honestly don't know what to do with myself.

This is insane. Just when I thought life couldn't be any more of a dream come true this happens. A week ago, I became a New York Times bestseller.

Today, I've been offered an opportunity to make a movie out of one of my books. I'll be helping with the adaption of the book and everything.

This is all happening so fast. At least it seems that way. I feel like in the blink of an eye, all my dreams have come true.

I've been sitting here for about an hour thanking God repeatedly. However, all of this will be happening overseas in Ireland of all places. This is so unexpected.

I don't even know how I'm sitting here with this opportunity. I'm waiting to wake up from this dream, but there is a voice on the inside of me that keeps telling me this is real. This is so big for my career.

I want to ride this wave, but Dae-Dae is turning four soon. I can't just uproot his life yet again and drag him around the world. He'll be in preschool.

Dae-Dae loves my parents and grandparents. I couldn't possibly pull him away from them. Yet, this is a chance of a lifetime. An entire year away, that's a lot.

I think of Felix and my heart sinks. I'll be leaving him behind. I know he can't come with me.

Both Dae-Dae and I will miss him like crazy. I don't know what to do. I need to decide soon though.

The agent who called me to make the offer explained that I have to get back to them sooner than later. My head is still spinning. I don't know how my work ended up on her desk in the first place.

I think my head is going to explode any second now. I'm totally awed. My stomach rolls again.

I force myself to breathe. I try to think of all the pros and cons to this. Going means I'll take my career to the next level.

I'll have a movie on my resume. This could mean a traditional deal or more exposure as an indie author. I mean, the possibilities are endless.

Dae-Dae could experience a different culture. I'd need someone to watch him. Dean has been wanting to get away.

She could always come along. My head is spinning at the thought of this actually happening. Yet, at what cost?

Leaving everything behind just doesn't seem right. My heart literally aches with the thought of sacrificing one for the other.

Remembering how hard it was to be away from Felix when I lived in New York, I let out a shuddered breath. Heck, I pout when he can't come spend the night here at the house. He refuses to let me take the long drive in when he knows he can't make it.

I've been to his apartment once to sleep over. He prefers to be at the house with Dae-Dae. Another nod to the importance of stability.

I've talked about us moving closer to Felix and my family. My grandparents moved out of the guesthouse last month. Most of their friends live around my mother and father's neighborhood.

Felix agreed that it would be a great idea for me to move, but I get the sense that he's been waiting for something. I guess that's for the best. I would have hated for him to purchase yet another home for me if I do decide to up and leave.

My phone rings and hope blooms in my chest that it's my girls calling. We are due for a writer's chat. When I look up at the clock, my hope deflates.

It's too early for either of them. I look at the phone and groan. It's Bonnie.

I'm not in the mood today. To be honest, if I take this offer, I'll have to cancel the signing with her group.

Not that I believe I'm going anyway. Something about her hasn't been sitting right with me. I've been avoiding conversations with her more and more.

I've actually been annoyed by the fact that she wants me to do so much of the promoting of her event. I mean, it's way more than others have wanted.

I don't see the other authors she's mentioned doing much. In fact, I don't see many readers buzzing about it either, which is odd. Then again, I've had my head down working on my books and plotting my next move.

When the phone stops ringing, I pick it up to call Felix. I think we need to talk. Before I can swipe to dial his number, Bonnie's number comes up again.

"She can't be serious," I mutter.

Her partner Lisa emailed me once. It was short, sweet, and to the point. This chick is working a damn nerve. What the heck could she possibly want that she's calling me back to back?

I let it ring out again. I'm not in the mood to get caught in her rambling. She keeps going and going and going. I've told her many times I've had to go, and she'll just roll right into the next conversation that she carries on her own.

I toss the phone down, too annoyed now to call Felix. I need to clear my head. I get up and go into the bedroom to put on the new yoga pants and top I purchased the other day.

I'm starting to feel like my weight is becoming a problem. I was running after Dae-Dae in the back yard the other day and I was so winded I thought I'd pass out. Not to mention, my knees and back have been hurting from sitting and typing so much.

Maybe a little yoga will help whip me back in shape. It's sure to help me clear my mind. I change and make my way back out to grab a bottle of water.

When I pass my phone, it's lit up. Reaching for it, I tap the screen and see five more missed calls from Bonnie and a voicemail. Starting to get concerned that something might actually be wrong, I listen to the voicemail.

"Hey, girl. It's me. I had some questions about those chapters you sent me. Oh, and you won't believe what's going on in Diane Spark's group—"

I cut the message off right there, baring my teeth at the phone. I don't have time for this bull crap. Why would you blow up my phone just to tell me some gossip I don't give a crap about?

This isn't high school. I have real things going on in my life. Not to mention, I haven't sent her chapters in, I don't know how long.

I stopped asking for BETA readers after the last book. Dean and Kia give real feedback and professional critiques. I found Bonnie and the few other readers I tried didn't give any useful feedback, if any at all.

I was starting to feel like they were taking advantage of me, which wasn't fair to me or the readers who get the end result. I always want to give my best work. Every useful critique helps.

I breathe through my frustration and storm out to the backyard. Yeah, I need to do this yoga session before I lose all my marbles. As for that bus tour—I'm not going even if I don't go to Ireland.

Enough is enough. I'll email Lisa once I've calmed the heck down. I'm over Bonnie. I don't even know who Diane Sparks is.

Lord, give me strength.

CHAPTER THIRTY-SEVEN

Will You—

Felix

This is it. I'm going to propose this weekend. I've been getting everything together for weeks to do this right. It's all set.

I've been avoiding calling Kaye all day. I'm scared shitless I'm going to fuck this up before Saturday. I shouldn't be going out to the house for just that reason, but something was off when I talked to Kaye briefly about two hours ago.

My heart is racing as I pull into the driveway. I just don't have a good feeling. Throwing the car into park, I get out and make my way to the house.

It's like I'm moving in slow motion. I hear every sound around me as if it's amplified. Pushing my key into the lock, I walk into the house.

All the lights in the front of the house are out. However, I can see that the master bedroom light is still on. Drawing a hand down my face, I move toward my fate.

When I step into the bedroom, our eyes lock. I know I'm right. Something is wrong.

Kaye's face is covered in worry and anxiety. Stepping out of my shoes, I move to the bed to climb in beside her. I gather her in my arms and shift her into my lap. She places her head on my shoulder.

"Talk to me," I murmur. "What's going on?"

She blows out a shaky breath, reaching to toy with the buttons on my shirt. I start to rub her back. At this point, I don't know which one of us I'm trying to soothe. On the outside, I'm showing my patience. Inside, I'm falling apart, and I don't know why yet.

"This should be one of the best times in my life," she murmurs. "I'm doing things I used to only dream of. I just don't know what to do."

"Hold on, I feel like I'm missing something," I say, trying to put the pieces together.

Kaye releases a deep, long breath. Lifting her head, she looks into my eyes. I can see the conflict and war within her pretty orbs.

It's like she's slipping through my fingers. I sense it. I want to stop it, but I can't.

"I … I got a call today. It was from an agent. I'm being offered a movie deal—"

"Baby, that's totally fucking awesome," I croon, cupping her face.

"Yeah, it is. They want me to help adapt the script and everything. I'd be involved in the project for a year," she says with a weak smile.

I draw my brows in. I'm not understanding why this is a problem. We should be celebrating and jumping off the walls.

"I don't understand, what's the problem. Do you need me to look into things and make sure it's all above board?" I offer, trying to grasp what I'm still missing.

Her eyes lower to her lap, where her hands are now fidgeting. I swallow hard. I see the wrecking ball coming.

"I'd have to live in Ireland for a year. Maybe a bit longer. It's where they're going to film the movie," she says just above a whisper.

It's like I'm watching all my plans for the weekend crumble. I know I can't ask her to marry me now. If I do, she won't take this opportunity.

I know Kaye too well. My throat is clogged with so many emotions. I want to be selfish and tell her everything.

I want to tell her that we can still get married before she leaves or at least get engaged until she comes back. Yet, I know, if I utter a single word about an engagement, marriage, or anything remotely close to where I want to take our future— she's not going to go.

"It's only a year," I manage to push out.

I surprise myself with how strong my voice comes out. Within, I've died a thousand times already. Being away from Kaye always leaves me looking for my next breath.

"But that's a year without you and what about Dae-Dae. I'm going to be dragging him away from everyone. I mean, do they have preschool at his age in Ireland? Will they take him as a student? I could homeschool I guess," she rattles off.

It slays me, but my brain starts working out the details. I know we can make this work because it's all a part of her dream. Once I look into this and make sure it's legit, I'm going to do everything in my power to make this happen for her.

"Your parents would take him," I say, feeling the pang that tears through my chest.

Dashawn is Kaye's son. She may not have given him birth but she's the only mother he has ever known. She loves him as if she did carry him for nine months herself.

I know leaving him behind will be the hardest thing Kaye has ever had to do. Just as I thought, she stiffens in my lap. I see the stubborn look that comes over her face.

I'm ready for the fight. She deserves to have this.

"I'm not leaving him behind. I'm his mother. My parents raised their children. I'm not going to saddle them with a four-year-old," she grunts, folding her arms across her chest.

"You're not saddling them with anything. They want to help out. Besides, I'll be here. I can help out," I offer.

"You don't have time for that," she mutters.

"I always have time for him. How much time do we have before you have to leave? We can move you guys closer to everyone. Get him settled into the new place and I'll move in with him when you leave," I muse. "That way I can drop him off in the mornings and pick him up at night, but he's in a familiar place."

Her face softens. She leans in to place a tender kiss against my lips. Her hand caresses my cheek.

"I love you. I love you so much more for always trying to make my dreams come true, but I can't ask you to do that," she says.

"You're not asking," I reply.

"Don't." She shakes her head. "Don't do that. I'm no fool, Felix. Your job is demanding and at times dangerous. You don't have time to play daddy for my responsibility."

I look away from her. Her words cut deeper than she knows. Dashawn is as much my son as he is hers. They are my family. Shit just keeps getting in the way of me making it official.

"I'll make it work," I mutter.

Kaye tips my face toward her with her fingertips. When I look in her eyes, I see it. She's made her decision. I think I'm going to bleed out.

"You've done so much for us. I won't ask you for a thing more. Everything I've worked for has led up to this. I want this, but I'm not going to burden anyone to have it," she says.

"Kaye, you're not burdening anyone. If anything, you've been the one carrying the burden."

I know I've said the wrong thing the moment the words are out of my mouth. Kaye climbs out of my lap and off the bed. She's pulling away from me and I'm at a loss to stop it. I'm too stunned that she might be moving over five thousand miles away from me.

"Dae-Dae has never been a burden to me. I probably never would have been bold enough to do any of this if it weren't for him. This is the least I can do for Danny," she sobs. "I thought you of all people would understand how important it is to me that I give that little boy the life I know my brother would have wanted for him—"

"Kaye, don't blow this out of proportion. You know that's not what I meant," I interject.

She swipes at her tears shaking her head at me. I get up, moving toward her. I just want to hold her in my arms. Kaye lifts her hands to halt me.

"Maybe this is what we need. We should probably take a break. You've done enough taking care of us," she chokes out.

"I'm glad you're choking on that bullshit. I love you. You have no idea how much I love you. I see what you think you're about to do. Not with me, baby," I growl.

"What are you talking about?" she grunts back.

"I'm not having that shit. You run your ass off if you want. I guarantee you; I'll be right on your ass. You don't have to hurt people for them to let you go when it means bettering yourself," I reply.

"You don't understand," she pleads.

"Bullshit," I snort. "I want this for you as much as you want it for yourself. Don't try to make this into something it's not. This isn't one of your books. I'm a real man." I point to my chest.

"I know how to let you go follow your dreams. If you want me to help with Dashawn, I'm here for that shit all day. If not, I'll support you taking him with you." I pause to get in front of her, ducking to be face to face with her.

"For keeps, Kaye. I'll be here waiting for you as long as I have to. I love you and need you as much as my next breath.

"I've told you before. I'm not your father. Stop trying to treat me like I am. You fight with me, fine, but before we go to bed we're making up and fucking.

"Simple as that. There's no silent treatment for three years or the year you're away becoming an amazing filmmaker. Don't even try it," I hiss and cup the back of her neck.

I crush my lips to hers and show all the love I have for her. I can taste her tears on my tongue, driving me to kiss her deeper. I know Kaye better than she knows herself.

"I love you," I say against her lips. "We'll never sacrifice us. We don't have to. We'll make this work."

"Okay." She nods, her fingers clinging to the collar of my shirt. "Okay, you're right."

"I know I am," I tease. "Now come here. We need to make up for all the time we'll be missing each other."

Kaye

He is gorgeous when he sleeps. Reaching to brush a lock of hair from his forehead, I smile down at him. I don't know what I was thinking earlier.

I figured it would be easier if … I don't know. Felix is right. I tried to fall back on a bad habit that's childish.

This is going to hurt so it is. If I would have succeeded at hurting us both, I don't think I would have made it a month much less a year. We both deserve better.

Please wait for me, Felix. I'll be back. I promise.

Those are my last thoughts before I snuggle into his side and pass out. I fall asleep trusting my man. Like he said, we'll make this work.

CHAPTER THIRTY-EIGHT

Cancel

Kaye

One week later ...

I'm wary of using my cell for business calls after how things turned out with Bonnie. She's still calling my phone at all hours. I haven't told Felix. He would flip out.

I think he's stressed out enough. I know Dae-Dae and I leaving has been a big blow, but I can't help feeling like there's something else going on. He keeps telling me that everything is fine, but I don't believe that.

I almost talked myself out of doing this. I saw the look on his face when I found out I had a week to make the move. This has been so hard on everyone.

I had to do things so quickly. Felix handled a lot of the details, but there was still so much for me to do. Dean offered to come along before I could ask. She had already wanted to make a change, and this was right up her alley.

The best surprise was Connie's call to let me know she would be in Ireland. For some reason that made it easy to breathe again. I made it through telling my parents and explaining to them that I wasn't going to leave Dashawn behind.

My dad was upset. I knew he would be. He glared at Felix the entire time as if Felix was supposed to make me change my mind.

In the end, both of my parents gave their blessings and offered to come help out anytime I needed. I got all of that squared away, but I totally forget to contact Lisa. There is no way I'm making that book tour.

At this point, I just want to deal with Lisa. I'll let her know I can't make it and that will be that. Making the call through my google line, I wait for someone to pick up.

Dae-Dae and Felix are at Felix's grandmother's house. Connie is here with me, helping me to get settled in while one of Felix's uncles made the trip to pick up Dean.

"Hello," a voice finally says on the other end.

"Hi. May I speak to Lisa, please," I reply.

"This is she."

"Oh, great. This is Kaye Blaze, the author."

"Hi. It's so nice to hear your voice. You're such a talented author. I truly enjoy reading your books," she says.

"Thank you. Thank you so much. I was calling because I needed to inform you guys that I won't be able to make the book tour," I say.

There is an awkward pause on the other end. I bite the pad of my thumb. I truly hate to disappoint her and the fans. There is just no way I'll be able to get back and not for that many days.

"I'm sorry, Kaye. The tour was cancelled months ago. I thought you were informed. You should have received your twenty-five dollars back by now," she says nervously.

I whip my head back then I look at the phone like I can see her and gauge if she's crazy. First, I've been pushing the event and I've seen posts about it. Second, I paid a lot more than twenty-five dollars.

I put the phone back to my ear and start to count backward. I can feel I'm about to get placed in the middle of some mess. I don't need this right now. I have to report to work in the morning and Felix flies back to the States tomorrow night.

"I truly am sorry. I haven't been on social media much, so I didn't make the announcement. I had a fire in my home and my laptop was ruined. Then, there were a few other issues. Bonnie promised she'd take care of everything," she continues.

As I said, this is my first time talking to Lisa. We've emailed once. I don't know what's going on or what to believe at this point. I'm so pissed off. I know the last thing I need to do is to get caught up in this.

"Okay, well, thank you for your time," I say. "You have a good one."

"Yes, okay, thank you," she says still sounding uneasy.

Twenty-five dollars? Ain't this about a—. Calm your nerves, Kaye.

Felix

It's always great spending time in Ireland with my family. I can't begin to tell you how relieved I was when I found out they would be producing the film not far from them. I was able to take the reins and set things up for Kaye and Dashawn.

Yes, there are cams all over the cottage. Carrick took care of that for me. That will allow me to breathe easier.

Connie has been in Ireland a lot lately. When I reached out and told her Kaye would be here, she was ecstatic. Granted she's much further out, but still within driving distance.

This will be okay. It's just a year. I'll be on a plane to come see them every chance I get.

Too bad I haven't been able to convince myself of my own words. I haven't slept well since Kaye made the announcement that this all had to be done in a week. Contracts were signed, the house was packed up and rented out, Kaye and Dae-Dae spent their last days in the States with me in my apartment.

That place is going to feel so lonely without them. I've been toying with selling the place. We already have a home waiting for us when Kaye comes back home.

It was a part of her engagement gift. My chest hurts when I think of the ring in my top drawer back home. Temptation almost caused me to place it on her finger.

However, I've been watching Kaye watch me. She's been waiting for a reason to back out of this. I'm not giving her one.

She's going to see her dreams come true and then she can come home. I'll be there waiting.

"Hey, you." The sound of her sweet voice comes up behind me.

I've been standing out here looking over the view, while she put Dae-Dae to bed. My grandmother spoiled us with food and attention. Dashawn wore himself out trying to hang with the big guys.

"Did Dean get settled in?" I ask, pulling her into my arms.

Kaye laughs, throwing her head back. She looks gorgeous. I've thought about extending my stay a few times, but the office is already short staffed. Wyatt and Noah have been out on assignment for going on two months.

"She's not here. She took off with your uncle and Connie," Kaye giggles. "I think your uncle has a thing for my friend."

"Uncle Ronan has a thing for women, period. You'd be doing your friend a favor by telling her to leave him alone," I warn.

"She's a big girl. She'll be okay," she says. "This place is great. I think Dae-Dae will enjoy it here."

"Yeah, we loved coming here when we were little. Some of our best memories come from visits to my grandmother," I reply.

"Is it weird that hearing that makes me feel like we'll be closer to you?"

"Not at all. I'm glad things worked out for you to be here. There are some shitty areas that I wouldn't have been too happy about," I murmur.

"Thank you, Felix. Thanks for always being there," she says.

"I'll always be here when you need. I mean it, Kaye. If you need me, you tell me."

"We'll be fine," she says with a small smile.

"You're amazing. This is going to be awesome for you. It'll go by faster than you know."

"I'll be counting down." She gives a small chuckle.

"That makes two of us. You'll be back home before you know it."

"Just a year. Nothing to it. What could happen in a year right?" she asks nervously.

I groan internally. As a PI, I know those are famous last words. All hell has broken to those words more often than not.

I don't say that to Kaye though. I cover her lips with mine and kiss her like it's my last. I'm going to miss her soft lips.

Next, week. Next week, I'll try to make it back.

CHAPTER THIRTY-NINE

BFF

Kaye

People are so grimy. I can't believe the screenwriter they hired on this project tried to throw me under the bus. Like, who does that? I'm fuming.

I didn't sign up for this BS. If I wasn't under contract, I'd be ghost. That asshole, Rodney has been getting on my last nerve. He makes the dumbest changes to the screenplay and then blames me for being an amateur. I'm tired of it.

I've been pacing for the last ten minutes. I want to call Felix but between the time difference and all the things that have been going on with Nellie back home, I don't want to bother him.

Felix was so upset while Nellie was in the hospital. Hearing the tension in his voice had me ready to get on a plane and go back home. I sort of wish I had.

So much is going on in Felix's life and I want to be there for him. He's an uncle now. I think getting to spend time with the twins has soothed how much he misses Dae-Dae.

Dae-Dae, on the other hand, isn't adjusting the same. It's killing me. We're both miserable. Connie said she would come by and take him to meet a new friend.

Dean is doing her best, but she's not totally sold on kids. She's great to Dae-Dae, but I think they're both over each other. Of course, Felix and his brothers have fond memories of being here.

They had family, cousins who were their age to play with. I feel so foolish for dragging Dae-Dae here thinking it would be so great for him. I think I rushed into this.

It seems like I always rush into things that I should spend more time thinking about. I start to fume more when I think about my conversation with Lisa.

I still haven't gotten to the bottom of that. At this point, I don't even care. I'm glad I dodged that train wreck.

However, *this* … this mess I'm dealing with at the moment has me seeing red. I'm so frustrated.

You should send him back home with mom and dad.

I start to rub my temples. I've had that thought a lot over the last few weeks. Knowing that Toby has little ones closer to Dae-Dae's age. Then the children at the church.

Am I being selfish?

I feel like it. Wanting Dae-Dae here with me, wanting this movie, I went as far as dragging a friend here with me. Me, me, me—that's how this is all starting to feel.

I should just pack us all up and go home. Maybe, just maybe I chased one dream too many. Heck, I don't even know if they've picked a cast worthy of my book.

The actors all start to arrive on location today. Yet, that jerk is making a mockery of my book. Well, wait, let me say that part right. He is making a mockery of my book only to turn around and present my ideas and suggestions when getting called out on the BS he tries to pass off.

Lord, give me strength. Please show me the right thing to do.

I'm about to explode. I need to get this off my chest before I punch a hole through something. Mainly Rodney's stupid face.

I snatch my phone from my pocket and pull up my social media profile. I don't normally rant about my personal life on here, so I keep it short and sweet. Enough to get it off my chest but not get into details. That's all I need.

I value trust, but I know it's not deserved by all.

I post the message and feel a fraction better. Although, ranting a full out page about this trip and working with that jerk would totally feel better. I miss my man.

"Hello there, Lass," I turn to the sound of a deep timbered voice.

I have to tip my head back to get a look at the source of the voice. Blue-green eyes are staring back at me from underneath thick amber brows. His face is covered in a full beard, but I can see the curve of his full lips.

Holy Cow! This better be my Tristan.

Tristan is the main character in the book and this guy nails him one hundred and fifty percent. The height, the broad shoulder, his accent—he is perfect for the role. Just wow.

"Hi," I reply when my thoughts stop rambling.

"You're the author, aye? Kaye?" he says.

"Yes, that's me." I nod.

"Grand, nice to meet you. I spent some time in the States while a young lad. I'll be honest. I think I fell in love with your characters. Makes me want to go back there to see if I can find that kind of love," he rumbles out.

"You read my book?" I ask with my brows knitted.

"Aye, I've read them all. Started with the one for the movie and couldn't stop there. Och, where are my manners. I'm Jacob McTavish, I'll be playing Tristan."

"*Yes*," I woot before I can catch myself.

I clamp my hands over my mouth. I want to crawl into myself. My face flames. I wish the floor would open and swallow me now.

"I haven't gotten that kind of reaction in a long time. Maybe there's something to dating American women," he teases.

"I'm so sorry. This has been the last few days from hell, and I've been so worried about casting. They were being so tight lipped about your role," I try to explain.

"Dinna fash yersel', lass," he chuckles. "That would be my own fault. I wasn't sure I'd make it in for the part until the last minute. I just made the trip over from Scotland."

"It's nice to meet you, Jacob." I hold my hand out, finally giving a proper greeting.

"You've already made the trip worth it. I'm a huge fan. I think we'll be good friends," he says with a wink, shaking my small hand in his. "You've already made this Scot feel welcome in this sea of Irishman."

"I guess that's because I'm in love with an Irish-Scot. I get the best of both worlds and can hang with the best of them," I reply to make sure he knows I'm taken.

"Och, should have known a beauty like you would be taken. I'll still take the friendship anyway. Rumor has it you have a lad my son and daughter's age. That's what made my decision. The producer promised there'd be a nanny for the three," he says.

"Really?"

This is the first I'm hearing of this. I thought no one was listening when I asked about daycare or something for my son. If they truly bring in a nanny that will be some time and stress off Dean.

"Aye, wasn't making the trip without them," he says firmly, all humor gone.

"Where's their mom?"

"You'll have to let me take you to lunch for that story," he says, his smile returning.

I eye him warily. When I see Rodney heading our way, I grab Jacob's hand and take off in the other direction. I'm not ready to be around that jerk again just yet.

A Fan

I've read Kaye's post over and over again. That fucking Lisa ruined everything. I know she went running to Kaye like she did the others.

They've all been asking for their money back. I had to create a second account and blocked most of them on the other one. I don't have that money to give back. If Lisa wasn't such a whiny bitch, I wouldn't have to give any of it back in the first place.

I would have made things work. It would have been just fine. So what her life was falling apart, I would have handled things. Now look.

I value trust, but I know it's not deserved by all.

"You can trust me," I shout at the computer.

I start to pace the room. Kaye was my ace in the hole. Her career is taking off. I could make so many things happen for myself through her.

"You can trust me! You didn't have to take this to social media and tell our business to the world! You could've come to me! We're friends. You should've come to me!"

My neighbor bangs on the wall. Fuck them, I hate them and their smelly dog. He's always barking at my cat.

Well, when I had a cat. Mr. Pennies hasn't been home in weeks. Everyone tries to leave me. Everyone except my book boos. They never leave.

"And they don't talk about me on the internet!" I shake my fist at the computer screen.

I shake my head, running a hand through my hair. She didn't have to do this. We were friends. I almost told her my real name. We talked for hours.

She listened to me. No one ever listens to me. She would let me say what I wanted without cutting me off. We had a connection.

"It's that bitch Lisa's fault. She ruined everything!"

Calm down. It's not over. We'll just call her. We can explain.

"Yes, yes, this can be fixed. You're friends. I'll fix this."

The sun will come out tomorrow and this will be right as rain. I'll just read a book for now to calm my nerves. This will all blow over.

You'll see.

CHAPTER FORTY

Dropping In

Felix

Three months later ...

Kidnapping, Kings and Queens, babies being born in the midst of this chaos, becoming a part of the Alliance we were trying to avoid. Yeah, life has been super fucked up around my family. I haven't been able to get away.

I miss Kaye so much it hurts. If I get a call about someone targeting my family—or any other shit that will make me have to turn around before I get to my woman to spend at least a few days with her—I'm going to lose my shit. No lie, I'm setting some shit on fire, blowing some shit up, feeding a few motherfuckers to the dogs.

I just want my girl. I need to be wrapped up in Kaye for as long as I can. I need to inhale her for a few hours before I let her up for air. I ache to have those thick thighs wrapped around me.

Kaye has been sounding a lot happier the last few months. The first few weeks I was sure she was going to come back home. She wouldn't say it, but she was miserable. I heard it in her voice.

She tried to hide it because I had so much going on, but I know things weren't going smoothly for her. Connie would only tell me that Kaye was trying to adjust. I got the feeling it was deeper than that.

I haven't told anyone that I'm flying in. I wanted to surprise Kaye. In a family as big as mine, I've learned that surprises only happen when you act fast and keep them to yourself.

I'm surprised no one has spilled to Kaye that I planned to propose twice. It's probably because the first time my mom and dad were the only ones who knew. This last time Kaye was gone before anyone could let the cat out of the bag.

My lips turn up as I think of the day when I finally get to place a ring on her finger. It's going to happen. This visit was a little too impromptu for me to move forward this time.

Rolling up to the cottage, I can't park fast enough. The lights are still on inside, which means Kaye is most likely still awake. It's ten in the evening here.

The nearly eleven-hour flight and the nine hour time difference is kicking my ass, but I'm not going to let that stop me. I feel my second wind kicking in just from knowing Kaye is in that house.

Cutting the car off, I retrieve my bag and the bouquet of roses. I start for the front of the house. When I push into the door, my smile falls from my lips. Kaye is sitting in the middle of the living room floor with a big ass ginger, and he isn't one of my cousins.

They both turn toward the door I just walked through. When the guy sees me, he stands as if he's ready to fight. I drop my bag, but before I can take a step or toss the flowers, Kaye gasps and rushes across the room.

She has those thighs wrapped around my waist, as she jumps into my arms and locks around me. Her soft lips are on mine, while she cups my face. I brace her weight against me with my arms under her thighs, still holding onto the bouquet in one palm.

When I groan into her mouth she pulls away with a giggle, kissing all over my face. I look over her shoulder at the guy standing in the middle of my woman's home. His look of disappointment both pisses me off and satisfies me at the same time.

Kaye seems to have forgotten all about her guest. She wraps her arms around my neck, squeezing the life out of me. I rub her back soothingly as her emotions hit me. She's not crying, but I can sense so much going on within her embrace.

She has needed me more than she let on. I knew with everything in me it was time to make this trip. It was almost as if I could feel her heart calling for mine as much as I felt my own calling for hers.

"I'm here now," I murmur when she tucks her face into my neck, pulling my attention back to her.

"I've missed you so much," she says on a sigh.

It's the sound of coming home after a long day and finally getting to rest your feet. She nuzzles my neck with her nose inhaling me. The cutest purr comes from her lips. I chuckle, turning to kiss her temple.

"I should be going, lass," the dude clears his throat and says.

I frown, picking up the Scottish note to his timbre. I still don't know who he is or why he's here and I don't like it. I place Kaye on her feet as she slides down my front. She takes the flowers from my hand, clutching them to her chest.

"Oh shoot, Jacob. I'm sorry. This is my boyfriend," Kaye says softly.

I look at her wondering why she's whispering. Kaye places a finger to her lips, leading me closer to the couch and this Jacob dude. He holds out his hand, drawing my eyes to it.

Kaye gives me a nudge, so I take his hand, but I put all my strength into the shake. He returns the gesture, trying to keep a straight face. I can see in his eyes he wants to pull back.

I release his hand, turning to the couch that was out of my view when I entered the cottage. Dae-Dae and two little gingers are fast asleep, all leaning against each other. It clicks in my head, these two must be Max and Gracie. Dashawn has been talking about them for months now. I think they made the difference for him.

I was concerned about him in the beginning. He whined for me a lot when I would call. Once he met his new friends, they've been all he talks about since.

"I'll collect my wee uns and go," Jacob says.

"Thanks for dinner. I know they all had a ball," Kaye replies, placing the bouquet down on the coffee table.

"I should be thanking you." Jacob's cheeks redden.

"It was fun," Kaye giggles.

"You work on the set?" I ask.

"Aye, I play Tristan. The leading role," Jacob says, his chest puffing up.

He says it like it means something. I don't give two shits. I know who the real Tristan is. I think his ass should as well.

I chuckle. "I enjoyed being the muse for that character. Actually, I love any time I can give her a new hero to write about."

Kaye places a hand over her brow and dips her head. I can see her cheeks glowing. She's probably going to tell me off when this guy leaves.

Fuck it. At least he knows.

"You're a lucky man," he murmurs, lifting the two children in his arms. "Some would kill to have a lass like her in their life."

"Or get killed trying," I boom.

"Goodnight, Jacob. Enjoy your weekend. I'll see you guys on Monday," Kaye rushes out.

"Aye, Monday," Jacob grumbles, heading out with the two children.

Kaye follows to open the door. A car is waiting outside. He must have called for his driver when Kaye and I were wrapped up in each other.

Kaye closes the door behind them once they are all tucked into the car. Shrugging out of my jacket, I turn for Dae-Dae to get him into his bed. Kaye follows behind me silently. I'm not sure her silence is a good thing. I can feel the daggers she's tossing into my back.

I move quickly to get Dashawn into his pajamas, like I've done a million times. He is knocked out for the count. He must have had an exciting day.

Placing a kiss on his forehead, I turn out the light and leave to close the door behind us. Kaye stops outside of the room with her hands on her hips. I know that scowl.

I didn't come all this way to fight. I duck to kiss her lips but she turns her face from me. Fine, she wants to set a challenge, I'm game. Reaching for one of her hands, I lace my fingers with hers.

I go to retrieve my bag before leading her to the master bedroom. Kaye doesn't protest, but she's not yielding completely either. I can still tell she's stewing.

Entering the room, I place my bag on the bed. Releasing her hand, I dig out my glasses a bottle of champagne and the book I bought for her. I see the little smile that twitches at the corner of her lips. She still won't give in though.

I put on my glasses, taking the book and champagne into the bathroom with me. I set the items on the countertop, moving for the claw foot tub to run the bath water. I find the bubble bath I've been shipping over once or twice a month in her care packages.

I always send little things to let her know I'm thinking of her. Books I hear her mention—because although she'll read on her e-reader—she prefers to read paperbacks. Socks to keep her feet warm when she mentions missing my heat.

Candy she can't find here. Name it, I try to send whatever I know will place a smile on her face. The bright smiles I get over Facetime whenever I send something over makes my life.

Dashawn's happy squeals are just icing on the cake. I never leave him out. I send him his own package every time.

Pouring the vanilla and pineapple scented liquid into the bath, I watch the bubbles form. I turn to find Kaye leaning against the doorjamb watching me, still fighting to keep that smile from her lips. I keep my eyes on her, as I come out of my shirt and toss it to the floor.

"Come here, baby," I coax.

Kaye

That sexy rasp is just not fair. I've missed him so much, but he didn't have to treat Jacob the way he did. Jacob and his little ones have been a saving grace.

Believe it or not, Jacob is the one reason I didn't walk off set and say screw it all. Rodney was working my nerves until Jacob set him straight in front of everyone. We truly have become friends.

I adore his son and daughter. They are so sweet, cute, and funny. Dashawn loves them. They have all become best friends.

I haven't mentioned much about Jacob to Felix just because of this reaction. I've seen the Blacks and the way they are with their women. Watching Wyatt with Nellie, Noah with Bean, and the times Felix and I have gone out. I knew this wasn't going to go over well.

I fold my arms over my chest, not budging from my spot. Trust me, the sound of his voice has my nipples hard and my core trying to drag me to him. I, however, allow my mind to remain steadfast.

"Suit yourself," he purrs, unzipping his jeans and stepping out of his shoes.

He pushes his pants down, stepping out of them. I fight not to bite my lip when his length bounces at attention. He's not playing fair. Those glasses, that body, and he bought champagne and a book.

"Where are you going?" he calls after me when I turn to leave out of the bathroom.

"I'll be back."

I sway my hips on my way to the kitchen. Taking my time, I fetch two glasses for the champagne. I allow the smile I've been fighting, when I think of the strawberries Dean and I found at the market yesterday.

We spent last night dipping them in chocolate with Dae-Dae. There should still be a plate of them left.

Dean took off to explore with Connie this morning. I doubt she'll be returning anytime soon. Grandma McGowan offered to babysit if I wanted to go. I almost took her up on the offer until Jacob's little ones asked for a play date with Dae-Dae.

Jacob looked like he could use a break and an adult to talk to for a bit. His schedule is insane on the set. When he's not working, he is always with his kids. My heart hurts for him. I can see when his mind wonders. His story is one out of a book.

I hope someday he finds the right one for him. Felix didn't have to behave the way he did. I see Jacob more like a big brother if anything.

I giggle to myself. It was kind of hot to watch Felix stake his claim—although unnecessary. Jacob has known from the beginning that I'm in a committed relationship. I think I've talked his ear off about Felix enough times already.

Turning back for my room—as much as I want to run to him—I take my time making my way back. I mean, he threatened to kill Jacob. I know Felix well enough to know that was not an idle threat.

When I get back to the bathroom, I expect him to be in the tub. Instead, he has his naked butt propped against the counter. His tanned skin catches my attention. I can tell he's been surfing lately.

I take my time to admire the artwork on his ribs. The picture of Dae-Dae and me always takes my breath away. It's so realistic.

My eyes lower to that killer v and the trail that leads down it. I feel like a waterfall starts between my legs. It's been so long since we've been together.

I tear my eyes away, remembering his words and treatment of my friend. I cross my arms over my chest, mirroring his stance. However, I don't close the distance between us.

He doesn't move to close it either. Nope, he reaches for the champagne as if we're standing in the middle of the kitchen. He opens it, then holds his hand out for the glasses. I take a step forward to hand them to him and groan internally.

Well played.

He has a sexy crooked smile on his lips. He knows exactly what he's doing, and I fell right in. I hand him the glasses.

Trying to recover my dignity, I reach past him to place the plate of strawberries on the counter. I turn to exit the bathroom. He snakes his arm with the glasses clenched in his hand around my waist.

I'm drawn back against his heated body. I can't help but to melt into him. His lips meet the skin on my neck, and I can't remember why we're standing off in the first place.

"Why didn't you tell me about him?" he whispers in my ear.

"There's nothing to tell. He's my friend. Our kids play together and share a nanny on set," I answer.

"That's on set. Why was he in our home?"

"First of all, Felix. This is my home, I can in—"

"Wrong." He cuts me off. "Wherever you are is our home. Whether I'm here twenty-four seven or not," he says.

There is something in his voice that sends chills through my body. Not in a bad way. It's confident, possessive, demanding, and dark.

Almost like a challenge for me to deny him this. I'm tempted to deny his words, wanting to know where that road can lead to. He places the glasses down.

His hands go to cup my breasts over my sweater. His erection is poking me in the butt. I cover his hands with mine.

"Excuse me," I say, halting his motion.

"I plan to be here for only a week. And that is only if something crazy doesn't call me back to work. We can fight about some dude who could never be me and ruin an entire night.

"Or we can get in that bath tub, sip this champagne while I read you that book, and then make love until you can't take me anymore," he breathes into my ear.

He has a valid point. I haven't seen him in over three months. I can fuss at him later. The thought of him getting called away before I get to have him for an entire week changes everything.

Yet, I'm still not giving in the easy way. I grin to myself. I have a trick or two for Felix.

With a wicked smile on my face, I step out of his hold. I hear the huff he releases before I turn to face him. He's convinced I'm going to be stubborn.

I am, just not the way he thinks I am. When I face him, he has a frown on those sexy lips. His ass is once again propped against the countertop and his arms are folded over his chest.

He's giving me attitude, while it's sexy as all hell, he can save it. I move to the sound system in the bathroom. I make quick work of turning the music on low.

I grin when the playlist from the last time I masturbated for him on camera comes on. That was another of our hot sessions. I move back to the center of the bathroom.

Bunching my dress up in my fist, I get the hem into my hands. Slowly, I tug the dress over my head, to the sound of Ginuwine crooning "So Anxious." I drop the dress to the floor and rock to one leg, dropping my hip.

I secretly smile to myself. I never removed the knee high black leather heeled boots I wore to work. Those gold eyes blaze from behind his glasses. He's watching me as intently as I've always imagined he watches the footage of me on those cams.

His eyes swipe me from head to toes and slowly back again. When I see he's had his fill. I reach behind my back and unfasten my bra.

I hold it out to the side and drop it to the floor. Sliding my other hand down my front, I slip it into my panties. I sink my teeth into my lip as I keep my eyes on him.

His nostrils flare. He knows this is a battle of wills just as much as I do. One of us is going to break, I'm determined for it not to be me.

I pull my hair free from its bun, letting my curls spring free. His lips kick up into a sexy smile. His tongue peeks out to wet his bottom lip.

Oh, I have him. He's going to make the first move. I stand there in my boots and panties, working my core, challenging him to come for it.

Widening my stance, I start to rock my hips. His jaw ticks but he doesn't move from the vanity. His erection twitches, pointing straight at me like a warning.

I don't take the warning. Instead, I pull my hand from my panties and bring my fingers to my lips. Licking my fingers clean, then suck them into my mouth.

They make a popping sound when I release them. It's the final straw. He pushes off the counter lightning fast.

One minute my feet are planted to the floor the next they are in the air. Felix is on his knees, with my legs over his shoulders supporting my weight.

He laps at me through the lace of my panties. One arm is banded around my waist, the other is maneuvering to unzip my boot. I hold on with one arm, reaching with the other to shove my panties to the side to give him access.

I wiggle my foot when he has the boot unzipped. It falls to the floor as he shifts, switching arms. He works on the other boot, while his mouth works on me.

I look down my body to see his glasses smashed against his face, with fogged lenses. I don't know why that turns me on so much, but it does.

With my boots free of my feet, I feel like teasing him a bit more. I shove and wiggle my way free. He looks up at me with red cheeks and blazing eyes.

I back up to the tub and climb inside. Once in, I sink into the bubbles. The water covers my breasts, but not my thick thighs. I hook one leg over the side of the tub. Pinching one nipple, I slip my other hand into the water and start to finish the job he was just calling his own.

He lifts to his towering height, watching me. Reaching for his shaft, he starts to stroke. The movement derails my entire plan.

I can't take my eyes off the glorious sight he makes. His eyes on me, the slow strokes—it's all enough to send me over. The water splashes as I truly lose myself. I cry out and he makes a rough growling noise.

Felix is in the bathtub with me before I can truly come down from my climax. I'm seeing stars when he thrusts into me beneath the water. It's been too long since I've had him inside of me.

"Felix," I whimper.

Felix

"That's it. Say my name," I hiss as I rock into her.

That little show has me so turned on; I can't see straight. I don't even take care for my knees. I thrust into Kaye like I've lost something inside her sweet tight pussy.

It's too good to stop. I push her legs into her body to open her up for me. I use every single tight inch of the tub to maneuver my way into her. I hiss through my teeth when I feel her tightening around me.

Water is splashing, Kaye's crying out, and I'm growling with ecstasy charging through my veins. She cups the back of my neck, pulling me to her lips. I devour her sweet mouth.

She moans as her own taste hits her tongue. I stick my tongue deep into her mouth so she can get a better taste. I break the kiss, grasping her throat as I dive forward.

Kaye's eyes roll. I can feel her on the verge of coming. She reaches to clear the fog from my glasses. We lock eyes and both smile.

"I'm coming, babe. Don't let me come alone," she purrs.

I suck my lip into my mouth and groan. This girl doesn't know how sexy she is. Everything about her is hot as fuck.

"Fuck," I roar as I spill into her.

I collapse against her, releasing her legs while burying my face into her neck. This is the way to come home. I care about why we were fighting. I'm just happy to have her in my arms.

She begins combing her hand through my hair. I want to stay like this forever. Nestled between her legs, wrapped in her love. It's my favorite place in the world.

"You missed daddy, didn't you?" I chuckle into her neck after a few minutes.

"Whatever, Felix," she giggles. "Get to pampering, Mister. You can apologize to me and my friend later."

"Um." I kiss her lips. "He can hold his breath for that."

She swats at me, but I move away too quickly. I stand up out of the water and hold my hand out to her. She gives me a puzzled look.

"You wasted our warm water," I tease. "Let's snuggle in bed, with the champagne and book. We can try this again later."

"I wasted the warm water?" she scoffs.

"Yes, you. Now come on." I smile down at her.

She shakes her head but places her small hands in mine. Pulling her up, I tug her against my naked body. I place my arms around her, holding tight.

"I missed you," I murmur.

"Missed you too. I'm glad you're here. Always right on time," she says and sighs.

"Always."

Kaye

I relish in the heat of his body as my back rests against his front. Felix started the fireplace in the bedroom, and we crawled under the covers still naked. We've been munching on strawberries, sipping on champagne, and he has been reading the book he brought to me.

I'm in bliss. Felix has always been the perfect boyfriend. Sending random gifts, calling at all the right moments, and showing up just when I need him. I truly couldn't ask for more.

"This shit isn't half as good as your work. It's putting me to sleep," he grumbles, placing the book down and kissing my shoulder.

I laugh, turning my head to look at him. He pecks my lips, tightening his arms around me. He starts to rock us from side to side.

"Why are you so in love with love?" he asks out of nowhere.

I think about the question. It's a good one. I never thought about it before.

"Honestly, I think it's because I've always been around it. Think about it. My parents, my grandparents, your parents, Danny and Alberto—I've seen so many forms of love.

"I was so angry at Alberto in the beginning. Danny's entire situation just sucked. Love shouldn't end the way it did for him, but I don't think he would have had it any other way.

"He was into that tragic love stuff. It's how I got into reading romance. I guess I owe Danny the credit." I pause and laugh.

"What?" he breathes against my cheek.

"There's one more factor," I admit. "I've always romanticized us," I say. Chuckling, I offer up one more admission. "I've been planning our wedding since junior high."

"I can't wait to see what all you've been planning," he replies.

I turn to look up at him searching his face. He doesn't have a single hint of mocking in his features. My heart begins to pound.

I won't dare ask him what I'm thinking. The Blacks have a reputation for being playboys. I've never seen that in Felix as much as the others, but I won't say a part of me doesn't wonder.

I come with so much. I've never thought as far as marriage. At least, not in the realistic sense. I've daydreamed about it of course. I remember him hinting at children before, but still.

"Don't look so surprised, Kaye. You know how I feel. For keeps, remember?"

"Yeah, but—"

I don't get to finish my thought. Felix's phone begins to ring. He kisses my forehead while reaching for it. I hold my breath until he hangs up.

"I'm not going anywhere." He reassures me once he ends the call. "I just need to work for a bit. Are you writing tonight?"

"Yeah, I planned to," I respond.

"Cool, sit with me. We can work together."

"Okay," I sing, happy. I get to have him at least for another few hours.

Please let him be able to stay the week.

CHAPTER FORTY-ONE

Don't Ignore Me

Kaye

I haven't stopped smiling since this morning when Felix woke me with his mouth. He called it a parting gift. I miss him already.

I know Dae-Dae does too. He clung to Felix all morning until we had to leave. I thought it would come to tears, but my little boy was brave and strong. Sending me into tears with his words.

"I love you, Lix. I'll take care of mama until you get back," he said.

When did my little boy grow up so fast?

Felix promised to make the trip back as soon as he can. I'm hoping it's not another three months before that happens. I know things get busy for him, but a girl can hope. Right?

"That smile is priceless, lass," Jacob rumbles beside me.

I turn my face up to look at him. I can't help smiling a little more. Jacob embodies my character, Tristan. From his thick red hair that is blowing in the wind, to the leather jacket and kilt he has on, as we wait for them to be ready for him on set.

I know the women who watch this film are going to swoon over this scene. If we can catch this sunset just right, this is going to be stunning. I can't wait to see him straddle that motorcycle and take off.

Not in a lustful way. For me, it's totally different. I'm watching the baby I created come to life. Each scene from the book that plays out perfectly is breathtaking for me. Jacob has been doing the character so much justice.

I can tell he read the book and he got it. He understands the inner workings of Tristan's mind and character. This is just one of those scenes that will make my readers that see it scream out, *yes*.

I can almost hear them in my head. I get all giddy inside and I know it shows. Jacob lifts a brow at me as his eyes bounce over my face. I shake my head to clear it.

"I have a lot to smile about," I chirp.

"Aye, I bet. Your boyfriend has brought out a new side of you. I'll hate to see him go," he says sincerely.

My smile falls just a little as reality sets in. Felix is already gone. When I go home tonight, it won't be to a home cooked meal and a waiting bubble bath. Nope, my week of pampering by my man is over.

"He's left. Hasn't he?" Jacob asks when my expression changes.

"Yeah," I say and start to pout. "I wish we had more time."

"If Rodney stops screw things up, we may be able to get ahead of schedule," he says hopefully.

"Yeah, that's great for you guys, but my contract has me here to help postproduction. Colton really wants me involved until the end. I don't get to go home until the reel is in the tin," I huff.

Jacob lets out a long whistle. "Well, I'll do my part to get this wrapped as soon as possible. That way you guys can get home sooner. That smile should be on your face all the time. Life is too short. You should be where your heart is."

"You're such a wise man," I tease, bumping my side into his.

He wraps an arm around my shoulder, smiling down at me. Jacob truly is a handsome man and so sweet on top of that. I wish he had someone to make him happy.

"If I were a wise man. I would have worn knickers under this kilt. My bum is starting to freeze up here," he teases.

I burst into laughter. The way he says it alone tickles me. The fact that I questioned whether he was wearing underwear when I first saw him in the kilt forces more laughter.

What? I know every other woman has thought the same thing.

"I hope you do come for a visit to the States like you promised. This would have been a disaster without you," I say through my laughter.

"Aye, you don't know how much you've been helping me keep it together. I've been thinking of a change. We'll see where the wind blows me," he says thoughtfully.

"McTavish, we're ready for you," the director calls.

"Let's go, *Tristan*," I sing.

I love that I can see him shift into character right before my eyes. I watch my friend Jacob turn into the character I wrote in seconds. His swagger shifts and his face changes.

I love it.

I take my phone out to check my messages quickly as they get ready to record the scene. I end up on social media somehow. My smile turns up a million times when I see Felix's last post.

Loving someone isn't the hard part. It's loving them so much you do what's best for them and not what you want for you.

I look up around me. The beauty of the hills and cliff side are breathtaking. In the middle of all this beauty, all these people are here to film a movie about a book I wrote.

Felix has always believed in me. He encouraged my writing, even through times when I wanted to give up. My dreams have always been a priority for him. With those thoughts, I think I fall in love with him all over again.

I decide to write my own post as my mind starts to spin. I'm so overwhelmed with love and happiness; tears start to well in my eyes. I need to share this somehow. A post is better than me bursting out into song, singing the hills are alive.

I've only told a few people about being here to film this movie. I haven't posted anything on social media about being here in Ireland. I'm not ready to share that with the world so my message is sort of cryptic. It says what I want to say in a roundabout way.

I value the relationships around me. Having all the right people in your life makes the difference. Living my happiness unapologetically. Love never abandons you.

With that, I log off and look up in time to watch the perfect take. Tristan riding off in the sunset—leather jacket, kilt, and all. It all comes to life.

This is my dream. I'm living it. I don't know if life can get better than this.

A Fan

How dare she? Kaye hasn't been on social media as much as she used to be. She won't answer my calls or messages and now this.

She's being petty. So I guess I'm one of the wrong people then? She's just going to put it out there like that.

"I loved you," I shout at the computer screen. "I didn't abandon you. You abandoned me!"

I stand and start to pace. I heard a rumor that Kaye has been out of the country. I've tried to tell myself that she's busy with making a movie. *Loving Tristan* was an amazing book. I've read and re-read it a million times.

It would be the perfect movie. Of course, they would have to get Tristan right. You can't fuck up a man like Tristan. He's one of my number one husbands.

Yes, if Kaye were working on a movie, that would be understandable. We are growing a brand. Kaye and I can take over the world together. She needs someone like me.

Yet, she's trying to push me out. I know it. I almost believed those whispers in the community about her filming, but this …

This post changes everything. I see it for what it is. She's not too busy for me.

Kaye's shoving me to the side, ignoring me. I tried to be a good friend. I was there for her.

"Why are you doing this?" I sob, shaking my fist at the computer.

I've spent so much time building what we have. Reading her books, watching her grow. It's Lisa. I know it is.

"You listened to that bitch and her lies about me. Didn't you?"

I throw myself back in my chair and start to type my own post. I'm fuming. Lisa ruined everything for me. Kaye is slipping through my fingers and it's all because of Lisa.

It's funny how you love people, and they act like you don't exist. They will abandon you and never ask you for your truth. It's okay. I see it for what it is and I'll do right by the relationships I value.

"Stop ignoring me, Kaye. Lisa is a stupid, lying bitch. Don't ruin us for her," I plead aloud. "I'm warning you."

CHAPTER FORTY-TWO

Lights and Words

Felix

Seven months later …

It's been seven crazy ass months. I've gotten to see Kaye once in the midst of that. She looked so beautiful all dressed up for Toby's wedding.

I couldn't keep my eyes or hands off her. It killed me to be in Ireland and not spend every single moment with her. Yet, I know Toby needed to have the support of his brothers and cousins.

Doesn't mean I didn't head right to the comfort of my woman whenever I wasn't needed. That first night I turned up drunk off my ass and horny as fuck, I thought Kaye was going to tear into my ass.

However, Kaye was so happy to see me nothing else mattered. Thank God for Dean because Kaye and I couldn't move out of bed the next morning. Dean took care of Dae-Dae while Kaye and I slept each other off.

I knew then I wasn't going to wait much longer to make her my wife. Two of my brothers have made it to the altar and I still haven't gotten my ring on Kaye's finger.

That's about to change. I've had a lot to think about after traveling to Africa with Toby and Kamara to take her kingdom back, then being tossed into the New York situation. I mean, seriously, all the craziness with the arrests, threats, more attempted kidnappings—enough is enough.

All I've been able to think about during these last few months is the fact that I have a woman I love and I haven't made her my wife. Sure, that may have been a good thing during all the chaos. Kaye was safe in Ireland under my family's watch.

Still, Nellie, Bean, and Kamara were there for my brothers to relieve their stress. Hell, Brax has Heather even though those two think everyone's blind or stupid. Yet, I'm limited in what I can share with Kaye from this distance and that stings.

I think the last few months have all been a reality check. I know Kaye still has a little bit of time left before she can come home, but when she does I want her to return to plan our wedding. Which is why instead of cleaning up the shit ton of files on my desk back in California, I'm landing back in Ireland.

I thought I was going to make this trip alone. It's been two weeks since we all returned from New York. I had booked a plane with plans to get to Kaye before anything else could get in my way.

Nosey Noah started asking questions and the next thing I knew my entire family was on the tarmac boarding the plane with me. The plane Wyatt switched out to accommodate everyone for this impromptu trip, including my future in-laws. I can't say that I don't appreciate it.

Fuck it, the shit choked me up. This feels right. This time I'm going to see this through no matter what.

One call to Connie and Carrick and they've been getting things ready for me. I've been barking orders over my laptop making sure they get this just right. It has to be perfect.

While Connie has been gushing about how romantic it all is, Carrick has been ribbing me for it. I don't care. Kaye is the one. This has to be from my heart. Better than any proposal she's ever dreamed up to write in one of her books.

Shit, Wyatt and Toby pulled off some amazing proposals. I've put some real thought into this. I think it screams Kaye, but most importantly, it speaks to how long I've loved her before falling in love with her.

"Ye did well. It'll be beautiful." My mom's voice cuts through my thoughts.

I noticed she changed seats to sit beside me when our descent was announced. You would think with seven boys it would be hard to show each one attention and love. That has never been the case with my mother.

She has been there whenever we needed her, including during times we didn't think we did. So much love in a tiny woman. I smile when I think of my choice in a woman for me.

Like my dad, I've chosen a small but fierce woman. Kaye's fierceness is just a little bit more hidden than my mother's. Although, I know if ever pushed, Kaye would unleash it all.

Sliding down in my seat, I place my head on my mother's shoulder. She cups my cheek and pats it with her small hand. My lips turn up when I feel her lips touch my forehead.

It's just like when I was a small boy. Her presence stopped me from questioning everything—why I was more interested in how things worked than just playing and horsing around like my brothers, why kids at school wouldn't play with me, why I couldn't speak up like Wyatt, Ryan, or Brax? I questioned so much.

Mom was always there to make me feel normal and okay with who I was. She never made me feel like I had to be like the others. I'll forever be grateful for that.

"I hope she likes it," I murmur.

"Like at it, she's going to love it," she replies.

I feel more than see her nod toward my laptop. Connie is testing out the lights. It's still early, but the sun will have set by the time we arrive there on location. It's going to be amazing. At least I hope it will be.

"Here goes nothing," I huff.

Kaye

"Please don't argue with me about this," I grunt at Rodney. He is getting on my last damn nerves.

We were moving through the edits and only needed a few reshoots, which Jacob and Shreya returned for. I want to be done with this. I want to go home. Why is this man always so damn difficult?

Lord, help me not to lay hands on this fool.

"I have to agree with Kaye. This is the reason for the reshoots. I didn't like that you changed that scene from the book in the first place," Colton, the director says.

"I thought it would work in film better this way," Rodney says defensively.

"I requested you on this job because Kaye is such a strong writer. I thought you would work well with her. Honestly, Rodney, you've been getting on my fucking nerves.

"You've cost us continuous blows to the budget that were unnecessary," Colton grinds out. "Pack your shit. Go home. Kaye has it from here."

I want to jump in the air and hoot. Who says God is slow to answer prayers? That was an instant blessing.

"Colton, you … you can't be serious," Rodney stammers.

"You're still here?" Colton says dryly.

Rodney's face turns red, but he turns and storms away without another word. I can't help the smile that comes to my lips. I turn back to see Colton watching me.

"You were waiting for that," he snorts. "He used to be one of the best. I think his ego has bested him.

"I just don't have the budget or the time to keep putting up with it. Besides, my little friend over there has been moping since Jacob's little ones left. I want to get you out of here."

I turn to see Dae-Dae kicking his foot at the grass beneath his feet. Dean had to head back State side for the roll out with her new publisher. The onset nanny was let go once Dae-Dae was her only charge.

Jacob was able to get a friend to watch over his two while he returned for reshoots. My son has become one of the crew around here, but it's still not the place for a child. When things get serious, and people need to do their jobs he is forgotten or pushed to the side.

I hate it and I've noticed the change in Dae-Dae myself. It's only a little while longer. I may call my mother this evening and

ask her to fly in, even if it's just to take Dae-Dae back until I
return.

Yes, it is time to finish things up here. I think we're both
ready to go home. It's like when we arrived all over again. I turn
back to Colton to reply, but Dae-Dae's squeal pulls my
attention back to him.

"*Lix.*"

I turn to see what's going on and find the last thing I thought
I would. All seven Black brothers are headed in my direction.
Felix is out front while his brothers flank his sides holding
bouquets of white roses.

I don't know what to do at first. I'm so relieved to see him.
I've missed him so much.

It takes a moment of watching Dae-Dae crashing into Felix's
legs for a hug, then Noah scooping Dae-Dae up into his arms
before I snap into action.

My legs carry me as fast as they can. The beanie I stole from
Felix flies off my head, but I don't turn back for it. I jump right
into his arms, wrapping my body around him. I knock him back
a bit with the force of my run and weight, but John and Wyatt
place a hand to his back to keep him stable.

Felix embraces me so tightly; I feel his muscles cord around
me. I haven't seen him since Toby's wedding. It's been a week
and four months. To say I miss this man is an understatement.

"What's going on? What are you doing here?" I breathe
against his neck.

He bounces me in his arms to get a better grip. I go to climb
off him, but he tightens his hold to prevent it. Lifting my face
from his neck, I look into his eyes.

"I needed to see you," he says simply, but his eyes say so
much more.

I look around behind him at all the handsome smiling faces. I feel like I'm being set up. When my eyes land on Dae-Dae and the light shining in his eyes as Noah whispers something to him, my heart aches.

We need to go home.

I turn back to Felix to catch him watching me closely. My eyes tear up. This is the weakest I've ever felt. I'm so homesick.

"He needs to go home," I say through a clogged throat.

"Yeah? Just him, or are you ready too?" he asks knowingly.

"This has been too long of a process. I'm so over it," I reply, blinking back tears.

Reaching to bring my forehead to his, he gives me some of his strength. It's right on time. I've needed Felix here for longer than I'll admit.

"I think I have something that will get you through. Ready to call it a day?"

"Yeah, just let me talk to Colton and get my things. I think I'm done for the day," I answer.

He releases me from his waist but laces his fingers with mine as I walk back to the director. I see the look in Colton's eyes as he looks at the scene that has played out around him. I'd have that look too if I were a director.

I'd have to have every single one of this family's fine men in my movie. Trust me, it has been a thought. I've toyed with writing a series about them. I think it would be a hot one.

"I'm going to take her for the rest of the day," Felix says, it's not a question, it's a very firm statement.

"Ah, this is the real Tristan," Colton chuckles.

I giggle, wrapping myself around Felix's arm. "Yeah, pretty much," I reply.

"Colton Rush, nice to meet you," he says, holding out his hand to Felix.

"Nice to meet you," Felix replies, returning the gesture.

I take note that Felix doesn't offer his name. Knowing him, I don't think it's an oversight. I don't really care. I just want to get out of here and somewhere alone with my man.

"Take the weekend. I think we have what we need for now," Colton says with a knowing smile.

"Thanks," I chirp.

I turn tugging Felix with me before Colton can change his mind or someone else finds something to need me for. As we walk back to the others, my mind registers the flowers all the guys are still holding. Curiosity piqued, I turn my face up to Felix.

"Hey. What are you up to?"

He looks down at me and winks. Dipping his head, he captures my lips in a searing kiss. I'm left breathless when he pulls away.

"Time will tell," he says in a silky-smooth voice.

With those words, each brother holding a bouquet hands it over. My heart and my arms are full as Felix leads me to the waiting SUVs. I have no idea what he has planned but it can't get any better than actually seeing his face in the flesh.

***

I remained snuggled into Felix's side the entire ride. I still don't know where we are. Felix told me to wait here in the car, while he and his brothers unloaded and took off.

I know this is Granny McGowan's property. This was where we came for the wedding. This place is so majestic.

I've written a few scenes about this place that I plan to build a story around. As I wait for the text Felix said he would send, I get lost in thought.

A transfer student that falls for a Duke, maybe. He keeps his identity hidden because he just wants to be normal and fall in love. Oh, yes. Where is my pen and notebook?

I start to dig my pen and journal out. This will work perfectly with the stuff I've already written. I need my laptop. I've been wanting to do something out of my norm.

My phone pings just as I get lost in my thoughts and notes. I frown at the interruption but remember that it's Felix—the real deal. I can get back to this later.

I want to know what Felix is up to. Retrieving my phone, I read his text.

Felix: *Follow the roses.*

I'm too excited to text him back. I shove my things out of my lap and pop the door open. With my phone in my hand, I look around for roses.

I spot two clay planters wrapped in lights, flanking the stone entrance to the side of the grounds. I rush down the path.

When I get to the mouth of the entrance, more rose petals cover the ground. They are creating a path, leading forward through the small iron gate. I move forward through the opening.

There are so many petals lining the path, I have to wonder if there are anymore roses left in Ireland. I stop in my tracks when the trail leads to a grove of trees.

It's not the trees that stop me, but the mason jars hanging from the branches. They look as if they have fireflies in them, but that can't be right. I saunter closer to a branch nearest me.

There are glowworms inside, not fireflies. The tears start to flow. There's a special story behind us and fireflies. I know they don't have them here, but only someone like Felix would know to find glowworms instead.

Reaching up, I touch the brown string attached to the bottom of the glass, to get a closer look at the paper attached to the string. More tears spill. It's a printed page from *Charlotte's Web*.

I move to another branch to see what's on the page at the bottom of the next jar. Wiping my eyes to see clearly, I gasp.

He remembers these?

"The mouse and the motorcycle," I breathe.

I float from branch to branch. *Stuart Little, Secret Garden, James and the Giant Peach*. Each sheet of paper has one of my favorites printed on them. Each one my favorites for one single reason.

"I loved you before I fell head over heels for you." His voice rumbles in my ear, as he embraces me with his arms.

"You remember all of this," I whisper.

"I remember you bringing me *Charlotte's Web* and looking up at me with those big brown eyes. I'd never been more proud of the fact that I could read.

"You were what? Five, I was six. You didn't go to Danny or Alberto. You came to me," he says.

I chuckle. "They couldn't read," I laugh. "I saw you with a big book. I wanted to know what the words were in these books."

"We spent hours sitting at the trunk of the treehouse tree. When it would rain, we'd hang in the treehouse. I've read every single one of these books to you," he says.

"The glowworms?" I ask, already knowing the answer.

"I've never seen a little girl so happy. We're taking our daughter to the East Coast as soon as she can walk," he chuckles. "I'll remember that trip for the rest of my life. When I captured them in the jar for you, the shine in your eyes made me feel like I was ten feet tall," he murmurs against my temple.

"You were to me. I couldn't catch them. But you got two and gave them to me."

I turn in his arms. My heart starts to pound. I think I know what's going on here.

Felix drops to one knee and that's when I see both our families behind him, holding lit candles in their hands. My mom, dad, and grandparents are here.

"Felix?" I sob.

"Kaye, I want forever with you. I want to read to our sons and daughters. I want to take our family on adventures like we made up in that treehouse.

"I want to write a real-life romance with you. I want to be there for Dashawn, not as an uncle, but as his father. We both see each other as father and son. It's time I make this the way it should be." He pauses taking in a deep nervous breath.

"Will you marry me?"

"Yes," I say it before he can finish the question.

We both laugh. His face scrunches up as his eyes drop to the unopened box. With a shaky hand he opens it.

I cover my mouth and stumble back. The ring is massive. I mean, I have no words.

I'm not even that type of girl. I don't know what he was thinking when he bought it.

"You underestimate yourself. I wanted to get a ring to remind you every day how precious you are to me. You're incredible, Kaye and I love you so much," he answers my unspoken thoughts, reaching for my hand to place the ring on it.

He stands tugging me forward into his arms. I wrap my arms around him and breathe him in. This is so unreal. I need to pinch myself to see if I'm dreaming.

"I love you too," I say into his chest.

Felix

"You did good," Noah says patting me on the back.

"Yeah, that was pretty cool," Ry says.

"Thanks. I can't believe it's finally done. I've waited so long. It's going to sting having to return home without her though," I wince.

"About that. It's only a few months, right? We'll cover for you. Stay," Wyatt says.

"Are you serious?"

"Yeah." He nods.

"Dude, that means so much. I'll do whatever I can from here. If you need me just say the word."

"We can handle it. Nellie has been holding things down when we need you in the field. She can take on a little extra while you're here," Wyatt replies.

"Are you sure? With the baby, bro—"

"You're fine. Mom will be all over helping with Nora. She's been busting my chops about spending more time with the baby," Wyatt groans.

"Aye, I could help out, I will," Uncle Ronan offers.

We all turn to look at him. Something's up with my uncle. I can't put my finger on it, but I know something is up.

"You're coming to California?" Noah says incredulously.

"You don't get more Irish than you and your brothers. I've been trying to get you over for years," Brax says. "What the fuck?"

"Och, I don't move to the beat of ya drum, I don't. I said I want to help. Maybe I want to spend time with me sister," Uncle Ronan grumbles.

"Bullshit," my brothers, cousins, and I say in unison.

"It's the lass with the dreads," Carrick snorts.

"Who?" I knit my brows.

"I'll batter ya, if ya don't shut yer gub. I said I'm going. Now leave it be," Uncle Ronan growls.

We all burst into laughter. Something is stuck in his craw. I'll have to do a little digging into that.

"I guess I'm staying," I say and shrug.

CHAPTER FORTY-THREE

Outrage

Kaye

I can't believe it. I'm engaged. I've called Kia and Hadiyah.

Jacob found out when he dropped in on an editing session. I usually don't share my personal life online, but I want my fans to know that true love does happen in real life.

"Here goes nothing," I murmur as I start to type the announcement.

I can't stop beaming as my eyes flicker to the ring. It's so insane. Felix went crazy picking such a big ring.

However, I loved his reason for it. I snap a quick pic to attach to my post. Tapping away at my phone, I bite my tongue nervously as I get ready to share my life with the world.

So this has happened. My fairytale come true. I've loved this man since I was a young girl. He has loved and supported me through everything.
I still can't believe he asked me to marry him. I still feel like his best friend's nerdy little sister with a huge crush that will never be returned. Yet, squee!
He wants to marry me. I said yes to my best friend, the love of my life, the man who owns my heart and soul.
All of that as we are drawing near the wrap of "Loving Tristan." Oh, yeah … about that. I've been on location for going on a year.
My book has become a movie!
I love my life! Can't wait to get State side to start planning our wedding. Love you, babe. I can't wait to be your wife.

A Fan

"Oh my God. This is so amazing," I gush as I read Kaye's post.

So she wasn't ignoring me after all. She has been in Ireland working on the movie. I'm so excited. Tristan on screen.

I'm so happy for Kaye. This means so many things for us. I have to get ready for her return.

She'll need a PA now. With releasing new books, a movie coming out, and now planning a wedding.

So much to do. I wonder when she wants to have the wedding. I can totally help her with that. First, I need to move closer to Kaye. I can do that now.

I've been doing edits for another author. She pays well enough. If only she knew I barely read the manuscripts.

Her writing is okay. I'm just not that strong in grammar or proofing. I needed the money. When I saw her post about an editor, I inboxed her.

She hasn't figured out yet that she's paying for shit edits. As long as she keeps paying, I'll have a ticket in no time. This is going to be just what I need.

"Okay, let's go apartment shopping. California here we come," I woot into the room.

I knew you weren't ignoring me, Kaye. That would just be stupid. We're friends. I'm sure you just had a bad connection while away. Or you could have not wanted to pay the roaming fees.

"Yeah, I get it. You couldn't be reached or take my calls. You were too far away, busy bringing my man to life."

I do a dance in my seat. This is going to be amazing. Oh, I can help her pick a wedding gown.

"So much to do, Kaye. We'll get it done."

CHAPTER FORTY-FOUR

Family Time

Kaye

It's as if the sun has come out just to warm this day for us. I have my palms behind my back as my face is turned up toward the sky. I'm basking in its rays, taking in the beauty of the day.

My own little slice of heaven. We left our laptops in the house, vowing not to work today. Since the families returned home to the States and it's just us, we wanted to enjoy some down time. It has been bliss.

Dae-Dae couldn't be happier to have his Lix here with him and I couldn't be happier to have my Felix. We've laughed more than ever, and life has been so simple in the last few weeks. We'll be leaving soon, hopefully, but it's been great to have Felix here with us.

Dae-Dae's giggle pulls my attention. I lower my head. My smile stretches impossibly wide. Felix is chasing after him, the two looking like they're having the time of their lives.

Dae-Dae's beanie bounces as he runs. He looks so much like Danny. His dimples pop just like his father's used to.

I feel a pang in my chest as I think of my brother. I miss Danny, but I couldn't imagine life without Dashawn. I strive to better every day for him.

Felix scoops Dae-Dae up into his arms and tosses him in the air. Dae-Dae's squeal pierces the air. It's a sound that warms my heart. I love these two with all of me.

I watch as Felix spins him around. The love Felix is pouring onto Dashawn is so real. It is written all over his face—my man loves my son as much as he loves me.

"Mama, Mama," Dae-Dae calls out for my help as Felix tickles him.

Felix rushes them both over to flop down on the blanket beside me. He then leans to kiss my cheek. Dae-Dae dives for my phone.

"Let's take a selfie," he sings.

"You have the best ideas," Felix coos.

"I know," Dae-Dae says with a sage nod.

Wrapping an arm around me, Felix drags me into his side. He settles Dae-Dae halfway on his lap, halfway on mine. Plucking the phone from my son's small hand, he holds the phone up and snaps a few pictures.

We all start to make silly faces for the last couple. I take the phone, laughing as I swipe through the pics we've just taken. Our happiness shines in our faces.

"Now that's one gorgeous family," Felix says.

"Yup! My mommy is so pretty and my daddy is handsome," Dae-Dae chimes.

I freeze, looking up at Dashawn. I've thought of him as mine for so long. He has called me his mama since he started talking. However, hearing him call Felix his daddy brings tears to my eyes.

I've never thought about how he sees Felix. I know how much Felix loves him. Hearing Dashawn's words just make this engagement so much more a reality.

"Not the first time," Felix chokes out. "Slays me every time. You know I want you both, right? He becomes a Black too."

I swallow hard. I can't speak so I nod. I'm so full. What more could I ask for?

Dae-Dae takes off running to play some more. Felix takes the chance to pull me between his legs, my back to his front. I melt into him as his arms wrap around me.

"Have you thought about where you want to get married or when?" he murmurs.

"A little. I want my dad to marry us. I just haven't decided if I want to do it in his church or somewhere else. Not sure what kind of wedding I want. Your brother's wedding was amazing," I muse.

"We can do whatever you want," he replies.

"I think I want to go for the big wedding. I know it will take a long time to plan, but in the end, it'll be worth it," I say.

"Yeah, it will be. Let's make it home and then you can talk with our mothers to see what you want to do. I heard them planning it on their own already. You might want to rein that in," he chuckles.

I turn my face up to look at him and he pecks my lips. I almost forget what I was about to say. The soft press of his mouth is so intoxicating.

"I love you," I murmur.

"I love you too." He smiles. "I can't wait for you to see the new house."

I sit up and turn to him. I knit my brows in confusion. My eyes widen. He did it again.

"You did not buy another house," I gasp.

"It's your engagement gift. I was going to wait until we got back to tell you. I've been holding it in for too long," he says sheepishly.

"Too long? Seriously?" I say incredulously.

"I bought it almost a year ago," he says, sucking his lip into his mouth.

My mouth falls open. My mind races. He can't be saying what I think he's saying.

"You were going to propose before I got the news about the movie, weren't you?"

"Yeah, that weekend actually," he replies.

"You've waited that long?"

"I've waited a lot longer than you know," he says, his cheeks turning pink.

"What?"

"I was going to ask you to marry me that night your family came to our place for the party."

"Are you serious? Why didn't you?"

"Do you not remember being so pissed off at me you didn't talk to me for weeks?" He snorts.

I tuck my chin into my chest and whisper. "Yes."

He lifts my head with his hand. His eyes locking on mine. A gentle smile is resting on his lips.

"I'd wait a million years for you. It wasn't the right time. Now is. We're not going to dwell on the past. I have you and we have our son. I'd say the world is perfect." He winks at me.

"I'd say so too," I reply, leaning in to kiss his lips.

"Daddy, come on," Dae-Dae calls making my heart squeeze.

I take full notice that there's so much joy in his voice as he calls Felix by that name. Felix kisses me quickly before getting up to run and join our son.

Wow, Danny. You managed to give me the world. Thanks, big bro.

CHAPTER FORTY-FIVE

Rumors

Kaye

Three months later ...

I give myself a mental hug. I'm still crazy busy, but it's so good to be back home. Dashawn got to spend his fifth birthday with his entire family.

I wanted to take a break, but this signing was a great opportunity. I've been away from my fans for an entire year. I figured I'd do this one, then I could slow down a bit.

I haven't had a chance to think about planning the wedding yet. I was offered a four book deal while in Ireland. My mind was blown by the offer.

I'm pulling in more than I thought would ever be possible with only five books out. I slowed down publishing while I was away. My books were doing well, which gave me some time to plan my next step. I decided to take the time to build up a few books. Two of which are a part of the ones I sold to a publisher.

"Hey, superstar." I hear sung behind me.

I turn to find Kia beaming at me. We both squeal, pulling each other into a tight hug, rocking side to side. It's been too long since I've seen Kia.

"Ugh, I missed you," I say.

"I missed you too. I thought that was you. You want some help?" she asks, pointing to my boxes of books and the retractable.

"No, no, I'm fine. Felix just went to grab a few things I forgot in the room. He'll be back to help me set up," I reply, waving her off.

"Oh my God, it's bigger in person," she gushes, grabbing my hand.

"Insane, right?"

"Gorgeous. I told you a long time ago that man was in love with you. Honey, a ring like this is a lot more than friendship," she says pointedly.

"Yeah, yeah," I grumble teasingly.

"Hey, Lakia," Felix says as he walks up behind her.

"Hi, Felix," she sings, giving him a hug.

"Where is your table?" I ask, looking around for her banners.

"I'm clear across the room." She purses her lips. "Wish I was closer to you."

"We're going to catch up after this," I insist.

"Of course, have you heard from that crazy ass Dean?"

"Nope, I don't know what she's up to. Last time we spoke was when she let me know she made it back home safely," I grumble.

"Yeah, that chick is up to something. I see her. I'm going to give her some space for now, but not for long," Kia says.

"Don't I know it," I laugh.

"Baby," Felix calls for my attention. I turn to face him. "You have a bit of time before things start. You guys want to go for a coffee or something. Text me where you are, and I'll find you. I got this."

I beam at him. He is totally focused on setting my area up. He already has books on the table and my banner up.

"Thanks," I chime.

"No problem," he murmurs, his focus on his task.

"You hit the jackpot. I can only wish," Lakia says, with a sigh.

"Your time is coming. I can feel it," I say, wrapping an arm around hers.

"From your mouth to God's ears. Toni has been working my last damn nerve. How can such an asshole be the one who gave me such a beautiful son?"

"God works in mysterious ways," I laugh.

"Umm," she murmurs. "Forget all that. I wanted to talk to you about something."

The change in her voice has my attention. We're walking out of the meeting room when she leans into me. I find myself leaning back in to listen.

"What's up with this Bonnie chick? At first, I heard her name in some bullshit and I was like whatever not my business. Then, I started hearing your name dragged into the shit," Kia informs me.

I whip my head back, my face compressing. Gossip is always rampant within this industry when you tune in. I tend not to tune in because I'm not for all that mess.

"What? I haven't talked to that woman since before I left for Ireland," I hiss out.

"I told you about these folks. She has your name in all kinds of mess. What pissed me off were the rumors that Felix beats your ass," Kia fumes.

"What?"

"Yeah." Kia nods. "I've met that man on a number of occasions. He's as sweet as can be. This chick is out here making it seem like you've been crying to her because he's fucking you up and shit. I don't like it.

"She has your name in author drama when you're the nicest person in the world. Authors I know you have met, but none of the shit they are saying sounds like you. Authors who gave her money for that event you were promoting or some shit.

"First of all, when do you have time for that messy shit when all you do is work and take care of your baby? And you never ask for shit or need to. I can't stand when messy folks try to drag good people into some nonsense.

"You know I'm the last one to get into some shit, but her ass can come up missing. I promise you we can ship her to my brother in pieces for him to scatter in the dessert."

My head is spinning. How the hell did all of this happen. Felix has never lifted a hand to harm me. Why on earth would anyone try to start a crazy rumor like that?

I knew something wasn't right with that woman. I start to play back conversations. It dawns on me that all she does is talk about people's business.

I never gave it much mind. I was either working or dealing with things in the house when she called. Never in my life did I think she would start telling rumors about me. I mean, she doesn't know a thing about me. This is so unreal.

"Come on, this can't be serious," I breathe out to Kia.

"Girl, we can get Vanity on the phone if you like. That Lisa chick who was supposed to be Bonnie's partner called her and spilled everything. Apparently, Felix came home cursing you out one day while you were on the phone with Bonnie or something," Kia says, lifting a questioning brow at me.

I draw my brows to the center of my forehead. I scrape my mind for what in the world she could be talking about. Felix has a foul mouth.

He curses all the time. You're not a Black if you don't curse like a sailor. However, I can't think of a time in my life that he has ever cursed me out.

Our little fights don't last long enough to be fights. Neither of us can stay mad at the other long. At least, Felix doesn't let me stay mad for long.

I think our longest fight was when my dad crushed the party Felix threw for me when I returned to Cali. Kia and I enter a restaurant and sit at a table, as I try to think of what in the world that crazy woman has been spreading around.

I shoot Felix a text to let him know where we are. It's in the moment, as I place my phone down on the table that it clicks.

"Oh my God. You have to be kidding me," I gasp.

Kia looks at me with concern in her eyes. This is so crazy. I remember the one time Bonnie has to be talking about. I'm so pissed I start to see red.

"What?" Kia asks.

"It was so long ago, I forgot. She called me while I was writing. I tried to get off the phone with her, but she just kept going.

"She mentioned something about my book reviews and I couldn't help myself. I went to look.

"Felix walked in and found me crying over what I'd read. All he said was, 'What the fuck?' He wasn't cursing at me.

"He was reacting to me crying and the reviews being up on my screen. That heifer has lost her mind. How are you going to take something so small and turn it into my man beating on me?

"Like, seriously. If she has that much time on her hands, maybe she should be the one writing books. This is insane," I grunt.

"That's what Vanity said. That the chick takes little conversations and turns them into elaborate tales. There's one more thing I haven't told you," Kia replies.

"Do I even want to hear it?"

"Hear what?" Felix rumbles as he sits beside me.

I turn to see his eyes searching my face. I can tell he's picking up on the change in my mood. That calculating mind is working overtime to find the problem, it's source, and a solution.

When I turn to Kia she's biting her lips, looking at me nervously. I nod for her to continue. I won't hide something like this from Felix. Especially with him being involved.

"Bonnie, the one who invited Kaye to that bogus event, she's been starting a lot of shit with Kaye's name mixed up in it. She's also been telling people she's your PA. Bragging about how close y'all are and that she works with you to hash out your books and she's apparently your editor to boot," Kia adds.

"The fuck?"

"The Hell?"

Felix and I bark in unison. Kia gives me a look, which I know means she thinks I should fill Felix in on the rest. I huff, turning to him to get him up to speed.

Felix's ears are so red when I finish, I know he's pissed. His knee is bouncing under the table. I wait for him to say something when I'm done. It takes him a few seconds while his jaw works under his skin.

"I looked into her before." He narrows his eyes. "I didn't find a Bonnie whatever her last name was supposed to be.

"I only left it alone because you left and didn't plan to do her event. I wanted to ask you more questions, but you had so much on your plate while the movie was being made, so I dropped it.

"I want everything. I want her number, access to everything she's ever sent you. Just give me your laptop," Felix fumes.

"Okay." I nod.

I know if anyone can deal with this, it's Felix. I'm not about to stress myself out about that nut. I can't believe the mess she's made.

Worse is the fact that some of the authors who believed her mess know me enough to come to me and ask. None of them have. If not for Kia, I would never have known about any of this.

Unbelievable.

CHAPTER FORTY-SIX

Cutoff

A Fan

"You bitch!"

I toss my tablet across the room. Kaye has blocked me from all her social media. Does she not know what I've done for her? I've moved here to be closer to her, to help her.

"Why did you block me?"

I start to pace the hardwood floors of my new apartment. I've been here for a month. I moved into this neighborhood with its overpriced apartments just for her.

Does she understand the things I had to do to get this place? Does she know how hard I had to work to make this happen? She doesn't know, she doesn't understand.

I've just been waiting for Kaye to come back and get settled. I was calling her today so we could get started on planning her wedding. Now, this. She has blocked me.

"I'll show her," I mutter, going to open my laptop.

I log into my other account, under my real name. I go straight to Kaye's profile. Scrolling through, I read all her recent posts. I stop and rage fills me when a long post grabs my attention.

I normally wouldn't address something like this. However, I'm saddened that someone would drag my name into so many things I have been totally unaware of.

I have not had a PA taking care of things for me while I was away in Ireland. If you have heard that I made comments or had discussions about you, please come to me and ask me.

I wasn't raised to sit around talking about folks. In fact, I automatically tune out when other people start that mess. If you know me, you know I'm a loving person.

I have a family to take care of and that's my focus every day. Social Media is just that, social media. I've been told that some of my posts were turned into drama by folks claiming I'm talking about this one or that one.

How? Was your name mentioned? I'm a direct person.

I would say your name. It's a shame that people would mislead you this way. Most times my posts are about my personal life without me mentioning my son or fiancé.

Those are the times that I chose not to mention names. To protect their privacy. Which shows you I'm not about to invade anyone else's privacy.

It has also come to my attention that remarks were made about my relationship and me being physically abused. Let me make this clear.

My father is still breathing and as long as that man is breathing there is no man in his right mind who would hit my father's child.

My fiancé is loving and protective. He has never harmed me and would never. This is frustrating to have to address. This will be the last time I do. I wish everyone the best.

"*No*," I scream. "No, no, no. You don't get to walk away from me."

I bang my hands against the table. I have to fix this. Kaye just needs to hear things from me. I can tell her my side and we can fix this.

"*Lies.* They're all lying on me because we're friends," I scream. "I hate them. I hate them all. They're trying to take you away from me."

I'll fix this. Yes, yes, yes. I can fix this.

CHAPTER FORTY-SEVEN

Lethal

Kaye

Seven months later ...

Since I was a small girl, my father has drilled into my head, follow my first mind. I don't know why but it's been heavy on me to take Dae-Dae to spend the weekend with my parents. I'm going to follow my gut on this one.

Besides, I have a few things to get done at the new house. I also have a ton of things to do for the wedding. I have no idea how Bean is planning her wedding in six months. It took five months for my dress to arrive at the dress shop alone.

Felix has grumbled about Noah rushing to get married before him a few times. I think he's only teasing. Our wedding is just a few months behind theirs.

I feel like there's still so much to be done. Thank God, I didn't decide to get married in Ireland. I think I would have lost my mind. My career hasn't slowed down nearly as much as I thought it would.

In all honesty, my life is the craziest it has ever been. I think the world has broken into wedding fever. There was Braxton and Heather's wedding in Vegas. Noah and Bean's wedding will be in four months and Lakia has asked me to be a bridesmaid in her wedding.

She and Parker aren't wasting any time. I told my girl her time was coming. I'm so happy for her.

Jake Parker is fine too. We know I have a weakness for men in glasses. Yup, these weddings are piling up and so is my work load.

I thought my work was done with the movie. Not even. It's just starting.

There's the entire media roll out that has to be done now that the movie will be coming out in a few months. I sometimes feel like an outsider when it comes to Nellie, Heather, Bean, and Kamara. Not that they don't welcome me in.

I'm just always so busy, I miss out on so much. I've been trying. The truth is, I get to spend the most time with them when I go to the gun range at the office.

Go figure.

Movies, books, wedding—I'd be excited if I wasn't so darn exhausted. I have two books I need to focus on in the next two months. If I can find a bit of time to myself, I'll get lost in those and crank them out.

Maybe that's why I feel this pull to let my parents have some time with Dae-Dae. Though, something else is nagging at me. I rub at my chest to get the humming sensation to ease.

It's like nerves or anxiety. The phone rings in the car, startling me. When I look to see its Felix, I smile.

I get the feeling he's up to something. All the brothers are. I had lunch with Heather and Nellie, and we picked up on our men acting a bit strange.

"Hey, babe," I chirp into the phone as I answer.

"Hey, baby. I miss you," he purrs into the phone, causing me to smile from ear to ear while squirming at the sound of his voice.

"Oh yeah? I was hoping you could help me out with this scene I'm working on," I reply.

"What do you need?"

I can hear the smile in his voice. He knows exactly the type of help I'm looking for. He'll enjoy it as much as I know I will.

"I was toying with the idea of a little rope play. Not sure, but I'm thinking honey should be involved somehow," I muse.

"Who's doing the bonding?"

"Oh, this hero is all alpha. He has taken control from the beginning," I laugh.

"I'm on it. I'll stop for some honey and a few other things I think will help out," he croons. "How far are you from the house?"

"Why ask questions you know the answer to?" I teasingly grumble. "You and I both know you have a tracker on me and Dashawn. You probably know what color my panties are and what I had for lunch. I don't know if I should be creeped out or turned on."

"We both know your pussy is wet and waiting," he says smoothly. "I don't have access to my equipment. How far are you?"

I frown. Felix is never far from his laptop and devices. Yup, this dude is so up to something. I have a million questions I know he won't answer.

"I'm actually turning into the gate," I reply.

"All right, I'm stopping at the store. I'll be there in a bit. Love you, Kaye."

"Love you too. See you soon."

I don't stop smiling as I grab my purse and step out of my car. I start to mentally plan the rest of the night. Work is forgotten.

I want to be cradled in the arms of my man for a few hours. That is until something in the house catches my eye. I have my key in the lock, ready to turn it, until I notice something is off.

The sun is starting to set so the automatic lights have come on outdoors. However, Felix has the lights inside set to turn on when you enter the house. I haven't pushed the door open.

Yet, I can see lights flicking inside. I squint to make sure I'm seeing right. I don't think twice, reaching in my bag I grab Maggie.

That's what I named the gun Noah gave me, what seems like years ago. I take comfort in her weight in my palm. In the back of my mind, I know I should get back into the car and call Felix.

Still, something draws me into the house. I press the button on the alarm system that shuts off the automatic light function and notifies Felix that something is wrong. I know when he gets the alert, he'll fly home.

Although, when I step inside the lights still come on. I curse in frustration, my face twisting in confusion. The red light lit up on the key fob. It should've worked.

"You're home," is cheered excitedly.

I know that voice.

I turn to find a woman dressed in the exact bridesmaid gown I picked a month ago. The same blue, the same style. Just a bit ill fitting. When I take in her feet, she's wearing the same exact shoes I picked with the girls and my mom.

"Oh, where are my manners. You've never seen my face. It's me, Bonnie," she chirps.

My face compresses. All the pictures I've seen of Bonnie were of a black woman, tall and slender. Standing before me is a woman who looks nothing like the profile pics from social media.

She is shorter than me, a bit on the plump side and her hair is dyed a platinum blonde. There's a crazy look in her eyes and something off about the way she keeps twitching. Her hands and arms are covered in henna tattoos.

This is a scene straight out of one of those crazy movies. She doesn't even seem to flinch at the gun I have pointed at her.

"What are you doing in my home?" I hiss.

"Honey, I know how much you need my help. There's still so much to do. I picked up your dress. I thought you could try it on, we could drink a bottle of wine, and then I could henna your hands.

"If you like it, we can do it for the other girls the weekend of the wedding. I think I finally got it down," she says, nodding her head at her own words.

"What? You have my wedding dress? How did you get in here?"

"I told you. I've been watching and waiting to step in. I finally figured out the system. That Felix is a smart one. This place is amazing, by the way," she replies.

"My fiancé will be here any minute. I tripped the alarm. You need to go," I say.

"No, you didn't silly. I bypassed that feature. It took me a while to read and learn how. It was quite easy after some practice. Oh my God, Kaye," she gushes. "I read what you've written for Wilson. I love it. We have to talk about where you're taking his story. He's my new favorite."

I feel so violated. This woman has been in my home, read through my work. She has been watching my life obviously. Oh God. My son could have been here with me.

"You need to leave now," I say more forcefully.

"Stop it! Stop it! Stop," she hollers, pulling her own gun out of nowhere. "We are friends. You can't ignore me anymore. I'm here for you."

This situation has just escalated from one to a thousand. I try to keep my head. I start to hear Noah's voice in my ear.

"You always keep calm. You control the situation."

I lick my dry lips. I have a son and fiancé I need to survive for. Felix said he was on his way after making a stop. I just have to make it that long.

"Okay, okay, we can figure this out," I say softly.

Dear god, please help me.

A Fan

Yes, we can figure this out.

She is starting to see it my way. I knew she would. I've gone through so much to get here. I've prepared for this day. I'm finally here. Kaye Blaze is standing before me.

"We … we were friends, right? Why did that change? We talked all the time," I say.

"Things have been so busy. Service wasn't so great when I was in Ireland. Then I've been busy since I've been back," Kaye replies with a smile.

"You have such a pretty smile," I say. "We should really pick different shoes for the wedding. These are so uncomfortable."

I kick off the too tight heels. They're killing my feet. I wanted Kaye to see me in the dress.

That stupid clerk kept telling me they couldn't get it in my size. I'm thinking of dying my hair dark for the wedding.

"Are we straightening your hair for the wedding. It's so pretty straight. You should wear it down more. I like it wild and curly too. You seem to like those messy buns," I muse.

"We can look through some of the magazines I have for ideas," Kaye replies.

"Oh, yes, I brought some more with me. You know what I was thinking. You should totally take one of the wedding themes from your books. It would be so amazing. You think Felix would agree?"

"We have to ask him. Bonnie, don't you think—"

"My name is not Bonnie," I yell at her.

"Oh, I'm sorry," she coos.

"You're full of shit. Stop talking to me like that." I blink a few times trying to focus.

This isn't going the way I planned. The candles are melting down and the wine I poured is going to be warm. I hate warm wine.

"Put the gun down, please," Kaye says, interrupting my thoughts.

"You put the gun down. I'm here to be your friend and you have a gun pointed at me. This is not how you start a friendship, Kaye."

"How about we both put them down," she replies.

"No, I don't think we're ready for that. You don't trust me. Lisa ruined the trust you had in me. This is all her fault," I growl. "Don't fucking move."

I raise my gun higher. I don't like her moving closer to me. I want her to stay right where she is.

"I just thought we could go and sit and talk this out. It's been a long day. It looks like both of our feet are hurting and tired," she says, that smile back in place.

"No, no, no," I reply.

"I'm sorry. What is your name again?"

"I never told you my name," I hiss.

"Well, my real name is Kaye Porter. It's nice to meet you."

"I know your real name. I know everything about you. My … my name is Mona. I'm your biggest fan."

"I'm honored, Mona. I have a few books upstairs. I'd love to get a few to sign for you," she offers.

I'm shaking with anger. My finger wraps around the trigger. I hate the tone she's using with me.

I hate it.

"*Shut up, shut up, shut up.* You're doing it again. Stop talking to me like that. I'm not crazy. You're talking to me like I'm crazy. I can hear it in your voice," I rage.

Bang.

I gasp at the loud sound moments before realization hits. This didn't go the way I planned at all. This has gone totally wrong.

Stupid, stupid, stupid. I'm sorry, Kaye. It's all ruined.

Felix

I've been jacked all day. Me and my brothers got to talking about treating the girls after all the crazy stuff we've been through, and we all decided on buying them cars. Wyatt told Nellie that Noah wanted to get Bean a new car as a wedding gift and coaxed her into starting a conversation about dream cars with the other girls.

What Nellie didn't know was that she was being set up to find out what all the girls wanted, including herself. When Kaye said she was taking Dae-Dae to stay with her parents for the weekend, I figured it was the perfect time to surprise her.

I was going to wait, but I couldn't after Toby sent pictures of the car he got for Kamara. I still don't know how he managed to pull that off as fast as he did. I mean, it took a little work, but it wasn't easy getting Kaye a powder blue Aston Martin on such short notice.

I know she's going to love it. I can't wait to see her face. This is just one of the many ways I plan to spoil Kaye for the rest of her life.

"What the fuck?"

The front door of the house is sitting wide open. I look at my phone, but there are no alerts flashing on my screen. The alarm should have tripped to notify me and all the males in my family that something is wrong at my place.

Maybe Kaye is taking packages inside or something.

I know that's bullshit even as I think it. Something is wrong. I berate myself mentally. I should've patched the system into Kaye's new car before I started home. I was just in such a rush to get to her.

It wouldn't have taken me long to do it. I can't believe I didn't listen to my gut. I would have had eyes on the house on my way in, the way I always do.

I rush out of the car and race to the front door. Not knowing what I'll find inside, my guns are already drawn. With getting involved in this Alliance shit, I shouldn't be slacking at all.

"Baby?" I choke in confusion. The smell of gunfire permeates my nose. "Holy shit, baby."

I drop to my knees beside Kaye, pulling her into my arms. She's ice cold. I know instantly she's gone into shock. I look over her head at the lifeless body on the floor.

Mona Richards.

Bonnie was an alias. She's wanted in several states for credit card and check fraud, identity theft, and she's a suspect in a few missing persons cases. I've been tracking her for weeks now. I couldn't let it go after the things Kia told us.

I was just one move from finding her. The trail went cold a few months ago. She's been lying extremely low. I guess now I know why.

"Shh, baby, shh," I soothe a sobbing Kaye.

"I … I killed someone," she sobs out.

"In self-dense. You did what you had to do," I reassure her.

"She was irrational. Her finger was on the trigger. I saw the shot and took it. I … I. Felix, I shot her," she gasps and sobs.

"Shh, baby. I'll take care of it. You know I always take care of it."

Pulling my phone from my pocket, I dial Toby first. His house is the closest to mine. He'll get here the fastest. When he answers the line, I say all that needs to be said.

"I need you."

"I'm there," he replies.

"Never a dull moment," I mutter to myself, dialing Noah next.

CHAPTER FORTY-EIGHT

No Judge

Noah

"Noah, I can't take anymore," Bean cries as I sit beneath her, devouring her core.

"Don't move," I grumble into her pussy. "I'm not finished."

"*Noah,*" she whimpers as I hold her in place.

I smile wide as her pussy drips all over my face into my beard. I can't get enough of her taste. I plan to be at this shit all night.

"Please," she pleads as her body convulses over my face.

I release her long enough to slip from under her. Once I'm up, I turn and flip her onto her back. Rebecca looks up at me with a lazy sated smile. I love that dazed look in her eyes.

Lifting her hands above her head, I slide into her tight body nice and slow. Her mouth falls open and her eyes roll back. I know the feeling.

Between her taste on my tongue, the scent of her sweetness, and the feel of her squeezing around me—it takes all I have not to lose all control and pound into her. I promised myself tonight would be a long leisure fuck. Nothing rushed, nothing rough.

Just me and my Rebecca making love. I want to clear her mind of everything but me.

"Noah," she groans in that sexy voice.

I can't wait until we're married. Just a few more months and life will be complete. Just knowing that alone makes this feel so much better.

"Aw, fuck no," I hiss as my phone begins to ring. "Shit, come on. *Fuck.*"

I stop thrusting to reach for the phone. Turning onto my back, I tap Bean's ass, prompting her to ride me. She sits up, placing her tits in my face, and starts to bounce her ass on me.

"Yo," I grunt into the phone, while flicking my tongue across Rebecca's nipple.

"I have a problem," Felix's voice greets my ear along with sobbing in the background.

I sit up immediately stilling Bean against my chest. The sound of Kaye's cries sends a chill through me. I'm protective about all my family, but my brother's girls have all become like little sisters to me. I hate it when they're upset, but this sounds beyond that.

"Where are you?"

"Home."

"I'm there."

I hang up the line, expecting to find Rebecca pouting. However, when I let her go, she jumps up into action. Tossing clothes at me, she starts to wiggle into her own.

"Where do you think you're going?" I grunt as I start to pull my things on.

"That was Kaye crying. I'm coming with you," she says without batting a lash.

"I thought you didn't even like her," I say, side glancing my girl.

"Never said that. I get her. She's an introvert and she's always in her head writing her books. I give her, her space." She shrugs.

I shake my head. I'm not touching the fact that my brothers and I have a common trait we're attracted to. Maybe with the exception of John. Although, when it comes to John he always does his own thing.

"Whatever, let's go."

Felix

My dad and my brothers are all here. Nellie, Heather, Kamara, and my mother arrived after my brothers and Bean assessed the situation. Wyatt and Dad called in a favor to keep this scene controlled.

I'm thinking of Kaye's career and the movie she has coming out. This isn't the type of press she needs. I wanted to keep this as quiet as I could.

My girl is still in shock. Although, I couldn't be prouder of her. She kept her head and got out of a sticky situation alive.

I will forever owe Noah my life. Because of him, Kaye isn't the one they took out of here in the body bag.

"The lass just needs a bit of time. She'll be fine," my mother says as she sits beside me on the sofa.

"Is she talking yet?"

"A wee bit," mom replies. "She called her father."

"How did I let this happen?"

"Oh, no ye don't," she chides. "Ye don't go feeling sorry for yerself. Ye couldn't have done anything differently. Ye heard Ry and Noah. She had an apartment filled with research and all types of things to get her way in here. She planned this for months."

"What if our son was here?" I grind out.

"We'll be thankful he wasn't," she says, patting my cheek. "I'll get these fuckers out of ye hair. Ye get in that room and pour all that love ye have into her. That's what the lass needs."

"I love you, mom," I say, wrapping an arm around her and pulling her into a tight hug.

"I love ye too. Ye did well, Felix. Ye found a lass as tough as me. Next time she'll fire first and take names last," she chuckles.

"Better not have to be a next time," I mutter.

"We're Blacks. There will always be a next time," Mom says ominously.

I groan and palm my head. Her words are the truth and I know it. There is always some shit going on around my family.

"All right, the lot of ye. Get yer asses out of Felix's house. We'll check on them tomorrow," Mom calls like the warden she is.

I can't help cracking a smile. Leave it to my mom to clear a place out. Not one person here is willing to argue with her. Although, I can see some of the girls looking as if they want to.

"If you need us, call," my father says before pulling me into a hug.

He releases me, waiting for my mother to finish embracing me before he wraps an arm around her and leads her out. Once everyone clears out, I make my way back to our bedroom, where Kaye has been since after giving her statement.

She barely made it through. Once she finished crying her way through the account, she shutdown. She wouldn't or couldn't say another word.

At least Mom said she called her dad. That's good. I didn't want to alarm her parents. Her being able to make the call is a start. I'll take some responsiveness over nothing.

When I enter the bedroom it's completely dark, except for the moonlight spilling in. I can make Kaye out on the bed. She's lying upside down, her head facing the foot of the bed with her feet propped up on the headboard.

I pad closer. When I get to the bed, I can see her eyes are open, glued to the ceiling. I climb on, hovering over her face.

She doesn't move or respond. I'm concerned, but my mother's words come back to me. Kaye needs my love more than anything.

I dip to softly kiss her face, catching her lower lip and chin with my lips. When I pull back to look into her eyes again, her focus is on me. Tears begin to roll back into her ears.

I climb over her, placing my back against the headboard. Grasping her ankles, I gently tug her until I've positioned her against my chest. She comes willingly, her limp body melding against mine.

We sit like that in silence for a long while. I stroke her back to sooth her, kissing the top of her head every now and then. I pour every ounce of love I have for her into my embrace.

"I could've just disabled her," Kaye whimpers. "I didn't have to kill her."

"I watched the footage, baby. You did the right thing," I murmur.

"Would you have done the same thing? You or your brothers? I killed someone."

"If it means me coming home to my family or keeping my family safe, every fucking time. We'd be eating pizza and drinking beer right now," I answer.

"That seems so cold," she says softly.

"Not in my line of work. The things I've seen and done—I'm not losing sleep over a mad woman who's been stalking you and held you at gunpoint, Kaye. You shouldn't either."

"Clearly she needed help," she replies.

"Yeah, she did. But baby, she was far past getting it. Do you want to know what my brothers found in her apartment?"

She turns her face up to look at me. I hate seeing such sadness in her eyes. She looks so fragile, not my strong girl at all.

"What?"

"They found the owner of the place stuffed in a closet. The ID in Mona's wallet was her picture, but the tenant's identity. That's how she hid under the radar. She was living that poor woman's life.

"We know for a fact she researched for the right person. Someone who had no family, very little friends, a decent bank account. She watched and waited, killed that woman, and took over her existence.

"So you tell me. Did you do what you needed to do to protect yourself?" I ask pointedly.

"Oh my God. Felix, that's crazy," she gasps.

"Kaye, it's her MO. She was watching and studying you just the same. I'm just so fucking happy Dashawn wasn't here and that Noah turned you into a precision shooter."

"I owe so much to him. I just kept hearing his voice in my mind. It's what kept me calm to wait for the right moment.

"I was so scared. She was coming apart right in front of me," she whispers, a shiver running through her.

"We'll get through this," I reassure her.

"Yeah, that's what my dad said. I called him to pray for me. I told him what happened. He said ... he said there are no accidents in the universe. She walked in my home with the intent to harm what belongs to God. No weapon formed.

"I ... I want to believe him. I want to see this from his point of view, but I'm no judge. What gives me the right to be an executioner?"

"Your God given right to be safe in your own home. Dude, I've been to your dad's church. I've gone with Danny to bible study a million times. All throughout the bible God teaches his people to fight for what's theirs. You think that stopped for us because times changed, or we have different weapons.

"I understand you, sweetheart. Kaye, you wouldn't hurt a fly, but tonight, you did what you had to. I have no doubt in me that you wouldn't do it again if your children were in danger.

"You're a fighter. This time you just fought to the death, and you came out the victor just like you should. Either way, this was that woman's last day. If she would have harmed you. She wouldn't have been breathing long after," I say tightly.

"Your mother probably wants you to call off the engagement. All of your brothers have such sweet wives and girlfriends, and you get me—Annie Oakley," she pouts.

I throw my head back and roar with laughter. I laugh so hard tears spill over. She did not just say that.

"Hold on, hold on. You can't be fucking serious," I say through my laughter.

"Why are you laughing at me?" she huffs.

"One, you've seen my mother's guns over the front door, haven't you?" I look at her with my brows raised.

"I've seen the guns. Didn't know they were hers."

"My mom would have walked in the door guns blazing. Kaye, seriously. Nellie, Bean, and Heather could have and would have killed that woman with their bare hands. Bean wouldn't have bothered coming in the house.

"She just would have picked that looney tune off with her sniper rifle out the trunk of her car. Kamara is the most innocent next to you and that's not saying much. I've watched her smack a guy across the face with a hot frying pan.

"I want you to think about something. Every single person who spent time in your New York apartment was there as a bodyguard. Male or female," I say, watching my words sink in.

I see the moment it clicks. Her eyes light up with understanding and her mouth falls open in shock. Her eyes bounce over my face as if to decipher my words. I shrug.

"Connie and Kate?" she breathes.

"Yup, and trust me, what you did tonight was child's play to them. Don't torment yourself. She had knives, ropes, and all types of other shit—I'm not going to clutter your head with—in her bag. No matter what she said. She didn't come here to play," I say to drive my point.

"Okay, I hear you," she says slowly with a matching nod.

"Good, but seriously, baby. We have to get you around the family more," I snort before bursting into laughter once again.

"Stop laughing at me," she whines, but I can hear the life and playfulness coming back to her voice.

Yeah. My girl is going to be just fine. Maybe a few days in Ireland after Noah's wedding will help. I'll get her through this.

"I love you, Kaye. Just the way you are," I murmur.

"Yeah, I'm definitely starting to see that something is wrong with you," she teases. "I love you too, Felix. Wouldn't change a thing about you."

"I wouldn't let you," I chuckle.

"Yeah, I know. That's one of the things I love."

I kiss her forehead and we fall silent again. This time I can feel my girl with me. When I look down into her eyes she's there.

Damn, we've come a long way. A really long way. I remember my shy little church mouse. Now, I have a gun slinging, book slaying, freak and I couldn't be happier.

CHAPTER FORTY-NINE

Here We Are

Carmen

I'm speechless. I have no words. I've been hanging onto every word since Felix and Kaye started talking. Their love for each other is so clear.

"I love how supportive you are," I gush.

"Why wouldn't I be? Kaye has so much talent. I'm not going to get in the way of that if I can help it," Felix says and shrugs.

It's the most I've ever heard him say outside of helping Kaye to tell me their story. Damn, I agree with Kaye. Felix has one sexy ass voice.

All that phone sex they used to have. There's another Black who has a voice just like his. Only that voice has a hint of humor and a tiny rasp when it drops and gets dirty.

Felix's eyes lock on me and I swear I see a secret little smile on his lips. It's as if he can see my thoughts.

Mm. Note to self. Beware of wearing my thoughts on my face around Felix.

He releases a small laugh. I can't help but think he just read my thoughts. It's a bit unnerving.

"I'm glad all of that is behind us. We'll finally be married in three more months," Kaye coos, looking up at Felix dreamily.

"Do you think you'll ever write about what happened?"

Kaye pauses. I can see the wheels turning inside her head. Her face screws up before she shrugs.

"You know. I see it this way. Inspiration comes from life experiences. You never know." She winks at me.

"I'll tell you one thing. That shit'll never happen again," Felix mutters.

"Yeah, because you screen everyone with a full-blown background check. I haven't proved it yet, but I swear he goes through my social media list to screen my followers," Kaye teases.

"Whatever," Felix grumbles.

"Who's pregnant, me or you? You're so grumpy today," Kaye cracks up.

"You're pregnant?" I gasp.

"Oh shoot," Kaye groans. She looks up at Felix apologetically. "Sorry?"

It dawns on me that Kaye has been drinking water all night. Her being pregnant would account for the glow she seems to have. It also says a lot about how watchful Felix has been over her.

Felix looks at me and winks. "She'll keep our secret."

"We're waiting until everyone returns home. We didn't want to take Noah and Bean's shine," Kaye whispers.

"Your secret is safe with me. Congratulations," I whisper back.

"You know my brother is a great guy. Don't let the teasing fool you. He'd treat you just as good as the rest of us treat our women," Felix says with those watchful eyes on me again.

"Oh, that's not going to happen. I'm not his type and I don't think he's mine." I wave him off.

"You could have fooled me. I see sparks fly whenever you two are next to each other," Kaye beams.

I shake my head. She writes too many of those books. Ryan and I would crash and burn before we ever start. We're just too different.

"I don't think so," I reply.

"None of us started out easy. Give him a chance. I've never seen him work this hard for a female's attention," Felix says warmly.

"He can stop wasting his time. I'm not that type of girl."

"What type?" Ryan's voice startles me.

He had gone to get drinks as Kaye and Felix finished telling me their story. We've been sitting in the back of the bar, while everyone else has taken over the pool tables. From what I understand, the O'Brien's own the place.

"Um, that's it right? The last of the stories?"

"Yes and no," Kaye giggles. "We'll see you at the wedding, right?"

"Oh, I ... I hadn't planned to be there," I reply.

"Nonsense. You have to be there. It's sure to be eventful." Kaye wiggles her brows.

My interest is piqued. One of these days my curiosity is going to get the best of me. I know it is.

"She'll be my plus one," Ryan says in that cock sure way of his.

"I don't know about that," I scoff.

Ry leans over me until our faces are just a breath apart. I stop breathing. I'm so still I could be a statue. He licks his lips and I feel the heat of the gesture against my own.

"You know all about my family, but what do you know about me?" He breathes, causing my nipples to tighten.

His voice alone is like a bolt of lightning. I hate that I have this type of reaction to him. This pull seems to be getting stronger, not weaker.

"Cat got your tongue, Nene?" he asks, my nickname rolling off his tongue.

"No," I say breathlessly.

"Um. Well, let me tell you a few things you need to know about me. One, when I know something is mine, I'd move heaven, hell, and earth to get to it. Two, I never give up. Three, it's all fun and games with me … until it's not.

"I knew you were mine the first time you fell into my arms. I'm patient, Carmen. As a matter of fact, I prefer to take my time. I hate to rush. Things get missed when people rush. You'll know when I'm done teasing you, gorgeous.

"When you lose your breath, and you need me to think straight. When *my Ryan* is the only thing that comes to mind. You'll know. We're done dancing around this and I'm coming to claim what's mine," he says so slick, my mind is convinced he just licked me between my legs.

"Well, damn. That's going in a book," Kaye says after a low whistle.

"Really?" Felix laughs beside her.

Ryan

"Aye, ye have a glad eye for that lass, you do," Carrick says beside me.

I roll my eyes. I don't have to turn to him to see the smile on his face. I can hear it in his voice. I don't reply.

I'm too focused on Carmen. She's so cute. She's been nursing the same beer for about an hour now. I can tell I fried the fuck out of her brain.

Felix got roped into a game of pool once he and Kaye finished dishing their story to Carmen. He's been cleaning Jeremiah out since. A glance over at the pool table tells me it won't be much longer before Felix finishes the job.

"Hey, I wanted to talk to you."

I snap my head in Carrick's direction. He has curbed his accent, grabbing my attention. I know he's serious and the look in his eyes confirms it. I focus on my cousin and the haunted look in his eyes.

I knit my brows. Carrick is older than I am. I've always looked up to him like I do Wyatt. He's more like a big brother to me.

"What's up?" I ask, showing him, he has my full attention.

Carrick looks down at his hands. I watch as he blinks slowly a few times. The wheels in his head are turning so hard, I promise you I can hear them.

I wait patiently, knowing he's putting his words together. When he speaks and his accent is tuned down again, I lean in closer.

"It's been almost two years since we talked of me coming to the States. Felix has Kaye and Dashawn. He says I can still come stay with him, but I don't want to be a bother.

"Have ye moved out of yer condo?" Carrick lifts his blue-hazel eyes to lock with mine.

"Not yet. I've been thinking of moving out or getting a roommate," I reply and shrug.

Carrick nods, licking his lips. Once again, I wait him out. I can feel the tension surrounding him.

"This will always be me home. I just need a change. Have you ever felt like yer body is in one place, but yer heart be in another?"

He shakes his head as if to clear it. I think on his question, my eyes travel over to Carmen. I absently rub at my chest. Yeah, I guess I do understand what he means.

"I think I know what you mean." I nod.

"It's odd. I have no clue why I've been feeling this way, but it's been weighing on me lately. I just feel like maybe what I'm looking for is on the other side of the pond," he muses.

"Dude, without question, my door is open, whenever you're ready," I reassure him.

A relieved smile takes over his face. I watch as his demeanor changes back to the confident, playful Carrick I know. He pats me on the shoulder, his mischievous smile in place, right where it belongs.

"Aye, glad ye be ken on the little lass. More nex for me when I arrive," he teases, nodding at Carmen.

I turn to see her staring over at us. She turns away the moment my eyes find hers. My lips pull into a grin.

I look to Felix to see him laughing his ass off at a sour looking Jeremiah. Uncle Ronan is in the corner nursing a beer, looking like a grumpy bear. It reminds me that he's been in the States going back and forth between New York and LA for a while now. I know there's a story there, but he hasn't been willing to share it.

"I tell a lie, I don't like ye," Jeremiah booms at Felix.

"I guess that game is over," I chuckle.

"Aye, I don't know why Jeremiah loves giving away his money," Carrick snorts. "Ach, I won't complain about collecting me fees though."

I laugh as Carrick heads over to the pool table. His steps seem to be lighter. I wonder what all that's really about, but I shake it off and head for the table my little reporter is sitting at.

It's time to get to my end game. Enough dicking around. It's time to create our story.

Brotherly Love

Felix

Two and a half years later …

I'm going to fuck Noah and Brax up. I know this was them. Sweat is pouring from my forehead. I knew I shouldn't have touched those brownies.

Jordan and Dae-Dae were distracting me. I swear these kids will drive you insane. Try listening to an eight-year-old and a nearly two year old explain to you how one of the other kids wronged them will drive anyone to grab for the nearest thing to chew to keep from cursing.

It's just dawning on me that Noah had just appeared with the plate of gooey treats. Fucked up part is, that shit wasn't meant for me. I know which one of my brothers those two were after.

"Fuck," I groan.

I'm sweating my brain out as I fuck this bathroom up. I don't know how long I've been in here. My stomach is killing me.

Noah is wrong for this shit. Payback is a motherfucker. We're all grown ass men with wives and kids. Why the fuck are we still feeding each other shit cakes?

Noah's vindictive ass has it coming. We'll see how he likes it when I lock him out of his house or some shit. I'm going to come up with something. He should have been paying closer attention. One of the kids could have eaten one of those fucked up brownies.

"Shit," I groan.

I pull my beanie from my head and toss it into the sink. My t-shirt is next to come over my head and get tossed. I flush, reaching for the spray.

"Are you fucking kidding me?" I hiss.

There's no spray or toilet paper. I look around and confirm that I'm shit out of luck. Nothing. This has my brothers written all over it.

I'm pissed as fuck now. Pulling out my phone I text my wife. I need her to come to my rescue. This shit is so embarrassing. I'm going to kick their asses.

Shooting off a quick text all I can do is wait, which isn't a problem. Apparently, I'm not done. I close my eyes and groan as my ass feels like it's exploding.

"Babe." I hear Kaye outside the bathroom door. "I was wondering where you've been. You okay in there?"

"No, I'm going to kill them," I growl.

I roll my eyes when my wife bursts into laughter. This shit is not funny. I just sit and wait for her to get it out.

"I'm sorry, honey. I'm sorry," she giggles. "Bean is trying to find the toilet paper. You guys are going to have to hold on for a minute."

"You guys?" I ask with my brows furrowed.

"Yeah, Ry and John are—" she cutoff, bursting into more laughter. "Let's just say you're not the only one in need of toilet paper and air refresher."

"Assholes," I mutter.

"Babe, I'll come back when I find paper and some spray. You kind of stink," Kaye giggles.

"Whatever, Kaye," I huff.

"Pee-yew," I hear Jordan's little voice outside the door.

I roll my eyes. Of all the kids, she's the last one who needs to be outside the door. It just keeps getting better.

"Is that Uncle Lix?" Riley's voice comes next.

"Oh God, really?" I groan.

Kaye hoots with laughter. I push a hand through the front of my sweaty hair. This has become my life. All these crazy ass kids, my brothers still acting like kids and my wife creating story after story from all our antics.

"Come on, girls," Kaye coos. "We might need to go to the store."

I shake my head. I can hear her laughing as she moves away from the door with the girls. This is some bullshit.

Just you wait, Noah.

Kaye

I swipe at my tears. I love this family. I couldn't have asked to marry into a one. I enter the family room still laughing my butt off.

"Noah and Wyatt just rushed into the bathrooms at the back of the house," Nellie laughs.

"You know you're so wrong for this," I say through my laughter.

"Ye get as old as me and ye will learn a thing or two. They all think they're too old for me to put them in their places. I think the fuck not," Cass huffs.

We all crack up. All the ladies are sitting around for the baby shower games. Joe and some of the other male guests have the children. I dropped Jordan and Riley off before coming in here.

"Felix thinks his brothers did it," I giggle.

"Aye, he would," Cass mutters.

"Remind me never to piss you off," Val says through her laughter.

"I shouldn't have to tell grown men to clean up after their wee un. I asked repeatedly for them to clean up before they left with the babes. I had a damn headache that day or I would've done it me self," Cassy fuses.

"That's the problem, they're so used to you doing it for them," Nellie says.

"I nearly broke me neck on those fucking toys last week. I told them I'd get them," Cass says.

A gasp draws our attention. We all turn to find Jordan and Riley standing in the doorway. I cover my mouth to hide my laugh.

"Bad word, Grandma," Jordan chides.

"Not today, lass. I be cheesed off, I am. Ye get yer wee butt back with rest of the chisellers. I've had enough of the lot of ye, I have," Cass fusses, folding her arms over her chest.

I promise you, Jordan's eyes round and get large in her head as she gives her grandmother a pleading pout. Imagine Puss in Boots from Shrek, Jordan has perfected that look. I watch Cassy turn into putty, opening her arms for Jordan to run into.

"And this is why Jordan is Jordan," Nellie says, palming her face.

"Tell me about it," I giggle.

"That little girl is something else," Pam says.

"Aye, has me wrapped around her finger just like her father when he was her age," Cass says with a sheepish look on her face.

We all start to laugh again. Like I said, I love my family. Every single one of them—and boy there's a lot of us these days.

I can finally say I have that smile—one like Danny's. A smile that brightens my days and feels freeing. I'm living my life without apology.

Blue Collection Character Tree

Legally Bound 1

Bobby Mairettie and Paige Kemble-Mairettie *father and mother of:*

*Peyton and James Mairettie (*twin boys*)
*Sydney Mairettie and Maria Lynn Mairettie (*twin girls*)

Legally Bound 2

Marcus Mairettie and Rita Briggs-Mairettie *father and mother of:*

*Daniel Mairettie
*Hannah Mairettie

Legally Bound 3

Nathaniel (Nate) Briggs and Pamela (Pam) Kemble-Briggs *father and mother of:*

*Tiffany and Tracey Briggs (*twin girls*)
*Nathaniel Briggs Jr.

Legally Bound 4

Jasper Briggs and Marie Mairettie-Briggs *father and mother of:*

*Clay Briggs

The Mairettie Family

Grandpa Marcello Mairettie and Grandma Marie Ann *father and mother of:*

*Marcello Mairettie Jr.
*Andrew Mairettie

*James Mairettie
*Jessie Mairettie
*Lynn Mairettie
*Gianna Mairettie
*James Mairettie and Minnie Mairettie *father and mother of:*
    *Bobby Mairettie
    *Sam Mairettie – (Ellen Kensington-Mairettie, *wife*)
    *Marcus Mairettie
    *Marie Mairettie

The Briggs Family

Thomas Briggs and Raquel Marinos-Briggs (*Deceased*) *father and mother of:*
    *Nathaniel Briggs
    *Rita Briggs

Earl Briggs (Thomas' younger brother) and Caitronia Marinos-Briggs (twin sister of Raquel) *father and mother of:*
    *Kelly Briggs-Fecteau (Alexie Fecteau, *husband*)
    *Jasper Briggs

The Kemble Family

Peyton Kemble and Davina Kemble *father and mother of:*
    *Pamela Kemble
    *Paige Kemble

Other Important *Legally Bound* Characters

Camille (Cam) Mc Wien-Carter (Seth Carter, *soon-to-be ex-husband*) *father and mother of:*
    *Seth Carter Jr.
    *Eddie Carter

*Aiden Carter

Austin Mc Wien (*Camille's father*)

Baroness Olivia Kontos (Baron Kontos' widow; Jasper's ex-lover; Thomas Briggs' new love interest)

Vanessa (Julissa) Smith-Mims (Patrick Mims, *husband, Deceased*)

Hush 1
Uri Donati and Valentina Caprisi-Donati *father and mother of:*
  *Vita Khayla Donati
  *Nori Donati
  *Inzo Donati
  *Eva Donati

Hush 2
Luca Donati and Shannon Caprisi-Donati *father and mother of:*
  *Carlo Donati (Introduced in **Ballers 2**)

The Donati Family
Angelo Uri Donati (***Deceased***) and Donatella Manzo-Donati-~~Zuko~~ *father and mother of:*
  *Uri Donati
  *Nico Donati ~~Zuko~~
  *Annabella Donati ~~Zuko~~ (*Nico's twin sister*)
  *Michael Donati – ~~Zuko~~

Nicholas Donati (Angelo Donati's brother) and Ava Donati *father and mother of:*

*Luca Donati

The Caprisi Family
Vincent Caprisi and Khayla Grant-Caprisi (**Deceased**) *father and mother of:*
  *Valentina Caprisi
  *Lissette Caprisi (**Deceased**)
  **Shannon Caprisi (*Vincent's daughter*)

Other Important *Hush* **Characters**
Uncle Valentine Caprisi (*Vincent's brother; head hitter*)

Iman Grant (*Khayla's sister;* **Shannon's mother;* **Deceased**)

Roberto Donati-Zuko (*Donatella's husband;* **Deceased**)
**Posed as Dale the accountant from Legally Bound 3*

Cole 'Brooklyn' O'Brien

DJ

Ballers 1
Bradley Monroe and Tamara Hathaway-Monroe *father and mother of:*
  *Brielle Monroe
  *Ashley Monroe and Ashton Monroe (twins)
  *Corey Monroe (*Baby Tam is pregnant with at end of* **Ballers 1**)

The Monroe Family

Vernon Monroe and Gloria Monroe *father and mother of:*
*Trevor Monroe (Donna, *soon to be ex-wife*)
*Bradley Monroe
*Ann Monroe (Bradley's twin sister; Tom, husband)

Trevor Monroe and Donna Monroe *father and mother of:*
*Jessica Monroe
*Toby Monroe and Paige Monroe (*twins*)
*Jonathan Monroe
Tom Rivers and Ann Monroe-Rivers *father and mother of:*
*George Rivers and Melissa Rivers (*twins*)
*Amy Rivers

The Hathaway Family

Byron Hathaway and Fiona Hathaway *father and mother of:*
*Ellerie Hathaway
*Tamara Hathaway

Other Important *Ballers* **Characters**

Stacey (Tam's best friend)

Reese (Tam's best friend; Nico's girlfriend in *Ballers 1*)

Alee (Tam's best friend)

Cyrus Pierson (Tam's boss) *father of:*
*Tommy Pierson
*Carey Pierson

*Stephanie Pierson

Ballers 2
Nico Donati and Reese Bridges-Donati *father and mother of:*
   *Nico Donati Jr.
   *Lanya Donati
   *Orso Donati
   *Santo Donati
   *Stefano Donati

Other Important *Ballers 2* Characters
Tiberius Roman (Reese's ex-husband)

Symphony (Michael's right-hand)

Brothers Black 1
Wyatt Black and Lanelle (Nellie) Bryant-Black *father and mother of:*
   *Nora Black
   *Evan Black

The Black Family
Joseph Black and Cassidy Black *father and mother of:*
   *Wyatt Black
   *Noah Black
   *Johnathan Black
   *Felix Black
   *Toby Black (Kamara, baby mother) and father of:
      *TJ and Lulu (twin brother and sister)

*Braxton Black
*Ryan Black

The Lockhart Family
Rob Lockhar and Faith Lockhart *father and step-mother of:*
*Heather Lockhart

Steve Lockhart and Nora Bryant-Lockhart (***Deceased***) *step-father and mother of:*
*Lanelle (Nellie) Bryant-Black

Chase Lockhart and Jennifer Lockhart *father and mother of:*
*Rebecca (Bean) Lockhart (Noah's best friend and love interest)

Other Important *Brothers Black 1* Characters
Missy (Johnathan's ex-girlfriend, ***Deceased***)

Lucy (*Heather's girlfriend*)

Barry Coleman (***Deceased***)

Brothers Black 2
Noah Black and Rebecca (Bean) Lockhart-Black *father and mother of:*
*Brodie Black
*Connor Black
Baby on the way

Other Important *Brothers Black 2* Characters

Joshua (*Deceased*)

Carmen (Nene) Nash (*reporter; niece of Mariah Briggs from Yours Series; Ryan's new crush*)

Logan O'Brien

Brothers Black 3
King Toby Black and Queen Ogeima Feechi (Kamara) Abioye-Black *father and mother of:*
*Lulu Black
*TJ Black
Baby on the way

Other Important Brothers Black 3 **Characters**
Missy (Johnathan's ex-girlfriend, *Deceased*)

Lucy (*Heather's girlfriend*)

Barry Coleman (*Deceased*)
King Elijah Abioye aka Mr. Naidoo

Queen Ada Catherine Naidoo-Abioye

King Kwäzē Naidoo-Abioye

Celeste (Kwäzē's ex-girlfriend)

King Afafa (*Deceased*)

Missy (Johnathan's ex-girlfriend, *Deceased*)

Lucy (*Heather's girlfriend*)

Barry Coleman (*Deceased*)

Joshua (*Deceased*)

Carmen Nash aka Nene (*Reporter, Mariah Briggs, from Yours Series, Niece, Ryan's new crush*)
Logan O'Brien

Dylan O'Brien

Jamie O'Brien

Cole 'Brooklyn' O'Brien

Uncle Jonah McGowan

Uncle Jack McGowan

Uncle Raymond McGowan

Uncle Ronan McGowan

Carrick McGowan

Malcolm McGowan

Graham McGowan

Jeremiah McGowan

Reilly McGowan

Brothers Black 4
Braxton Black and Heather Lockhart-Black *father and mother of:*
*Riley Black
*Rowen Black

Other Important *Brothers Black 4* **Characters**
Debbie ~~Lockhart~~-Kline (Rob's ex-wife, Heather's Mother)

Lucy (*Heather's pretend girlfriend*)

Amanda Kline (Heather's half-sister)

Ernest Kline (Heather's Stepfather, *Deceased*)

Eugene aka Crooked Nose

Logan O'Brien

Dylan O'Brien

Jamie O'Brien

Cole 'Brooklyn' O'Brien

Uncle Jonah McGowan

Uncle Jack McGowan

Uncle Raymond McGowan

Uncle Ronan McGowan

Carrick McGowan

Malcolm McGowan

Graham McGowan

Jeremiah McGowan

Reilly McGowan

Nicholas Lincoln

Sephora Lincoln

Thomas Briggs

Brothers Black 5
Felix Black and Kaye Porter-Black aka Kaye Blaze *father and mother of:*
*Dashawn Black
*Second child unannounced

Other Important *Brothers Black 4* Characters
Lakia Redding (*Kaye's writer friend*)

Dean (*Kaye's writer friend*)

Hayidah (*Doll for Club Desire*)

Pastor Wayne Porter (*Kaye's father*)

Danesha Porter (*Kaye's mother*)

Danny Porter (**Deceased** *Kaye's brother and Felix best friend*)

Grandma Reid (*Kaye's grandmother*)

Grandpa Reid (*Kaye's grandfather*)

Alberto Perez (*Felix's best friend*)

Jacob McTavish (*Lead actor in Kaye's movie*)

Mona Richards (**Deceased**, *a fan)*

Logan O'Brien

Dylan O'Brien

Jamie O'Brien

Cole 'Brooklyn' O'Brien

Uncle Ronan McGowan

Carrick McGowan

Yours Series
Nicholas Lincoln and Sephora (Sophi/Soph/Lilla du) Emilsson *father and mother of:*
    *Nicole Lincoln
    *Nadia Lincoln
    *Nicholas Lincoln Jr.

The Lincoln Family

Dean Lincoln and Shelly Lincoln (***Both Deceased***) *father and mother of:*
    *Nicholas Lincoln
    *Rick ~~Carbon~~ Lincoln
    *Gavin ~~Carbon~~ Lincoln

The Emilsson Family

Liam Emilsson (thought to be deceased) and Faraz Emilsson father and mother of:
    *Lucian Emilsson
    *Ettie Emilsson
    *Sephora Emilsson

Lucian Emilsson and Kimberly Ann Clove *father and mother of:*
    *Lilla Emilsson

Other Important *Yours* Characters
Mark Fienberg (Sephora's best friend)

Ivana Graves (Nick's ex-girlfriend; ***Deceased***)

Bianca (Liam's mistress; ***Missing***)

Winton (Nick's driver and security)

Jillian Carver (Nick's ex-temporary PA; *Deceased*)

Harvey Carver (Jillian's father; Nick's family friend; *Deceased*)

Bailey Wilder (waitress; Mark's girlfriend)

Dylan O'Brien
Nick's Crew
Wyatt Black
Kevin Briggs (Mariah Briggs' husband; Nick's PA)
Craig Hilton
George Ligal
Lucian Emilsson
Andrew Connor (Ettie's husband)

ACKNOWLEDGMENTS

This book!! I'm so happy that I took my time and changed directions from where I started. This book was everything to me. I think this may have been the toughest to write so far, as it was both personally and technically challenging.

Thank you to all of my readers for your patience and support. I poured a piece of me into this one, I think more so than any of the others. I'm just glad that I can create humor from issues and situations that I actually lived through.

Felix has been one of my most challenging and dominating males yet. If it were up to him this book would have been a lot longer. LOL. In the end, I think I was able to get everything I wanted out of this book. Watching my husband laugh, get upset, and talk so enthusiastically about the emotional scenes solidified this fact for me once he finished reading it.

Thanks so much to the team that worked so hard to get this book done.

It is more than necessary to thank God. I would not be able to do any of this without my Source. God is in everything. I'm glad to have learned that so early. It's a revelation that allows understanding of life, love, and hurt. If we can find God in the root, we can find peace and strength. Thank you, Lord, for your Grace and Favor. With all I am, I give you the highest praise.

Next and ready! Ryan, Ryan, Ryan. Phew, let's go big boy.

ABOUT THE AUTHOR

Blue Saffire, award-winning, bestselling author of over seventy contemporary romance novels and novellas, writes with the intention to touch the heart and the mind. Blue hooks, weaves, and loops multiple series, keeping you engaged in her worlds. Blue writes for her own publishing company, Perceptive Illusions as Blue Saffire, as well as Royal Blue.

Blue and her husband live in a house filled with laughter and creativity in Long Island, NY. Both working hard to build the Blue brand and cultivate their love for the arts. Creative is their family affair.

Blue holds an MBA in Marketing and Project Management, as well as an MED in Instructional Technology and Curriculum Design. She is also an NLP Master Practitioner.

Wait, there is more to come! You can stay updated with my latest releases, learn more about me the author, and be a part of contests by subscribing to my newsletter at

www.BlueSaffire.com

If you enjoyed Brothers Black 5, I'd love to hear your thoughts and please feel free to leave a review on Amazon Click Here. And when you do, please let me

know by emailing me TheBlueSaffire@gmail.com

or leave a comment on

Facebook https://www.facebook.com/BlueSaffireDiaries

or Twitter @TheBlueSaffire

Other books by Blue Saffire

Placed in Best Reading Order
Also available …

Legally Bound

Legally Bound 2: Against the Law

Legally Bound 3: His Law

Perfect for Me

Hush 1: Family Secrets

Ballers: His Game

Brothers Black 1: Wyatt the Heartbreaker

Legally Bound 4: Allegations of Love

Hush 2: Slow Burn

Legally Bound 5.0: Sam

Yours 1: Losing My Innocence

Yours 2: Experience Gained

Yours 3: Life Mastered

Ballers 2: His Final Play

Legally Bound 5.1: Tasha Illegal Dealings

Brothers Black 2: Noah

Legally Bound 5.2: Camille

Legally Bound 5.3 & 5.4 Special Edition

Where the Pieces Fall

Legally Bound 5.5: Legally Unbound

Brothers Black 4: Braxton the Charmer

Broken Soldier

Brothers Black 5: Felix the Watcher

A Home for Christmas

Doctor Feel Good

Brothers Black 6: Ryan the Joker

Brothers Black 7: Johnathan the Fixer

Wild Hearts

Pieces of Trevor's Heart

Ballers 3: His Team

Coming Soon...
King of Gods Book 4: Immortal Iron Brothers Series
King of Past Book 5: Immortal Iron Brothers Series
Ronan Book 1: Kings of New York Series

Other Blue Saffire Series

Hold On To Me Series
My Funny Valentine
Be My Valentine

Hitter Squad Series
Remember Me

Work Husband Series
Unexpected Lovers
My Best Friend's Wish
The Ones Left Behind
The Last Ones Standing

The Lost Souls MC Series
Forever
Never
Always

The Moran Brothers Series
Love Notes
Stay With Me

The A**hole Club Series
Pit Book 1: The A**hole Club
Ox Book 5: The A**hole Club
Kelex Book 6: The A**hole Club

Immortal Iron Brothers Series
King of Knights Book 1
King of Inferno Book 2
King of Tides Book 3

Check out Blue Saffire exclusives on the

BlueSaffire.com website
The Fixer
His Miracle Baby
Razor
Dane
Trip
Professor Jones
Room 112

Other books from Evei Lattimore Collection Books by Blue Saffire
Black Bella 1

Destiny 1: Life Decisions
Destiny 2: Decisions of the Next Generation
Destiny 3 coming soon…

Star

Other books from Royal Blue Gay Romance Collection written by Blue Saffire
Kyle's Reveal
Beau's Redemption